Sweet Expectations

"When Daisy McCrae's already semi-scrambled life abruptly turns even more upside down, it leads to deeper soul-searching, the exploration of family ties, and a quest for the ultimate meaning of her purpose and direction. . . . With Daisy's narration alternating with her sister Rachel's, the story unfurls at a slow yet steady pace, nicely layering characters, subplots, and backstory." —*Booklist*

"Sweet and totally satisfying . . . Absorbing characters, a hint of mystery, and touching self-discovery elevate this novel above many others in the genre." —*RT Book Reviews*

"This novel satisfied my craving. . . . [A] sweet little read." —*Night Owl Reviews*

"[A] charming and very engaging story about the nature of family and the meaning of love, all set in the most delightful bakery one could ever imagine. The story is full of sugar and spice and is highly recommended for anyone looking for a pleasant and well-written novel." —*Seattle PI*

The Union Street Bakery

"Like a good recipe, the new novel *The Union Street Bakery* has a little bit of everything that makes a satisfying experience. . . . Taylor pairs the past with the present to please history fans as well as those who like tales of family secrets, reinvention, and renewal. . . . Taylor, who lives in Virginia, conveys the essence of the community, of regular shop patrons and history literally around every corner in centuries-old buildings. . . . Taylor serves up a great mix of vivid setting, history, drama, and everyday life in *The Union Street Bakery*. Here's hoping she writes more like it." —*The Herald-Sun*

continued. . . .

"A wonderful story about sisters, family, and the things that matter most. I loved this beautifully written journey of self-discovery."   —Wendy Wax

"Interesting and intriguing. . . . [A] fast-paced story of sisters, family, what really matters, betrayal, faith, healing, and life in general. If you enjoy historical facts, heritage, adoption, family, and love you will enjoy *The Union Street Bakery*. . . . [A] wonderful story!"   —*My Book Addiction Reviews*

"An excellent job of showing how important a family can be and who your real family is. Ms. Taylor . . . makes you care not only about Daisy but about all the family and friends involved. . . . Get a copy and settle in a comfortable chair with a cup of tea or coffee."   —*Long and Short Reviews*

"Marvelous!"   —*Chick Lit Plus*

"Readers will love Daisy and the McCrae family and be engrossed in both the historical and the present puzzles Daisy and her family must solve. Taylor never takes the simple plot path or gives in to melodrama . . . Highly recommended for anyone who loves family stories with intelligence and heart."   —*Blogcritics*

"I found myself so caught up in this family's lives and turning the pages late into the night. You will not be able to put this book down until you turn the very last page. . . . I can't wait to read more by Ms. Taylor."   —*Fresh Fiction*

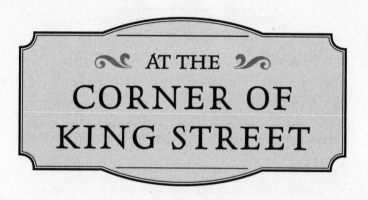

AT THE
CORNER OF
KING STREET

Mary Ellen Taylor

BERKLEY BOOKS, NEW YORK

BERKLEY

An imprint of Penguin Random House LLC
375 Hudson Street, New York, New York 10014

AT THE CORNER OF KING STREET

This book is an original publication of the Berkley Publishing Group.

ISBN: 978-0-425-27825-3

Library of Congress Cataloging-in-Publication Data

Taylor, Mary Ellen, 1961–
At the corner of King Street / Mary Ellen Taylor. — Berkley trade paperback edition.
    pages ; cm. — (Alexandria series)
    ISBN 978-0-425-27825-3 (softcover)
    1. Single women—Fiction.   2. Life change events—Fiction.
    3. Self-realization in women—Fiction.   4. Self-actualization
(Psychology) in women—Fiction.   5. Domestic fiction.   I. Title.
    PS3620.A95943A95 2015
    813'.6—dc23
    2015002636

PUBLISHING HISTORY
Berkley trade paperback edition / May 2015

PRINTED IN THE UNITED STATES OF AMERICA

10 9 8 7 6 5 4 3 2 1

Cover art by Alan Ayers.
Cover design by Diana Kolsky.

Penguin
Random
House

August 12, 1745

A cold rain pelted Aberdeen when the magistrate found Faith Shire innocent of witchcraft. The judge, a pious old man, found no legal reason to imprison Faith, but he feared the dark arts. Wishing to be rid of her, he determined transport to the Virginia Colony the best solution for all.

As the lowland woman was pulled over slick cobblestone streets to the docks, she screamed, her high-pitch shrill cutting through the rancorous crowd. Some looked away. Some left. But I stood firm as I watched her climb the plank of the *Constance*, the three-masted ship weighed low in the water with other indentured men, women, and children bound for the colony.

As Faith turned to steal one last look at Scotland, a sudden wind stirred up her red locks into a fiery halo. Watery, vivid blue eyes scanned the onlookers until they settled on me. She held my gaze until the guard yanked her below deck.

May God have mercy on me.

Prologue

❦

The Universe has sucker punched me twice. The first nearly cost me my life. The second changed it forever.

But near-death or life-altering experiences weren't on my mind when I flipped the Open sign to Closed on the front door of Shire Architectural Salvage.

On this warm August evening, my nerves were shot and my head rattling from an argument I'd had hours earlier with my brother-in-law, Zeb. Furious, he'd curled calloused fingers into fists, paced, and shouted so loud his voice reverberated down the rows of reclaimed doors, stacks of lumber, stained glass, claw-foot iron tubs, marble mantels, and bins filled with odds and ends.

"Addie, how could you do this to me?"

To calm my racing thoughts, I shifted my focus from invoices to cast-iron keys, antique doorknobs, and back plates assembled by my

Aunt Grace during her three decades of salvaging. For years, she'd been tossing keys and locks into a big bin, never bothering to sort or catalogue. With the keys, at least, I could transform chaos into order.

"How long have you known she was sick?" Zeb shouted.

"I tried to warn you!"

"You didn't try hard enough!"

"I thought she'd tell you," I stammered.

"She didn't tell me shit!" Eyes once friendly, burned with scorn.

Trembling fingers brushed over a large tarnished brass key, three inches long. Its lopsided heart-shaped handle created an ornamental air that set it apart from the other utilitarian keys designed for heavy-duty locks. Where had it been found? Grace never worried about documentation. She simply collected, her aim to keep alive as much history as she could cram into the two-thousand-square-foot warehouse on King Street. For every item here there was a second chance for some kind of life.

As I closed my fingers around the old key, a heavy energy reverberated through my hand and up my arm. Dust flecks danced like fireflies in light generated by countless rescued crystal chandeliers, copper ship lamps, and dozens of other salvaged fixtures. Images of sky and wide-open seas flashed in my mind. Outside, thunder cracked.

Breathless, I nearly dropped the key back into the box. For a few long, tense seconds, I stared at the lopsided heart, not quite sure what to do with it. The sound of a car door closing caught my attention and I slid the key in my pocket, determined to ask Grace about it later.

A heavy August rain pelted hard against the salvage yard's glass window when I heard the hard, fast rapping on the front door. Glancing up, I saw my sister, Janet, standing in the rain, holding up a soggy paper bag. Water dripped from her mascara-smudged eyes, which blinked fast, like windshield wipers. Raindrops flattened her thick blond ponytail and soaked her red sundress.

My relationship with my older sister was forever contentious. There'd never been a time of calm or sisterly love. She was the fun, energetic one, whereas I was the safe, steady one. She made messes. I cleaned them up.

I'd hoped we could find a peaceful middle ground after Janet married Zeb at Christmas and then gave birth to a son, Eric, days after Easter. Healthy, with a lusty cry, the boy inherited his father's dark hair, olive complexion, and long limbs. The day Eric was born, I held him in my arms and, after counting all his fingers and toes, I said a prayer of thanks that he was a boy. He was safe.

You see, Janet and I come from a long line of women who are cursed.

No one can pinpoint how far back the curse reaches, but I know for certain that Janet, our mother, grandmother, and great-grandmother were all burdened with the same affliction. Mom's doctor was the first to give it a name. He'd called it bipolar with psychosis. Drugs could balance and treat, he'd said, and for a time, there'd been some hope a modern miracle drug would counteract what centuries of prayers couldn't. The medications did offer brief tastes of normalcy, but neither Mom nor Janet liked the side effects, so neither stayed on their medications long. Calm waters never lasted.

Whatever hopes I nurtured that day in the nursery quickly crumbled. Janet, under the twin weights of wife and mother, dipped back into depression within weeks. At first, Zeb and his parents attributed Janet's mood to postpartum blues. However, those theories shattered when she quickly soared, like Icarus toward the sun, into mania.

Janet knocked harder on the door, shifting her stance from side to side. "Addie, open up!"

My sensible tennis shoes squeaked on the cement warehouse floor as I crossed the main floor and opened the door. "Zeb's looking for you."

Janet brushed inside quickly, tracking mud on my freshly swept floor, and held up a prized bag from the Union Street Bakery. "Happy Birthday, Addie."

I folded my arms, bracing. "Janet, did you hear me?"

"Zeb is fine. Don't worry."

"He looked mad."

She waved away the comment with long, elegant fingers. "You thought I'd forget your birthday, didn't you?" Grinning, she was pleased she'd remembered and bought a cake. Details were hard for Janet, just as they were for our mother. Remembering was a prize not to be downplayed. "It's chocolate. Your favorite."

My birthday was two weeks ago. "I love chocolate."

Janet meant well, but her illness stole time. She often lost months when the depression hit or the mania whipped up into full swing, her racing mind moving so fast that life zinged past her in a colorful blur.

Grinning, she fumbled for pockets at her side only to realize she wasn't wearing her coat. "I wanted to light a candle for you, and I was careful to put matches in my pocket." Nervous laughter bubbled. "Now I just have to find the pocket."

Accepting the bag, I fished out napkins, a couple of plates, a plastic knife, candles, and matches. Janet would not have remembered this detail. That was someone at the bakery's doing. "It's all in the bag."

"Oh, great! You can make a wish like you did when you were little."

I lifted the cake out of the damp, crumpled cake box and set it aside before I scooped up the soggy carton and dropped it in the trash. "Why don't you let me light the candles?"

"I can do it." With a trembling hand, Janet settled several candles in the center of the cake. "I'm not such a lost cause after all."

I wiped the flecks of sticking cardboard from the counter as she dug a match from the small box and struck it. The tip didn't flare or light, and so she attempted a second and then a third match. Finally, Janet handed me the matches. "I think they're too wet."

I removed one from the box. "How you been doing?"

"Been doing okay. Got new medicine, and I'm feeling real good. Life's feeling steady." She tugged the folds of her wet skirt.

I struck the match again. Too wet to ignite, it snapped in my hand. I chose another and tried again. It failed. "Zeb said he hasn't seen you in four days."

She flinched. "I've been busy. Lots to do."

"What about the baby?"

"Zeb has him."

The last match sputtered and finally caught fire. I held the glowing tip to the candle's wick. Slowly, the circle of candles came alive and cast a soft glow over the waves of chocolate. I blew out the match.

"What have you been up to?" I asked.

She clapped her hands together. "Addie Morgan, today is about your birthday. I want to talk about happy things."

"How about the demons? Have they been bothering you?"

The demons, the witches, even the lady of the lake, they'd all come to see Janet over the years. The apparitions, which the doctors said were caused by a terrible lack of sleep, were rarely kind to my sister. They taunted her. Told her she wasn't good enough and, sometimes, they suggested I was a threat.

Janet swiped her finger along the rim of the cake, gathered up icing, and licked. "So what are you gonna wish for, Addie? What do you want more than anything?"

My wish was simple. I wanted a normal life. One where my sister and I were friends. A world where the demons didn't come around to taunt her. A world without curses. "I wish we could be normal."

Janet smiled as a shadow darkened her gaze. "I wish it, too, Addie. And you know what? I think this time I might be able to hold on. I might not fly toward the clouds or fall into the swamp."

"Well, then it's the official birthday wish." I blew out the candles, and we both clapped. I laid out the paper plates and with a plastic knife sliced each of us a piece.

She accepted her plate, jabbed her fork into the cake, moved it around, but didn't eat. "This is nice."

And on the surface, it was kinda normal. A birthday. Two sisters.

I bit into the cake. Stale and dry—she'd bought it weeks ago and forgotten about it. Smiling, I chewed and swallowed. Carefully, I stabbed another piece, moved it around but didn't eat it. We sat in silence for a few minutes, both of us pretending to eat the soggy, stale cake.

"What kind of meds do the docs have you on, Janet?"

She dragged her fork over her icing. "I can't remember the names. But I have all the bottles in my pocket."

"In the pocket of your jacket?"

"Yes." Her fingers again slid down the sides of her dress and then curled into fists. "I forgot. I'm not wearing my coat. I must have left it in the car." A shrug of the shoulders reminded me of a twelve-year-old girl, carefree and unworried.

"When are you supposed to take the meds, Janet?" Somewhere along the way I became the oldest child.

"It's not for a while. I'm fine. You don't need to worry."

I swirled my fork in a lump of chocolate icing. "I'm not worried. Just wondering when you're due to take the meds."

She sighed. "Not until six o'clock tonight. So there. You don't need to worry."

I glanced at the clock on the wall. "Janet, it's after eight."

She stared blankly at invisible puzzle pieces lying in a jumble. "It can't be after eight, Addie. I left the bakery at four with your cake and came straight here."

"You sure you came straight here?" Sheila McCrae would not have sold her a stale cake.

"I didn't stop at a bar, if that's what you think."

"I didn't think that." The edges of Janet's plateau cracked and crumbled like the dry cake. "Why don't you let me call Zeb? He's worried about you."

"No. Don't call Zeb." She dragged the tips of her plastic fork against the paper plate until she dug a rut.

"Why not? He's a good guy, Janet. He loves you."

A deep frown furrowed her brow. "You and Zeb think alike. All you two see are my screwups. I'm always wrong where you two are concerned."

This fake normalcy thinned like ice cream on a hot day. Soon it would drip, run, and melt away. "Maybe we should go get your medicines. I'll drive you home."

"No. I don't want to go home."

"Why not?"

She jabbed agitated fingers through her hair. "Because."

I dropped the fork and knife, no longer able to keep up the pretense that I was enjoying the stale, soggy chocolate mess. "Why, Janet?"

She tightened her jaw and moved to slide her hands again into pockets that weren't there.

I met her gaze and could see the confusion mingling with the frustration. "What's happened? Are you and Zeb having trouble?"

"No trouble. Not exactly." She fisted her fingers. "I moved out. It was all getting too crazy in the apartment. The baby was crying. Zeb was upset and frustrated. I couldn't take it."

Even Zeb's once-steady demeanor couldn't navigate these waters. "Where are you staying?"

"In a motel."

"Which one?"

Janet sniffed. "I hate it when you judge me. First, you light the candles, and then you ask me about meds, and now you want to know where I'm staying. So many questions. You were always like that. Asking questions."

And with that, the ground under the almost peaceful moment vanished, and we plunged. I collected our dishes and dumped them in the trash. "Let me drive you. Is your car parked out front?"

Janet flipped a lock of her wet blond hair out of her eyes. "I can drive myself."

"Let me drive, Janet. The rain is coming down hard, and I know you don't like the rain."

She turned to the glass storefront window and stared at the pelting rain splashing on King Street and washing into the gutter. "I don't like rain."

From under the counter, I grabbed my purse. "I can drive."

She moved to the door, opened it an inch, but let it close immediately when the water splashed her face. "The demons like the water."

I grabbed my rain jacket, too tired to point out that the demons weren't real, and laid it over her shoulders. "Let me have your keys."

"They're in the car."

"Where's the car?"

"Down the block."

"Let's get to the car."

Cringing, she stared at the rain pelting the windows. "I don't want to go."

I held out my hand. "We'll go together. I'll drive."

Eyes wide with fear, she shook her head. "You'll protect me?"

"Yes."

She took my hand. "You fix everything, Addie."

Outside under the awning, I locked the front door and then, hand in hand, we rushed through the rain to the white Volvo sedan. By the time I slid behind the steering wheel, my hair and coat were as soaked as Janet's. Inside the car, the faint scent of old pizza and hamburgers drifted up from a backseat packed full of her clothes, an assortment of groceries, and empty boxes.

"Do you remember the name of your motel?"

"The blue one."

"Riverside?"

"Yes." She let her head fall back against the headrest as her gaze drifted out the side window.

I started the car. The gauge registered a quarter of a tank of gas. It was enough to get us to the motel on Route One and then to the apartment she shared with Zeb.

Seeing Zeb didn't thrill me.

"I haven't seen her," I'd told him. "But she'll be back. She always comes back."

"Always? How many times has this happened before?"

"A few times when we were teenagers. I thought she'd gotten a handle on it."

"I can forgive her. She's sick. But you, I can never forgive." Anger had radiated from him. "You must have thought you'd found a real sucker when I came along."

Headlights cut through the rain as I backed out of the spot. We were on the main road in less than five minutes and headed across town toward Route One. "Janet, you're sure you're staying at Riverside?"

Long fingers flicked her bangs back and she folded her arms again. "I don't know why you keep asking so many questions."

"Just want to be sure."

"Riverside reminds me of the places we lived with Mom."

Faded gray carpets, dark floral bedspreads, cheap seascapes of clipper ships and mildewed bathrooms—there wasn't much to love about those places.

As I rounded the corner, I was distracted, worried and tired from the long day.

The windshield wipers fought, but failed, to keep up with the hammering rain. The road's center yellow line vanished.

Janet's gaze brightened with panic and she shook her head as if one of her demons flickered and danced in her peripheral vision. She covered her eyes with her long pale hands and began to moan. "I have to get out of the car."

I should have slowed, but an invisible clock ticked louder and louder in my head. Soon Janet's moans, like Mom's, would become screams. She needed her medicine and the sooner I got her to the motel and to her meds, the better for Janet.

She grappled with her door handle, desperate to get out.

Gripping the wheel with one hand, I glanced at Janet. "Janet, take a deep breath."

She shook her head. "I don't want to be here!"

"It's okay, Janet. As soon as we get your medicine, you'll be better."

She raised her fisted fingers to her ears and shrieked.

Distracted, I lost sight of the yellow line again and the car drifted toward the center. As Janet's screams shrilled, I glanced toward her. "It's okay."

Suddenly, headlights cut through the rain and blinded me. A horn blared. I swerved hard. Metal crunched.

Later, the officers would declare it an accident. They blamed it on the rain. Low visibility. No fault.

Janet walked away from the accident without a scratch. My arm was badly broken and I suffered a concussion.

Two days later, Janet vanished.

July 14, 1750

Traveling into uncharted territory has an exotic, lovely sound to it. It conjures images of sailing vessels, strange and wonderful lands, and fascinating, if not dangerous, people. In reality, traveling is difficult, filled with endless seasickness and the smell of unwashed men. Belhaven, or rather Alexandria, is not what I expected. As I stand on the deck of the ship, now moored in the crescent harbor, I see high up on the bluffs a small scattering of wooden homes. They are clustered near Mr. West's tobacco warehouse, perched on the eastern edge of the harbor. It's all so desolate. I fear I have plunged into the deepest end of an abyss. My dearest husband, Dr. Goodwin, is filled with excitement for this new opportunity to build his practice in the colonies. He is convinced the Virginia Colony is a land where fortunes can be made. He says we will become rich beyond our dreams. A faithful wife follows her husband, but I will confess, I fear this strange and savage land.

Chapter One

Glue. No one pays much attention to glue. Doesn't matter if it's the white, pasty elementary school, slightly sweet kind or the industrial strength, crazy variety capable of suspending a construction worker five stories in the air. Doesn't matter if the glue is the human kind that holds families together or keeps businesses running. No one really cares about glue. Until it's gone and life falls apart.

My cell phone buzzed with an incoming call and, without a glance, I hit Delay and continued to run through the sales projection numbers for Willow Hills Vineyards. The main thrust of the discussion was simple. Willow Hills Vineyards could not survive on wine alone. Weddings and other special events would be necessary to bridge the gap until wine sales reached their tipping point and would allow us to claim a profit measured in dollars and not pennies.

"Addie, how do the reservations look for next quarter?" The question came from Scott Cunningham, the vineyard owner and my boyfriend.

I glanced at my budget numbers. "We have two weddings on the books, but there are two other couples that might still book a last-minute gathering. I should know in the next day or two."

Scott swept thick blond hair away from his deeply tanned face. "Not perfect, but it'll have to do. My big worry is the launch of our new Chardonnay. How are the preparations for the event going?"

"All on track. All under control. Do you want me to run through the checklist?"

He glanced up at me and grinned. Just a shifting of muscles, but I drank up the love and gratitude in his eyes. "No. That's not necessary. I trust you."

We sat at the long oak farmhouse table centered in the new tasting room that had been completed months ago. The walls were made of a thick gray stone harvested from the western part of Virginia and the south wall, made entirely of glass, faced toward the rolling hills of the Shenandoah River Valley. Directly to the right of the glass wall stood the tasting bar, handcrafted from knotted pine reclaimed from a nineteenth-century farm in Kentucky. Behind the bar, wine bottles nestled on their sides in hundreds of cubbies. Pendant lights hanging above the bar illuminated sparkling glasses stacked in neat rows.

I loved the room's quiet stillness. The calm before the storm. Everything was clean, perfectly aligned, polished to glistening and in its place. Perfect. No chaos. I inhaled, savoring the scent of the lemon polish I'd applied on the hardwood floor early this morning.

He winked. "I don't know what I'd do without you."

"You'd be fine." I leaned a little closer to him. "You dreamed up the vineyard and gave it life when no one would have dared. This is your dream."

"Dreams need to be fed and nurtured. Without you, my dream wouldn't be what it is today."

Drawn, I leaned in another inch, waiting for him to close the gap and kiss me. When he held steady, I tilted forward the last inches and kissed him. His lips carried the flavors of this morning's taste testing, and he smelled of fresh air and the soft scent of his handmade favorite soap. "I love you."

"I love you, too, baby."

The display on my phone lit again.

I deepened the kiss, already looking forward to the end of the day, when we would share a glass of wine on the new stone veranda as the sun set.

As I drew back, I glimpsed my phone. The display read: Janet Morgan. Fingers of tension rubbed against the nape of my neck. "I have phone calls to make for the wine launch."

He winked. "Don't let me keep you."

I scooped up my phone along with my papers and hurried from the tasting room to my office, a small room located at the back of the building. The phone buzzed in my hand, insistent and demanding, but I refused to answer or look at the display. When the buzzing stopped, I shoved out a breath. I waited several minutes, gripping the phone and praying she didn't call me back.

Janet was the past. My future, my life, was here now at the vineyard.

Closing my eyes, I imagined the tasting room five days from now, filled with people from all over the region gathering to taste the new wine that Scott was launching. It was a Viognier aged in French oak barrels. Its smooth, honeyed flavor possessed a tropical twist. Scott had been nurturing these vines for ten years and these were the first grapes he'd withheld from the wholesale market so that he could make his own signature wine.

The terroir of the Willow Hills Vineyards, like the terroir of any vineyard, was unique. Terroir was not simply the soil, but also the way the sun warmed the earth, how and when the rain fell, and the mix of temperature in summer and winter. A mile or two east or west, north or south ensured the grapes grew differently. Perhaps they'd be better, perhaps not.

Scott's gift as a winemaker was his ability to use the land. He worked with the terroir instead of against it. He understood the synergy of man and earth.

My phone buzzed a third time. Janet. Again. Frowning, I stared at the display. "What do you want?"

The last time Janet called me, she was living in Chicago and working as a cocktail waitress. She was drinking again and facing a DUI charge. She needed bail money. When I said no, she cried and begged. I maxed out my credit card and got her out on bond. Two days later, Janet jumped bail, leaving me to eat the cost.

Janet always possessed a talent for reemerging when my life was perched on the edge of hopeful and good. An exam. A job. A new wine. Janet knew when to call and tip over the applecart that I carefully filled.

Tense seconds passed as I stared at the display. Finally the buzzing stopped. "Stay away from me."

The doors to the reception hall opened and, immediately, I lowered the phone and rose from my desk. I hurried into the main hall to find a tall, burly man wearing jeans and a work shirt bearing the name Billy stitched above the pocket.

"Where do you want the tables, Addie?"

I blinked, shifting my brain from the past to the present. Tables. For the tasting. In five days. "You brought rounds, correct?"

Billy owned a party rental company in Staunton, Virginia, which was about twenty-five minutes south of the vineyard. He and I had traded several e-mails, texts, and calls over the last few days as I revised the head count for the opening.

"Thirty rounds according to the e-mail last night. Looks like you're gonna have yourself a crowd."

"We're getting more RSVPs than I imagined. It's exciting."

"I'm glad for the business."

"You and me both. Start placing the tables in the center of the room, and then we'll work it out from there."

Billy nodded. "Will do." He headed back out the glass doors to a large yellow truck. As he unlocked the back of the truck and raised the door, Scott entered the room.

Seven years ago, I left Alexandria with no fixed destination, but determined to go far. And then two hours away, the rolling hills, the white farmhouses, and peace seduced me. The Help Wanted sign posted in the small town of Middleton caught my eye and I decided to apply at Willow Hills. I was hired as a picker during the harvest season, but within days I surrendered to the heat and my aching muscles, which were still strained from the accident. The I-want-to-work-on-a-vineyard was officially exorcised, and I wanted my city life back.

"Give me Park Avenue," I grumbled in my best Eva Gabor accent as I marched up to the vineyard's main office, which was little more than a trailer, to quit. Even five days at the vineyard was enough to show me Scott was a dynamic visionary who spoke passionately to his workers about growing the best grapes and creating award-winning wines. He was a man to be respected. But I wanted nothing more to do with grapes.

When I knocked on his door, he sounded gruff when he shouted, "Enter." Tonight, he wasn't the noble, sun-kissed man riding a tractor up between the rows, but a very tired guy, slumped over a secondhand desk, doing his best to make sense of the day's accounting numbers.

"Scott."

He glanced up, his gaze gutted with fatigue and confusion. "Addie?"

He knew my name. There were more than twenty of us working the fields, and I assumed I vanished in the masses. "Scott."

"What can I do for you?" Dirt-crusted fingernails dug through sun-drenched hair.

I stared at his lean face, vivid blue eyes, and deeply tanned skin, and fell a little in love with him at that moment. He was the poet, the dreamer. I never harbored any big dreams and found I was drawn to anyone who did. "I don't want to interrupt."

"You're not." A very disarming half smile flashed. "It's accounting and schedules, and I'm terrible at both."

With the rumpled resignation letter in my fist, I stepped forward. "Numbers are kinda my specialty."

"You signed on to pick grapes."

"I have an accounting degree. I was stepping outside of the box and thinking of a grand adventure."

"And?"

I held up the letter. "I hate picking grapes. I want back in the box."

He chuckled. "I love the fields. The sun. The smell of the wind. The feel of the rich soil in my hands. But I get that this life is not for everyone."

"Which is why you should be here, and I shouldn't. I'll finish out the picking season, but I'm gone in two weeks."

Scott nodded. "Fair enough. Fair enough."

I laid the note on his desk and glanced at the open ledger and the scrawl of numbers and words. "Thanks for giving me a try."

"No worries." He tucked the note in the back of the ledger and tapped the page. "Thanks."

Suddenly, I sensed a broken energy that tore at me. Maybe because

I grew up with so many wounded, I felt comfortable around the broken and bruised. "What are you trying to do there?"

"Payroll. But it's not balancing."

"Want me to take a stab at it?"

"No shit?"

Extending dirty and vine-scraped arms and smelling like the inside of a barn, I smiled. "Don't I look like I have an accounting degree?"

He laughed. "No."

"Give me a try. And if I can fix this, you pull me out of the fields and turn me loose here."

He studied me a long beat and then finally nodded. "Okay, Addie. Show me your stuff."

From that night on, I ran the office, finding I could love the vineyard through numbers, logistics, through marketing plans. And, of course, through Scott's eyes.

Now, as Scott stepped into the tasting room and whistled his approval, I couldn't resist crossing to him and stepping into his arms. I savored his embrace as he rested his chin on the top of my head. "It's all coming together."

"Yes. It's going to be perfect."

With an extra squeeze, he broke free of the embrace, but held me close at his side. His gaze scanned the room. "Addie, you've outdone yourself. The launch is going to be perfect."

The compliment almost filled the emptiness. "Willow Hills Vineyards will shine on Friday night."

He drew in a deep breath as he moved toward the polished granite countertop and smoothed his palm over the surface. "We've plenty of wineglasses?"

"Five hundred."

"They've been washed?"

"I inspected them all for spots when they came out of the sanitizer."

"And the caterer?"

"She's on target and will set up on Friday morning."

"The band?"

"Confirmed. Here midday Friday." And before he could ask another question, I said, "We've received one hundred and fifty confirmations to our invitation, and I'm sending one last e-mail to everyone on our list this morning to remind them. The web page was updated and table linens were delivered an hour ago. I'll have the room set up today."

He kissed me. "I love you."

"I love you, too."

My phone buzzed, sending a chilled warning up my spine. I didn't dare look at the display. *Please, Janet, for once, stay away.*

Scott drew back. "Aren't you going to answer that?"

"What? Oh, I suppose."

"It could be a vendor."

I looked at the phone and saw Janet's name. I silenced my phone and slid it in my back pocket. *No more car accidents. No more bail. No more fixes, Janet.* "No one that can't wait."

"You sure?"

"Very."

"Well, if you have it all under control, I'm going to check the north property. We're clearing the land today."

I never lied to Scott, but I also never told him about my family.

Long ago, I locked away Janet, my mother, my Aunt Grace, and my life back in Alexandria in a very small box, and I had never once been tempted to open it. I reinvented myself when I moved to Willow Hills and left my history behind.

One day, I might tell Scott, but for now, there was no reason. My sister weathered crisis after crisis and this one would likely blow over by tomorrow.

I watched him leave, but the lightness I had enjoyed ten minutes ago vanished. Pulling out the phone, I checked for a message. Four missed calls but no message.

Guilt chewed at me as I stared at 4 "Missed Calls" on my phone's display. Janet was back, no doubt bringing with her another wave of destruction.

July 15, 1750

We spent our first night in Alexandria in the tavern built in the shadow of the tobacco warehouse. Mr. Talbot, the tavern keeper, sent a female servant to attend me. Pale-skinned and gaunt, the servant kept her capped head bowed as she moved about my room. She barely spoke two words to me, but I felt her scorn. Thin as a reed, she moved as silently as a cat. When she finally lifted her face and I looked upon the ice blue eyes, recognition mingled with fear. I knew her. She is Faith. Witch of Aberdeen. A castout.

That night, nestled close to Dr. Goodwin, I asked him about Faith. He told me she is indentured to Mr. Talbot, who bought her contract from the McDonald family. Talbot says she is a curious woman but means no harm.

No harm. Mr. Talbot surely does not know his servant's dark past. I wanted to ask Dr. Goodwin more, but feared my questions would arise his curiosity. Better he never know my association with the witch.

Chapter Two

Minutes after two, the sun reached the hottest part of the day, its harsh light heating the rolling green hills of the valley and burning off the morning's cool and pleasant breeze. I closed the doors to the tasting room. The air conditioner now hummed, the vents gently fluttering the muslin curtains. A wine-bottle wind chime, hanging near a window, clinked.

All morning, I prepped for the launch party by setting up tables and chairs. The table linens were inspected and placed on each table. Table decorations—small wine casks with a bundle of white roses and grapevines in the center—would arrive Friday morning. Candles would be placed tomorrow, and the wine-cork place card holders would go out before the event.

With one table to dress, I stood back, savoring the order and organization. I invested energy and care into each place setting, hoping that by creating order on every eight-foot round, I somehow restored balance to the Universe tipped out of balance by Janet's four calls. The phone remained quiet since the initial burst of calls but, as much as I wanted to believe all was well, silence often came before disaster. I was in the eye of the storm.

As I smoothed my palm over the last white table linen, an old truck rumbled up the main drive, its engine grinding and humming as its tires crunched gravel. Gears shifted and groaned as the truck slowed. The old truck radio blared a country western song about wishes and moonshine. The song coaxed a smile. It must be Scott in one of the farm vehicles. Scott liked country western music. Though raised in an upper-middle-class home, he somehow fancied himself a good old country boy. Gentleman farmer described him best.

I expected the sound of his booted feet thudding up the steps to the porch, no doubt sprinkling clumps of dirt in their wake. Scott never was good about the boots or cleaning up messes. Never.

Scott worked harder than anyone else on the vineyard, so I couldn't criticize. But he expected hard work and productivity to end with the desired result. Two plus two always equaled four in his world. He never toiled toward a goal only to see it ripped out of his hands and destroyed.

Since this morning and Janet's call, I imagined Fate flipping a coin now flying high in the air, turning end over end. Soon, the coin would fall toward the ground losing side down.

When I didn't hear footsteps, I rose from the table. Suddenly, I pictured Janet standing outside the tasting room, staring at the building, ready to charge inside.

Heat rushed at me as I opened the door and, shadowing my eyes from the high sun, I didn't see a vineyard vehicle, but a red, rusted truck.

The door opened and an old woman got out. Her graying hair was pinned back in a tight bun; deeply tanned, well-lined skin surrounded her eyes and her mouth. She wore an old sweatshirt, faded jeans, and scuffed brown work boots. Crystal blue eyes snapped and bit as her gaze roamed.

Not Janet. My Aunt Grace. My mother's sister. The last time I saw her, I was packing up my car, my body still battered and bruised from the car accident. She asked me to stay. I refused.

My walkie-talkie buzzed with Scott's voice. "Addie, I'm headed up to the tasting room. Sorry, I'm late."

I plucked the walkie-talkie from my hip and pushed the red button, my gaze squarely on Grace. "Scott, head up to our house. Grab a hot shower. I'm minutes behind you. There's nothing else for you to do here."

"You sure? Thought you wanted me to check the layout."

"It can wait. I have a vendor onsite, and we're gonna have to talk for a few minutes."

"Ten-four."

Shifting focus, I clipped the walkie-talkie to my hip and moved across the open veranda and down the steps. I approached Grace much like I would a stray dog.

Grace was the strong one in our family. The summer I turned twelve and Janet turned fifteen my mother needed to be hospitalized. Social Services contacted Grace and she agreed to take us. Aunt Grace was never a chatty woman or very maternal, but those three months were delightfully predictable. I hoped to stay forever but then Mom returned. Janet was thrilled as we sailed away from Grace's safe harbor toward the choppy waters with Mom.

"Grace."

Grace eyed me for long, tense seconds. "You don't answer your phone."

"Lots of work today. I turned it off."

She rested bent hands on narrow hips. She was fifteen or twenty pounds leaner. "You turned it off when Janet started calling."

"Yes." Steel, which I kept in close reserve, molded around my heart. "I suppose she's in trouble again."

"You could say that."

I folded my arms over my chest, knowing I might not be cursed with madness, but I was indeed cursed with a sister who refused to release her grip on me. "What has she done this time?"

"She's in the Alexandria Hospital."

No insurance likely. No money. What was the issue? Overdosed? Fallen? Another car accident? "Did she toss out her meds again? Is she psychotic?" Seven years separated Janet and me, but in a blink, all the old fears and anger rushed me.

"She's out of it pretty bad." Grace approached, but neither of us made an effort to close the remaining feet between us and hug the other. "She also gave birth this morning. This time it's a girl."

I sensed a shift in the earth under my feet and a wave of nausea passed over me. Another female in the clan. More madness. "A girl."

"Six pounds. Six ounces."

"Physically healthy."

"A miracle, considering how Janet must have lived the last nine months."

Oddly, we Shire women enjoyed strong constitutions. Physically, we rarely were sick. Pregnancies and births were easy. We could count many among us who lived into their eighties and nineties.

But I wasn't worried about the child's physical health. Selfish, maybe, but my focus rested solely on her mental state. Of course, it would be too early to tell. The madness didn't show itself right away, and though some would argue it might not ever come, the odds were stacked against us.

This morning, mere phone calls from Janet stoked my imagination with a thousand disaster scenarios. Now with the actual news in, the burden nearly made my knees buckle. I shifted, hoping maybe I could shake it off. But like a perched hawk, it clung with strong, sure talons.

"Who's the baby's father?"

The lines around Grace's mouth, which some might have mistaken for laugh lines, deepened as she frowned. "I asked, but she's too far out of it to know."

"What are the chances that she'll ever know?"

Grace held up her palms in surrender. "I'm not here to defend your sister or what she's done."

"Why are you here?"

"To ask you to come home."

"I am home."

Her frown deepened. "Home to Alexandria."

I touched the walkie-talkie, wishing I could call for help. "No. I am not going."

Grace shifted her stance. "I know you love this fantasy life you've made for yourself here. I know you want to forget you are a Shire."

"I'm a Morgan."

"You're half Shire. And the days of pretending you don't have a family are over. We need you."

"I'm not pretending." The pitch in my voice rose before I caught myself. "This is my life, and I love it."

The lines deepened around Grace's mouth as her forehead furrowed. "It's not a real life. It's pretty. It's neat and clean, but it's not really your life."

In the distance, I heard Scott's truck rumbling in from the fields. My heart slowed as I waited until I heard it make the turn toward our house. "How can you say that?"

"Do your new friends know about your mother? Do they know what you did to yourself in college?"

A jab of ice sliced through my chest right into my heart. "What I have with these people is none of your business."

My walkie-talkie squawked. "Heading home, Addie. See you soon."

My eyes on Grace, I lifted the radio to my mouth. "See you soon, Scott."

Grace nodded. "Scott. That's a nice name. I bet he's handsome. Nice. Great smile."

My fingers gripped the hard edges of the walkie-talkie.

Grace's head tilted. "He doesn't know, does he?"

My teeth ground so tight I feared my fillings would crack. "Would you lower your voice?"

"Addie, my back is to the wall with your sister." Her voice was a raspy stage whisper. "I can't do this without you. You need to come home for a few days or until we can figure out what to do."

The walls inched a little closer and the air grew stale. "I don't want any part of Janet's latest drama."

"You think I want to deal with this shit? Do you think I want to clean up another mess? For all the dramas you cleaned up with your mother and Janet, I've done the same plus more with my own mother."

Steel wrapped my heart. "Janet is not going to ruin my life."

"I will if you don't deal with this."

A cloud passed in front of the sun, blocking its rays. The glare from my eyes was gone and I could really see the disaster shaping up before me.

"She doesn't know where I am."

"But I do. And if you don't come back with me now, I'll smash this life to bits. No Shire woman gets a free ride."

I stepped toward her, my temper heating. "That's crap. You've no right to come here and threaten me."

Grace arched a brow. "If you've been honest about your past, then the truth I got to share won't matter a bit."

My jaw clenched. "I don't want you talking to anyone here."

"I didn't think so."

Outrage collided with fear. "This isn't fair, Grace."

That prompted a laugh. "Fair. Don't toss fair at me, girl."

As the cloud moved away from the sun and the light shifted again, I noticed the slight tremor in Grace's left hand. Her shoulders stooped forward an inch or two more, and though she was now threatening me, I could feel the desperation rumbling under each word. Calling the bluff of someone with little to lose never ended well. She drove two hours south from Alexandria to find me. She played every card in her deck. And if we went head to head, I'd lose. "What do you want me to do?"

"Help me deal with the social workers. I don't have patience for those people and all their questions and forms."

The stone under my feet turned to sand, shifted. "If I talk to the social workers and get the baby placed and Janet committed, you'll leave me be?"

Grace's well-lined hand pushed back a shock of gray hair from her sharp eyes. "Sure. I'll cut you loose. But you've got to deal with the city people. You know I don't do that."

My calloused fingers clenched and unclenched. "I want to be clear. I'm not staying past tomorrow. I have a huge event here on Friday. I have to be here."

"I'm not asking for your life, Addie. Just a day or two to help me get this fire put out. It's been a long time since I handled this kind of situation, and I don't have the spirit to do it."

"You have the fire to drive here and blackmail me."

Grace rested a clenched fist on her thin hip. "I still have a move or two left in me."

I ran a hand over my tight ponytail. "Put one fire out and then another starts. That's how it goes with our family."

With squinting eyes, she stared off toward the mountains, the longing for the quiet and stillness burning in her gaze. "It's always the way, Addie. It's always the way. But I can't worry about a new fire when one's raging at my feet."

I looked back into the reception hall, so pretty and neat. So perfect. This was my world. My perfect life. "This is bull. I don't want to deal with this."

"Are you coming or not?" Grace sounded weary but determined.

My gaze shifted from the neat and organized to the road that snaked toward the main road and eventually the city. I lost the coin toss. "I'll see what I can do, but I'm not staying. I swear to you, Grace, I'm not staying."

August 1, 1750

Barely a year old, Alexandria is a collection of half-built wooden structures, muddy streets etched with deep ruts, and none of the culture we enjoyed in Scotland. The doctor enjoys his clay pipe, puffing tendrils of tobacco smoke that permeate the hot, humid air of our one-room cabin. My new home is a single room with a dirt floor and a large stone hearth. One roughly hewn table and four chairs dominate the space and serve as a place to prepare meals, mend clothes, and on very rare occasions transcribe my thoughts. The doctor tells me he was lucky to acquire a lot of land this close to the thriving port. Of the sixty-plus surveyed plots last July, all sold within days during the land sale. He tells me Virginian and British gentry desiring a home closer to the bustling warehouse purchased the lots, so we will be in good company. Mr. Carlyle, a second son of a Scottish lord, is building what promises to be the largest home in the city for his new bride, Sarah Fairfax of Belvoir. Made of limestone, it sits on two lots on the newly named

Fairfax Street. The doctor assures me our wooden house is temporary. He has vowed we will live in a brick home by next summer.

He presented me with a serving girl to assist me in my daily chores. She is not more than sixteen. Plump and strong-boned with skin the color of mahogany, she promises to be a good worker. Her name is Penny.

Chapter Three

"What do you mean you're leaving?" Scott looked up from his wine journal, his eyes wide with a touch of panic, and his mouth slack. I couldn't have surprised him more if I told him dinosaurs roamed the vineyards.

"I wouldn't go if I absolutely didn't have to."

He drummed his pencil on the journal. "What could be more important than the launch of this wine? I can't think of what matters more than this."

Guilt chewed. "I agree. But I have to go back to Alexandria and take care of some family business."

"Family business. You never talk about family."

"We're not close." The door to my past creaked open wide enough for me to hear the whispers of self-doubt and fear. "But I'm the only one that can help."

He rose, and I wanted him to wrap his arms around me and tell me it would all be fine. The secrets and decisions I made long before loomed between us, silent and threatening. I didn't want my life—our life—to shatter, and I feared it would collapse under the weight of too much truth. "I'll drive into the city in the next hour, and then I'll be home by tomorrow afternoon. I'm ahead of schedule, and there really isn't much I can do until Friday."

Scott shook his head. "I don't like this, Addie."

"Neither do I, Scott. But it can't be helped."

"What's so dire that you have to take care of it?"

Telling one bit of the truth was akin to tugging on one loose thread. How much would make it all unravel? "The details don't matter."

He sighed out what sounded like the weight of a great sacrifice. "I'll see you tomorrow."

"Yes. Tomorrow." He wasn't pressing for details and that eased some of the worry. But then Scott never really pressed for details. He always assumed I'd handle it.

"Okay." He leaned forward and kissed me lightly on the lips. "Be safe."

"I will. I love you."

A smile tweaked his lips. "I love you, too."

He sat and turned his attention back to his notes.

There was no reason to linger, but I wished like hell I could stay as I packed a clean shirt and a second pair of jeans along with a tooth-brush in a duffel bag. I walked to my car, a dusty white CRV. I tossed my purse and bag on the passenger seat and slid behind the wheel. Gripping my keys in my hand, an odd energy surged, and when I opened my palm, my gaze was drawn to the old key I'd found in the box at the warehouse so many years ago. After surviving the accident, I thought of it as a lucky charm and kept it on my key ring.

For a moment, my grip tightened around the old key. "Damn you, Janet. Damn you."

I jammed the car key in the ignition. A turn of the key and the engine roared to life, and I drove the narrow dirt driveway toward the main road. Dust and rocks kicked up under the tires. At the end of the drive, I glanced at the Willow Hills sign, the dangling Welcome sign, and the bright yellow marigolds planted days ago.

My life. My home. I didn't want to leave.

Shoving out a breath, I turned right and headed northeast toward Alexandria.

Country roads that rolled past barns, green fields, and split-rail fences gave way to bigger routes, which quickly fed into I-66, the main artery between the west and east in Northern Virginia. By the time I reached the Washington, D.C., Beltway, traffic was heavy, nearly bumper to bumper, and the sixty-plus-mile-an-hour pace I enjoyed outside the city slowed to a crawl.

Traffic moved along the hot paved roads bracketed by tall concrete sound barriers. The only hints of green now were clumps of weeds that grew at the base of the barriers or around a few guardrails. My chest tightening, I opened the window, expecting fresh air. The hot breeze carried with it the heavy scents of gasoline and oil. Damn. Welcome back, Addie.

I slunk around the Beltway until I spotted the Telegraph Road exit. More inching and moving forward at a snail's pace away from my life, toward insanity, followed.

"Leave it to you, Janet."

By the time I parked in the Alexandria Hospital parking lot, the traffic and fatigue had wrung out some of the anger. Resolved, I made my way to the nurse's station, where a tall, lean woman dressed in dark slacks, a white shirt, and a pink smock stood. Her nametag read Molly Burns, Volunteer, and she wore her long brown hair swept into a thick ponytail. A ready smile reached her green eyes.

"I'm looking for the maternity ward. I'm here to see my sister."

She grinned. "Maternity is on the sixth floor. There's a nurses' station to your left when you get off the elevators. And congratulations."

"Thanks."

I'd not been in a hospital since my car accident, but I could see little had changed. The air still held that stale antiseptic smell and the glow of the fluorescent lights made everyone look sallow. I punched the Up button and when the doors opened I stepped inside. The elevator stopped at the third floor and a young Indian couple stepped inside. They spoke in whispered tones, but when they saw me they grew quiet. We all rode the remaining floors in stiff silence.

When the doors dinged open, I flinched. The couple exited and turned toward the nursery. I didn't want to see the baby. Janet was the real issue now. Getting her fit and healthy was the priority.

I found the nurses' station easily and waited while a short, round woman in her mid-fifties and dressed in scrubs finished a phone conversation. When she glanced up, I shifted, nervous and edgy. "I'm here for Janet Morgan Talbot." I didn't know if she still used her married name.

The nurse glanced at her patient list and then back up at me. "You're her sister?"

"That's right. I'm Addie Morgan."

Concern deepened her frown. "You're on the list of approved visitors."

"Do all the patients have lists?"

"No. But she's different."

Different. "How did the delivery go?"

She smiled, but it didn't quite reach her eyes. "C-section, but it went textbook."

"What about the baby?"

"The baby is doing well. She's small. But that's not a surprise. I don't think your sister was eating regularly, based on her weight."

Janet didn't eat much when she was manic or depressed. "Has a psychiatrist been in to see her?"

The nurse set aside her papers. "Yes. He wants to talk to your aunt, but she left this morning and hasn't returned."

Because she was busy dragging me back into this mess. "Can you page the doctor and tell him I'm here? If we can't meet today, maybe tomorrow."

"Okay."

"Where is my sister?"

"Ms. Morgan is in room 606."

Along this long hallway, a new mother was gingerly walking the halls with her attentive husband. Two grandparents admired a picture on their phone. A care partner carried a stack of blankets. Normal life continued.

I paused before I reached Janet's open door. I moved into the room and carefully pulled back the curtains encircling her bed. Janet lay still, her eyes closed, her pale blond hair hanging around her slender shoulders. She wasn't wearing makeup but her cheekbones cut high, thick eyebrows arched smoothly, and skin remained as porcelain as ever.

Janet possessed a vulnerability that made people want to help her. Her whimsical regard for responsibility branded her fun-loving and carefree. Anyone having a party in high school wanted Janet to attend. She was quick to laugh and never refused a dare. When she was fifteen, a couple of boys at a party dared her to run naked along King Street. She took the dare and with a crowd of twenty high school kids watching, dashed down the busy street without a stitch. She was arrested, of course, but laughing when the cops put handcuffs and a blanket on her. Even the cops were amused.

As I moved closer to the bed, I saw the wrist restraints binding her arms at her sides. Thin white scars marred her arms. She was cutting herself again. An IV ran from her arm to a bag hanging by the bed.

There was a knock on the door and I turned to see a tall, young man dressed in a white coat. Thick dark hair swept over his wide forehead. Dark circles hung under his eyes. His name tag read Dr. Mike Reed.

"Ms. Morgan?"

"Yes."

His gaze, which swept over me quickly, reflected surprise. I was short, with dark hair that skimmed my shoulders. There was nothing about my round face or pug nose that would link me genetically to Janet.

"I'm Dr. Reed," he said. "I'm the psychiatrist who evaluated your sister."

"That was fast."

"I happened to be on the floor."

"Good timing."

He cleared his throat. "Have you heard what happened?"

"Not the specific details but I can easily imagine."

He rubbed the back of his neck. "Has your sister ever been diagnosed with a mental condition?"

"When she was twenty, she was diagnosed as bipolar with psychosis."

"Was she under a doctor's care?"

"For a while. I haven't seen her in seven years. I don't know what kind of treatment she's undergone in the interim."

"Okay." He opened the chart at the foot of her bed and made notes.

"Is she going to be hospitalized?"

"Yes. She was in active labor when she was brought in by police."

"She called me several times this morning. I missed the calls. I hear her C-section was textbook."

"It was. If you go to the nursery, they can update you on her status."

I didn't want an update or status. I didn't want to get pulled back into this cursed world that had plagued my family for as long as I could remember. "How long will she be in the hospital?"

"Three days minimum, but I'm going to encourage her to stay for thirty. She'll need to be really stable before she can think about caring for the baby."

The nerves in my back fisted. "Is there any record of the baby's father?"

"He's listed as unknown."

"How long will my sister be unconscious?"

"Until morning. She's heavily sedated."

At least one of us would get a good night's sleep. "Okay."

"Do you know if she has any drug allergies?"

"She doesn't have any that I know of. As I remember, she responded well to her meds before. The trick will be to keep her on them."

"Right." He clicked his pen closed and popped it in his front pocket. "When she wakes, we can figure out what's next."

"Okay."

"Are you going to see your niece?"

A sigh shuddered through me. I didn't want to see her. I didn't want this nightmare to be real. "Yes."

I thanked the doctor again and then headed into the hallway. The buzz of machines, the hum of the overhead lights, and the rattle of a gurney swirled around me as I stood frozen. What the hell was I going to do?

The friendly nurse from the nurses' station approached me carefully. "You've seen your sister?"

With effort, I shifted my attention to her and tried to smile. "Yes. She's sleeping."

"That's for the best. Dr. Reed is very good. All the nurses think a lot of him."

"Good. My sister is going to need the A-Team and then some. Where's the nursery?"

"Let me show you the way."

As tempting as it was to run screaming from the building, I followed. When we arrived at the large glass window, I scanned the couple of dozen bassinets. Immediately, I shifted focus from blue blankets to pink, but I couldn't pick my own flesh and blood out of a crowd.

"She's on the end," the nurse said.

I moved along the glass wall until I stood in front of the last bassinet on the end. The baby was pink, round-faced, and crying. Judging by her balled fists and the extra red in her cheeks, she was furious. "What's wrong with her?"

"She's hungry. And from what the nurse told me she likes to be held."

High maintenance. Figures. "Is anyone going to feed her?"

"Would you like to?"

That was her mother's job, not mine. My grip tightened on my leather purse strap. "I've never fed a baby before. What if I make a mistake?"

"It's not hard. I can get a nurse to show you."

I scrambled for a decent excuse to get out of this. I wanted to run back to the country and worry about place settings, caterers, and polished wineglasses.

"You should learn." She dropped her voice a notch. "I've treated patients like your sister before. They don't just pop back after a few pills. It's going to take her some time and this baby is going to need someone who is stable to take care of her."

That startled a laugh. "And who says I'm all that stable? I feel like I'm going a little insane right now."

A sad smile curled the edges of her lips. "That sounds pretty normal to me. Only a crazy person wouldn't be worried right now."

Standing here with this stranger, it was easy to open up and be honest about what I'd denied for years. "The women in my family have a history of mental illness. My mother was ill most of my life and Janet's been ill since she was a teenager."

"What about you?"

I stepped back from the glass. "I was once insane enough to think I could help them both. Now I know better. Whatever I do for Janet, she'll find a way to undo it. It's always a matter of time."

"Want to hold the baby?"

I looked at the baby's little clenched fists. Giving her a bottle would make her feel better now, but in the long run, I knew she was screwed if she stayed with Janet.

"She needs you."

A warning voice in the back of my head screamed for me to run. *Don't hold this baby. She'll steal your heart. You're not that strong.* "Sure. Fine. I'll give her a bottle."

I followed her into the nursery and was immediately struck by the volume of my niece's crying. The sound scraped along my spine. "Kid's got some lungs."

The nurse reached for a pile of gowns and handed one to me. "She's been crying nonstop since she was born."

"Is she sick?" I set my purse down and slid my arms into the gown.

"No. She's physically healthy. Apgar score was a ten."

I washed my hands in a small sink and dried them with paper towels. "Has she been tested for drugs?"

"Yes," the nurse said. "She's negative."

"What about signs of fetal alcohol? Any signs of that?"

"The staff pediatrician checked her out. She shows no signs."

"So why is she crying?"

The nurse opened a sterile bottle filled with sugar water as she moved to the bassinet. She picked up the baby with a practiced ease. "I think she's stressed. Babies pick up a lot when they're in the womb, and your sister was clearly in crisis when she arrived." She nodded toward an empty rocker.

I sat in a rocker, grateful to be off my feet. The baby's wails echoed in the room. "Did my sister say anything about where she was or what she was doing before she returned to Alexandria?"

"No." The nurse cradled the baby in the crook of her arm and swayed gently back and forth. I sat stiffly, afraid and wanting to run.

The nurse settled the baby in my arms. She didn't fit as neatly in my arms as she had in the nurse's arms. In fact, she felt rigid. Her crying grew louder.

"You need to relax," the nurse said. "If you're tense, then she's going to be tense."

"Well then, we're in for some real trouble because I'm about to have a nervous breakdown."

The nurse pulled up a chair beside me. "You're folding her up like a wallet. Relax your arm. Breathe."

I jerked my arm down so the baby wasn't scrunched. The nurse moved my arm gently back and forth in a rocking motion. The baby settled a little, but she still continued to whimper.

"She likes to be held?" I asked.

"When we're stressed, we like a nice hug now and again."

I blew a stray strand of hair out of my eyes. "I'm feeling like I could use a good hug. And a few glasses of wine."

"Are you a drinker?"

My feeble attempt at humor fell flat. I could taste wine all day long because tasting required swirling the wine in your mouth and then spitting it out. I could tell you if a Cabernet was good or not or if a

Riesling was too sweet or tart. "Sorry, bad joke. I'm good for a glass once in a while."

The nurse smiled. She held up the bottle. "This is sugar water. We'll start her on formula tomorrow. Unless you think your sister will breast-feed?"

"Not likely. The psychiatrist is going to put her on heavy-duty meds, and it can't be great for the baby."

She handed me the sugar water bottle. "Brush her lips with it. She'll know it's there and suckle."

"I'm not sure why I'm doing this. I'm not in a position to take care of a baby right now. I don't live in Alexandria. I have another life that is so far away from all this."

The nurse smiled and gently nudged my hand so that the tip of the nipple grazed the baby's lips. "Would you like me to contact Social Services?"

I stared at the baby. The waters around me might look calm, but I was like a duck, paddling as fast as I could below the surface to keep it all together. "What will Social Services do?"

"They'd find her a foster family until your sister gets well."

"And then what?"

"I'm sure they'll keep tabs on the baby."

No one kept tabs on Janet or me that summer with Grace. She was good to us but we were lucky. The baby began to grunt and nudge the nipple and then finally latched on. She began to suckle.

The nurse patted me on the arm. "Look, you've got her eating."

"I wish a bottle would fix all her troubles."

The nurse rose. "I'm gonna leave you two for a few minutes."

Panic cut through the worries. "I shouldn't be left alone. I'm not licensed to do this."

"You're doing fine. When she's done with the bottle, give a shout out."

Fear scraped against my gut. "But what if she chokes?"

The nurse slid her hands in her pockets. "She won't choke. You're both doing fine."

The nurse ignored my pleading gaze and moved back toward her desk, where she typed into a computer.

I looked at the baby—a blood relative, but a stranger. She seemed to sense this, too, as she suckled, but she wasn't really relaxing into my arms. Her little fingers clenched into fists, and her body remained tense. I suspected if she could, she'd have jumped up and run away.

"I feel ya, kid. I do. Janet hasn't done either one of us a solid. And you know, I don't have any answers. I'm as lost as you." I leaned back in the rocker, willing my back to relax against the spindles. On high alert since this morning, I felt the flood of adrenaline slow to mere drops. Fatigue washed over my limbs and a weight settled on my chest. "Janet's not going to be able to take you. Not now, anyway."

Suckling, the baby opened one eye. Babies were born farsighted so I knew she couldn't really see me. But it didn't feel that way. I imagined her wondering what kind of crappy karma from a past life landed her in this family. "You and me both, kid."

Her other eye opened. She suckled harder.

"I have so much that needs to be done between now and Friday. And I don't know much about babies. I've never changed a diaper." Bubbles gurgled in the bottle and I raised the end until they slowed.

"You really will be better off if I get Social Services involved. They'll find someone who can really take care of you."

The baby flexed her fingers and closed her eyes. Clearly, I'd get no argument from her.

Her fingers were long and slender, unlike the customary chubby baby fingers. The nail beds were deep and the fingertips neatly rounded.

They were Mom's hands. Janet's hands. Delicate. Lovely. These fingers were created to be painted a bright shade of pink and to wear diamonds. Perhaps to glide over piano keys.

My fingers were short and stubby, destined for gripping a crowbar, scrubbing rust from an old metal lock, or wrestling weeds from the hard dirt.

The baby's hair color was a soft, pretty light brown. Little ears curled into a cherubic C shape and her pink lips dipped gently in the center.

Her limbs were long, and I imagined she'd be tall like Janet, with an athletic build. She looked underweight, but I wasn't sure if that was stress or if she'd inherited Janet's knack for burning calories with little effort.

Her nose turned up at the end and her face was round. Not long and lean like Janet's, but kinda like mine. "At least you didn't get my short legs."

Cataloguing her features and finding a bit of me was unsettling. Whereas I could never see myself in my nephew, I could see a bit of me in this baby.

I closed my eyes. In the end, it didn't matter if her legs were long or if her face was round or lean. The only factor that mattered was that she was a Shire female. And Shire females were cursed.

"I've lived with this curse all my life," I whispered as I rocked. "I wish I could help you, kid, I do. But I couldn't fix my mother or your mother, and I won't be able to fix you."

The baby's body relaxed a fraction, accepting that we were in this together.

When the baby finished the bottle, I pulled the nipple free of her lips and we sat in silence for several minutes before the nurse came back and took her. Free of the child's weight, I rose, wishing the tension gripping my shoulders would ease.

I stripped off the gown, took my purse, and left the nursery. Out in the hallway, I didn't bother a glance back at the baby.

Tears tightened my throat and welled behind my eyes. "God, Janet, why would you do this?"

A woman dressed in black slacks, a white shirt, and sensible shoes caught my gaze. Her dark hair was pulled back in a ponytail and horned-rimmed glasses accentuated green eyes, the singular trace of color on an otherwise colorless woman. "Are you Miss Addie Morgan?"

"Yes."

"I'm Kathleen Willis. I'm with Social Services. The hospital called me a few hours ago."

I folded my arms over my chest, pushing back rising defenses and tears. "Oh, right."

"Janet Morgan, the baby's mother, is your sister?"

"Yes."

"You've been in to see the baby?"

I cleared my throat. "Yes."

"I've been told that your sister won't be able to care for the baby right away. She could be hospitalized for weeks."

"If she agrees to stay. She's over eighteen so I can't force her into any kind of mental health care as long as she's no danger to herself."

"You understand the laws."

"We've been through this before."

She glanced in a file, clearly double-checking a fact. "Well, it's my understanding that she's willing."

"She's signed papers?"

"Not yet. But I plan to see her in the morning once she's recovered from the delivery."

"Until she signs those papers, I wouldn't count on her going into treatment."

Ms. Willis gently thumped her clipboard against her leg. "Will you be willing to take the baby?"

"Me? No. I'm not in a place where I can take a child. Don't you have foster families help in times like this?"

"We do. But right now we don't have many on the register, and it may take a week or so to place the baby."

"A week. What happens if she can't be placed? Does she stay here and wait for a family?"

"She's not going to be able to stay here. The hospital doesn't have the bed space or resources."

"Why not? I saw lots of empty cribs."

"She's not sick. And this isn't a place for healthy babies. Healthy babies belong with a family."

"Maybe if I talked to the nurses."

"It's hospital policy, Ms. Morgan. The baby cannot stay here beyond the first forty-eight hours."

"So where does she go?"

"There's no way you can take her on a temporary basis? For a few days?"

"You don't understand; this is how it always goes in my family. A little favor. A minute or two here or there, and I'm suddenly taking care of yet another person who does not want my help. I get tied up in knots. I can't sleep or eat and in the end, nothing changes."

"She's got to leave the hospital by day after tomorrow."

Tears tightened my throat. I glanced up, hoping someone would rescue me from the next Shire family quagmire threatening to swallow me whole.

And then I saw him. Zeb Talbot rounding the corner. Out of the frying pan and into the fire.

August 2, 1750

Our baby stirs in my belly often and promises to be a lively child. My best guess puts the child's delivery close to Christmastime. The doctor spends long days seeing patients.

Yesterday, he bled a tobacco farmer by the name of McDonald. The doctor expects the young man to regain his health. Though he says the family has been beset with bad fortune for years.

The doctor has bought shares in the *Constance*, which is now being filled with barrels, called hogsheads, brimming with Virginia tobacco. Once the ship's captain delivers his cargo to London, he will sail to the West Indies to pick up newly acquired slaves from Africa. The doctor expects high profits upon the ship's return.

Mr. West's tobacco warehouse and tavern does a steady stream of business catering to planters in town to sell their wares. Early this morning, I spied Faith staring at our house. She didn't speak and, when I met her stare, she turned and left.

Chapter Four

The last time Zeb and I saw each other was the day of the accident. He came to the warehouse looking for Janet. Furious. Frustrated. And so damn afraid of the total unfixableness of Janet.

And now Janet was back.

Zeb's dark hair grayed a bit around the temples now, but remained as thick and wavy as I remembered. He wore a blue T-shirt that read Talbot's Construction over the left breast pocket. The shirt, like the jeans, was well worn but clean and crisp. Scuffed work boots were laced tight and carried with them a dusting of construction dirt. Zeb clearly still ran his life as tightly as when he served in the Marines.

If I thought he was going to sail in and offer Janet another lifeboat, the deep frown lines grooved around his mouth and across his forehead sunk that idea. His rigid stance telegraphed displeasure.

My gaze flickered to a young boy standing at his side. He was a little Zeb. Dark hair, olive skin, and vivid blue eyes that held a determination any Marine would have admired. The kid must be Eric.

"Zeb," I said.

He put his hands on the boy's shoulders. "Addie."

I turned to the social worker. "This is Zeb Talbot. He and Janet were married." I moistened my lips, rummaging for a smile I couldn't seem to find. "And I'm guessing this is my nephew, Eric."

The boy's eyes widened with a hint of surprise at the sound of his name.

Zeb nodded. "Eric, this is your Aunt Addie. She and your mother are sisters."

Eric studied me a beat. "You don't look like Mom's pictures."

Natural for the boy to want to know his mother, and it was so easy for a disgruntled husband to deprive the child of contact, especially after a painful divorce. But whatever Zeb might have been feeling toward Janet, he kept enough pictures of her so Eric knew her face.

"No. We don't look much alike." I dug through my heart for a trace of love or emotion for this boy, my flesh and blood, but like the baby, I discovered my reserves were empty. "You look a lot like your dad."

The boy nodded, solemn. "I know."

Zeb squeezed the boy's shoulder gently. "Grace called you?"

Tempted to fold my arms over my chest, I slid hands in my back pockets so I didn't look as defensive. "Yes."

"Have you been in to see her?" He didn't use Janet's name, as if it was too sour to stomach.

Aware of Eric's keen gaze, I chose my words as gingerly as I could. "I have seen her. She's sleeping now. Heavily sedated, and she won't be able to see anyone until morning."

Relief unbound the muscles in Zeb's shoulders a fraction. He didn't want to see Janet. Today. "Okay. But she came through it fine."

"Yes. She's physically healthy."

He knelt and looked Eric in the eye. "Did you hear that? Your mother is sleeping now. She's doing okay, but she won't be able to see you until tomorrow or the next day."

"She's sleeping because she made a baby," the boy said.

"Yes. It's hard work having a baby." The words carried a weight of meaning that the boy missed, but neither Zeb nor I did. "When she's better, we'll try to see her."

"Are we going to try or *do*?" the boy asked.

A half smile flickered at the edges of Zeb's lips, suggesting he heard his own words tossed back at him. "One way or the other, we'll see your mother. But I can't make promises about when."

"I know. She's sick." Eric sniffed, his gaze focused and clear. "What about my sister? Is she sick?"

"I don't know much about your sister." A fresh ripple of tension washed over Zeb as he rose. "Let's ask your aunt." His gaze settled on mine, above the boy's head. Dark eyes shot a warning for me to tread lightly.

I didn't want to dash the kid's hope about his sister, who, assuming from Zeb's stoic expression, was definitely his half-sister. But I also didn't want the social worker to think that I was a solution to this problem. "She's in the nursery right now."

"Can I see her?" Eric asked.

The Morgan family hooks sunk a little deeper into my skin. "Come to the window."

The boy glanced up at his dad, who nodded his approval, and the boy came to my side. He was tall for his age, and would likely top six foot three like his dad, but he was still too short to see above the lip of the nursery room glass window.

"Can I pick you up?" I asked.

He gripped the slim sill of the window and tried to peer over the edge and through the glass. "Yes. I want to see her."

I wrapped my arms around his waist and hefted him up to the glass.

Unlike the baby, his body was relaxed. He didn't have the buzzing energy pulsing through his body, or the hum of quiet desperation. He felt normal. No curse. No madness. But then he was a male, and though the Shire men's blood may have carried the curse and passed it on to their daughters, they never suffered the weight of mental illness.

I tapped the glass. "She's in the bassinet on the end."

He pressed his nose a little closer to the glass. "The one that's crying?"

"Yes."

He traced the outline of her bassinet on the glass. "Why is she crying?"

"I don't know," I said. "I just fed her a bottle."

His head turned partway toward me. "Did I cry a lot as a baby?"

Soft, firm footsteps moved behind me as Zeb closed the distance between himself and his son. This close, I smelled the fresh air and lumber mingling with a faint soap. As I remembered, summer was the busy season for Zeb and an afternoon off was a precious gift for him to give.

"You didn't cry much at all," I said. "You were a happy baby."

Eric frowned, pressing his nose to the glass. "Why isn't she happy?"

"I don't know. She might not be feeling well or maybe she wants another bottle. I met the nurses, and they are nice. They'll take good care of her."

"Will she stay here until Mommy can take her?"

"She'll be in there a day or two." Sidestepping, I avoided answers involving Social Services, foster families, and my inability to take the child.

"Eric, there's a candy machine right around the corner." Zeb fished four quarters from his pocket as he looked at the social worker. "Would you mind taking the boy for a candy bar? Addie and I need a moment."

The social worker, realizing she might have an ally, smiled. "Be glad to." She held out her hand to Eric. "It's a really good candy machine. I saw chocolate bars."

Eric glanced at his dad and after another it's-okay nod the boy took her hand. "Is there Skittles? I like Skittles."

Ms. Willis grinned. "Let's go see."

Zeb handed the quarters to the boy, who clamped his fingers over them with a dedication that reminded me of Zeb. "Can I spend it all?"

"You bet."

The boy rattled the coins in his small palm. "So, if I see two candy bars that are fifty cents each, can I have them both?"

Zeb smiled. "You can."

Eric grinned and hurried alongside the social worker. As I watched the two walk away, I wondered what happened to the baby boy I once held. Until this moment the passage of time had gone unnoticed.

I couldn't help but say, "You've done a great job, Zeb. He seems like a great kid."

"He's one in a million." His words were crisp, clear, and confident.

"He's a lot like you." I let the words linger, not wanting to give voice to the fear that Eric might really be like his mother.

"He *is* me." His words held as much force as fear.

"Yeah. I didn't think he'd get sick."

"Why?"

"My mother's people are Shires and as far back as I can remember the men in the Shire family don't get sick."

"Really?" His naturally honed gaze sharpened.

I rubbed the back of my neck. "I never knew of one."

Reluctant relief skittered across his gaze as it shifted toward the nursery. "What about the baby? What's going on with her?"

"I just held her for the first time. She's agitated and cries." The baby's little fingers were balled into tight fists.

"I called a couple of my cop buddies. Janet was found at a bus stop in Old Town in active labor. The police were called. She got upset. She fought them and tried to resist, so they restrained her and took her to the hospital."

"She called me this morning. Four times. I ignored the calls. I didn't realize there was a baby." Would I have taken the calls if I'd known about the baby? "I thought it was another one of those Janet moments. And I didn't want to deal with it."

He shifted his stance, bracing for a familiar unsteady path. "So what happens next?"

"Janet needs to be evaluated. The mental health doctor would like to commit her for thirty days."

His gaze grew vacant as time transported him back to another similar conversation. "You think she'll agree to that?"

"If she stays three days I'll be shocked. But three days is better than no time."

"And the baby? What about the father?"

"We'll have to wait for Janet to stabilize before we figure out that one."

"And in the meantime?"

The questions came with a crisp punch of frustration that I found irritating. I wasn't giving a report to a boss or a commander. Hell, I shouldn't be here now. "I'm talking to Social Services about finding a foster home for the baby."

"What about you?"

I turned from the baby. "I don't live here anymore. I have a job. No time for a baby. Maybe Grace can help."

His frown lines etched a little deeper. "You know she's been sick, right?"

It shamed me to say, "No. We don't talk that often."

A muscle in his jaw pulsed. "Eric likes to visit. She's all the family he has on his mother's side. We see her about once a week. She suffered a mild stroke about eight months ago."

"No one told me."

"She didn't want me to call you. She was very clear about that. And because she seemed to get better fairly quickly, I let it go. The stroke has taken the wind out of her sails. I've tried to send salvage jobs her way, but she's said no to all of them."

I rolled my head from side to side. If I were at home on the vine-yard right now, I'd crawl into my bed and pull the sheets over my head. "I need to go see Grace."

"And then? Are you going to run away like your sister did?"

The words smacked like an open hand. "I don't run."

His hands rested on his hips, a calloused finger tapping the worn leather. "Run, walk, stroll. You're leaving. Like her."

Before I could fire back, Eric rounded the corner with a piece of candy in each hand. "Dad, I got two pieces."

The blue depths of Zeb's gaze reflected annoyance and acceptance. "Good job, Eric. Ready to hit the road?"

The boy grinned. "Can we come back? I want to see the baby again. And Mommy."

"Sure, pal. We'll be back."

"What about Addie?" Eric asked, looking at me. "Are you coming back?"

Under Zeb's and Eric's gazes, all the excuses that made such good logical sense when they marched single file across my mind vanished like faithless traitors.

Are you going to try or do?

"I'll be by early in the morning to see the baby, Eric. I have to go see Grace." The sentence came attached with an unspoken asterisk, which clearly stipulated that I was not staying and that I was going back to my old life.

Eric heard my words, but Zeb noted the caveat. The look of disgust that flickered across his face made me want to punch him.

August 28, 1750

The *Constance* sailed away three days ago and the doctor packed a bag so that he could make rounds at several plantations. I was left alone with only Penny for company. Work continues on our house and I long for the day we will live in a real home again. The doctor has promised that the *Constance* will return with fine English furniture for our home. He plans many purchases with his profits.

I found a bundle of purple wildflowers lying by my front door this morning. They reminded me of Scotland. And of Faith.

Chapter Five

ᘛᘚ

The drive to Grace's warehouse on King Street took close to twenty minutes. As the crow flies it was a five-mile journey, but winding in and out of the steady commuter traffic added to the trip. I didn't mind the delays. As anxious as I was to get back to my life, I was in no rush to talk to Grace.

Turning onto Seminary Road, I made my way past the strip malls toward Old Town Alexandria. Concrete gave way to green lawns and century-old homes and the road curved left past the tall spire of the George Washington Masonic Temple, fashioned after the ancient lighthouse in Alexandria, Egypt. Soon I was in the heart of Old Town, driving past eighteenth-century brick buildings that now housed a collection of shops, pubs, and bookshops.

The summer season brought lots of tourists, who meandered and crowded along the Mount Vernon trail that snaked along the Potomac River, visiting the tony shops.

A half block before the end of King Street, I turned into a side alley and parked in one of the spaces marked Shire Salvage Yard Parking. I shut off the engine and, with a sigh, got out and walked down the alley, dodging potholes, to the corner and the salvage yard's main entrance. Block letters still arched over the main glass window, now covered with thick metal bars. The front door, once a vibrant red, was faded and chipped. Hanging in the front window was an Open sign that tipped slightly to the left in a half-hearted greeting.

Seven years since I last stood in this door, weeks after the car accident. Janet was nowhere to be found and my body was bruised and battered. As I'd hauled myself up the stairs, the pain had convinced me that if I didn't break free, this family would drown me.

I gave Grace my notice that day, went to my apartment, sold what little I owned, and packed the backseat of my car with the remains of my possessions.

Holding tightly to my purse, I pushed through the door only to be greeted by a familiar musty smell that followed the old and discarded. There was a time when I welcomed the scent, but now it carried with it memories past I did not want to remember.

You could say my Grandmother Lizzie founded the Shire Architectural Salvage Company when she was in her early twenties. She hated how the old Alexandria homes in the 1940s were falling into disrepair, so she drove the streets searching for signs that houses were on the verge of ruin or demolition. Whenever she saw demo crews assembling, she'd be there with her 1941 black Ford pickup truck to collect whatever the crews discarded. Lizzie began with fireplace mantels, chandeliers, and doorknobs.

She stored it all in her father's side barn, located on his farm south of Alexandria in Prince William County. On one of her salvage missions, she met Philip Shire, a third cousin. The two quickly fell in love and soon married. As a wedding gift, Philip, charmed by Lizzie's quirky love of the past, gave his wife the warehouse property at the corner of King Street. Lizzie's father, it was said, was as thrilled to see his daughter wed as he was to rid himself of her junk.

Philip Shire, my grandfather, understood the madness plaguing the women in his family as well as his own wife. His mother often talked to spirits and rarely left her house. He prayed the curse would leave him alone. He prayed for sons. Lizzie gave him two daughters, Elizabeth and Grace.

By today's standards, Lizzie might have been called a hoarder, but back then she was simply a beautiful woman with an infectious laugh and a big empty warehouse to fill. Her need to collect was part of the package.

Philip's architectural practice grew, as did his girls and Lizzie's collection. For a time, both girls were healthy as if the curse passed over his family.

When Lizzie and Philip died suddenly in a car accident in their late forties, Grace, just eighteen, was one of the first to inspect the warehouse, now crammed to the rafters. She began sorting the goods her mother so lovingly collected and slowly began to find buyers who shared her love of the past. Elizabeth, my mother, showed little interest in the warehouse full of junk, as she called it. Her dream was to be an actress on Broadway, so two weeks after her parents' funeral, twenty-year-old Elizabeth left Alexandria. She never became an actress. Seven years after leaving Alexandria, she returned, newly widowed, with four-year-old Janet and one-year-old me in tow. And, of course, voices rattling in her head.

When I left Alexandria, the front end of the warehouse was crammed full of items. Now the space was as nearly empty. All that remained was a marble mantel, an old elevator, doorknobs, and a handful of stained glass windows, all coated in a thick layer of dust. There was a time we were a regular stop for designers and builders and items didn't linger long enough to gather dust.

"Grace!"

She kept an office in the back, behind rows of reclaimed doors, and she also maintained an apartment upstairs on the second floor.

"Grace!"

When she didn't answer, I climbed the stairs to the sprawling space, divided into rooms that ran the length of the building.

"Grace!"

From the back of the space where the kitchen was tucked away, I heard the rattle of pots and pans. I wandered through the living room and past the three small bedrooms that lined the center hallway. There were bathrooms, each tiled with reclaimed subway tiles and sporting claw-foot bathtubs. All the rooms were located on the east side of the building and their small windows offered a wonderful view of Union Street and the Potomac River. This was a nice piece of real estate and I was somewhat surprised Grace hadn't sold out yet.

I ducked into the last room on the right before the kitchen. Narrow, it sported two beds, a low three-drawer dresser in between, and a round braided rug. The walls remained a light blue and the twin beds were still dressed in the handmade quilt comforters. Even the gray and blue rag rug on the floor was unchanged. Rehang my posters and put my lava lamp on the dresser and it was the room I lived in twenty years ago.

I turned from the room and found Grace in the kitchen. Like the rest of the apartment, it was furnished with salvaged items, including a white stove that dated back to the nineteen forties, a large farmhouse sink that predated World War I, and a white block refrigerator with a long silver handle that dated to the fifties. The countertops were butcher block, rescued from an old restaurant, and the kitchen table was built out of salvaged planking from a Fairfax County barn.

The room should have looked like an outdated hodgepodge of stuff, but Grace wove it all together in an oddly pleasing sort of way.

The retro decorating magazines would have loved it. During my short tenure here at the warehouse, I wanted to reach out to several publications that catered to designers. She thought it was a great idea, but nothing ever came of it.

The evening summer light, still bright and warm, streaked in through the small window above the sink that overlooked Union Street. The light illuminated the silver in her hair. "Would you like a cup of coffee?"

The coffeemaker looked like a prototype of the first automatic coffee makers.

She dumped grounds into a white filter and settled it in the machine. "Zeb bought me a fancy coffeemaker as a thank-you for watching Eric from time to time. But I've never seen the point of using those little cups. Seems a waste." As the machine gurgled, she leaned against the counter, folding her arms. "Eric's a bright, happy child and he loves exploring the warehouse."

"It's a great place for a little boy. I loved it here as a kid."

Grace looked at me, her gaze searching and a bit lost, before she turned toward the counter where a plump cherry pie cooled. She reached for a knife and two plates and dished up two slices.

I remembered begging Grace and Mom to let me stay beyond the summer and go to school in Alexandria. Both women refused, and I was whisked away from the orderly chaos of the warehouse to the hardcore chaos of living with Mom again. Grace understood the depth of Mom's illness, but couldn't deal with it. I once thought I was different than Grace, more dedicated to family, but time proved otherwise.

The coffeemaker gurgled. I rose and got cream from the fridge. Grace set the pie and the coffee on the table and lowered slowly into the seat across from me. For a few minutes we both ate and drank, savoring the bitter and the sweet. We both knew there was a mountain to climb and neither of us wanted to start the conversation. So we kept eating.

"Pie's good," I said.

"Came from the Union Street Bakery. Daisy's doing a good job with the place."

The bakery was located a block south, around the corner on Union Street, in the heart of Old Town Alexandria. I remembered the Mc-Crae sisters and the Union Street Bakery. Daisy and I went head to head over a book. Each of us grabbed one end and yanked. The book ripped in half. "When I left, she was working in Washington, D.C. Some kind of rising star in finance."

"Lost her job. Moved back home."

I stabbed a juicy cherry with my fork. "That couldn't have been fun."

"She's made the best of it. She got married and produced a baby."

"That, I cannot picture."

"She drools over the kid."

That jostled a laugh. "What about Rachel? Pregnant and married as I remember."

"Her husband died, so she and her twin girls live on the second floor of the bakery."

"Damn." I didn't have a lock on trouble. "And Margaret?"

"Back in town. Drifts from job to job. Helped me a few times last year."

"At least some things don't change." I couldn't picture Daisy pushing a stroller with a fresh baked pie in hand. "Daisy wearing a white apron and slinging crust? I've lived to see it all."

"She does real well. Life's softened her a little. She came by an hour ago with the pie. I told her about Janet and the baby."

I cringed a little. One thing to have a troubled family, but another to have people know it. "I suppose it's not a secret."

"No hiding a baby."

I pressed my thumb against the crumbles of crust on my plate and savored the last bit of sweetness. "Grace, we've got to figure out what we're going to do."

The lines in her face deepened with her frown. "I'm out of steam, Addie. I don't know what to do, and there's no one in the family other than you that I could ask for help."

I pushed the plate away. "You called Zeb."

Dark eyes flashed and narrowed. "I called him after I saw you."

"When you came bearing threats."

"Not threats. Just a reminder that you have family who know you better than most."

"Why call him?"

"He's got a right to know what's happening."

The sweetness of the cherry pie melted and a bitter taste settled in my mouth. "We all know where each other's skeletons are buried."

"You've always carried with you a strong sense of family," she said, ignoring me. "You kept your family together when your mother couldn't. You know how to handle this kind of burden."

"You must have lived through this before with Mom when you were younger."

"Maybe I did. But that was a long time ago. Like I said, I'm old."

As easy as it was to remind Grace that she backed away from my mother when she was a much younger woman, who the hell was I to judge? Being AWOL for seven years undercut any claims to self-righteousness. "Mom used to call Janet her superstar and me her glue. Janet shined and I was invisible."

Grace dug her fork into a plump cherry, but she didn't raise it to her lips. "She was giving you a compliment and didn't even realize it."

"How's that?"

Grace inspected the cherry and then lowered her fork. "Without a superstar, life is quieter. Without glue, it all falls apart."

"She always smiled when Janet walked into a room. Hell, everyone did. And I bet they still do. I bet Janet can still turn any dull day into a tremendous adventure."

Grace swirled the cherry on the plate. "She's sick, like your mother. Maybe worse."

I wanted to disagree, but couldn't. "She was sleeping when I saw her today. She looked peaceful, and even after what she's been through, beautiful."

"She was raving mad when they brought her into the delivery room. Screaming that a witch cursed her and that she needed to get away before it stole her soul. It took a couple of men to restrain her so that the doctor could sedate her."

The scene played in my mind: Janet's arms flailing, and yelling doctors scrambling to restrain her and deliver the baby.

"The baby was born by C-section," Grace said. "She was breech."

"Didn't want to come into the world? I can't blame the kid."

"Addie," Grace warned.

I shrugged, the bitterness tightening around my heart like a vise. "I lived with a crazy mother. It's horrible."

"So did I, Addie."

"She wasn't a Shire by birth," I said.

Grace tapped her finger on the edge of the plate. "She and my father were third cousins. Go back far enough in her tree and you find a Shire."

"Yours wasn't crazy. She collected things."

"She packed every square inch of this warehouse, including this floor. She did the same to our home. And I can promise you that not all of it was lovely, salvaged goods. In the last years, she took to stowing her garbage."

The vignette irritated rather than mollified me. My skin prickling with frustration, I rose and moved to the counter and the cherry pie plate. I sliced another piece of pie and stood at the counter, eating not for taste but because eating was better than thinking about this mess.

"Pie's gonna make you fat, Addie. It isn't going to solve a damn thing."

I took a third bite. And a fourth. "Maybe. But I don't know what else to do." I set my fork down. "The social worker said she could find a foster home for the baby."

"A foster home." The words drifted with her sigh. "I was hoping you could take her."

The kitchen window faced Union Street and, beyond it, the waters of the Potomac River. Past the traffic and the buildings across the street the river meandered, unaware of the city's chaos, drifting out to the Chesapeake Bay and finally the Atlantic. A gentle, warm breeze carried the brackish scents up through the open window. "You and the social worker collaborating together on this?"

"We talked on the phone. I said you were young and smart and not like Janet. Said you'd be the wisest choice for the child."

"In whose mind?" The solution solved everyone's problems and gutted my life. Damn it.

Grace sat back in her chair. "Can you take the baby or not?"

Anger and frustration caught the sharp words in my throat. I ate another piece of pie.

"Addie, look at me. My health is not great. I don't have the energy for a baby, especially a difficult one."

The child's cries rattled around in my brain as I swiped away a tear. "I have a huge deadline at work this week. We're launching the vineyard's new wine. A lot is riding on this. I can't have a wailing kid strapped to my chest while I discuss grapes, growing seasons, and sunlight. I can't."

"Foster care, Addie. I've heard the stories. Overcrowded homes, babies forgotten or not fed."

I turned from the river view and faced her. "The media always picks up on the worst of the worst. There are a lot of loving families out there that could look out for the baby for a few weeks. And if Janet can get some hospital care, then they might be able to stabilize her, and she can take the baby back."

The words rang hollow like a cracked church bell. Mom did have good times. She was stable for months at a time. But those times never lasted. I hated our life. Hated it. And now I was asking this kid to live it with Janet.

Grace pressed wrinkled lined hands to her forehead. "Can you at least deal with the social worker for me tomorrow? If you can't take the baby, at least see that she ends up in a good home."

I owed the kid that much. My running tally of lost moments and stolen time was so huge that another day or two wouldn't matter much to me, however it could really matter to the kid. "I can do that. I can make sure the baby gets a good home."

Grace nodded, but there was no gratitude in her expression. The solution I offered wasn't one she wanted, but it was all I could give.

"Thank you."

I pushed away from the counter as I dug my cell phone from my pocket and walked into my old bedroom. I sat on the twin bed made with the same red-and-blue quilt that smelled of fabric softener. A very old painting of a lady still hung over the bed. Its patina was cracked and faded and the frame, once gilded, was not dulled by time. I often stared at the delicate brown curls framing her pale white face and her lace-trimmed collar and wondered who she was to us. Grace muttered the name Sarah, which only fueled my imagination.

The bedsprings groaned and squeaked as I sat and stared at my phone's screen saver, a photo taken of a smiling Scott and me at the vineyard in front of the new tasting room. Angry, frustrated, and backed into a corner, I closed my eyes and tapped my index finger on the image.

To discuss a piece of my history with Scott could open the Pandora's box of my past and let loose questions I never intended to answer. As panic pulled and tugged, I drew in a breath and released it slowly. "Don't do this to yourself," I whispered. "If I handle this right, maybe I won't have to tell him."

I took another deep breath. Scott always admired my crisis management skills, but this would put it all to the test.

"Breathe, Addie. Breathe. Think."

It was Monday. The wine reception wasn't until Friday evening, so there was a day or two that I could spare. I worked ahead and planned to spend the week tweaking final details in my OCD way, but if push came to shove, I could handle it all in one very hectic day.

I dialed Scott's number, half hoping he shut it off or was in the fields where reception was spotty. He picked up on the second ring. "Addie. Thank God. Tell me you're on your way home. I got a call from the caterer, and she has questions I couldn't answer."

Pressing fingertips to my temple, I rose. "What was the question?"

"Availability of shrimp I think."

A normal, everyday kind of crisis. I liked those. "I'll call her in the morning and sort it out."

"I knew you would." He yawned. "Are you coming back tonight?"

"It's getting late. Better to drive when I'm fresh. Plus I have more loose ends to clear up here." The next words rushed, carrying an apology woven in the tone. "I'll be back tomorrow, and I'll get it all on track. Don't worry."

After a long silence, he sighed into the phone. "Baby, what's going on there? Is everything all right?"

"Nothing I can't fix." I'm Addie the Glue. I hold it all together.

"Where're you staying?"

I moved to the window that overlooked the alley.

"I'm staying at my Aunt Grace's house on King Street in Old Town Alexandria."

"You've never mentioned her."

"I used to work for her in her architectural salvage business."

"She has property in Old Town Alexandria? That's got to be worth some money."

"I suppose it is. My grandfather bought the land when it was cheap."

"What kind of property is it?"

"It's a warehouse."

"Could it be a wine warehouse?"

"What?"

He chuckled. "Just thinking, baby. We expand our wine empire, we might need a city location."

"Our wine empire." The words tripped off his tongue without effort, and it warmed me more than a thousand *I love you*s.

"Of course, our wine empire," he said softly. "I wouldn't be where I am without you, Addie. You're the center of my life."

Wine or empire didn't matter. *Our* did. "Really?" I nestled closer to the phone, trying to imagine the clean scent of his skin, which smelled like wine and sunshine.

"Baby, you know that."

More anxious than ever to return to the vineyard, I sat up straighter, determined to fix this issue and return to my real home. "We don't talk about us all that often. We're so busy."

"After this Friday, we're going to talk more about us. I've been putting it off and that's bad. Too much work filling my head. But we'll talk long and hard this weekend."

He ended the sentence with a sensuous chuckle, which coaxed a smile. We'd not made love for a few weeks. He chocked it up to work and stress and, though I missed the reassurance of his touch, I understood.

"I love you," I said.

"Me, too. Me, too. Hurry home. We all miss you. I miss you."

When I hung up, the worries melted and, for a moment, I didn't think about Janet, the baby, social workers, or Zeb's annoyed expression. I imagined my life with Scott. Sitting on the back porch, sipping a glass of wine, and watching the sunset. In my daydreams it was always just the two of us. Enjoying each other.

I tucked the phone back in my pocket and found Grace standing over the sink, washing the pie plates. She left the coffee cups on the table and refreshed both. "I'll put a call in to the social worker in the morning and get this sorted."

"Who was that you were talking to?"

"Scott. He owns the vineyard."

"The boyfriend."

"Yes."

She placed the first dish in a rack by the sink. "Does he want children?"

"He says his sole focus is the vineyard. The grapes are his children."

"Been my experience that most men, when they reach a certain age, want a child, a legacy."

Not a child who's cursed. Not a child who swings between highs and lows and doesn't know when to stop spending money or cut back on the drinking. Not a child who yells and screams at imagined monsters in the shadows. Not a child who has no future.

When I turned twenty, I feared I'd have a child cursed with madness. My mother was dead by her own hand and my sister off on another manic adventure. And so I arranged to have my tubes tied. The doctors spoke to me over and over about the consequences of the surgery. *Just wait. What's the harm in waiting?* At the time, I saw no other resolution to a problem that would never go away and I refused their counsel.

"Eric is doing all right," Grace said.

I pictured my crying niece with her red face and tight belly. "What if Scott and I have a girl?"

"You've a fifty-fifty chance."

"You and I both know that's one hell of a dice roll."

September 5, 1750

I had the good pleasure to meet Mistress Smyth, wife of Captain Smyth, owner of the *Constance*. The Smyth's home is also to be constructed of brick, but unlike our home they have yet to lay down their foundation.

Mistress Smyth and I shared a honey cake and tea in her temporary wooden home. The air was so hot and thick and I longed for Aberdeen. It does my heart good to know I am not the only one without a permanent place to call my own. I summoned the nerve to ask Mistress Smyth about Faith. Her face turned sour. She told me Faith is an indentured servant who fancies herself a midwife. Always growing herbs in her gardens and mixing concoctions. She warned me to, "Stay clear of that one."

Chapter Six

Sleeping at Grace's warehouse apartment bordered on miserable. The lumpy mattress squeaked and groaned each time I rolled on my side or back. A draft blew above the floorboards and shadows played on the walls, dancing and swaying in time with the moon. I forgot how creepy this place could feel at night. As a child, it took me weeks to adjust.

At three A.M. I stared at the ceiling, listening to the chilly whispers of wind whistling down the center hallway. A cool breeze blew under my threshold and across my face like fingertips.

The warehouse's quirks were easy to accept when I was a kid because, honestly, imagined ghosts and spirits were an improvement over shouting drunks lingering near the motel room Mom and Janet and I shared. The spirits didn't argue or create such a disturbance that the cops were summoned.

Janet feared the warehouse's ghosts and specters hovering in the fragments of older homes destined for demolition. They played havoc with her already failing sanity, so she spent most of that summer living with the McCrae sisters. The summer of endless sleepovers. Janet was nearly the same age as Daisy and Rachel and the trio spent the summer running around the city.

Janet missed the excitement and stimulation of life with our mother, but I adored the quiet of the warehouse. I read. Slept late. And though Grace and I never talked much, I always found an excuse to help her in the shop downstairs. Grace taught me how to take the fragments of old homes and either spruce them up for resale or dismantle them and refashion them for the endless stream of customers. Old doors became coffee tables. A large round gear from an old sugar-processing plant became a round end table. A rusted refrigerator from the 1930s was sanded, repainted, and fashioned into a bookshelf. The old and broken found new life.

Restless, I rose and slipped on my shoes. Moving quietly, I walked the hallway to the door that led to the stairs. Carefully, I unlatched the deadbolt and clicked on the staircase light. Quietly, I moved down the stairs, wincing when one or two creaked.

In the warehouse, I flipped on the main light and took my first really good look around.

Again, I was struck by the emptiness. Once, nearly fifty lights hung from the ceiling. Lanterns, chandeliers, sconces, and pendant lights cast a warm glow over the rows of reclaimed doors, stained glass windows, fireplace hearths, and so many odds and ends I didn't think it possible to catalogue them all.

Moving toward the counter where I'd worked, I pressed my hands on the dusty countertop, taken aback that time had whittled this vibrant place to what amounted to skin and bones. One of my last jobs here included cataloguing keys and locks. I glanced under the counter, half expecting to see the dusty box filled with keys. All I found was a stash of papers and invoices that looked in dire need of sorting. I grabbed a handful of papers and glanced through bills, flyers, site directions, and receipts. There was no real order to the stack.

"Oh, Grace."

Instead of returning to my bed and certain tossing and turning, I began to sort papers. Making order out of chaos calmed my nerves.

By six in the morning, I'd sorted through all the papers and discovered that Grace's salvage yard was on the verge of closure. She received several generous offers, which it seemed she ignored. Zeb said she'd suffered a stroke in the last year, but judging by the ignored papers, she'd started unraveling long before.

Guilt jabbed me in the back. Grace was thrilled when I joined her company after college. Once or twice she mumbled I was her saving grace. And then I left.

"Damn it." I neatly stacked all the sorted receipts and put them back under the counter. I thought about calling Scott, needing to hear his voice, but decided against it. He was already headed into the fields and out of cell phone range. I'd try Scott around ten, when he normally returned to his office.

Rising, I shoved fingers through my hair and padded down the hallway to the single bathroom in the apartment. A flower mosaic made up of black and white hexagon-shaped tiles covered the floor of the small room. There was no shower but rather a claw-foot bathtub that Grace and I salvaged the summer of my twelfth birthday from a farm an hour west in Middleburg, Virginia. The pedestal sink, another rescue, offered a few slim ledges barely wide enough for my toothbrush, and above it hung an oval framed mirror with silver backing that was thinning and fading on the bottom edges.

I turned on the tub water and stripped. Thankfully, I packed a small bag, somehow remembering or knowing that no Shire disaster was as quick as anyone thought.

The bath restored a little of my energy and by the time I redressed into the one change of clothes, a pot of coffee brewed in the kitchen.

Without a word, Grace poured a cup of coffee for me in a large blue mug and splashed in a dollop of milk. Breakfast was fruit and toast. Neither of us spoke as we ate.

I glanced at my watch. "It's seven. Hospital visiting hours start in thirty minutes and doctors will be making their rounds. I want to catch Janet's doctor and find out how she's doing."

Grace's lined thin hands cradled her mug. "What about Social Services?"

"One problem at a time."

Grace rose from the table and made herself a second cup of coffee. She cradled her large white mug in hands bent by arthritis. "Don't toss that baby away, Addie. Don't do it."

Anger snapped. "I'm meeting with Janet's doctors."

"I heard you the first time. But you're going to talk to that social worker and I want you to do right by that baby."

Rising, I grabbed my purse and fished out my keys. "I'm not a monster."

"Don't have to be a monster to do wrong."

"Damn it."

"There was a time when you were brave and not afraid to ruffle feathers. I need you to be that person again."

"Stop. I will figure this out." Keys gripped in my palm, I left, stomping down the old stairs to the first floor.

Outside, a breeze from the Potomac was warm and heavy with moisture that promised heat and maybe a storm this afternoon. A filmy haze of clouds softened the sky's crystal blue. A typical day in the city. Hot and muggy.

I checked my cell for a weather report. Ninety degrees today and tomorrow. Scattered showers today. At the vineyard, I became adept at watching the weather and tracking storms and heat waves. As glamorous as some might have considered owning a vineyard, the bottom line was that we were farmers and as much slaves to the weather as the tobacco farmers who settled this area three hundred years ago.

Not bothering a glance toward the warehouse, I got in my car. Damn. "Is it really that wrong to want my own life?"

Traffic was already thick, clogged with tourists and commuters, and it took me twenty minutes to travel the half-dozen miles to the hospital. I parked in the lot and sat in the car for a moment. My heart raced and my hands sweated as I thought about what waited for me. Circumstance swirled up around me like a hurricane, sweeping away all the joy and excitement this week originally promised.

I wasn't supposed to be here. I belonged in the country at the vineyard at Scott's side.

Before my self-pity could grow out of control like a weed, I got out of my car quickly and moved past the receptionist toward the elevators. Elevator doors dinged open as if expecting me. Inside the car, I pushed number six for the maternity ward. Inside the elevator, soft, nondescript music played from a hidden speaker. I stood straight, hand clenched on my bag, wanting so much to run away. But when the doors opened I moved to the nurses' station staffed by an older woman with red hair and glasses. She glanced up at me. "May I help you?"

"I'm Addie Morgan. I'm here to see my sister, Janet Morgan."

"Do you have identification?"

I pulled out my wallet and handed her a driver's license. "I was here yesterday. Is Dr. Reed here yet?"

"He's in with her now." She handed me back my license. "Room 606."

"Right. Thanks."

As I moved quickly, overhead lights hummed, like buzzing flies chasing me to room 606. I stopped at her door when I heard the murmur of conversation. A man, who I recognized as Dr. Reed, was talking to a soft-spoken woman. My sister. Janet was awake.

Clearing my throat, I moved into the room and peered around the curtains. Janet lay back on her pillows, her long face as pale as the over-bleached bedsheets. Blond hair, stringy and oily, draped over the pillow like the roots from a tree. Her green eyes, as wide as an owl's, were haunted and scared as she stared at the doctor. I recognized the expression, which was so like our mother's. Most days when I was at school, Mom drank. Gin was her first choice and though she swore each morning that today would be different, every day at two-thirty I found her in the same spot on the couch half asleep. *"It's okay, Mom. I'll brew coffee. You'll feel better soon."* And I would gently pull the glass from her hands and head into whatever room served as our kitchen and make coffee.

I stepped around the curtain. Dr. Reed looked at me, a hint of relief fluttering over his mocha skin. "Ms. Morgan. Look, Janet, Addie's here."

Janet shifted her gaze to me and like Mom, hope flickered. Her narrow shoulders looked so slight and slim, even childlike, in the bulky blue hospital gown. She was drowning, and I was the life preserver she expected would save her.

"Hello, Janet." I should have smiled or softened my voice but the edges, honed by too many rescue missions, sounded brittle.

"Addie?" Long, lean fingers gripped the sheets. "Addie, you came."

Dr. Reed's smile came from relief more than joy. "Yes, it's Addie. She came to see you."

Janet's gaze locked on me, not wandering toward the sound of the doctor's voice. "Addie, I think I messed up again." Her voice turned soft, and I remembered the ten-year-old girl who broke Mom's crystal vase and begged me to help her glue it back together.

Suddenly, I craved a coffee and my old quiet routine of sitting, cigarette in hand, breathing in and out. "We do have a problem, Janet. You have a baby girl."

Delicate eyebrows drew together in worry and confusion as her hands slid to her belly, still distended from the birthing. "A girl."

"Yes. A girl." I moved closer to the bed, wanting to stay mad and pissed and struggling to hold on to both.

She picked at her blanket. "I called you yesterday. You didn't answer."

"I was in meetings. I couldn't take the call." The lie tripped over my lips so easily I believed it. "I'm here now."

She leaned forward, glanced from side to side, and whispered, "I don't know what to do. I don't know how to fix this."

And on reflex I heard myself say, "You think I can fix this?"

"You can," she said, her voice barely above a whisper.

"I'm not sure how to fix this, Janet. This is big."

Tears welled in Janet's eyes. "I thought I could deal with it. I thought I could make it all right. Thought maybe I could be a good mom this time around. And then the voices came back. And they got worse and worse."

"Did you take your meds while you were pregnant?" I knew enough to know her kind of medications moved from the mother's blood to the baby's, and the effects weren't good.

"I stopped before I got pregnant."

And she spiraled out of control. How long before Janet lost her grip on reality? Days? Weeks? Months?

"Do you want to raise the baby?"

"I thought maybe I would if I were better. And then, when the baby really started kicking and moving, I freaked. I thought about how babies get bigger and bigger and they need, need, need." Her fingers tightened around the folds of the blanket, her knuckles turning as white as the sheets. "Addie, I don't have anything to give."

"I know."

"Will you fix this?"

You'd have thought seven years away would have created new habits and different ways to cope, but old habits do indeed die hard. I had mended problems and smoothed the waters since preschool. I heard myself say, "Yes."

Janet relaxed back against the pillows and her grip on the sheets loosened. "I knew you would. I knew you would make it all better."

Dr. Reed slid his hands into his white lab coat. "I have a bed for Janet at the mental hospital. We can admit her for three days right now based on circumstance, but better to keep her there for thirty days. However, she'll have to agree."

My mind jumped from today into the future thirty days. The launch party would be a memory and the Willow Hills wine would be launched. The grapes would have ripened and, if not ready for harvest, on the verge of perfection. Scott would be clearing the north property and readying it for planting.

The baby's life would also change in thirty days. While Janet struggled to regain control, the baby's life would move forward. Weren't the first months critical for bonding? Didn't their little brains grow or not grow based on outside stimuli?

"I'll go to the hospital for as long as necessary." Janet's voice was small and quiet as she looked at me, expecting approval. "That's what you want, isn't it, Addie?"

The enormity of this made me dizzy. In the span of twenty hours, Janet reached into my life, tugged on a critical thread, and unraveled the fabric. I wanted to leave this room, find a waiting room, and sit. Smoke a cigarette. Drink coffee. Figure a way to get my life back.

"What do I do?" she whispered.

Thirty days. Gone. "You need to go into the hospital for as long as they'll keep you."

She closed her eyes, nodding. "I want to go. I want the voices to get quiet. I want to sleep."

Fingers gripping my purse strap, I faced the doctor. "When can she go?"

"She can go tomorrow. According to the OB she's healing quickly."

"Her first birth was very easy. She was running days after her son was born." At the time, her resilience impressed Zeb, who didn't see the storm on the horizon.

"You'll have to make arrangements for the child," Dr. Reed said.

"Yes. I know."

Janet relaxed back against her pillows, and her eyelids dropped as exhaustion washed over her. Her face was now serene—as if she didn't have a care in the world. Which, of course, she didn't. They all now rested on my shoulders.

"The social worker should be here any minute," Dr. Reed said.

I straightened, preparing much like a weightlifter did before hefting a record-setting weight. "I'll go find Ms. Willis."

"Thank you, Addie." Janet's voice sounded far off, childlike. She drifted to her peaceful place.

I moved out into the hallway, assailed immediately by the bright lights, the rattle of carts, and the chatter of nurses and patients.

"Ms. Morgan."

I turned to see Ms. Willis headed my way. Her sensible shoes clipped on the white tile floor and her pageboy bangs brushed the top of her dark eyes.

"Have you seen the baby this morning?" she asked.

"No. I was in to see my sister." I recapped Janet's decision. "Is the baby all right?"

"She's still very fussy. Didn't have a good night. The nurse said she was quiet yesterday when you held her. She was wondering if you could give her a bottle."

"Any luck with a foster family?"

"I'm looking but, so far, not yet. Can you keep the baby for a day or two?"

That delayed leaving until Thursday. I could do that, couldn't I? "Okay."

"If I get a line on a family I'll call you." The social worker smiled, as relieved as Janet. Another brick on my chest. "I have papers for you to sign. And then you two can go home."

"I don't have anything for the baby. Grace can scramble some kind of crib, but I don't have a car seat or bottle or formula."

"I have it all in my car. I was hoping we could work something out and I wanted to be prepared."

"Am I that predictable?"

"I saw someone that I believed would step up."

We walked to the nursery and at the nursery window I saw Baby Morgan crying, her fists balled. Her little pink stocking cap was askew and I imagined she'd tried to pull it off. I didn't like hats much, either. "If there's anyone in this show less happy than me, it's Baby Morgan. She is not a happy camper."

"She's waiting for you to bust her out."

Nodding, my fingers touched the nursery glass as I traced the baby's outline. "You said you have baby stuff?"

Ms. Willis adjusted her glasses. "I do. I'll be right back."

As her determined footsteps clicked on tile floor, I rested my head on the thick glass. "How am I going to do this?"

The nurse in the nursery spotted me and smiled. She indicated that I should move to a side door, which she promptly unlocked. I washed my hands, donned a gown, and before I sat in the rocker the nurse put Baby Morgan in my arms. She handed me the bottle and instructed me to rub the nipple against the baby's lips. When I did, she cried.

"Come on, kid. I know you want it. Give it up and latch."

At the sound of my voice the baby's cries eased and she began to root for the nipple. I tucked it between her lips and she immediately suckled. She snorted, sucked, and snorted again, reminding me of a little piglet. She smelled fresh from clean blankets and gentle baby soap.

I leaned my head back against the rocker, all the while keeping a careful gaze on the baby's face. Feeding her today didn't feel as awkward as yesterday, but I was not a pro at this baby thing.

"Baby Morgan," I whispered. "We're in a pickle. Aunt Addie is kinda freaking out here." The baby gurgled. "Your mom has to go away for a month, and you and I are stuck together for a few days. Then Ms. Willis is going to find you a nice home where you'll be so happy. And Aunt Addie can return to her real life."

The baby relaxed, her face as serene as Janet's minutes ago.

Addie to the rescue.

Driving home with a baby in the backseat for the first time was an unnerving task that stretched my nerves to breaking. The baby carrier was in the center of the backseat, buckled in tight by Ms. Willis, who had shown me how to jam my knee into the base as I hooked the seat belt through it. "For an extra tight fit," she said.

She'd settled Baby Morgan's seat into the base and snapped it in place with practiced ease. She'd armed me with a box filled with bottles, pre-mixed formula, a pack of diapers, and a couple of onesies—my starter kit.

Baby Morgan's seat faced away from me so I couldn't see her face. She was so quiet that once I pulled to the side of the road to make sure she was still breathing. She was sleeping, clearly falling for the lull of the car.

As I drove, five miles under the speed limit, I avoided my customary rolling stops and optional yellow lights, which now seemed dangerously reckless.

I slowed for my third yellow light and a brown SUV behind me honked. "Baby on board, asshole," I muttered as I glanced in the rearview mirror, hoping he saw I was more angry and frustrated than he ever could be. "Baby Morgan, don't cuss. It's a bad habit. And stay away from the cigarettes. And men, until you're thirty."

We reached the warehouse parking lot before noon. The sudden stillness of the car startled the baby awake and within seconds she drew in a deep breath and began to cry. I now knew two facts about Baby Morgan: She was quiet when I fed her and she liked driving in the car.

Grace came out to meet us. Her face was stern, and her crossed arms unwelcoming, but to her credit she was there as promised. She peeked in the backseat at the crying baby and then stepped back as if she spotted a snake or a large spider.

"You actually brought the baby here."

I got out, slung my purse over my shoulder, and very quietly closed my front door. "I did."

"I wasn't sure you would."

"That makes two of us." Aware of the rising heat, I opened the back door and reached for the baby seat. I fumbled around the base for the release button that Ms. Willis pointed out. She'd removed the seat easily, without a bit of effort. And what looked so simple twenty minutes ago was now frustratingly complicated. I smoothed my hand over the base but couldn't find the button. "Damn."

"What?"

"I don't know how to get this car seat out."

"There must be some kind of release button."

Baby Morgan cried louder and the midday heat beat on my back. Sweat trickled along my spine. "That's what the social worker told me, but I can't find it. I don't suppose you have a set of bolt cutters."

"You're gonna need that seat. You can't go hacking into it."

The baby cried louder. My fingers skimmed over the base, searching. "For the love of God, release."

Sweat dripped. Finally, I found the button and pushed. The seat loosened and I was able to lift it and Baby Morgan out of the backseat.

Baby Morgan looked at me. She cried louder.

"Shoot me now," I muttered.

"What?"

"Never mind." I handed Grace the bag of bottles and formula and diapers. "This should get us through until Thursday."

She inspected the bag. "What if we need more?"

I shook my head. "Grace, the social worker said she'd try to have a home for the baby by tomorrow."

There were calls to make for the vineyard, and I needed to touch base with Scott, but none of that was going to happen with a crying baby. The first priority shifted from much-needed work to getting the kid settled.

"I made up a bed for her in your room," Grace said.

"So you knew I'd cave."

She shrugged. "I hoped."

"Great." Balancing the baby seat, we climbed the front steps to the second floor. I dropped my purse on the couch and settled the baby on the kitchen table as Grace unloaded the supplies on the counter. "Do you know how to make a bottle?"

Grace held up a jar and, eyes squinting, studied the directions. "No."

I unhooked the kid and, supporting the back of her head with my fingers like Ms. Willis showed me, I lifted her out of the seat. Her diaper, tripled in size in the last hour, sagged. "I think she needs a diaper change."

"I can't help you with that."

"How about you spread a blanket on my bed?"

Grace hurried to the bathroom and returned with a clean towel, which she spread out on my bed. I laid a wailing Baby Morgan on the towel. "Chill, kid. Chill."

She kicked and flailed her arms.

Grace produced a bag of disposable diapers and wipes. "Here you go."

I opened the diaper. "Are there instructions on the bag?"

She flipped it over and pointed to a small diagram. "It says the wide part goes in the back for girls. Front for boys."

I opened Baby Morgan's old diaper, which was soaked. I tugged it out from under her and accepted a wipe from Grace. I swiped the kid's bottom with a wipe and waved my hand around her to dry off her wet skin. Grace, her expression as grave as a surgeon's, handed me the clean diaper.

I guess this stuff came naturally if you were a real mother, but I didn't have a clue. Real moms got nine months of prep time.

I wrangled her little bottom into the diaper and pulled the edges close as I peeled back the adhesive tab. I secured the first tab mid-center of the front and the second too high, creating an awkward fit.

"Looks like a drunken sailor diapered the kid," Grace said.

I tried to peel off the adhesive so I could straighten out the tabs, but the diaper's plastic tore. Cutting my losses, I resnapped her little one-piece outfit. "Now no one will know that Baby Morgan was diapered by a drunken sailor."

"I suppose as long as it doesn't leak, it doesn't matter."

The baby's cries now scraping against the back of my skull, I cradled her in my arms. "The nurse said she eats every three hours, and it's been . . ." I checked my watch. "Three hours."

"Kid has your sense of time. You liked your meals when you were a kid."

"Yeah. Well, I learned early on with Mom to eat when the food was there. Never knew when the next meal was coming."

Grace straightened. "A few of the bottles looked pre-made. Let me open one."

"Thanks."

She hurried out of the room and by the time the baby and I made it to the kitchen, she'd opened the bottle and screwed on a nipple. "Hot or warm?"

"I don't know. Warm."

"Should I put it in the microwave?"

"It's got to be room temperature," I said.

"Is that too cold?"

"I don't know. Shit. What does warm feel like?"

Grace scanned the sheet. "No."

"Damn."

She unscrewed the nipple and put the bottle in the microwave for thirty seconds. As the bottle turned round and round, the bells on the door downstairs clinked. "I better go check," Grace said.

"Ask them if they've ever fed a baby before."

"We don't know who it is."

Baby Morgan turned up the volume on her cries. "As long as they know babies, I don't care."

As I rocked my body from side to side, the phone in my back pocket buzzed. I fished it out and read the display. Scott. With the baby's cries bouncing off the rafters, I let the call go to voice mail.

Steady and quick steps hurried up the stairs. Zeb and Eric rounded the corner. Eric was grinning, carrying a pink teddy bear, and Zeb look solemn and resigned. As he took in the image of me holding the baby, his expression darkened. For some reason, I thought he'd be pleased I was doing this, but he wasn't. Maybe it was because the baby anchored Janet to Alexandria, his son, and his life.

Baby Morgan cried louder. The noise, coupled with my fatigue and frayed nerves, reinforced that I was not good enough to do this. God, help us all! Unshed tears clogged my throat as I sniffed and pointed out the bottle to Zeb. "Can you tell me if the milk is too hot?"

He crossed, took the bottle out of the microwave, and screwed the nipple back on. His tanned, calloused fingertips barely missing a beat, he upended the bottle on the underside of his wrist. He skillfully drizzled a few drops. "You shouldn't feel hot or cold. If it's as warm as your skin, you won't feel it. That means it's just right."

"Is it too hot?"

"Yes. She's gonna have to wait a minute."

I cradled Baby Morgan closer. "She's not good at waiting."

Zeb crossed to the sink and turned on the cold water. He put the bottle under the cool stream. "Surprised?"

"No, just desperate."

"Can I hold her?" Eric asked.

I glanced at the sole cheerful, bright face in the room. "Eric, when she settles. Right now I need to feed her."

"I can feed her," he said a little louder, over the baby's crying. "I bet I know how."

Zeb placed his hand on his son's shoulder. "Let Aunt Addie handle this feeding. You'll have your turn."

Eric frowned but accepted his father's tone, which left no room for arguments. "Does she have a name yet?"

I glanced at the baby's wristband. "Baby Morgan."

The boy wrinkled his nose. "What kind of name is that?"

Jostling didn't slow her cries. "I don't know. It's the one the hospital put on her wristband."

"It's not a name." Zeb shut off the water.

"Janet didn't name her."

"Can I name her?" Eric asked. "I know lots of good names."

Zeb tested the bottle again, dried it with a towel, and handed it to me. "Good to go."

Grateful, I sat in one of the kitchen chairs and teased Baby Morgan's mouth as before and she accepted the bottle. Her cries slowed as she rooted and then latched. When she quieted and suckled, the adults in the room sighed.

Eric moved closer and studied her face. "She doesn't have much hair."

"No," I said. "And she pees in her pants."

He giggled. "She's a baby. They do that."

"I know. I have to remind myself to check."

Eric touched the crest of her head with his fingertip. "She is soft."

"Be careful, pal," Zeb said. "The top of her skull is soft."

"Why?"

"Her brain is still growing."

Eric touched the top of his head and ran his fingers along the edge. "My head is hard. You say so all the time."

Zeb smiled. "When you were a baby, it was soft."

"Has my brain quit growing?"

"No. But you don't need the soft spot anymore."

Eric nodded, his expression as stern as his father's as he considered Zeb's words. "She still needs a name, Addie."

"I know." I didn't have the right to give her a name she'd carry for the rest of her life. Wasn't that Janet's job? I suppose I couldn't keep calling her Baby Morgan, and if she went into foster care she'd need a full name.

"Can I name her?"

I looked up at Eric. "What kind of name do you have in mind?"

He studied the baby. "My dog's name is Shep, but he's a boy."

His serious expression charmed me. "Better stay clear of boy names."

He nodded thoughtfully. "There's a girl in my class named Hanna, but she smells funny and likes to kiss boys." He touched the baby's hand. "There's a girl named Emily in school, but she's always laughing."

"So no to Hanna and Emily."

The boy nodded again.

"Is there a name you like?"

He looked at the baby and traced his hand over her head. "I like the name Carrie."

"Carrie?" Movie images flashed of the fictional Stephen King character, blood-soaked and screaming at her prom tormentors. "Carrie?"

"Yeah." Eric brightened. "My teacher's name is Carrie, but we don't call her Carrie. We call her Ms. Thompson. She's really nice. Brings candy on Fridays. I like her. And I like this little Carrie."

"Carrie Morgan." Out loud, the name sounded good. I could picture it on a business card one day. "Okay, Carrie works for me."

Eric grinned. "Do you mean it? Can we really call her Carrie?"

"Sure. Carrie Morgan has a nice ring to it."

"Why isn't it Carrie Talbot? I'm a Talbot."

Zeb kept his expression neutral. "I'm not her dad, pal. You and Carrie have the same mom, but you have different dads."

"But she has mom's name. Why doesn't she have her dad's name?" Eric traced a gentle finger over Carrie's foot.

"I don't know, pal." Zeb struggled to suppress his frustration around Eric, but I could hear it bubbling to the surface. Some questions didn't have good answers.

I nestled the baby close, interested in Zeb's reaction. "What do you think about the name?"

He cleared his throat, but emotion still clung to him when he spoke. "It's a good name."

Seven years ago, when he left me standing in front of the warehouse, near tears, I thought he was an unfeeling jerk. I could not see past his anger to his fear.

I saw it now. Dark circles under his eyes coupled with flashes of worry humming in the background. He was wondering how to handle it all in the shadow of Janet's return. The two of us were a part of a very special club created by Janet.

"It's official. When the social worker asks me what her name is, I'll tell her Carrie."

September 28, 1750

When I came outside this morning, I saw Faith standing across the way, staring at my house. She did not speak, but her thin, waiflike body reminded me of a spirit. She raised a long, thin arm and pointed at me and simply stared. My baby kicked hard in my belly and I feared Faith bewitched me. I told her to leave or I would tell Mr. Talbot to beat her. She slowly lowered her arm, turned, and walked away. A cold shiver passed up my spine. I dreamed that night of Faith's stark blue eyes staring, accusing me.

Chapter Seven

From a grocery sack, Zeb produced a baby front pack that he had used with Eric. Though the edges were faded and a bit tattered, it was clean. "Easy to use and it will help," he said.

Had he also expected me to give in and take the baby? "Looks like a straight jacket."

"You will thank me."

I pulled the bottle out of Carrie's mouth and she started crying. I rocked her, whispered promises of chocolate and gold, but she kept wailing.

Eric pressed his hands to his ears, shouting, "She sure does cry a lot."

Zeb quickly made excuses for them to leave and Grace quickly followed suit. I was alone, abandoned.

My phone vibrated in my back pocket, and I didn't need to look to know it was Scott. It was two in the afternoon. Damn. I owed him and the caterer a call. God, the time was racing so fast.

As Carrie cried and fussed, I spread out the baby pack on my bed and tried to figure out how she fit into it. As I dug out instructions, the baby wailed louder. Finally, I realized this was a sling.

"Carrie, you do understand that crying doesn't help, right?" The baby kicked and wailed. Tears welled in my eyes.

I put the baby on the bed and she fussed louder. I threw the sling over my shoulder and then picked up Carrie and settled her in the pouch. At first, she scrunched into a ball on the bottom and that made her cry louder. My hands trembled as I fumbled to straighten her out and tighten the straps in place. As her cries cut through my head, I settled my hand under her bottom and moved across the room. "This is what a nervous breakdown feels like. Funny, it's far more stressful than I ever realized."

The sound of my voice seemed to catch her attention and for a moment she silenced. Grabbing my cell, we headed down the stairs. "Might as well give you the grand tour of the joint, kid. Who knows, this salvage empire could be yours one day, because it sure as hell isn't going to be mine."

Down the back staircase, I cradled her bottom in my hand as her wails echoed in the stairwell.

As a fussing Carrie and I moved onto the large first floor of the warehouse, I strolled down the nearly empty first aisle. It occurred to me that babies liked to hear singing, but I didn't know any baby songs. "Come on, Addie, you've got to know a song." I sang the words. The kid grumbled and fussed. "Baby, baby, you can stop crying now. Auntie Addie is going insane," I sang.

Her cries suggested if she could speak she'd have cussed.

My pace quickened as I moved past a row of fireplace mantels, swaying from side to side with each step. Carrie's cries silenced, started back up, then silenced. The stutter-step cry was an improvement. I kept walking, swaying. The silences grew longer and the fussing shorter until finally it stopped.

I reached for my cell and considered a call to the caterer, but Carrie's radar sensed this and she wailed. We kept walking.

At the end of the row, I turned around and walked back past the mantels. A few were made of white marble with gray veins running through them. Several more were made of mahogany. One was inlaid with carved roses whereas another sported simple, smooth lines. I ran my hand through the dust along the smooth, cool lines of another mantel made of a dark marble, imagining the house that once displayed such a lovely piece of art. It would have been early nineteenth century. A Federal-style house. Brick. Hardwood floors.

"Carrie, Carrie," I sang. "Do you think the house was pretty? Do you think a little girl lived there that loved to play with dolls?"

As we moved deeper into the musty, dimly lit space, the baby's body relaxed into the sling. Again at the end of the row, I stood swaying my body back and forth. In a darkened corner, I heard little feet scurrying and knew the mice set up new nests. Grace wasn't setting her traps.

I swayed back up the second row. This section was once the home to all the stained glass windows, but most of the shelf space was filled with dust. The inventory consisted of a circular rose window ringed in walnut and a few small pieces. The next row, which held the doorknobs, was filled with bins that were mostly empty. From one bin, I pulled out a crystal doorknob cracked through the center.

"Baby Carrie, Grace hasn't been collecting, has she?" Grace loved the salvage business. Loved the idea of saving properties and bits of history and people's lives. I thought about her long, lean face and the deep lines grooved in pale skin around her once vivid blue eyes. The stroke stole so much.

Another problem. Another worry. Another compulsion to fix. And then I reminded myself that I wasn't in the fixing-of-lives business anymore. "Baby Carrie, how did my life get so screwed up?" I sang.

The baby settled against my chest and soon her breathing was deep and even. Patting her bottom with one hand, I dug my cell out of my back pocket, scrolled through the numbers. When I found the catering company's number, I hit Send. The phone rang. I rocked back and forth.

"Addie" came a breathless feminine voice. "Where've you been? Crisis!"

Suzanne owned Sweet Treats in the Shenandoah River Valley near the city of Staunton. She did small jobs for me and the events went smoothly. The Friday reception was our biggest job together to date, which was why two days ago we reviewed all the details.

"What crisis, Suzanne?" Tension crept through my body, twisting already tense muscles.

Metal clanked and rattled over the line, and I imagined red and yellow bracelets rattling on her wrist as she dug fingers through her hair. "I tried to talk to Scott, but the boy is clueless. He sounded a bit panicked when I asked about you."

"I'm in Alexandria for a day or two. I'll be back by Thursday afternoon." I glanced at Carrie, wondering if the lie reverberated in my tone. "What's the problem?"

"I can't get the shrimp from the supplier. We'll have to make a swap."

"A swap?"

"I know. I know how much you wanted the shrimp. And I'm so sorry, but I can get these lovely beef tips."

Carrie shifted and fussed. I realized I wasn't swaying. I swayed. "Fine."

"Fine what? Fine like okay or fine like I'm really pissed."

Carrie wrinkled her face and made more noise. "Fine like it's okay. Beef will pair with the reds, and we already have chicken for the whites. We can do without the shrimp."

"The beef does cost a little more."

I tipped back my head, wishing that a little bit more money could solve all problems. "Just work up a price and e-mail it to me. I'll pull it up on my phone and send you back a response."

"Thank God."

"Is that it?"

"Yes."

"Great."

"You okay, Addie? You sound stressed."

Sway walking along the near-empty bins that lined the row, I smiled, thinking if I could fool myself, I could fool her. "Just a tad stressed over the opening."

"You'll run the night like a general."

"You know me. Just a worrier." Carrie mewed out a half cry, half yawn.

"Is that a cat I hear?"

"Yeah, it's a couple of old tomcats. They're all over Alexandria."

"Sounds like a mean one."

"You've no idea." We traded more quick pleasantries and I hung up. "Carrie," I sang. "If you blow my cover, I'll have to tell Scott about my family. And I swore that would not happen." I ended the song on a deep and moody note. My half-baked singing did the trick again and she settled back. When her breathing sounded deep and even, I pulled up Scott's number.

On the second ring the call got tossed into his voice mail. Closing my eyes, I listened to his voice and tried to squeeze strength and courage from the deep tones. I imagined he was saying, "It's okay, Addie. I'll love you no matter what." But at the beep, I did as I was told and left my message. "Scott," I said, with a bright smile on my face, "this is Addie. All is solved with the caterer. Not really an issue. I'm still in Alexandria, and it looks like I might have to stay until Thursday, but don't worry. I got this. Friday is going to be great. I love you!"

I hung up and held the phone to my chest, wishing I could reach out and share with him pieces of my life. But when I moved to the vineyard I swore the past and the curse would remain forever buried. My baggage was mine alone to carry. And I wouldn't share the weight with anyone. Not now. Not ever. Somehow, I'd solve this alone.

Grace stood on the edge of the Potomac and closed her eyes, savoring the brackish scents of the river. The day's once-hot air now cool brought tourists out to amble the bike trail, which ran from Alexandria to Mount Vernon.

This was her favorite time of the day. The sun hung low, as if refusing to let go of the light. Knowing the day would soon end added a bit of urgency to the remaining hour of daylight.

She had gone to the grocery store and bought supplies for the baby as well as a couple of shirts and shorts for Addie. It wasn't much, but a small gesture to ease the guilt weighing on her shoulders. She'd failed Addie once and for years after swore, if given the second chance, she would stand by her side. But her second chance had arrived and she'd shrank from Janet and her baby and dragged Addie, the remaining uncursed Shire woman, back.

Grace was a coward. She knew this. She was afraid of the curse. Once she was given the chance to face it head on, but she'd failed herself, her sister, and her nieces.

She glanced at her hands, bent and weakened by arthritis. She tried to make a fist, curling them in on herself, but she couldn't endure the pain. She studied her lined knotted hands and cursed old age.

A boat sailed by and several laughing children rode colorful bikes along the path.

She turned from the water and moved slowly toward the parking lot and her car. The drive back up the George Washington Parkway toward King Street took fifteen minutes, and by the time she parked and unloaded her bags, the sun had surrendered to darkness.

Through the front doors of the shop, she found Addie standing by the old cash register, arms crossed in front of a baby front pack. The child had nestled into the pack and fallen asleep.

Addie, however, looked wide-eyed and crazed, and reminded Grace so much of herself that summer Social Services had dropped off her two nieces.

"Grace, I was worried about you."

Soft steady breaths came from the front pack. "I went to the store."

Addie took the groceries. "That was five hours ago. Are you okay? Zeb told me about the stroke."

"You don't need to worry about me." Anger for Janet, Elizabeth, and her own failures sharpened her tone. "You look tired.'

"I've been pacing all afternoon. The baby wakes the instant I stop moving."

"I got formula and diapers. Couple of shirts for you. Looks like just in time. You stink."

Addie's steps echoed up the stairs. "I smell like spit-up."

"When's the last time you changed that baby?"

"An hour. Maybe two. It's all running together." She set the groceries on the counter in the kitchen and began to unpack them. "Thank God, you got coffee. I scraped the bottom of your coffee tin an hour ago and made a half cup."

"You sit. I'll heat up the soup."

"I'm afraid if I sit, Carrie will cry."

"Carrie." The new name sounded awkward, foreign.

Grace opened the refrigerator and loaded in a quart-size bottle of milk and butter. Two staples she hadn't bothered with for a long time, but did now, for Addie. She grabbed the last cold soda from the fridge and handed it to Addie. Addie popped the top of the can, taking a long sip. "I haven't drank one of these in ages. I've missed it."

"They don't have diet sodas in the country?"

"Scott's not a fan of soda. And I totally get where he's coming from. Water and wine."

"I don't see why you can't enjoy what you love."

"I love my country life." She sat in the chair, grateful to have the weight off her feet and lower back.

Grace removed an old dented pot from the shelf and set it on a gas stove. She switched the burner on and reached for a can opener. The summer Addie stayed here, she made her tomato soup and grilled cheese every night for supper. The kid savored the routine and never minded that Grace's cooking skills were limited to heating and toasting.

Grace reached for the can opener her arthritis had forced her to buy a year ago. Though its special handle allowed her old bent hands to get the job done, she resented it.

Time had caught up to her and there was no fixing the mistake she made when she allowed her sister to take the girls. But maybe she could prevent Addie from making the same mistake—hopefully freeing her from the curse.

October 2, 1750

With Penny at my side, I ventured to the small market in the town center. There I saw Patience McDonald and her husband. They own a small tobacco farm a few miles west of town. I inquired about storm damage and Mistress McDonald told me she and her husband and their indentured man harvested most of their tobacco crops before the skies opened. What remained in the fields was crushed. If the storm arrived weeks earlier, many would have seen their livelihoods ruined. I was tempted to ask Mistress McDonald about Faith but feared my interest would arouse suspicion about my own connection to Faith.

Chapter Eight

The first rays of light cut through the blinds into my room and reached into a restless sleep, pulling me toward consciousness. I didn't want to wake up. I wanted the sun to go away and the silence around me to last forever. Pushing a strand of hair out of my eyes, I imagined Scott's body nestled close to mine, his unshaven chin teasing my shoulder. I conjured the scent of his aftershave mingling with the scent of grapes and sunshine. Curled on my side, I smiled.

The nightmare of yesterday with Janet and the baby was just that, a nightmare. I wasn't back at the warehouse in Alexandria. I wasn't hot, sweaty, and too tired to eat. It was over, and I was back to my life.

The sun brightened and coaxed my itching eyes open. The worn ceiling and the room's fading white walls were not mine. I sat up and swallowed. Saw the portrait of the dour lady staring at me. The steady tick-tock of a clock echoed. *Tick-tock. Tick-tock. Tick-tock.*

Grace's clock. I wasn't wrapped in my large queen bed back home, but in a twin, twisted up in faded pink sheets embossed with roses and vines. Alexandria. The city.

The nightmare continued.

Ticking clock. The pink sheets. Silence.

Where was the baby? I rose and tiptoed across the floor to the dresser drawer lined with blankets. Inside, Baby Carrie slept on her back, her eyes shut tight and her small lips moving as if she were mumbling.

I stared at the steady rise and fall of her chest. One. Two. Three. Alive.

Rubbing the sleep from my eyes, I pinched the bridge of my nose. Carrie had been up half the night crying, and now, as the sun rose, she slept hard. Holding my breath, I backed up a step and tiptoed out of my room. Floorboards creaked at the threshold and I paused. The baby shifted, yawned, but didn't wake. I hurried toward the kitchen, determined to have coffee before she awoke.

Standing over the old farmhouse sink, I stared out the window at Union Street and, beyond it, the Potomac. The city streets were empty but, on the river, a sailboat skimmed along the early morning waters, enjoying the breeze yet to warm under the summer sun. A couple of joggers passed by on a trail by the river. The city wasn't really awake and the peace reminded me of the country, where life meandered at a quieter pace. I missed Scott and our life desperately.

"Soon," I whispered. "I'll be home soon."

I opened the coffee jar and nearly wept when I discovered Grace had refilled it last night. Jamming as much coffee as I could in the filter, I closed the lid and filled the carafe with water. Soon, the machine was loaded and gurgling.

From a wooden breadbox hand painted with strawberries and

vines, I found a bag of cinnamon raisin bagels. My stomach grumbled. Did I last eat yesterday morning?

As the coffee dripped, I pulled butter and milk from the refrigerator. I dragged the knife over the butter and then covered the bagel in a thick coating. Normally, I'd have skipped the extra fat calories, but today I deserved them.

As I leaned over the sink and ate the bagel, the faint scent of formula wafted over. A glance at my stained shirt and I realized I still wore yesterday's shirt. Pride should have made me care that I looked one step away from homeless but I kept eating. Chewing, I rolled my head from side to side, working the kinks from the stiff muscles.

Sipping coffee, I moved through the kitchen into the living room. A thick marble mantel inlaid with angels sported a collection of silver frames filled with black-and-white photos and paintings. The first dated back to the nineteen twenties. A woman with a pageboy haircut wearing trousers and a safari-style jacket stood on the plains of Africa. She wore a wide-brimmed hat, sunglasses, and a long dark scarf curled around her neck. Another small painting dated back to the late eighteenth century, perhaps the seventeen nineties. The unsmiling woman stood next to a mantel much like this one, and wore her dark hair coiled in a tight bun. Next to this frame was a plain glass bottle no more than eight or nine inches high.

The bottle's long neck was corked and sealed with red wax, which dripped blood red down the forest-green glass. Thick and sturdy, the bottle clearly once held wine. I held it up to the light and could see objects inside, but the wavy, hand-blown glass was thick enough to obscure my view. Shaking the bottle, I heard the faint click of metal.

Footsteps creaked behind me and I replaced the bottle on the mantel. Turning, I found Grace standing there with a full mug of coffee.

She was dressed in clean clothes, and her hair was brushed and in place.

"Been a long time since I woke to the smell of coffee."

"The baby didn't sleep well."

Grace sipped her coffee. "When did she finally fall asleep?"

"About three A.M., I think." I savored the coffee's bitter taste, hoping it would compensate for no sleep.

"What's the plan for today?"

"I need to check in with Scott, and then I'll meet with the social worker. She's supposed to update me on a foster family."

Grace's lips flattened into a frown. "It's important that it's a good family. You or me might not want to be a mother. Janet might not ever be able, but Carrie deserves a strong mother. She's gonna need one if she's cursed."

Staring into the milky depths of my coffee cup, I pushed back resentment. "I never said I didn't want to be a mother. I said I never wanted to pass mental illness on to a child."

"I guess those that really want to be a mother are willing to take the risk. I wasn't. And you weren't. I'd call us smart."

"If I'm so smart, what am I doing here? Why aren't I back in the country, living my life?"

"It isn't always about what we want, but what we got to do."

"I've never been able to fix this family. At best, I'm a Band-Aid that slows the hemorrhaging but never really stops the bleeding."

"Maybe you buy enough time until the real fix arrives."

As much as I wanted to believe a new family could save Carrie, I feared the baby would be traveling a hard path most of her life, and whoever walked the path with her would suffer right along beside her.

I reached for the bottle, needing a distraction. "Grace, what is this?"

She turned and studied the jar. "Just a little curiosity I found in your grandmother's belongings."

Morning light bounced off the impenetrable glass as restrained energy seemed to vibrate through the bottle. "What is it?"

Grace let a sigh trickle over her lips. "A witch bottle."

"A witch bottle? Like to cast evil spells?" It didn't feel full of magic, but rather fear.

"No, to protect against a witch's spell."

Just when I thought my family couldn't get any weirder. "We have witches in the family."

"No witches. We feared witches and curses."

My fingers tightened around the bottle as the energy seemed to grow stronger. "We all talk about curses in the Shire family, but the bottom line is we have bad genetics."

"It started somewhere."

I gently shook the glass, hoping to disrupt the odd sensations. "What's inside?"

"Metal pins or nails, likely some hair, and maybe a bit of blood." Bent fingers grasped her warm mug, clearly welcoming the heat into the swollen joints. "It's to ward off evil energy. Keep away what we fear most." She studied the jar. "Can't say it worked so well."

"Why pins?"

"Not really sure. I suppose whoever made it knew the answer."

"How old is it?"

"Close to three hundred years old."

Hearing its age, I wrapped a second hand around it. "Seventeen hundreds."

"As I've been told, it dates back to when the city was first founded. Around 1750."

"Shouldn't this be in a museum?"

"It belongs to our family, not a museum."

I moved toward the direct sunlight and held up the bottle. "You said there's hair and blood inside?"

A smile tweaked the very edges of her mouth. "I like to think it's blood. Some of those protection bottles used urine instead of blood."

"Two days ago the mention of urine would have grossed me out, but considering I smell like spit-up and baby pee I can't criticize." I rattled the bottle again, suddenly annoyed. "If it's a protection bottle, it's not working well."

"You would be right."

I replaced the bottle on the mantel next to a black-and-white picture of a woman dressed in a long dark dress. For a moment my fingers hummed and I flexed them several times before they relaxed. "We've been in Alexandria for a long time."

"Since the 1740s. Our first man in town was a doctor who came from Scotland with his new wife, Sarah, to set up a practice. I believe the portrait in your room is of Sarah Goodwin."

"Not a happy-looking woman."

"No."

A glance at the clock and I realized it was quarter after seven. "I don't know how long the kid is going to sleep. Might be minutes or hours or seconds, but I need a shower and to make a few calls."

"You got that bag of T-shirts I picked up. Not fancy. Just plain black, but they'll do the trick."

"Thanks." I plucked at the fabric of my shirt. "Maybe in some cultures baby throw-up is considered chic."

"No."

"Right." I plucked at the sleeve of my very ripe T-shirt.

"Get into the shower. I'll make a couple of bottles of formula and put them in the refrigerator."

"You know how to do that?"

"If I don't have a baby screaming, I can read instructions as well as the next person."

"Tick-tock. She'll awaken soon." I swallowed the last of the coffee. "And thanks."

"Addie?"

"Yes."

Ice blue eyes bore into me. "It's going to be all right."

Unexpectedly, her words soothed. "Why do you say that?"

"It has to be, doesn't it?"

The grandfather clock ticked steady and even in the hallway. "I don't know what we did to offend the cosmos, but somewhere along the way, we really stepped in it, and now we're getting paid back."

The shower washed away enough fatigue so that my eyes didn't itch and the ache in my muscles faded a fraction. The T-shirt Grace bought me was an off shade of black and a glance at the red-stickered price tag told me she found it on the clearance rack. It was a size too big, but it was clean and would be serviceable enough for my meeting with the social worker. I'd toss it in the trash before I returned to the country.

I ran a comb through my hair and was just brushing my teeth when the baby stirred. She barked out a cry, a testing of the waters, and for a moment was silent. I stopped brushing and stood, silently praying for fifteen more minutes. Fifteen minutes. No, I'll take ten. Five.

But the kid's cries returned, growing loud and insistent very quickly. I finished brushing my teeth and went into my bedroom where Carrie kicked and screamed, her fists balled and her face turning as red as a tomato.

"Hold your horses," I said. I fumbled in the grocery bag for a fresh diaper and wipes and a changing towel. I spread them out on my bed. Last night, she woke me sometime after midnight and I stumbled around in the dark as I searched for the bag with the diapers, stubbing my toe. Not today. Today, I would be more organized and figure this out just as I'd learned the vineyard business step by step. If I could manage three hundred acres of land and fifteen workers, I sure as hell could keep a kid clean and fed for a few days.

I picked up Carrie, cradling her head in one palm and her bottom in the other. "God, I feel sorry for you, kid," I whispered.

She cried louder.

It took me an hour to get her changed, fed, and cleaned up enough to put her in fresh clothes. I grabbed one of the outfits from the white plastic bag without really inspecting it. It was a baby blue jogging suit trimmed with gray and bunched at the baby's ankles and wrists. I laid Carrie on my bed and as she kicked and cried, I unsnapped the outfit's midsection and yanked off the clearance tab. "Hey, don't blame me. I didn't pick a boy outfit for you. That would be your Aunt Grace. Take it up with her."

She squirmed and fussed as I struggled to get her into the outfit. I started counting the minutes, seconds, moments, until I could return home to the country.

With her finally dressed, I tugged a pair of socks onto her feet. I didn't have a diaper bag so I stuffed an unopened can of formula, a bottle, and a couple of diapers into my purse. My hope was that we would arrive at Social Services and, though it was only Wednesday, the nice social worker lady would have a great home lined up for Carrie.

After snapping her in the car seat, we headed down the stairs, her cries echoing along the stairwell and through the warehouse. I clicked her seat into the attachment and closed the car door. Sliding behind the wheel, I turned the ignition and glanced in the rearview mirror, which offered a great view of the back of her seat. "Please, fall asleep. Aren't you tired?"

Her cries rose up from the backseat, madder and deeper.

"I know this is tough, kid. I know. But Social Services knows what they're doing. They'll know what to do. You want people who know what they're doing. Lord knows you don't want me in charge of your life."

The words rang clear with my desperation and fear. Carrie cried louder. I shoved the car into drive, turned right onto Union Street, and headed south toward Duke Street. Up and around the block I headed back down Prince Street, which was lined with cobblestone. The route was a little longer, but I hoped the jostling would soothe the kid. I drove slowly up the street, the car rocking and bumping on the uneven road. Carrie's cries vibrated with the car, but the extra motion slowed her wails. By the time I drove up King and turned right on Washington Street, her breathing was slow and deep. The car was silent by the time I turned up Mt. Vernon Avenue toward the Social Services office.

The tree-lined street looked friendly enough and the brick façade gave me a little hope. It looked inviting. Nice.

I circled the block twice before I found street parking. The instant I stopped the car and shut off the engine, Baby Carrie woke up and cried. "Of course."

Digging coins from the bottom of my purse, I got out of the car to feed the meter. I was struck by the quiet and how a little distance from the baby could lower my blood pressure. As I fished for quarters, I glanced in the backseat. Carrie was red-faced, mouth open in a full scream, and her fists were clenched.

My hands trembled a little as I found four quarters, which bought me about an hour's time. Confident that we would be finished sooner, I opened the back door and the remaining cool air rushed out as I wrangled with the release buckle on the baby seat. The heat of the day was rising and my blood pressure was bumping against the upper lim-its. I ignored the sweat trickling down my back.

"How did I get here?" I mumbled as the button finally gave way and the seat came loose. With a crying baby in the car seat and my purse slung over my shoulder, I glanced both ways and crossed the street to the department's main entrance. "I'm a good person. People like me. I *am* nice."

As I stood in front of the double doors, the bagel and three cups of coffee weighed heavily on my stomach. Grabbing the door, I yanked it open and stepped into the cool lobby, which magnified Carrie's cries. Several people in the waiting area glanced at me. More disapproval.

I hurried to reception, separated from the lobby by a thick glass partition. I leaned toward the microphone and in a voice loud enough to drown out Carrie I said, "I'm here for Ms. Willis. Addie Morgan. She's expecting me."

The woman nodded. "I'll page her. Have a seat."

Instead of sitting, I began to pace, swinging the car seat a little, hoping Carrie would fall asleep. She fussed. Wailed. Fussed. And though she wasn't quiet, the full screamfest eased.

Ms. Willis entered the lobby from a side door and smiled. Her gaze reflected hope until she met my eyes. "You doing all right?"

"Long night. Babies don't sleep."

"That's true." Smiling, she reached out for the handle of the car seat, which I gratefully gave her. Free of the child's weight, some of the tension in my shoulders eased as I followed Ms. Willis through a door and along the carpeted hallway lined with cubicles. Overhead fluorescent lights buzzed, mingling with the hum of conversations. Ms. Willis ducked into a tiny cubicle.

She took a seat and set the car seat on her desk while I sat in a hard gray chair. The walls of the cubicle were decorated with hundreds and hundreds of children's faces. Some of the kids were smiling, but many were not. I focused on the smiling kids.

"These are the kids you've placed?" I asked.

"Yes. I've been at this almost twenty years."

"Wow. So you really know what you're doing?"

She smiled at the baby and jostled the child's foot. Carrie, for whatever reason, was not happy and her cries grew louder, rising above the padded but short walls of the cubicle. I reached for a pre-packaged bottle in my purse, rose, and took Carrie from her seat. Cradling her awkwardly in my arms, I stuck the bottle in her mouth. Silence.

What did I do to deserve this?

Ms. Willis visibly relaxed. "You seem to know what you're doing."

"I have no idea what I'm doing," I said. "I'm totally lost." I lowered my voice. "I'm in full panic mode, Ms. Willis. Janet is leaving the hospital today and going straight to a mental health facility for thirty days. I have an aunt who's suffered a stroke and her business is failing. And I've an almost-fiancé who is letting all my calls go to voice mail because he's pissed that I'm not there to help him with the biggest day of his life. I can't keep doing this. Please tell me you have a family for Carrie."

"Carrie?" She picked up a pencil and wrote it at the top of a form. "So her name is Carrie? Did you pick the name?"

I blew a strand of hair from my eyes. "No, her brother, er, half-brother picked it."

"So he's excited to have the baby?"

"He's the only one. His dad, Janet's ex-husband, isn't thrilled by any of this. But he's trying, for Eric's sake."

Ms. Willis made a note on her form. "Janet said the divorce was friendly and she and her ex-husband enjoyed a good relationship."

"That's not true. They've not spoken in years. Honestly, I don't know if Carrie is the only child she's delivered in the last seven years." The thought made my head spin. "Shit, what am I going to do if there are more babies out there?"

Ms. Willis set her pen down. "Why don't we worry about this baby and you? The rest, I can't help with, but I can help now."

"So you've found a family?"

"I've found a family. They are a nice older couple and are currently fostering six other children."

Carrie gurgled and burped, forcing me to pause while she read-justed and latched back on. "Six other children? Carrie would be their seventh child?"

"Yes."

I pictured myself holding a crying Carrie as six other children clamored for my attention. As loud as Carrie was, she'd get lost in the shuffle. "There aren't any other families that have fewer children?"

"None that are set up to take an infant on a short-term basis."

"What about other counties?"

"I can try."

"How long will that take?"

"A few days."

"It's Wednesday. I'm supposed to be back in the country on Friday morning."

"Have you told your almost-fiancé about the baby?"

"God, no."

"But he's your fiancé. Don't you share burdens?"

"I don't share my burdens with anyone. No one wants to hear me go on about my crazy family. I don't need people wondering when I might go off the rails like my sister or my mother."

"You think you're going to have mental health issues?"

"Both Janet and Mom showed signs of illness in their late teens. So far I'm fine." The fear always lurked in the shadows. "But it runs in my family."

"Are you two planning on having children?"

"We won't be having children," I said.

She tapped her finger on the form. "You've discussed this?"

"No. Not in so many words."

She shook her head. "How can you be sure there will be no children?"

"Because I had my tubes tied right after my mother committed suicide." The words came out with an exasperated breath. "There will be no accidents."

This secret, only shared with Grace, rolled out, clamoring for freedom all this time.

When I drove to the outpatient clinic almost ten years ago, I was alone. They almost cancelled the procedure when I couldn't produce a friend or family member, but I convinced them that a work friend would pick me up. The nurse wheeled me to the back and the rest, to this day, remains a blur of surgical greens, hushed tones, and lights. After the procedure, when the nurse realized I didn't have a ride, she insisted I wait while she called a cab. But I rose, dressed gingerly, and left alone. The deed was done, and rides didn't matter. That night, I lay in bed and cried.

Ms. Willis stared at me a long moment. "Okay."

"You don't approve."

"I didn't say that."

"You don't have to."

"I think it's important to be honest with your partner."

"When the time comes, I will." But I wouldn't. Instead, I would find a million ways to make his life perfect without children.

Carrie relaxed into my arms, and her mouth went slack as she fell into a deep sleep. I raised her up on my shoulder and patted gently. No cloth on my shoulder, so I prayed she didn't spit up.

Ms. Willis shifted to a stack of papers on her desk. "You're good with her."

"I'm not a mother."

"Then I'll call my foster family. They'll come get her in a couple of hours."

Carrie's cheek rested on my shoulder and a little sigh shuddered from her lips. I might be a screwup excuse for a temporary mother, but she didn't seem to mind. "What does the baby do until this new family arrives?"

"I've cared for my share of babies. I can watch her."

The carpet, walls, and furniture were a sickly gray color and reinforced my unease about all this. "Can I meet the couple?"

Shaking her head, she shuffled through the papers, seeming to move on to the next problem. "I can promise you they're good people."

The knot in my stomach twisted tighter. "I don't doubt your word, Ms. Willis. But I want to meet them."

"I could arrange a visit in a couple of days. With six children, my foster mom doesn't have a lot of time, and she's said she can only duck in and get the baby and duck out."

I imagined Carrie in a room alone, crying in a crib while six other children ran around outside her bedroom door. "You said you could find another family for the baby in a few days."

"Sure."

"Early Friday?"

"Yes."

If she picked the baby up by eight on Friday and I drove like the wind, I'd be in the country by noon, which was time enough to pull the party together. "You *think* or know you could have a family by Friday?"

Ms. Willis looked at me with vague curiosity. "I'm fairly certain."

I nestled the baby very carefully back in her bucket seat. I adjusted the child's arms into the straps and held my breath when I clicked the lock in place. She settled back into her seat, asleep.

"I'm keeping her until Friday. I can juggle, take care of her, and get my work done over the phone."

Ms. Willis leaned back in her chair, studying me. "Are you sure?"

No. "I'll make it happen."

Ms. Willis smiled. "I know this is hard for you, but you're the best fit for this baby right now. She's more relaxed when you're around."

Carrie's sock dangled halfway down her foot. I tugged it up. "Tonight at two A.M., when her head is spinning like Satan because I'm not making her bottle fast enough, I'll tape it and send you a text. Then we'll talk about relaxed."

Ms. Willis patted my arm. "You're doing a good job."

"I'm not, but it's nice you said so." I picked up my purse and the arm of Carrie's bucket seat. "You won't tell anybody about what I told you in here, right? No one knows."

She touched the baby's foot. "I won't tell anyone."

"Thanks."

Outside the front door of Social Services, the heat of the day hit me hard. The glass doors closed behind me. How was I going to make this happen? Carrie fussed and kicked, and I hurried to the car, anxious to get the engine started and the wheels moving.

Carrie and I were halfway home and I was still processing this entire mess when the Check Tire light blinked red and bright. Silence from the backseat told me Carrie slept. But when the car stopped, I was fairly sure all hell would break loose. "Please, let me at least get home."

The light stopped blinking, but it now burned a bright red. Not good. I kept driving until the car bumped, lopsided and unsure.

Gripping the steering wheel, I glared at the bright, bright light. "Haven't I paid enough today? Please don't do this to me."

The car, stubborn and mutinous, wobbled, and the steering wheel jerked, and finally I pulled over to the side of the road and slid into a parking spot. For a few long, tense seconds, I sat and didn't move, my heart hammering in my chest as the air conditioner blew cold air. Tears welled in my eyes. "Universe, what have I done to deserve this?"

When no answer came, I left the engine running and got out of the car. I left the door slightly ajar, fearful if I closed it, the doors would lock. Visions danced of breaking the door's window glass with a brick to rescue a crying baby as the cops arrived.

The front tires were full and hard. The trouble came from the back driver's side. Flat. As a pancake.

Chest tightening with a frustration not really felt since Mom died, I kicked the tire. Traffic buzzed past, and I glanced up and imagined the remaining walk home. Temperatures were forecasted to reach ninety today, and I pictured walking the additional two miles carrying the car seat while sweat soaked my blouse and the baby wailed. I got back in the car and dug out my cell and wallet. Exactly twenty-one dollars and six cents. Enough for a taxi ride, but I'd be cleaned out.

The baby stirred.

With the baby time bomb ticking in the backseat, I searched on my phone for cab companies in Alexandria.

Seconds passed as I waited for the search engine to find a cab. The baby squawked. *Tick-tock. Tick- tock.* "Go back to sleep, Baby Carrie," I sang. "Sleep is our very, very good friend and Aunt Addie's nerves are shot."

A knock on the window made me jump and turn to find a curious Zeb Talbot staring at me. What were the odds? Top off this stellar day with a heaping helping of embarrassment.

I rolled down the window. "Flat tire."

"So I see." He wore a dark T-shirt branded with Talbot Construction over the left breast pocket, worn jeans, and scuffed work boots. A thick belt looped around a narrow waist and a brass belt buckle was engraved with the letter T. Dark sunglasses tossed back my haggard reflection.

"I'm calling a cab."

"You don't have to."

"I do, if I don't want to walk." The less we interacted, the better. He didn't have much use for the Shires, and I wasn't in a mood to be judged.

"Stupid for you to wait in the heat with the baby. I'll take you where you're going." Without waiting, he reached into the backseat and easily unhooked the car seat. Seconds later, he untangled the seat belt from the base.

The efficiency with which his strong fingers worked annoyed me more. He glanced at the fussy baby, frowned, then strode toward his red truck, easily loading the baby in the backseat. Irritated, I shut off the engine and locked up my car as my phone's search engine finally found cab companies. I hurried after him.

"Thanks."

He clicked Carrie's seat into place and shut the back door. "I'll send one of my men to change the tire if you leave me a key."

I paused, my hand on the front passenger door handle. "Really, you don't have to do that."

"Do you have AAA?"

"No."

A brow arched. "I'll need your car key."

Judgment rolled off him without a word spoken as I unfastened the car key from my ring and slid into the passenger seat. The cab was spacious and large and the cool air a welcome relief. He slid behind the wheel, his large, broad shoulders eating up the space and his body filling the cab with the fresh scent of soap and lumber. I handed him the key, which he tucked in his pocket. "Where to?"

"Back to the warehouse."

"Don't you have an appointment with Social Services today?"

"I did." I half wondered if that's why he was in the area, to check up on me.

He shifted gears and pulled into traffic. "And?"

Closing my eyes, I rolled my head from side to side. "I'm keeping Carrie until Friday. The foster family the case worker picked already has six kids."

For a long moment, he didn't speak as he drove through traffic, expertly weaving in and out of lines of cars. "And after Friday?"

"The case worker has promised to get a smaller family."

"And if she doesn't?"

Another weight settled on my shoulders. "I'm only crossing the bridges in front of me right now. Distant, far-off bridges are too much to worry about."

"So, you don't know what you're going to do."

Ass. "Nope. I have no plan other than to go back to the warehouse and feed the baby. If I get really lucky, she'll fall asleep, and I'll be able to make business calls this morning."

Silence settled, and I assumed we would not speak for the rest of the drive. Good. I wasn't in the mood to chat. Carrie, lulled by the car's movement, grew silent.

Zeb pulled onto King Street and wound down the road until he reached the warehouse on the corner. He pulled into the alley and parked. He threw the car in park but didn't rush to turn off the engine. "I remember days like this when Eric was a baby. Trying to take care of an infant and working is tough."

"Any words of wisdom?"

"Keep putting one foot in front of the other, and you'll make it."

I rubbed my eyes, which now itched with fatigue. "God, I hope you're right."

He turned toward me and slowly pulled off his sunglasses. Words seemed to catch in his throat and, for a moment, I thought he'd say more but he simply nodded and got out of the car. He unloaded the baby and when I got out and came around the car to take the car seat, he shook his head. "I'll get her upstairs."

Grateful for the help, I climbed the front stairs to the apartment. "I've got a makeshift crib for her in my room. This way."

Steady booted feet followed me into my room. His shoulders filled the door frame as he surveyed the room: unmade bed, three half-empty coffee cups on the nightstand, and a spit-up shirt dumped on the floor. Overseeing it all, the woman in the portrait, frowning. Always frowning. "Where's the crib?"

I eased past him and moved to the dresser lined with blankets. "Not fancy, but it gets the job done."

He didn't speak as he set the car seat on the bed. He unfastened the straps and carefully lifted her up. In his large calloused hands she looked so, so small and helpless. He laid her on her back in the make-shift crib. "I'll have my guy bring your car back in an hour."

"Thanks, Zeb."

He turned to leave. "Sure."

"Zeb?"

He hesitated, his gaze still turned toward leaving.

"I know this isn't easy having Janet back. Eric wanting to love her . . . It has to be hard."

He reached for sunglasses tucked in his pocket and stared at the dark lenses. One earpiece was well worn, chewed a thousand times while he worried. "It's natural for him to want to love her."

"Has she seen him in the last seven years?"

"Seen? No. A few random phone calls, but they always came at night while he was sleeping. She sent a card or two, which he still has. But that's about it."

"But he's still excited to see her. I'm guessing you've only kept your words kind, so he thinks she'll be easy to love."

He shook his head. "I never meant to mislead the boy, but to talk against Janet didn't make sense either."

My purse slid from my shoulder to the floor. "Do you have any idea who Carrie's father might be?" I asked on the off chance he knew.

"No." The short, curt word cut. "She hasn't called for a couple of years." He lifted his gaze to mine, and I saw his struggle with anger and frustration. "Car will be here by lunch."

"Thanks."

His booted feet echoed in the hallway and down the stairs. The front door closed behind him and I was alone with Carrie. I slid to the bed and my weight quickly settled. A few minutes of sleep would do the trick.

I lay on the bed, wincing as springs squeaked, and very carefully brought my feet up to the mattress. Slowly, I closed my eyes to Carrie's steady breathing.

Thirty minutes later, I woke to her crying.

October 2, 1750

Two young boys were stricken with typhus. Dr. Goodwin went to attend them but said there was little he could do but bleed them. He told their mother to say her prayers for God's good grace.

Mr. Talbot, who is fond of the boys and their families, sent Faith to attend them. Mistress Smyth told me Faith mixed some of her potions and gave the boys an elixir. Both boys showed steady improvement and I've been told they are both eating again.

Dr. Goodwin fears Faith is spinning magic, for no medicine he knows of would have assisted the boys. Mention of Faith struck me with a shiver of fear. My hand went to my belly, and I wondered if she cursed my child when she stood on the street corner and pointed her pale, slim finger at me.

Chapter Nine

That afternoon while the baby slept, I took the chance Carrie would sleep five more minutes while I called Scott, knowing that this was a quiet time of day for him.

The phone rang once, twice, three times, and I expected his voice mail again. But on the fourth ring, Scott's breathless, "Addie" touched my ear.

"Scott." I turned away from the baby and lowered my voice a notch.

"Where are you? God, I've been so worried."

"I'm still at Aunt Grace's."

"Addie, what's going on?"

"She's not been well." That was not a complete lie. Grace wasn't herself. "I'm trying to get her situated with doctors."

His breath rushed over his lips in a frustrated sigh and I imagined him digging his fingers through his thick blond hair. "Honey, are you all right? I'm worried about you."

To know he was thinking about me and worrying, warmed my heart so fully, tears filled my eyes. "I'm fine. I just have to take care of this family issue. I'll be home, come hell or high water, on Friday morning. I've talked to the caterer and texted all the vendors, and we're set. The wine is going to enjoy a beautiful launch."

"You're sure?"

The baby curled her fingers into fists and squawked, so I crossed to her and gently jostled her seat. Her face relaxed and she quieted. "I'm very sure. Grace is doing much better, and I've been able to meet with her doctors to get her medicines figured out." The trouble with lies wasn't creating them, but remembering them. By the time I entered kindergarten I was an accomplished liar. I understood telling the truth about Mom's sickness caught the attention of the teacher, which eventually led to Social Services. *Where's your lunch, Addie? Is your mother okay? Where are you living now?* By the time I was ten, I told stories better than a seasoned con man.

"When you get back and we get this opening behind us, I want us to spend some alone time. If this break has taught me any lesson, it's that we need to talk more."

Gently, I rubbed my thumb along the bottom of Carrie's foot. "We talk plenty."

"Lately, it's been the vineyard or my dreams. It struck me today, we never talk about you."

"I can promise you, Scott, my story is not interesting."

"Everything about you is interesting."

His kindness was nearly my undoing. Here was a man who I loved with my whole heart, and I was hiding so much of my life from him. What was wrong with me? Why didn't I share my stories with him? As much as I wanted to tell him now about Janet and Carrie, I couldn't. Blame it on old habits, but I truly feared my family's past would taint my future with Scott. "Thanks."

"I miss you. And, I miss the vineyard." The front door on the first floor opened and closed, and I quickly glanced to Carrie to make sure she was still sleeping. "Scott, it sounds like Grace is home from the doctor's. Let me get her settled for the night."

"Call me tomorrow."

"You can count on it."

"Addie, I love you."

"I love you, too."

I hung up and held the phone to my heart, pushing back the tears welling in my eyes. My chest tightened and my breathing grew shallow. A tear spilled, but I quickly swiped it away. I would make all this work. I would get Carrie to a good home. Janet would come out of the mental hospital with her meds balanced, and my life in the country would resume. This story would have a happy ending.

As I tucked the phone in my back pocket, I turned to see Grace entering the room. A glance at me, and her expression soured. She didn't spare a glance toward the child as she moved to the refrigerator and pulled out a cold beer. She twisted off the top and took a long drink.

"Wow, Aunt Grace, bad day?"

"You could say that." She glanced at the beer bottle, judging what remained.

"What's going on with you? Other than the obvious with Janet, what's bothering you?"

She held up the bottle. "Isn't all this enough?"

"More than enough, but there's something else."

"I got an offer on this place. A good offer. More money than I could make in a lifetime. I've always known the land was worth a small fortune, but no one gave me hard numbers to consider."

"I didn't realize you wanted to sell."

"I don't. I love this place."

"But it's getting to be too much."

Grace's gaze widened a fraction as she stared at me. Instead of answering, she took another long pull on the beer. "You've been talking to Zeb."

"I've got eyes. I walked the warehouse a couple of times. I noticed the inventory was very low. How long has it been since you took on a job?"

"About a year. I lost my manager, and I couldn't find anyone to take on this place. I figured there was time to sort it out. The warehouse was full. But I never expected inventory to dwindle so fast."

"No jobs in a year?" In this business, you built connections with local contractors who were scheduled to demolish a home. You built connections with designers who visited your shop weekly, looking for the next trend. You built by word of mouth in the community. Everyone, especially the contractors, expected you to be there and ready to act. Disappoint these folks a few times, and you fell off their radar.

Grace dug her fingernail into the beer bottle's label. "I got a call from Zeb this afternoon about demolishing an old stone fireplace. It's all that remains of a small house once part of the McDonald Plantation. The hearth dates back three hundred years. Two years ago, I'd have jumped at the job."

Working at the warehouse, I made a point to learn the area's history well. Alexandria became an official city in 1749, and when the first lots in the city went on sale in July of that year, they all sold within days. The primary stipulation of each land sale required that a permanent house be built on the lot within two years. A few brick homes were constructed, but most were wooden structures that didn't survive the test of time. Surrounding the new city were hundreds and hundreds of miles of Virginia farmland dedicated to growing the highly profitable crop of tobacco. Our warehouse now on King Street was only blocks away from the original Hunting Creek warehouse built to receive, inspect, and pack tobacco for shipment to England.

"Why haven't you? You could always hire day workers."

"Yeah, I suppose. And then what? I'd have a bunch of stones lying in my warehouse."

The market for old stones consisted mostly of high-end designers who wanted to create a unique feature for a client. "Do you still have the list of designers?"

"I have the list, but I'm not sure how active it is."

"Give them a call."

"I can't pull this off fast enough. I have to be on site tomorrow to haul away the stones."

"Zeb can't give you more time?"

"He placed the first call a month ago. I've been putting him off."

"The stones would be an easy flip, Grace."

She raised the bottle to her lips and drank. "Not sure I care enough to try anymore."

"What if I picked up the stones? I could bring them back. Make a few phone calls and see if anyone wants them."

Grace's face softened with amusement. "One job isn't gonna do me much good, Addie. This whole operation is on borrowed time."

"I'm stuck here until I hear from the social worker, Grace. I could do the job and see if I could sell the stones or sit around here and go insane. Honestly, the insane option doesn't appeal, and I would like to get out in the fresh open air and move a little."

"You got the baby."

"I also have you. You work with me, and we could make this happen. We both could ride out to the property and have a look. The truck still runs, because you drove it to the vineyard."

"Yeah. It's tip-top." She dug deeper into the beer bottle label with a thumb made crooked by arthritis.

"You want me to call Zeb?"

"Honestly, Addie, I don't care." She lowered into a seat, no longer able to shoulder the weight.

"Grace, is there more going on that I should know about?"

"I'm running out of steam. It's all getting to be too much for me."

"What's getting to be too much?"

"Life."

I reminded myself that my plate was full as I reached for the phone in my back pocket. I scrolled through the numbers and found Zeb's number. I hit Send. The phone rang once and Zeb's crisp, "Hello," cut through the line.

"This is Addie."

"The baby okay?"

"Baby's great. Sleeping for now. And thanks for the car. Really helped."

"You didn't call to say thank you."

"I called about the job you offered Grace. The stone job."

Silence crackled. "I put one last call in to her today, Addie, but if she can't handle it, I'm gonna demo the rocks. I've an addition to build for this client, and I can't put her off any longer."

"What if I came out tomorrow with a few guys, and we hauled it off?"

Silence crackled. "I can give you until noon and then my grading crew has to get started."

"Where's the job site?"

"Not fifteen minutes from you, down Richmond Highway. The property was the old McDonald Plantation."

"Grace told me. Can you text me the address?"

"Sure." A chair squeaked and I imagined him standing from his office chair. Seven years since I stood in his office, but I suspected he still owned the beat-up pine desk that once belonged to his grandfather.

Behind it stood a tall bookshelf crammed full of construction manuals and supply catalogues, model airplanes he made as a kid, and pictures of Eric. There were also pictures of Janet, but I assumed they were gone. On the wall was his diploma from the Virginia Military Institute, an old Virginia college, ripe with tradition. Zeb was the first in his family to attend the school and graduated with honors in Civil Engineering before he went into the Marines and served for eight years, including two tours in Iraq. Within months of arriving back in Alexandria after leaving the Marines, he met the vivacious Janet and fell head over heels in love.

"Thanks. I've got this."

"Addie, are you sure you can tackle this? The baby's a handful."

"I'll bring her along with Grace. The kid seems to be happiest when we're on the move. She only has an issue when I do selfish things like sit or close my eyes."

His heavy sigh cut through the phone. "Okay. Address is on the way."

"Thanks."

I hung up and looked at the sleeping infant. "Grace, you'll have to watch over the kid while I manage the site."

"I don't know anything about babies."

"All you have to do is watch her. Keep her out of the sun. If she has an issue, get me."

"It can't be good for a baby to be outside."

"If we keep her out of the sun and heat, she'll be fine." The kid stirred and a glance at the clock told me it was feeding time again. Damn, this kid is punctual. As I moved to the social worker's bag of formula, I flipped through a mental Rolodex of people who could help us. "Do you have cash in the business account?"

"Some. A thousand maybe."

"It's enough for a couple of day workers. Who have you used lately, or, at least, most recently?"

"Not anyone in a regular way in a couple of years. But last year, Margaret McCrae helped me out. You played with her and her sisters, Rachel and Daisy, that summer you lived here."

"I remember. Do you have Margaret's number?"

"Sure. In my office."

I cracked the top of the formula bottle and secured a nipple as the baby's eyes opened. She looked around, clearly searching for a reason to cry. Her gaze drifted toward me and she found her reason.

Ready this time, I picked her up and put a bottle in her mouth. "Can you get the number while I feed the baby?"

Grace nodded. "I knew you were the one who could fix the mess."

"Addie, Fixer of Messes. It'll be engraved on my tombstone one day."

Grace shrugged unapologetically. "You were always good at helping, even when you were a little kid. Janet was older. Your mom was the parent. But you ran the show."

"That's not my job anymore. Right now, I'm trying to fix a crappy situation and see that we all come out of it with what we want. You might not want the money from the sale of the stones, but I'm betting Janet could use it."

Grace snorted. "She won't know what to do with the money. I don't care how many medications her doctors put her on, she'll spend it on crap."

"Then I'll put it in an account for her."

"And what? You'll keep helping her after she gets out?"

A bank account was one of those distant bridges I couldn't consider crossing now.

Grace found Margaret's number, and once Carrie was changed and settled back in her dresser drawer cradle, I dialed the number. If Margaret couldn't help, I hoped she could at least point me in the direction of someone who could. I really didn't want to call Zeb back and tell him we couldn't do the job. He sounded so unsure of me, and I needed this. I couldn't really fix my family, but I needed to prove, to myself more than Zeb or Grace, that I could at least do this.

On the third ring, I heard the shatter of glass hitting a floor, muffled curses, and then, "Margaret McCrae."

Clearing my throat, I leaned forward on my bed. "Margaret, this is Addie Morgan. My Aunt Grace owns the architectural salvage company on King Street."

"Yeah. Sorry about the crash and the curses. Just knocked my coffee cup over." She cleared her throat. "It's been a long time, Addie. Like twenty years. How's Grace doing? I haven't seen her in a year."

"Great." The lies tripped easier and easier. "I'm in town for a few days, and she's gotten a lead on a salvage job. She said you helped her with the last job, and I was wondering what you're doing these days?"

"Still chasing any historical gig I can find. Landed a job in St. Mary's County, Maryland, last year but that ran its course. Working part time at the Archaeology Center, and if the Universe really hates me, I help at the bakery."

"I don't think I've been in the bakery in over seven years."

"A lot has changed. Daisy is running the joint along with Rachel. My parents finally retired. Hard to keep them in town much. Have Winnebago, will travel. They're always on the go."

Hard to forget Mr. and Mrs. McCrae from that summer. I visited the bakery more to see them than to play with Daisy and Rachel. They were solid, hardworking people and they seemed to really love and care for each other. That kind of respect and affection between a husband and wife was foreign to me, and I savored it as much as Grace's routines. "Good for them."

"You know Rachel's husband died."

"Grace told me. I'm sorry."

"Yeah. But she and the girls are good. She was dating a French baker, but is single again. And old Daisy got herself hitched last year and made a baby. Never, ever thought I'd see that day."

Her candor teased a laugh. "She's a tough customer."

"I think Mom still has the book that you two ripped in half. She pulls it out every so often and tells the story. If Mom is telling the story right, you give as good as you get."

"No doubt."

"So what are you doing these days?"

"Work on a vineyard in the Shenandoah River Valley. Started off as a picker and I now manage the place."

"And Janet? She was always a firecracker."

"Around."

"Ah, more to that story, I sense."

I glanced at Carrie. "You'd be right."

"So, you said you have a job?"

"It's an old stone hearth. I don't have a lot of info on it, but I've been told it dates back to the early eighteenth century. Located on what was the McDonald Plantation. The owner wants the hearth removed so she can build a garage or expand her driveway."

Margaret sighed. "How much history has been lost because someone needed more parking?"

"This job will give you a chance to dig into a bit of local history. The McDonald place was a tobacco plantation."

"We're the city tobacco built." Interest warmed Margaret's whiskey voice, and I sensed it wouldn't take much to hook her.

"I dismantled a few hearths in my time, and I always found something unexpected hidden in the rocks."

She chuckled. "You know how to sweet talk a girl, don't you?"

I smiled for the first time in days. "I'm giving it my all. If you say no, I have to hustle and find someone else."

"I'm not saying no. This sounds good. So what do you need from me?"

"I've got the truck, but I need day laborers, and if you've got the time, I'll pay you to be on-site. The more I know about the site's history, the higher the price the stones will fetch."

"What time tomorrow?"

"It's going to be early. I've until noon to clear the site."

"You telling me a developer is going to destroy the site right after they take a lunch break?"

"Zeb Talbot is trying to work with us. He's been asking Grace for a couple of months to clear the site, but she kept turning him down."

"Is she really doing okay?"

"She's old, Margaret. She wants to do this, but even though she won't admit it, the job's too much." That wasn't true, but Grace was family, and I lied for family.

"Might be fun, and if we go super early I can push back my work at the bakery. They're very used to my tardy, delinquent ways."

A small weight lifted from my shoulders. "That would be great, Margaret. Do you have any muscle men?"

She chuckled softly. "I can always round up muscle. Now tell me again where the property is. You've peaked my interest, and I'm feeling the need to do a bit of pre-dig research."

I checked my texts and found one from Zeb. I read off the address. "Can you go as early as six or seven?"

"Split the difference. How about six-thirty?"

"Great."

November 1, 1750

Captain Smyth arrived home today on the *Constance* safely. So excited was his wife to see the white sails on the horizon that she bade me to run with her to the bluffs. We watched as sailors, anxious to be ashore, unloaded their cargo of dark-skinned creatures onto barges as they also tossed rocks used for ballast overboard.

When the captain reached shore he hurried to his goodwife and gave her a fierce hug. My nose wrinkled over the wretched odor that clung to him. He smelled of human waste and despair. When he saw me raise my handkerchief to my nose, he grinned and replied the stench of money was not always sweet.

When I arrived home, Penny was silent and hovered in the corner. Dr. Goodwin arrived home for lunch, grinning. The cargo, he said, would fetch handsomely on his investment. Penny turned to the fire and prepared him a hot cup of broth, and when she turned again and handed the mug to him, she was her old smiling self.

Chapter Ten

C arrie woke at midnight and then again at three in the morning. Though her cries startled me awake each time, my heart didn't race as fast or as hard as last night. My body was trying to adjust to this new, temporary routine.

On the vineyard, there were plenty of times we rose as early as four. Harvest season was a three-week stretch of days that began long before the sun rose and ended hours after sunset. The grapes were planted and designed to ripen in one section of the vineyard after the other, and it was important to be ready for the grapes because, if left too long in the sun, they withered, and if left too long in damp soil, they rotted. Grapes required a delicate balance that the grower carefully maintained.

The alarm on my nightstand went off at five-thirty A.M. and I quickly silenced it. I needed to be downstairs, ready to go with Grace and Carrie at six-thirty.

Carrie slept in her dresser drawer bed, her little lips slightly parted as her chest rose and fell steadily. "As tempted as I am to wake your little ass up, I won't. I'm the bigger person in this relationship." I also reveled at the idea of taking a quick shower, dressing, and guzzling coffee before the kid awoke.

I found Grace in the kitchen setting up a pot of coffee. "I've made sandwiches," she said. "And I've packed the last pre-mixed bottles."

"That's great." I didn't expect the gesture.

"Get your shower. I'll scramble a few eggs."

Whoever whisked the real Grace away and brought this Replacement Grace was my new best friend. "Will do. Thanks."

I hustled into the shower and turned on the hot water. Aching and tired muscles all but groaned their pleasure as I stepped under the hot spray and soaked up the warmth for a minute or two before I was out of the shower. I was half dressed when Carrie started to wail. Pulling a quick comb through my hair, I hauled on a T-shirt and moved toward the kid. I found Grace standing over the child, frozen.

"You can pick her up," I said.

"No. You're better with her than me."

"She's pretty tough." I leaned over, my damp hair falling forward, and lifted Carrie. "I think she's gaining weight. Or her diaper is a real mess."

Grace backed out of the room. "I'll let you figure that out."

I cleaned up the baby, who squawked and cried as I wiped her off and fitted her with fresh diapers. I dug out another outfit from Grace's clearance-rack run and found a long-sleeved jumpsuit covered with a commando print and sporting a duck in the center of the chest. As I wrestled her into the outfit, I said, "Sorry, kid, but you don't look so hot."

Carrie cried.

I hefted her on my shoulder. "Yeah, I'd cry, too, if I were wearing a camouflage outfit with a duck on it."

Grace handed me the bottle as we entered the kitchen and grimaced when she saw the baby. "It was only a dollar."

I sat and tucked the kid in the hollow of my arm. Within seconds, she was suckling hard. "It doesn't really matter. Soon, we'll have her with real parents who'll know what the hell they're doing. She can spend her days in a crib staring at mobiles instead of a bare ceiling."

Grace poured me a cup of coffee, her expression grim. "A kid does deserve a real home."

"We're the temporary harbor and not the final destination." The idea of sailing to a new port buoyed my spirits. As hard as this seemed, it wasn't forever.

Carrie finished up her bottle as I gulped coffee and ate a piece of toast. I rested her on my shoulder and eight pats on the back later she burped like a field hand. "Good girl."

As I was about to load her in the front pack, she did a number in her diaper, which required a revolting change of diaper and apparel. I tossed the damp and very smelly commando duck outfit in a paper bag for dirty clothes and dug out another jumper. This one was navy blue with sailor stripes on the collar. The red clearance tag read fifty cents. "Your aunt knows how to squeeze a dollar."

We found Margaret McCrae on the first floor studying an old marble fireplace. She wore faded jeans rolled up to her calves, Chucks, and a loose green shirt. Her red hair was fastened in a knot with a black scrunchie. In the last twenty years Margaret and I had crossed paths a couple of times, but she hadn't really changed much. Still the same free-spirited geek.

"Margaret," I said.

She turned with a grin that vanished as her gaze swept over the baby. "You dropped a kid?"

Away from the vineyard, it was easy to discuss my well-known family. "She's Janet's baby."

"Where's Janet?"

"In the hospital."

"Complications?"

"Not the medical hospital."

Her eyes narrowed and then her head nodded with understanding. "She's sick again."

"Yeah."

"How bad?"

"She made a baby, nearly gave birth on the street corner, and now can barely communicate."

"Sucks."

"Yep."

She glanced at the baby, but didn't ooh or ah like some women might. "You already enlisted the kid in the Navy."

"Yeah, meet Ensign Carrie Morgan."

"Morgan? So Zeb wasn't a part of this?"

"No."

Margaret rested her hands on her hips. "And you're keeping it together?"

"For a few days."

"And then?"

"I'd rather talk about my stones and all the great history behind them."

Margaret's grin was swift and genuine. She rubbed her palms together, her ringed fingers catching the light. "I can't say for sure if I know who the property once belonged to, but I have an idea."

"Let's load up the truck, and you can tell me as we go." I glanced toward the stairs. "Grace!"

Footsteps sounded on the stairs and her head poked around the corner. She carried the baby seat and the cooler stocked with lunches and bottles. "Addie, I've gotten a call."

"I didn't hear the phone ring."

"It's important." She glanced toward Margaret. "Good, you're here to help."

"At your service. How you doing, Grace?"

Grace arched a brow, her expression saying, *You've got to be kidding.* "Great. Did you get those men we used the last time?"

"More or less. Two men. Very strong. And hard workers."

"Then you don't need me."

"You said you were going to help with the baby," I said.

Grace shook her head. "I can't. Not today. Besides, Addie, the baby likes you better than me."

Annoyance snapped and stirred old feelings of resentment. What was the deal with this family? Did anyone ever go the distance? "Grace, I think you can pull it together enough today to help."

Grace's frown deepened. "I'm not coming and I'm fairly sure Margaret doesn't want to hear our argument."

Margaret shrugged. "Grace, I never mind a good family argument. It's much like being at home. You two have at it."

Arguing in front of others might not have bothered Margaret, but it bothered me a lot. As much as I wanted to yell and scream, with Margaret standing feet away, I swallowed all my frustration. "We'll see you when we see you."

Pissed, I picked up the car seat and loaded it in the backseat of the truck. My familiarity with the belts and hooks was growing at an alarming rate. I installed the kid in her seat and then turned on the truck engine and the air-conditioning. Margaret slid into the passenger seat beside me.

As I backed out of the parking lot, I caught sight of Grace standing in the door of the salvage company, staring at me with a stony face.

I pulled into traffic and wound my way up King Street. A turn on Patrick Street and I was headed south toward Richmond Highway.

"So you want to hear what I found out?" Margaret asked.

Shoving out a breath, I loosened my grip on the steering wheel. "I sure do."

"If I have my property correctly identified, then you're going to love this." She dangled the historical tidbit much like a mother used candy with a child.

"Spill."

"Do you have a basic history of Alexandria?"

"For the most part. Most of my knowledge centers around architecture because it helps to know a little when you're demolishing a place."

She winced. "Taking a place apart. Makes me want to cry."

"The way I look at it, I am saving history."

Margaret swiped away a loose curl. "In the sixteen hundreds . . ."

The truck frame shuddered a little as I slowed. "We're going back that far?"

"I pulled up your job site on Google Maps. And yes, we're going back that far."

I downshifted at a stoplight. "Give it to me."

"You know about Jamestown?"

"Sixteen oh two."

"Sixteen oh seven. Basic American history, Addie."

"Understood. But can you give me the CliffsNotes version?"

She sighed. "I'm dealing with peasants."

"Work with me."

She turned sideways in the seat so that she faced me. "In 1607 the

English created the first settlement in America. As you may or may not know, it didn't go so well."

"Right. Pocahontas."

"Right, Ms. I-Get-My-History-from-a-Disney-Cartoon. Anyway, the first settlements didn't go well, but settlers kept coming and, after a decade or so, discovered that tobacco was a major cash crop. Thank you, John Rolfe, Pocahontas's husband. Long story short, the Virginia settlement spread west toward Williamsburg and into the Chesapeake Basin and around the banks of the Potomac. In 1732, the plantation owners along the Potomac River were doing a bang-up business of growing tobacco, but trading it with the English was cumbersome. And the English were finding that sometimes the tobacco reaching their shores had rotted. The Crown decreed the establishment of to-bacco inspection warehouses. Long story short, Mr. Hugh West's Hunting Creek warehouse thrived."

"On the corner of Union and Oronoco Streets." The site was five blocks north of our warehouse.

"Give or take. Yes." She settled back in her seat, as comfortable as a history professor at the lectern. "I could get into the land grant, the survey-ing of what would become Alexandria, but that lesson's for another day."

"So who did my stone hearth belong to?"

"I know there were a few families that lived in the area south of town. Technically, they would have leased their land from the Berke-ley family, who really owned all of Northern Virginia and as far west as the Shenandoah River Valley."

"Margaret, you're getting too deep in the weeds for me. What about these stones would help me sell them?"

She fiddled with a red beaded bracelet on her wrist. "There's a men-tion of a woman named Faith who lived in that area. She was brought to Alexandria in the mid-1740s and, from what I can tell, she was accused of witchcraft in Scotland and her punishment was indentured servitude in Virginia. This is the first time Faith has popped up on my radar, so I've definitely got to do more digging on her."

"Witchcraft." I sensed Margaret would connect the witch to the stones.

"Fears of it were alive and well, even then."

"I thought all the witch stuff was limited to Salem in the sixteen hundreds."

"Nope, fear of witches thrived in Scotland around that time. And Virginia can claim a lapse in judgment when it comes to witches. There was a case in the Tidewater area around seventeen hundred. That woman was convicted and sentenced to seven years in jail."

"Seven years? What did that woman do?"

"Basically, she was an independent woman. She grew herbs, wore trousers, and refused to remarry after her husband died."

"But she is not connected to our stones."

"No." Margaret rubbed her hands together, the rings on her fingers clicking against each other. "But stories about witches will sell those rocks."

"For the right buyer, they sure could."

"To be fair, a lot of people believed in witches in Faith's time. England or Virginia weren't easy places to call home in those days. Disease, hunger, and the Indians all made life tough. Death was always close and when the sun set, there was only a handful of candles and hearths to chase the dark away. It was easy to assume the unnatural lurked in the woods."

"So you think Faith is attached to this property?"

"I do. On microfilm I found her indentured servant contract. It was first owned by the ship's captain, then it was sold to a man named McDonald."

"The current owner of the land is a McDonald."

Margaret ran her hands along her arms, chilled by a sudden breeze. "No shit?"

"Yeah. It's a woman. Rae McDonald."

Bracelets rattled as she fist pumped her hand in the air. "I love it when the past connects to the present."

"So we have a connection to a witch. Then our stones will be enchanted?"

Laughter rumbled in her chest. "Hey, you wanted a story that would sell them."

We drove down Richmond Highway past the older subdivisions filled with mid-century modern homes and fully thick mature trees. I reached for my phone in my purse and pulled up the job site address. One mile to go.

"So Zeb Talbot is working this job, too?"

"He is."

Margaret jabbed her thumb over the back of the seat toward the baby. "So that's got to be weird."

"You've no idea."

"And Janet's okay with you having the baby? As I remember, you two didn't get along so well."

"She needs me, and whether she likes me or not really doesn't factor into the equation."

"How long do you have the baby?"

"A few days."

"Damn. I can do an hour with my nephew and then I need a drink. He's a great kid, and God knows Daisy adores that boy, but wow, a real live kid to raise? Too scary."

"I try not to think about it."

A soft laugh rumbled in her throat. "That's why we're on for this excursion. You need something to do so you don't go crazy taking care of the kid."

"I'm getting a little claustrophobic. But this should be an easy job, and the stones are going to be worth good money to the right buyer. I hate to see opportunity lost."

The GPS on my phone warned me a quarter mile remained before I needed to take a right-hand turn. As I slowed, not wanting to miss the turn, I spotted the twin white brick pillars, surrounded by a riot of purple and yellow pansies, marking the entrance to a newer neighborhood. Gold letters that read *Belle Haven* sprawled across the white brick.

"Belhaven used to be the name of Alexandria," Margaret said almost to herself. "George Washington surveyed this area when he was a young man and referred to the city as Belhaven."

GPS silenced my questions and told me to turn left and then to take another quick left past newer homes and then finally into a cul-de-sac that faced Richmond Highway but was buffered by a thick stand of trees. Centered on the cul-de-sac sat a large brick colonial house surrounded by a thick stand of boxwoods. In the center of the yard stood a tall oak tree with a full and thick canopy of leaves. Hanging from the lowest limb was a thick rope that dangled above the grass, its end frayed and broken. Somewhere along the way, it had been a rope swing.

Margaret sat forward in her seat. "Nice house. This the McDonald house?"

I reached in my back pocket and pulled out the rumpled note with the name and address of the owner. "Yes. The owner of the home is Rae McDonald. She's putting on an addition or building a garage."

No sooner were the words uttered than a large, rumbling red truck moved down the center of the street and parked behind me. I didn't need to see the driver clearly to realize it was Zeb behind the wheel.

I glanced at the baby in the backseat, figuring in five minutes she'd realize the car wasn't running. With the air-conditioning blowing cool air, I slid out of the car and came around to Margaret. "You have men coming, correct?"

"Should be here any minute. Grad students. Not day laborers, but they love this kind of stuff and they're very cheap."

"That works for me."

I moved toward Zeb's truck, not sure if he were here to help or check up on me. The Morgan sisters were not known for their staying power, and we did break our word from time to time.

He got out, pulled off his glasses. "Glad to see you made it."

Hearing the challenge, I silenced a petulant quip begging to be voiced. With all the trouble in my life, I did not need a war with Zeb Talbot. "Let me introduce you to Margaret McCrae. She works at the Archaeology Center and helps Grace from time to time."

Margaret thrust a calloused hand forward and took his in hers. "Been a long, long time. I was at your wedding."

A muscle tensed in his jaw. "Right. Good to see you again."

"This should be an interesting job," Margaret said.

"Stone removal is interesting?"

"It's history, dude. And history makes me weak in the knees."

A hint of a smile tweaked the edges of his mouth. "Glad to hear it."

A beat-up VW van rumbled onto the cul-de-sac and the driver ground a couple of gears as he downshifted and slowed.

"That would be my crew," Margaret said. "We're going to dismantle the chimney carefully. We don't want to wreck any historical findings."

Zeb rested a fist on his hip and looked at me. "We don't have weeks to do this, Addie. I can stretch this to this afternoon, but my men have to grade the land tomorrow morning."

"Understood. Let me get the baby and Margaret and I'll go visit with the land owner."

"You brought the baby?" Zeb said.

"I didn't have a choice. Grace won't watch her."

"It's going to get hot today."

"I know. But the truck has air-conditioning, and I'll keep her out of the sun. I have a hat for her."

"Not really ideal, Addie."

"Doing the best I can, Zeb." Irritated, I turned and went back to the truck and dug the baby sling out of the diaper bag. I hooked it over my arm and then, unfastening Carrie, slid her into the pouch.

I came around the truck and Margaret and I walked to the front door. A large brass doorknocker in the shape of a lion glared at us, a large ring dangling from his mouth. I lifted the knocker and banged it against the door a couple of times.

"I'm dying to know when this place was built," Margaret said. "I'm betting 1820s or '30s."

Inside the house, high-heeled footsteps clicked against a hardwood floor before the door snapped open to reveal a young woman. She was in her early thirties and her neat blond hair brushed her sharp jawline. A delicate strand of pearls hung around a pale slim neck above a cream-colored silk top that vanished under the waistband of a navy blue pencil skirt. Her legs were long and she wore no stockings. It wasn't odd for women not to wear stockings this time of year but, for this woman, I guessed the move was more a silent rebellion than a nod to the heat. She wore no trace of makeup, but on her, added color would have looked garish.

"I'm Dr. McDonald. May I help you?" she said.

I shifted, doing my best to feel like a professional and not such a clumsy hack, which would be a neat trick with a kid dangling from around my neck. "My name is Addie Morgan and this is Margaret McCrae. We're with Shire Architectural Salvage. And back on the street"—looking irritated, I thought—"that's Zeb Talbot."

Dr. McDonald's gaze flickered in Zeb's direction. "I've worked with Mr. Talbot before. If you'll follow the stone path around the side of the house, I'll meet you in the backyard."

"Will do."

The heavy lacquer door closed, leaving the brass lion to glare at us. Margaret and I glanced at each other and followed the side pathway made of stone that cut through a tall stand of yellow dahlias. At first glance, the pattern appeared random, but a second take and I could see the root of each plant was spaced at equal distance. After the dahlias, clumps of hostas clustered around a tall wooden archway covered in a rich clinging vine of honeysuckle. Though most of the sweet buds were gone this time of year, the faintest trace of their scent hung in the air.

In the backyard, Zeb's red flagged stakes marked the outline of the new garage.

Rae McDonald came out a side utility door. She'd changed her shoes into a set of more practical flats and easily crossed the neatly trimmed backyard toward us. She extended her hand and my gaze followed, settling on the stone hearth.

The base was ten feet wide, and the stack rose up about ten feet in the air, though judging by the random stones scattered around the base, the original stood several feet taller.

"My hope is to build the new garage on the back portion of the property, but I can't do that with the fireplace there. I hate to remove it. It's been there since I was a kid, but a couple of months ago it was struck by lightning and several stones were knocked loose. I'm not so sure how safe it is anymore, and I suppose it's time to let it go."

"Do you know how long it's been here?" Margaret asked.

"My great-great-great-grandfather built this main house in 1815 and his diaries mention the ruins of the hearth."

"I'm surprised no one ever pulled it down before. That's good stone," Margaret said.

The woman's gaze remained fixed on the hearth. "Rumor has it in the family that the hearth was cursed. No one could say why, but all my ancestors assumed there'd be trouble if the hearth were destroyed."

"And you're not worried?" I asked.

A delicately plucked brow arched. "No. It was a nice conversation piece, but now it's a safety hazard and it has to go."

Questions sparked in Margaret's eyes. "Did your ancestors keep detailed diaries?"

"Not really a diary, but there are letters and logbooks detailing the goings-on in the house and the area. The hearth was mentioned only once by my accounting."

Margaret tore her gaze from the stones. "I'm with the Archaeology Center. Would you ever allow me to look at those house accounts?"

Dr. McDonald's chest rose and fell with a delicate yet determined breath. "Not at this time."

The rebuff sent a cold bristle up my spine. Margaret's smile froze. She opened her mouth to reply, but I quickly spoke up.

"Ready to get started on the hearth?" I asked. Redirecting was a trick I used when my mother was ranting about anything and everything.

Margaret nodded, seemingly soothed by the mystery that might lie before us. "We need to start at the top. If we do this right, I should photograph the site, and we should be numbering the pieces so that the next person who wants to reassemble can do it properly."

"A buyer will reconfigure them however they choose."

"Maybe, but having the history and the deconstruction documented will boost the price. This won't be a pile of stones, but a chunk of living history."

Carrie fussed, but a pat to the bottom settled her. I understood the scope of the job and understood what it took to keep this kid happy, but I think I'd misjudged the toll juggling the two would take on me.

"I'm going to get my camera," Margaret said. "It's in my purse in the truck, and if you don't mind, I'll dismantle this hearth. You can help, but my guys and I have done stuff like this before, and I want to see it done right."

Dependence was a slippery slope. Initially, help is a relief. The next day the hope for it is strong, but soon enough you grow to expect it. I didn't want to rely on anyone. My mother taught me the downfall of dependence.

"I can help."

"You can help by watching," Margaret said, glancing at the baby pouch. "I know this is your company, and your job, and your gig, but history is my specialty. Give me a couple of hours to do this right." She smiled. "Please. This is my passion and it's almost my birthday."

"Really? When's your birthday?"

"Seven months."

Humor eased the sting, but it still hurt to accept help. "Happy Birthday."

Margaret dashed to her car and got her camera and sketchpad from her purse, leaving me with nothing to do and wondering why we were even here. The stones would fetch a thousand dollars, but they wouldn't change much. Fixing the details of Janet's and Carrie's lives wasn't as simple as harvesting hearthstones or launching a new wine. Check one item off the "to be fixed" list and it reappeared at the bottom of the list within minutes.

Zeb walked up to me and stood with booted feet braced, much like the captain of an ancient sailing vessel. "I've got a couple of my men who can help with the stone removal."

"That's not necessary," I said. "Thank you, but you've done enough."

"I haven't done anything."

I glanced at the collection of stones, weighing the debt of each one. "You sent this job to Grace. Even when she turned it down, you kept sending it to her."

"I was hoping it would excite her."

As much as I wanted to know what was going on with Grace, I couldn't ask him.

He stood silent, expectant, but when no question came, he nodded, almost relieved. He'd tried to help a Morgan woman before and was burned.

Margaret stood in front of the stone hearth and snapped picture after picture, moving around it, studying it like a painter studied a masterpiece. Finally, after she took several dozen images, she pulled a sketchpad from her bag and began to draw and make notes.

Dr. McDonald ran a finger along the strand of pearls circling her neck. "I thought you were going to carry them away. I didn't think this was going to be such a project."

Addie Fixer of All Things smiled. "It won't be long now. If we can document the removal, it will help us with resale."

Dr. McDonald watched curiously as Margaret gingerly touched a stone. "I've got a client coming in fifteen minutes. I can't wait any longer."

"Oh, please go inside," I said. "We'll take care of this. I'll come and get you when we're finished."

"If you have any questions, ring the front doorbell. I'll see you in a few hours."

"Will do."

I moved toward Margaret. "The client is restless. I think we'd better start moving rocks."

Margaret's gaze lingered on the stone hearth another long moment before she shoved her pencil in her topknot. "Ready to roll."

Margaret and her workmen settled a ladder on the side of the hearth and began to chip away at the mortar. The mortar joining the stones, beaten and worn by the weather, crumbled easily, almost turning to dust in their hands. The top pieces all but fell into the workmen's hands and they carefully began to stack the rocks in a wheelbarrow.

Carrie fussed and pounded a tiny fist against me, expecting to be fed. I moved toward the truck and took one of the pre-mixed bottles and popped the top. I sat in the shade of an oak tree with the baby and fed her. "Carrie, be careful about needing too much. You can't count on your mother and you can't count on me."

She suckled, her eyes moving toward the sound of my voice.

"I'm sorry, am I boring you? "

Carrie grunted softly and kept eating.

"No one seems to believe me when I say I'm not the person to fix all this. I'm not."

Carrie didn't bother a glance or a sound as she ate. I watched the crew move quickly and efficiently with the stones. Zeb and his men, no longer willing to stand on the sidelines, transported the stones to the bed of my truck, moving as one unit. His operation was a well-oiled machine, whereas mine was working but was held together with bubble gum and string.

Carrie finished her bottle easily. I burped her and changed her diaper before repositioning her back in the sling. She fell asleep, her face relaxed and peaceful.

She was learning to depend on me. Learning to expect that when she cried I'd be there with a bottle, a clean diaper, or a soft word. My words of warning fell on deaf ears. I only hoped she would have someone she could really trust.

An hour later, the chimney of the hearth was dismantled as well as half the base. The job I thought was out of reach this morning was nearly done.

Margaret knelt in front of the hearth and then rose, waving me over. "Addie, come over here and see this. Very interesting."

I moved across the thick grass and, tucking my hand under the baby's bottom, knelt. "What is it?"

"Look inside the hearth."

I glanced at the stones long ago blackened by fires that kept a home warm. Weeds grew among the soot-stained stones, sticks blown in by wind clustered in a corner, and dozens of large ants scurried toward one of the cracks. Time never waited. "What am I looking for?"

Margaret pulled a small flashlight from her back pocket and shone it in the corner. The light shimmered off a near-invisible surface. "See that?"

"Yeah." Cupping Carrie closer, I leaned in, feeling the same pull of energy felt years ago when I touched the key and more recently when I looked at the portrait in my room. Unsettled, I tensed. "What is it?"

She reached in with a small stick and gently chipped away at the dirt around the object. Her hands moved methodically, reflecting the experience earned over a decade of dusting away the past. Slowly, the dirt fell away to reveal the shape of a bottle turned upside down in the dirt. With her fingertips, she scraped away more dirt until she was able to wrestle the bottle from the earth.

Margaret slowly turned the bottle right side up. It was short, made of brown handblown glass, caked in dirt. The cork, blackened and coated with age and filth, was sealed in place by wax.

"What's that?"

"Judging by the glass, I'm guessing it was made in the mid-seventeen hundreds, give or take a decade or two."

"That dates the fireplace."

"It does." Margaret held the bottle up to the light and, as she moved, a metal-like object rattled inside. "This is truly amazing. I can barely breathe. I can't wait to show the folks back at the center."

"Grace has a bottle like that."

"Like this?"

"She calls hers a witch bottle."

"I think that's what this is." Margaret shook her head. "I doubt it's as old as this one. We have only one or two in museums that have survived intact."

"Maybe hers isn't so old, but they do look the same." Carrie fussed and squirmed. "I should offer this to Dr. McDonald. We're here to remove the stones. The rest really belongs to her."

Margaret frowned. "Can we just hang on to it for a few days? Give me a chance to figure out what it is. I'll clean it up for her."

"I can't, Margaret. I have to show it to her."

"Can I go with you? Maybe I could make a case for history and the center."

"She wasn't open to sharing the ledgers."

Margaret pushed out her bottom lip in a pout. "I'll be nice."

"Let me talk to her. I'm good at turning a no into a yes."

"Really?"

"It's not possible to run a vineyard without getting a lot of personalities to work together."

Margaret pressed her hands together in prayer. "I would really like to study the bottle. You know my birthday is soon."

"Give me the bottle, Birthday Girl, and let me ask."

She reluctantly held it out to me. "I suspect you can be nicer than me."

The energy from the bottle all but hummed as I reached for it. For a moment, I hesitated to touch it. Finally, drawing in a breath, I wrapped my fingers around the bottle's neck. An odd sense of unease shot up through my fingertips. Sadness and fear collided. My breath hitched.

What the hell? I studied the simple bottle, half tempted to hand it back to Margaret. The same thing happened when I held Grace's bottle.

"You okay?"

"Sure. Fine."

"You're pale."

The vibrations around the bottle waned, softened, and then vanished, leaving me to wonder again if magic or madness was at play. "Be right back."

Heading toward the house with the bottle in my right hand I was struck by its weight. Not that it was heavy or fully loaded, but it pulled toward the earth, seeming to wince against the bright light. The bottle was very similar to the one on Grace's hearth.

I knocked on the back door and seconds later heard the clip of high-heeled shoes. Dr. McDonald opened the door and the rush of cool air blended with her perfume and swirled around me. She glanced toward the hearth. "It appears to be almost done. Progress."

"Yes. We should be finished within the hour." Carrie squawked and squirmed. Patting her bottom, I held up the bottle. "We found this at the site."

Dr. McDonald took a step back and straightened. "What is that?"

"An old bottle. Handblown. Margaret thinks seventeen hundred-ish."

Her noise wrinkled. "What do you want me to do with it?"

"We found it on your property. It belongs to you. I'm contracted to take the stones only."

Dr. McDonald's gaze settled on the bottle and for a moment her eyes lingered. Her face paled as her fingers reached for the top button of her silk blouse. I was ready to hand it over to her when she shook her head. "Keep it. I don't want it."

"You're sure? It's old and might be of value." Carrie fussed louder, so I swayed, hoping the movement would lull her back to sleep. Her fussing slowed to grumbles.

"I don't want it. You're welcome to it and whatever else you find by the stone hearth. Just get it all off my property."

"Okay."

Taking a step back, she stood rigid, her hand poised on the door. "Is that all?"

"Yeah. Just wanted to check in about the bottle."

"Okay. Let me know when you're finished." She closed the door and the high heels clicked, growing more distant as the house swallowed her up.

"Sure."

Margaret jogged across the lawn. "What did she say?"

"She said we could keep it." I handed it to Margaret. "And I'm giving it to you."

"Giving?" A million dollars in cash wouldn't have made her happier.

"The least I can do."

Margaret accepted the bottle and cradled it close to her chest. "This is so awesome."

"Happy Birthday." I glanced at Carrie and discovered she'd found her thumb. I was fairly sure in some baby book it warned that this was not good, but the kid sucked greedily, and I sure wasn't going to be the one to tell her she couldn't enjoy comfort when she found it.

Margaret held the bottle to the light, but caked dirt and mold blocked us from seeing through it. She gently jostled it and again we heard the clink of something inside. "If I find out any information about the bottle, do you want me to tell you about it?"

I'd be gone by Friday, so it didn't really matter about the bottle. "Sure."

December 22, 1750

A light snow fell today, blanketing the muddy streets with a pure white. Until today, Dr. Goodwin worked with the men building our house. He seems most anxious to have us all settled. He tells me he is using the profits from the last voyage of the *Constance* to buy fine furniture for us.

Though I am excited at the prospect of a real home, the baby weighs heavily in my belly and I find it hard to get comfortable. My time will come any day now.

Chapter Eleven

I dropped Margaret off at the Archaeology Center by three and then drove the few extra blocks to the warehouse. Pulling into the alley parking spot, I glanced in the rearview mirror. I couldn't see Carrie's face but the steady sound of her breathing told me she was asleep. Maybe I could squeeze out ten or fifteen more minutes.

Since arriving in Alexandria, I was always racing the clock. Racing to get Janet in the hospital, racing to a meeting with the social worker, racing to remove the stones today, and now racing to feed the kid. After the Friday morning meeting with the social worker, it would be a race against time to get back to the vineyard and finish up the details of the opening.

Tick. Tock.

The air conditioner still running, I sat back and leaned into the seat, willing knotted muscles to release. The pace might be crazy now but it wouldn't be forever. Days from now, I'd wake up in my own bed, refreshed and ready to face my real life.

Past the warehouse and through the thicket of trees, the waters of the Potomac flowed slowly. During my summer here, I often snuck down to the riverbanks and stuck my toes in the cool water. Once Janet tried to convince me to take a swim with her, but the current was so fast and looked dangerous. She called me a baby. She said I was scared, as she tugged off her shoes and jumped into the water. The chaos of her hyperactive mind couldn't override the strong pull of the water, which quickly began to pull her downstream. Panic flashed in her blue eyes as and she reached out to me. Without a second thought, I grabbed on to a tree branch and leaned out to take her hand. She took hold with a surprising grip. I pulled, fighting a current I thought would take us both. But I didn't let go. I held on to the branch and Janet.

"Karma, I've paid in a lot of goodwill over the years, and if there were a moment in time when I needed payback, it's now. Find me a good home for Carrie and make Janet better. I won't ask for another favor."

For a beat or two, silence swirled, making me wonder if Karma heard my plea. An expectant smile teased the edges of my lips and then the baby wailed.

"Thanks, Karma. Thanks." I shut off the truck engine and got out, opened the back door, and pulled the car seat free. "I know. It's been a long day. Hopefully you'll soon be in a nice new home, and I'll be back home. Auntie Addie is going to have a very big glass of wine on Friday." I kicked the car door shut with my foot, irritated at Karma and myself for expecting a miracle. "You'll have your new, happier home, and I'll get my life back. I'll make it happen."

I glanced at the pile of rocks now secured under the tarp and immediately filed them under tomorrow's agenda. Today demanded last-minute calls for the wine reception.

Climbing the stairs, I passed several packages addressed to me. More party details. As much as I wanted to dive into them, I went straight to my bedroom, where I found a fresh set of clothes for the baby in the clearance bag. Grace. Not helping and helping. Like me.

I changed the baby and hefted her up on my shoulder. The routine was becoming smoother and not as nerve-racking, and as tempting as it was to feel good about that . . . I didn't. I was her temporary fix, not her permanent solution.

Ten minutes later, I sat in a rocker in the living room, a bottle in the baby's mouth as she greedily sucked.

My back relaxed into the rocker, but as much as I wanted to close my eyes, I didn't. There were too many party details to handle. My printer shipped the guest cards to me here so that she could go through all the names tonight and arrange the seating chart. A few hours of work and then I'd call Scott, remind him that I loved him, and wait for him to say the right words that would soothe the numbing guilt overcoming me. I wasn't giving Carrie what she needed and I wasn't giving Scott or the vineyard all of me. This feeling of not being enough first flickered as smoldering embers and now burned brighter with each day.

Stomach grumbling, I didn't have the oomph to get up out of the chair and make a peanut butter and jelly sandwich. I couldn't take care of myself.

For an instant I half hoped Scott was climbing the stairs, rounding the corner, and smiling to greet me. As much as I didn't want to share this part of my life with him, I needed him to take me into his arms and hold me close. I needed to hear, "I love you, no matter what."

No matter what.

Tears glistened, and I closed my eyes to stop the flow of tears. *No matter what.* All love came with conditions. Unconditional love wasn't real. People loved each other for many reasons, but there was always a reason. I was loved because I was glue. I held lives together. My shining armor didn't glisten in the sun. It seeped into the cracks and crevices and held tight.

"God, but I need a *me* right now." The seams of my life were unraveling. And as much as I wanted to ask Scott for help, I knew it tempted ruin.

My gaze drifted to the mantel and settled on the witch bottle found the other day. Margaret's discovery of a similar bottle prompted several questions. In the mid-seventeen hundreds, Alexandria was a new, bustling city with a growing collection of wood-framed and brick homes. Though it was a far cry from its more sophisticated sister cities of Williamsburg and Richmond, Virginia planters saw a bright future. However, the bottle proved some superstitious people remained rooted in the past.

Two women. Two bottles. Could a woman like Faith have scared them so much that they cast a protection spell?

The door downstairs opened and closed and steady, determined footfalls moved up the stairs. Grace rounded the corner, carrying two plastic grocery bags. Silent, she moved into the kitchen and unloaded her purchases.

Carrie finished the remains of her bottle, and I slowly lifted her to my shoulder and gently rubbed her back until she burped. When her cheek relaxed against my shoulder her breathing grew slow and deep. I rose and carried the sleeping child to my room and tucked her in the makeshift dresser drawer bed.

In the kitchen, Grace opened a sleeve of white bread and was buttering each side as a skillet heated on the stove. She tucked cheese between the slices and placed two sandwiches in the pan. "I see the truck is full of stones."

"We salvaged nice pieces. And Zeb thinks he might have a buyer, a stonemason, who's been commissioned to build a hearth in a mountain home. The man is supposed to come by and look at them tomorrow."

Grace flipped over the sandwiches, turned down the stove, and reached for two mismatched plates in the cabinet. "What about Social Services?"

"Ms. Willis is still coming by the warehouse tomorrow at eight in the morning."

"Maybe we'll all have what we want by then."

"Maybe."

She slid a sandwich on each plate and handed me mine before she wordlessly sat at the table and began to eat.

"Thanks." I filled a glass with water from the tap and drank before I sat with my sandwich. Seemed a sin to enjoy such a simple dish that was loaded with fat and refined wheat, but the grilled cheese sandwich soothed nerves firing nonstop.

The silence settled between us, trapping me in my thoughts and Grace in hers. Neither of us wanted to be here, but here we sat, each controlled by an illness that seeped into so many lives.

"Are you going to see Janet before they move her to the mental health facility?" she asked.

"I'll ask Janet's doctor about her, but she needs to focus on getting well."

"Focus. That's never been her strength."

"Nope." I tore off a piece of butter-soaked crust and ate it.

Grace set down a half-eaten section of sandwich and wiped her fingers on a paper towel. "Janet reminds me so much of your mother when she was younger. Pretty, vivacious, and full of life. I never met a man that wasn't drawn to her."

I couldn't imagine my mother as a young woman. My memories were of an exhausted woman overwhelmed by the demands of motherhood and mental illness. Mom would sit for hours in front of the television, watching game shows and soap operas, drinking cup after cup of coffee. She dozed during the day on the couch and then roamed the house until dawn. There were times when she made a grab for sanity, but it always remained out of her reach.

"She was always asleep when I came home from school."

Grace studied me for a long moment. "Janet's going to be different."

"Is she? Or are we good at telling lies to ourselves?"

I ate the last of the sandwich and rinsed off my plate. "I'm going to rest for a few minutes. The baby will be up around midnight and neither of us slept well last night."

"I bought that powdered formula. The pre-mixed stuff from the doctor is about gone. I priced the big cans of ready-mixed formula, but it's too expensive so I bought the powder. I don't know how to mix it, but it can't be too hard."

Unless it's midnight, and you have a crying baby in your arms. "Where is it?"

"On the counter."

A glance at the canister told me instantly it was more work than popping a top and putting it in the baby's mouth. I read the instructions, pulled several of the baby's bottles from the sink, and rinsed them out with hot soapy water. Carefully, I scooped formula into each bottle and mixed in six ounces of water. Fifteen minutes later, there were three bottles to go in the refrigerator. "That should get me to breakfast."

Grace bit into her sandwich. "See you in the morning."

"Right."

In my room, I glanced at the sleeping baby and sat on the edge of my bed. My gaze drifted to the portrait of the stern woman, Sarah Goodwin. Energy pulled. I wondered if she and the witch Faith crossed paths. Though her dark gaze appeared so practical and sound, I wondered if she could have been swayed by fear of the dark arts enough to make a witch bottle.

I yawned and rolled my head from side to side. Too tired to worry about Sarah let alone shower the day's sweat and grime off me, I kicked off my boots and lay back on the pillows. I thought about the place cards and the seating charts. Damn. I still needed to review them. Five minutes. That's all I needed. Two seconds later, I was out.

It was past midnight when Zeb tossed his pencil and pulled off his glasses. He pinched the bridge of his nose. Eric was asleep and the house silent. He rose, moving to the shelf holding a picture of a smiling Janet holding baby Eric. Her blond hair was bright and her eyes vivid.

Her leaving ripped through him and for a long time life was simply putting one foot in front of the other. Eric kept him going and slowly life found a new normal. Somewhere along the way, he assumed Janet would never come back into his or Eric's life. He believed the stability he and his son enjoyed was rock solid, and that she couldn't upset it.

But the last few days proved him wrong. Janet stumbled back into town, a new child in her belly, and they were all paying the price.

Eric's questions about his mother were frequent before, but then, Janet was a far-off smiling figure captured only in photographs. Forever smiling, she was the happy, vibrant woman in the slim-fitting white wedding dress grinning beguilingly as Zeb gazed at her. She was the young mom holding her infant son in her arms hours after his birth, or she was the pretty, slim woman at Eric's christening.

Sometimes, when he looked at the pictures, he forgot all the turmoil and remembered the woman he loved.

Zeb rose from the desk and climbed to the second floor of their house. A pull-down attic string hung from the ceiling and very slowly he tugged the steps and climbed into the attic. At the top of the ladder stairs, a tug on another string clicked on a bare lightbulb.

The space was mostly full of old furniture, business files, and Eric's forgotten toys. Seven years didn't seem so long until he came up here and stared at the relics of so many memories.

Zeb straightened, but the limited headspace required he walk stoop-shouldered past a collection of boxes, toys, and the footlocker that held his old uniforms. Reaching a darkened corner, he found the cradle that he'd built for Eric. Though dust covered it, the smooth walnut lines remained straight and sturdy.

He could build anything. He didn't need plans or patterns—just give him a picture, and he could figure out the construction. Janet found the picture of this cradle in a baby magazine, and she'd been so excited about the piece, she'd asked him if he could build it. Grateful to see his wife smiling, he tore out the picture and the next day began the project. It took him several months, working on the cradle after twelve-hour shifts in the new construction firm, but as Janet's belly grew, the cradle slowly took shape.

Janet loved the cradle, declaring it better than the picture in the magazine, and the day they placed their son in it was one of those perfect moments life rarely offered.

Janet's problems distracted Zeb from his son, who was growing so quickly. What should have been a joyous time was riddled with strife and fear. By the time Eric was four months old, he was too big for the cradle and Janet was gone from their lives.

Zeb stowed the cradle away and with it the happiness and hope for his life with Janet.

He ran a calloused thumb down the smooth spindle, trying to recapture the few months Eric slept in the cradle. He reached back, hoping to catch a memory, but most flittered out of reach and the few he caught were tainted by Janet's problems.

When she finally vanished, he searched for her with no luck. When it became clear she wasn't coming home, he was relieved. The roller-coaster ride was over.

And now, Janet was back and she'd given birth to another man's baby. He traced his hand over the end of the cradle where he'd carved an elaborate "T" for Talbot.

Images of Carrie lying in the dresser drawer pushed to the front of his mind. She was safe and secure, but the makeshift bed was as rigged and half-assed as the life that waited for her.

Eric had him forever. Carrie had Addie, but for how long?

"Dad?" Eric's voice drifted up from the bottom of the attic stairs.

"Yeah, bud?"

"Can I come up?"

A smile tweaked the edges of Zeb's lips. When Eric was three, Zeb left the attic steps down as he was hauling up their lone box of Christmas ornaments. The boy scrambled all the way up the ladder and stood in the attic before Zeb realized what was happening. Seeing the boy perched on the lip of the attic landing with a dozen steps and a ten-foot fall inches behind him nearly gave Zeb a heart attack. He calmly coaxed the boy into the attic closer to him. The boy was thrilled to oblige. Only when Zeb had wrapped strong arms around the toddler did he release the breath he held. Eric knew no fear and spent the next ten minutes asking about all the items stored in the attic.

"I'll be right there, Eric. Remember our deal, stay off the stairs."

"But that was when I was a baby."

"I think we agreed you'd not come up here alone until you were thirty."

"Daaaaad."

Zeb released his hold on the cradle and moved toward the steps where he found Eric waiting, foot poised on the first rung. With one last glance toward the cradle, he clicked off the light and climbed down the stairs.

"What were you doing up there?" Eric backed up a step so Zeb could fold the stairs and push them back up into the attic.

"Just poking around."

"Why?"

Zeb jostled Eric's hair. "I was looking at the cradle that you slept in when you were a baby."

"Why?"

"I don't know. Seeing Carrie made me think about you when you were so small."

"So, is she my sister?"

"She's your half-sister. You two have the same mom."

"You aren't her dad."

"No." Whatever annoyance he felt wasn't over Janet's sex life. He knew she'd moved on to other men a long time ago. His annoyance stemmed from the wreckage Janet created without a second thought.

"Who's her dad?" he asked.

"I don't know."

His head tilted. "Does Mom know?"

"I suppose." He searched for any jealously over his ex-wife's love life but found none. "But that's not exactly our business."

Eric raised a finger. "Does Addie know?"

"I don't know. That's between the two of them."

Eric padded back toward his bedroom and climbed in the bed shaped like a race car. When Zeb had bought the bed for the boy, it all but swallowed him up. Now he could see the bed might last another year before it was too small.

"Is Addie going to keep Carrie?"

"I don't know." He'd expected her to bolt by now. He was surprised when she didn't accept the first foster family proposed by Social Services. Though she wasn't committed to raising the baby or embracing the family, she did seem to care about the child.

His mom and dad loved him and gave him a stable home. Janet only hinted about her childhood but from what little she said about motels, going hungry, and periods without her mother, it couldn't have been easy for her. And Addie—well, as the lone sane one in the family, she surely suffered more.

Addie broached the subject of her family to him the night before his wedding to Janet. But he was too damn in love with Janet to care. Whatever might be wrong with his bride-to-be wasn't too big a burden for him. He would summon the discipline and love to fix it. He considered Addie weak when she reiterated Janet had problems that weren't easily fixed. He disagreed, insisting that her lack of commitment was the root of the problem.

And so, when he and Janet ran into trouble halfway through her pregnancy, he refused to reach out to Addie for advice. He dug in his heels. But the harder he worked to keep Janet stable, the farther she drifted away. Everything he did was wrong. He spent too much time with her or not enough. He was too controlling or too uncaring. He hovered, was gone too much.

After the car accident, she checked herself out of the hospital and vanished. He still believed he could make it work and it wasn't until he tracked her to Seattle and found her high and wearing a skimpy cocktail dress that he realized he could not fix Janet or break the curse that ailed a Shire woman.

Zeb could have dusted off the cradle, polished it until it shined, and delivered it to Addie. But in the end, the crib wouldn't make a bit of difference in Carrie's life. He couldn't help her any more than he could have helped Janet, his own wife, the mother of his child.

January 10, 1751

My labor pains have begun. The doctor took a sudden chill days ago and can barely sit up. I fear he will not be able to help me with the birthing. Penny suggested the midwife, Faith. At first I could not give her an answer. Did I fear giving birth in this unholy land without my husband's help more than Faith's assistance? I wanted this child more than anything and would do what I must to usher it safely into the world. When another pain gripped me, I gave my consent to summon Faith.

Chapter Twelve

Janet had been moved to a mental health facility on Thursday. I arranged for the social worker to take her, fearing if she saw me, she'd change her mind. Ms. Willis reported that Janet seemed relieved to enter her new room and refused to discuss the baby.

On Friday morning, Ms. Willis was due to arrive at the warehouse at eight. Rising early, I fed Carrie and dressed her in a clean outfit. However, the best I could do for myself was to pull a comb through my hair and put on the last clean T-shirt in Grace's clearance-rack bag. However, my jeans remained dusted with the dirt and dust of the hearth's deconstruction. Food amounted to a spoonful of peanut butter and a half a cup of coffee.

I rushed to the door, anxiously glancing around the place, expecting Ms. Willis to find us lacking. From the moment I could walk, I sought approval first from Mom and then Grace. I lapped up Scott's approval, always a little hungry for more. Maybe I'd never feel full and would continue to gobble up approval whatever I could find. Whatever the reason, I needed the social worker to think the best of me.

"Why're you glancing around like a nervous cat?" Grace asked. She leaned against the kitchen door, a cup of coffee in her hand. "The place looks fine. The social worker won't find this house lacking."

Her defiance did little to ease my nerves. "I want it to be perfect."

She studied the black depths of her mug. "She'll like us just fine."

"How do you know?"

Grace shrugged. "It really doesn't matter. The baby isn't staying."

I reached for a rag and wiped the counter for the third time. "Don't you care about what other people think about us?"

"Nope. And you shouldn't either."

I rubbed a scratch on the counter over and over until I realized I'd never be able to wipe it away. "Maybe."

The bell downstairs rang.

Hands trembling, I draped the washcloth back over the sink and hurried down the stairs to find Ms. Willis standing on the landing.

Dressed in a dark pair of pants and a crisp white shirt, the social worker fastened her hair into a practical knot. "Ms. Morgan."

"Ms. Willis. Please come up."

Ms. Willis followed me, her practiced gaze sweeping over the eclectic furniture in the living room. "I've driven by this place a million times but never been inside. I was always curious about the business."

"It's my aunt's business," I said. "Her mother started a collection and Grace turned it into a business."

Her eyes danced with fascination. "This is very charming."

Grace stepped out of the kitchen. "Can I offer you a coffee?"

"No, thank you," Ms. Willis said. "I have a full day and the sooner we can talk the better. You must be Grace Shire."

Grace did not extend her hand. "The baby's sleeping."

Hoping my smile softened Grace's tone, I moved between the two. "Would you like me to get her?" I asked. "She doesn't have much, but I've packed it. Extra diapers, formula, clothes." Clearing my throat, I stood straighter. "Did you find a family for Carrie?"

"Yes. It's not as large as the first and they are very adept at caring for special needs children."

"Carrie isn't special needs."

Ms. Willis frowned, and I sensed that after meeting Janet, she, too, worried about the child's long-term mental health. "I understand, but you said yourself she's not an easy baby."

"She's demanding and knows what she wants. As long as she gets it, she's fine." That was a perfect description of Janet.

"But you would agree she needs a parent who is skilled at handling babies with issues."

Issues. Carrie's issue was that she was born to an unstable woman, no father, and into a family known for having troubles. "To peg her as 'special needs' when she's only days old doesn't seem fair."

"I'm not pegging her. I'm trying to find a family that can take care of her and understand that she is not going to be an easy baby."

Grace shifted her stance, and a sigh that sounded like an oath spilled over her lips.

I folded my arms. "What are the special needs issues of the other children?"

Ms. Willis raised a brow. "I thought you needed to leave for a business meeting later today and you couldn't keep the baby any longer."

Her tone scraped over my nerves like fingernails on a chalkboard. "Yes."

"Then I don't see where you have a choice. You can't put a baby aside for a day or two when it suits you."

An invisible wall pressed against my back. Scott was the one person in my life who was stable and sure, but tossing the kid into the system branded as "special needs" or "difficult" dug into my gut like broken glass.

"How much time do you need at the vineyard?" Grace asked.

I didn't look her way, not really sure why she cared. "If I left now, I could be back by this time tomorrow."

"Twenty-four hours," Grace confirmed.

"That's about right."

"And after that, could you stay until Janet gets out of the hospital?" Grace asked.

"I suppose. That's about four weeks." I ran through the upcoming calendar at the vineyard. "We really don't have much going on at the vineyard for the next month."

"I'll watch the baby for twenty-four hours," Grace said. "Then you come back and see to her until Janet can."

Grace's expression was not filled with joy, but hardened with determination.

Ms. Willis glanced between Grace and me. "You're telling me you two will keep the child until her mother can care for her?"

Grace and I stared at each other and, without a word exchanged, entered into a pact. Together, we would find a way to care for Carrie.

"Yes," we said together.

January 20, 1751

I was well into my labor pains when Faith arrived. Pain tightened my belly and robbed me of breath and word. As Faith shrugged off her cape, I saw then that her belly was round and heavy with child. The doctor lay on a pallet by the hearth. The fever overwhelmed him and he could barely speak.

I heard Faith and Penny whispering and I demanded to know what they were saying, but Penny only pressed a damp towel to my head and told me not to fret. Before I could protest, Faith opened my mouth and poured a foul-tasting liquid into my mouth. I coughed and spit. The pains did not vanish, but suddenly I could distance myself from them.

My son was delivered two hours later—strong, fit, and with a lusty cry. Faith gave Penny a sack of herbs and told her to make a tea for the doctor. Penny did as Faith instructed and my husband's fever broke that night.

Dr. Goodwin and I named our son William. I am grateful to have my son and, if the truth were known, I am grateful to be spared the worst travails of labor.

I could not meet Faith's gaze or thank her for coming to our aid. I fear only witchcraft could free a woman of the childbirth or break a man's fever so easily.

Chapter Thirteen

For the first time in days, I was able to sit and simply be with my own thoughts as I drove through Old Town toward the Beltway encircling the Washington metro area. But as I settled into my car, tension, not relief, rippled up my spine. I was racing another clock. Tick. Tock.

A nervous energy buzzed as I changed lanes. Had I forgotten something? I made plenty of bottles for Grace to feed the baby. I washed Carrie's clothes last night so there were a half dozen outfits to wear. Janet would not be an issue. The stones were a problem for another day.

And still, this persistent fear that I missed an important detail dogged me as I drove around the Beltway and headed west on I-66.

I reached for my cell and dialed Scott's number. Three rings later, the call went to voice mail. A little relieved, I said, "Scott, this is Addie. I'm on the road and will be home in two hours. Looking forward to tonight. It's going to be a great success."

I had planned and over-planned for the event, but I wasn't at all confident that it would be a success. I glanced in the rearview mirror at the place cards. I never went through them or cross-checked seating charts. Damn. Such a small detail now, but tonight it could blow up into a disaster. Damn. A week ago, I would have freaked out. Now I did not have the energy. The event was now officially open seating and I'd deal with any problem that arose.

I began my calls to the vendors. The caterer was top of the list. The owner of the small firm answered on the third ring. "Sweet Treats Catering."

"Suzanne, this is Addie Morgan. Checking in on tonight." My heart beat fast, hard against my ribs, as I braced for trouble.

"We're all set, Addie, and will be at the property in about three hours."

"Great. I'll see you then. What do you need from me?"

"A check for the balance when I arrive."

"E-mail me the final balance, and I'll take care of it."

"Great."

And so it went with the calls. Next was the vendor who was delivering large potted ficus trees adorned with white lights. And finally the cake vendor, who made a specialty cake shaped like a bottle of wine. It was a surprise for Scott. The secret cake, like the place cards, seemed like such a big deal days ago. I worried over chocolate and vanilla, Italian buttercream and whipped cream. I even fretted over the raspberry filling. Now I didn't really care if he saw the cake early or never.

"Addie, we have the cake ready to go and switched out the flavors as you requested."

"I'm sure it'll be great. See you in a few hours."

"Would you like to go over the details one more time?"

"As long as it's cake, I don't care."

The baker hesitated and I could almost feel her relief wafting through the phone. "Sounds good."

The highways gave way to four lane roads, which quickly narrowed to two lanes. Concrete thinned until the landscape around me transformed into rolling hills.

During my first drive out to the vineyard seven years ago, I was running away from Alexandria. Still battered from the car accident, I was tense, scared, and praying that this new temporary job would work out so I didn't have to return.

My full-circle life brought me back to the same spot—only this time I wasn't running away from home, I was running toward it. I belonged here now. Not in the city. My life was with Scott. He loved me.

The shrill of my phone cut through me, startling me from my thoughts. A glance at the display and I saw Scott's smiling face. Drawing in a deep breath, I picked up the phone and grinned before I hit Answer and said, "Scott! I'm only a half hour from home."

"Jesus, Addie, this redefines cutting it close. The phone has been ringing off the hook today."

I never redirected the office calls to my cell. Damn it. That was a rookie mistake. "I've called all the vendors, and they'll be at the vineyard in about an hour. It's going to be fine, and I'll get right on the return calls as soon as I hit the door."

A forced breath shuddered through the line. "Addie, I'm going insane."

"It's going to be fine, baby. I'm almost home and will take charge."

"I really don't know what I would do without you."

"You never have to worry," I said. A speed limit sign warned me to slow and, though tempted to race past it, I didn't have time for a ticket. "Do you have all the wines at the tasting room?"

"We have one hundred bottles total. Thirty red and seventy white. It's warm and people will want the white. Do you think those ratios are okay?"

People would guzzle the wine and devour the food. Some would talk about bouquets and flavors and aromas, but most wouldn't know the difference. "They're perfect. It's going to be wonderful."

"A reporter called me today."

"From the wine magazine?"

"Yes. I used your cheat sheet of answers. It went smoothly."

"You are a charmer, Scott. The press will love you." That was a reminder to make press calls in the remaining twenty-eight-minute drive.

"I miss you."

"Me, too."

"See you soon."

"Can't wait." I hung up and dialed the editor of the local paper. The circulation was over ten thousand, but the editor was once a writer for *Food and Wine* magazine, and it didn't hurt to reach out. I also called the *Post* and a couple of D.C. area magazines that received releases. In all cases, I landed in voice mail, but you never knew who would show or what publicity would stick. As I rolled off the main road past the vineyard sign, I called Grace. She didn't pick up, and I left her a message. A glance at the clock told me that Carrie would be hungry now and no doubt Grace would be scurrying to feed her.

I parked in my spot next to the large tasting room beside two large white trucks. In the tasting room, I saw a befuddled Scott talking to a large, burly man with a clipboard. My purse still slung over my shoulder, and my cell gripped in my hand, I scrounged up a bright smile. "Mr. Warner. Do you have my ficus trees?"

Both men's gazes shifted to me and the relief was palpable. Scott crossed to me instantly and kissed me on the cheek. He smelled of fresh air and grapes, and I smelled of sweat and baby milk.

"Addie!" Scott said.

"I've got this," I said.

"Thank God," Mr. Warner muttered.

I kissed Scott quickly on the lips. His nose wrinkled, and I sensed the unasked questions about my appearance and smell. "Do what you need to do. Go."

He squeezed my hand and nodded. "See you soon."

"Can't wait."

Scott dashed out of the tasting room as I grinned at Mr. Warner. "You need a check."

He nodded. "Yes, ma'am."

"What about the centerpieces I ordered?"

He stared at me with a blank expression and then his skin paled. "Ma'am, we left them at the shop. I can run and get them."

The round trip would take over an hour and that was too late. "Deduct it from my total cost. I don't have time to worry about them."

"I can do that. Darn it all, I'm sorry."

"No worries."

He glanced up at me, bracing for anger and sarcasm, but found a woman on the verge of a nervous breakdown. "Right. Thanks."

And for the next two hours, I worked as a makeshift traffic cop directing vendors, writing checks, and arranging and rearranging tables and polishing wineglasses. A boost of adrenaline kept me moving, but if I sat for a moment, I'd never get up again.

By four, the room was a glittering display. Twenty round tables and the surrounding chairs covered in white linens filled the room. Sparkling wineglasses and polished plates and cutlery shined personally by me glittered in the soft afternoon light.

"Addie," George, our vineyard manager, called from the doorway. "I got those grapevines like you asked for."

"Excellent. Let's cut them into forty-inch strips and tie them in circles. They are going to be the centerpieces."

"Tied-up grapevines?"

Not the elaborate pieces originally made, but they would do. Outside, we cut and twisted the green vines into less-than-perfect circles, but when I set them in the center of the tables and placed the large white candles in the middle of the vines, it looked kind of rustic and quaint.

By the time the tables were dressed, less than twenty minutes remained before guests arrived, so I drove up the dirt road toward the small house Scott and I shared. Without a glance around the house, I stripped off clothes and moved toward the bathroom. A thinning mist in the room told me Scott already showered. The khakis and white shirt I pressed for him last weekend were missing from the closet so I knew he'd changed. As I turned on the shower, he appeared in the bathroom doorway. He glanced at me and frowned, but I silenced him with a raised hand as I ducked into the shower.

I dunked my head under the hot spray of the water and quickly lathered up shampoo. This was my first real shower in days. I'd have paid money to linger for five or ten minutes. But as I rinsed, the water grew cooler and cooler and by the time the last of the soap melted off my body, the spray of water was ice cold. Trembling, I shut off the water and reached for a towel, hoping to warm the sudden chill that iced my bones.

"Sorry about the hot water, babe," Scott shouted down the hallway. "Lost track of time while I was showering."

"That's okay."

"See you at the party."

"Love you."

"Me, too," he said as he left.

Out of the shower, I toweled off and then twisted my hair in the towel. I changed into a white sundress. In my former life, there would have been time to shop for accessories or maybe another dress, but in my new life, I was grateful to be clean. A quick application of makeup added pop to my features and instead of drying my hair I twisted the curls into a French twist. Ringlets framed my face and, again, it wasn't the super sophisticated look once planned, but it worked.

I dug a pair of older sandals from the closet, momentarily wishing for time to buy new shoes, and slipped them on before heading outside. The sun settled a little lower on the horizon and cast a warm, lovely glow over the rolling land covered with green vineyards. For a moment, I stopped and stared at the sunset, realizing how much I missed it the last few days. Soon, I'd be back. Soon my life would be normal again.

The crunch of gravel heralded the arrival of our guests and I forgot about sandals, sunsets, or normal.

The flash of a camera bulb told me the photographer was here. God, I'd forgotten all about him.

A grinning Scott stood at the entrance of the tasting room as the guests arrived. I nestled close to his side, and the two of us greeted guests before George drew me away with questions about serving sizes and limits.

"Everyone gets a half glass and we'll limit the number of servings to three."

"Some people will want more."

"I'm not sanctioning drunk driving."

George glanced at the bartender and held up his hand as the man prepared to pour a glass of wine. "We have a guest who's already on his second glass."

My gaze settled on the man at the bar. Mr. Dixon. He was a rich and well-connected landowner who was known in town as a drunk. "Three-glass limit, George. If he has an issue, send him to me, not Scott. I'll deal with him."

"Sure thing, Addie." As a waiter passed with a tray of whites, George grabbed one. "Have a glass."

I accepted the glass and took a long sip. The dry white slid over my tongue and I welcomed not only the flavor, but the kick of alcohol that softened so many edges that hardened over the last couple of days. I took a second sip. "Thank you."

"What the heck happened to you in Alexandria? You look like you've been hit by a truck."

"It was a six-pound, six-ounce truck."

"What?"

"Just family stuff. But thank you for asking." I dug my cell from my pocket to see if Grace called me back. No calls. Was that good or bad? Carrie wasn't easy and Grace wasn't patient. The two were not a good mix.

Scott came up to me, his grin nervous and expectant. "Are we ready to get started?"

I slid the phone back into my pocket. "We are in about five minutes. I have a detail or two to check and I'll kick off the night."

His grin softening to genuine, he leaned in and kissed me on the lips. "Have I told you how much I love you?"

"Never enough. Never enough."

"After tonight, I'll do a better job of it. I won't be so distracted." A local newspaper reporter moved toward us and Scott glanced away. "I'll be right back."

"I know."

I moved to the ladies' room and dug the phone out. I dialed Grace's number. She didn't have a cell but a rotary phone hung on the kitchen wall. No answering machine made the entire setup Stone Age. Who didn't have a cell? The phone rang three times, four times, and then a breathless, "What the hell?"

"Aunt Grace," I said, lowering my voice and moving into one of the stalls. I closed the door and locked it. "How's it going?" In the distance, Carrie's cries echoed off the high walls of the warehouse apartment.

"I called Daisy. She's got a boy who's only seven months old. She knows babies. She's come over to the house."

"Daisy McCrae."

"Daisy Sinclair. And yeah."

The girl I remembered was rough and tough and always looking to start a fight. That summer we all ran together, Daisy did a fine job of making her sister Rachel cry. "Can you put her on the phone?" Outside I heard the hum of the crowd blend with the guitar music. Laughter mingled with the clink of glasses.

"Addie?" The voice was feminine and gruff, and I immediately pictured the long-legged hellion.

"Daisy."

"The baby's fine. Cranky as hell, but fine. She was almost asleep when you called."

Picturing Carrie's red face crying, I jabbed tense fingers through my hair. "Sorry. You have plenty of bottles?"

"You'll be back tomorrow, right?"

The bathroom door opened, and I hunched a little lower. "Yes. Tomorrow."

"Where are you?"

"Long story. But I'll see Grace by ten tomorrow."

"Okay. We'll survive." Her voice softened. "Do what you got to do. We'll manage."

"Thanks."

"No worries. Got to go." The line went dead, and I was left to stare at the phone. A toilet flushed. I hurried out of the stall, washed my hands, and moved straight to the tasting counter.

The next several hours blended like a mixture of our grapes. Sweet moments mixed with sour notes, but all in all, the evening came together as planned. Scott charmed the crowd. The wines, for the most part, were a hit. The cake earned laughs as Scott cut into it and the photographer snapped pictures. Mr. Dixon found his way to several more wineglasses and when the man slumped in his seat, George and I escorted him out so his wife could drive him home.

We received dozens of orders—not a stellar breakout, but enough to generate buzz. Launching a wine was a building process. We pressed enough grapes this year to bottle thirty thousand bottles. Certainly the night was not enough to get us on the world stage, but it was a start.

Under the exhaustion, satisfaction hummed. Mission accomplished. I'd have savored the moment but there was still much followup to do. Guests to call about their reactions to the event and the wines. More media calls. So many plans . . .

It didn't matter what the plans were, because I was driving back to Alexandria to sort out an issue that refused to be settled.

Close to midnight, I was collecting glasses from the tables and placing them in the glass cases, which would be picked up tomorrow. George pulled all the extra bottles of wine and placed them in the fridge and boxed up what little food remained for himself and his wife. Scott was outside talking on his cell to a restaurant owner in Lexington who enjoyed the evening and wanted to schedule an event at his restaurant.

As I dropped glasses into their slots, the door opened and closed.

Scott leaned against the doorjamb, his face a blend of euphoria and exhaustion. I flashed back to the last time we made love and he wore a similar look. A good kind of exhaustion, he'd said then.

"Why don't you leave those for the morning?" he asked, crossing to me. He took a glass from my hands and wrapped his arms around me. "God, you feel good."

I relaxed into his embrace. "So do you."

"You did a stunning job."

"Thanks. So did you." I kicked off my shoes, put an apron on over my dress, and undid the French twist.

"We were a hit."

I ran my fingers through my hair and massaged my scalp. "It was a great start."

He leaned back and studied my face. "That's not the enthusiasm I expected."

"I'm excited."

"But not exuberant. Why not?"

"Always better to be a little excited and find out later it went so much better than you expected."

He kissed my forehead. "You're my serious Addie. The one who is always expecting disaster."

"And you're my dreamer. That's why we make such a good combination."

"We're the dream team."

"Yes."

He squeezed my shoulder. "Come to bed."

Resisting his gentle tug, I shook my head. "I really have to finish the glasses. They're being picked up very early. Why don't you go to bed, and I'll be in soon?"

He rested his chin on my head. "I should help."

"That's okay. You had a long day."

A sigh trickled from his lips and he leaned back and studied my face. "You wouldn't be mad if I left you to this?"

"No. No, I wouldn't. Just go."

He kissed me again, and I savored the touch of his lips against mine and the feel of his chest pressing against my breasts. I loved touching Scott, and in his arms I almost, *almost* felt like I was safe from the world.

He left me to load the remaining glasses. By two in the morning the last of the glasses were packed away, the table linens shoved in laundry bags, and the counters wiped. The tasting area sparkled.

When I slipped into bed next to Scott, I lay on my back, my body exhausted, my brain too jazzed with nervous energy and caffeine. A few hours sleep would have to do. Maybe tomorrow night, Carrie and I could sleep.

March 1, 1751

Dr. Goodwin remains fragile, but he is getting stronger. I saw Mistress Smyth at the market and she told me she heard Faith attended my son's birth. She tells me also that Faith delivered the pastor wife's baby. A girl. Mother and child are doing well. Mrs. Smyth heard Faith spun magic around the woman and relieved her birthing pains. "It's a sin," she whispered. "A sin."

Chapter Fourteen

"What do you mean you're leaving?" Scott stared at me over a toasted bagel loaded with cream cheese.

"I've got to run into Alexandria." I wriggled into clean jeans and a white top that floated above my waistline. "It's going to take me a couple of weeks to sort it all out."

"A couple of weeks?" He sat up, leaning heavily on his elbow. "But you just got back. I thought you'd handled your family crisis."

"I've gotten some of it handled, and I'll fix the rest in the next few weeks."

"Weeks?"

"Two or three." Okay, it was four weeks, but I'd tell him that later.

"Shit, Addie. You're going to be gone almost a month. Who's going to take the orders or coordinate the press?"

"I will. I've forwarded the phones to my cell and George will keep the day-to-day operations in play like he always does."

"What's going on with your family?"

From my top drawer, I grabbed clean underwear, T-shirts, and shorts. "Truly, it's not that exciting."

"If it's taking you away for three weeks, I want to know." He swung his legs over the side of the bed, pulled on his shorts, and crossed to me. He cupped his hands on my face, the worn callouses brushing my cheeks. "What's going on with you?"

His hands, warm and welcoming, tugged at the secrets locked away. "Family stuff."

His darkening gaze searched mine. "I don't know any information about your family. You never, ever talk about them."

"Because they're a lot of drama. And I hoped I'd left them behind for good, but more drama has caught up to me."

He rested calloused hands on my shoulders. "Let me help."

As much as I wanted to share this burden with him, I feared the telling of one secret would lead to another and another and then one day he'd know the darkest part of me that I could never share. "I don't want to drag you into this."

"Honey, you're important to me and whatever is an issue for you is an issue for me."

Scott believed what he was saying. He wanted to believe it. But Janet and Carrie were not sprint races; they were twin marathons that would exhaust the toughest of runners. Scott could lend his attention to events outside the vineyard for short bursts, but for him to put all this on hold to take care of a fussy baby and her mentally ill mother, well, that went beyond what he could handle. I wasn't sure if I could handle it.

His thumb traced my jawline as he held my face. "Honey, let me help."

I pulled his hands from my face and kissed the palms. "I'll make a deal. If I can't figure this out in a couple of weeks and put it behind me, then we'll talk."

A frown wrinkled his brow. "Either way, we need to talk."

In four weeks, with Carrie settled into a good home and separating me from Alexandria, I was fairly certain I could talk to Scott about my family. We would never get into the dark and dirty secrets, but I could skim the surface enough to satisfy him.

"Two or three weeks?"

A smile curved the edges of my lips. "Four at the outside. It won't be long."

"Four weeks?" He pulled me against him, and I could feel his erection pressing into me. "I don't like it when you're gone."

"I don't like being gone." Some of my resolve melted and for a moment, temptation whispered, "Stay. Just stay." I wanted the past to leave me alone. I wanted this life with Scott. I wanted . . .

My wants would have to wait. Like it or not, Carrie needed me and she was as stuck in this mess as I was. Neither one of us asked for the hand we were dealt.

Before temptation could speak again, I slipped out of his embrace and grabbed a handful of clothes from the dresser and shoved them in my duffel bag. I zipped up the bag and hefted it on my shoulder. "I've already packed my laptop and papers in the car so I can work remotely. This time of year, the work I do is all office related."

"What about the website and the pictures from the photographer?"

"I'll take care of it in Alexandria."

He shook his head and grabbed my wrist in his hands. "Four weeks, Addie, and if you're not home, I'm coming after you."

His declaration warmed my heart. "You won't have to track me down. I'll be here."

Fifteen minutes later, I drove the gravel drive of the vineyard, the dust kicking up around my back tires. Through the cloud of dirt I saw Scott standing by our house, waving before he turned and vanished into the house.

Tightening my grip on the wheel, I slowed at the main road, turned right, and followed the twisting pavement through the small town of Middlebrook and then toward the interstate. Five days ago, leaving the country, I was angry and filled with resentment I couldn't voice. Now, well, I wasn't happy about returning to Alexandria, but a grim determination settled over me. I wasn't embracing my past, but I needed to deal with it head on or it would chip away at my future.

When I arrived at the salvage yard at eleven, Grace was waiting for me at the top of the stairs with a crying Carrie. Without a word, I dropped my bag and purse in a heap at the top of the stairs and took the baby. A few days of experience taught me to check her diaper and ask, "When was the last time she ate?"

Grace turned toward the kitchen, her limbs moving stiff and slow, as if she aged twenty years in the last twenty-four hours. "She took a bottle at two but refused all since. I tried, but she won't take it."

"Where's the bottle?"

"Kitchen counter. By the sink."

As I moved closer to the kitchen, Carrie's cries grew louder and more impatient. I reached for the bottle and checked the temperature on my wrist. Warm enough. The nipple popped in her mouth, and she suckled immediately. Her little body remained tense and her tear-streaked face tight with tension. When I began to sway back and forth, she slowly relaxed.

Grace raised a brow. "She would not do that for me. Not once. Almost like she figured out the B-Team was in charge."

I moved to a kitchen chair and sat, cradling the baby in my arm. "I'm hardly the A-Team."

She poured a cup of coffee and then dug out a bottle of whiskey from the cabinet. She splashed a generous amount in her coffee before she took several slow sips.

She waved her mug toward the baby. "The kid isn't stupid. She understands you're the best person in her corner now. Without you, she'd be a number in a foster home family."

I settled Carrie a little closer to me and the remaining tension furrowing her little brow vanished. "I'm not a permanent solution, Grace. Janet is her mother."

Grace scoffed. "Janet's got a good soul, but she's not a mother. She'll maybe want to try at some point, but she won't be able to handle the heavy lifting. She never has been able to handle it."

"Just like Mom."

"Your mother had a soft soul. She loved you and Janet. She just couldn't do it."

I pulled the bottle from the baby's mouth to give her a chance to let her milk settle. Too fast down meant it came right back up. Carrie fussed a second or two before I settled the nipple on her lips again. "You could have taken us."

Grace sipped her coffee once, twice. "I'm not cut out for parenthood, Addie."

"Who's to say I am? I'm pretty darn good at running a business. I like my independence. I'm not so different than you."

"You are very different from me."

"How can you say that?"

"Because you came back. I'd have stayed at my vineyard and not come back." She finished the last of the coffee, grabbed the bottle of whiskey, and pushed away from the counter. "I need sleep."

As the baby suckled, I eased back in the chair and listened to Grace's feet shuffle along the hallway. Her bedroom door closed and the lock clicked.

The baby's eyes drifted closed as the bottle drained to large white bubbles. I gently pulled the nipple free and carried the baby to my room. The chest of drawers makeshift bed was gone and in its place was a real cradle outfitted with clean blankets and a sheet.

The craftsmanship on the cradle was amazing. Oval shaped, with whiskey-colored mahogany slats, precisely placed, curving with the top band and creating an egglike nest. On the headboard, tiny carved birds fluttered around an inlaid T. The polished, smooth wood smelled faintly of lemons.

T. Talbot. Zeb.

If I were sentimental, I'd have attached meaning to the cradle. But I wasn't and neither was Zeb. He owned a cradle and knew Carrie needed one, if only for a month, so he dusted off Eric's and brought it by. He was filling a need, as I was. Neither of us was attached to the baby or Janet. We were simply doing what needed to be done.

I situated Carrie in the bed. She moved her lips, mouthing some unintelligible word before her body relaxed into a deep sleep. Lowering my body to my bed, I knew there was so much to be done for the vineyard, mainly regarding followup calls. And I'd get on it right away. I fell back toward the pillows and closed my eyes. Just a few minutes of sleep. Maybe ten or twenty minutes. And I'd be refreshed and back on the job.

"Addie?"

The voice came from a distance and at first was easy to swat away like a fly.

"Addie?"

More insistent and impatient, the stage-whispered voice promised to grow louder if I didn't respond. "Yes?"

"Are you awake?"

My eyes fluttered open and, for a moment, I could not have told you where I was. The too-quiet room, the white-washed walls, and the tongue-and-groove ceiling did not register. "Yes, I'm awake."

I slung my legs over the side of the bed, rose, and wiped a bit of drool from the corner of my mouth. A glance to my right and I saw the sleeping baby. Baby Carrie. Alexandria.

Standing in the doorway was Margaret. Her hair sprung from her topknot, like a woman who always ran her hands over her hair. She wore a *History Rocks!* T-shirt and faded jeans.

"Good, you're awake." Margaret's now-familiar voice held a buzz of excitement. "I've been up all night reading about your bottle and your stone hearth."

Not my bottle. Not my hearth. Not my life. "And what did you find?"

"You think we could make a fresh pot of coffee? I'm on fumes. I snagged some day-old cookies from the bakery. Sugar and caffeine. My favorite food groups."

A smile tweaked the edges of my mouth. "Coffee coming right up."

"You're a goddess." She vanished from the door and padded down the hallway.

I rose, checked on the baby, and followed. In less than a minute, I made us both cups of coffee and cradled mine at the table. "You mentioned cookies."

Margaret dug a Union Street Bakery box from a tattered knapsack and set it on the table. Inside were six sugar and six chocolate chip cookies. I took one of each. "Thanks."

She sipped her coffee. "The kid is doing okay?"

"Sleeping."

"For how long?"

"What time is it?"

"Twelve."

I slept for an hour. "I don't think she slept much last night. So I'm hoping a little while longer."

"Good." She leaned back in the chair, her arm resting casually on the back like we were best buddies. "So how did the wine thing go?"

I yawned. "It went well. We were a hit."

"And was lover boy pleased?"

"Scott was very happy. He's worked hard for this moment."

"Sounds like you have as well."

"The vineyard is his dream."

"Dreams are all fine and good, but if there isn't a brain behind the dream, then it generally doesn't get far. Sounds like lover boy sees the forest, and you see the trees."

The sugar cookie tasted sweet and soft. "That's a good way of putting it."

"I'm a tree kind of person myself. Love digging into history."

"You love what you do. That's a blessing."

"Blessing and a curse. I can spend all day in the past, but can't really connect with the present or the future."

The hot coffee revived my brain a little. "I avoid the past as much as possible."

"Too bad, because your bottle is fascinating," Margaret said.

"You keep saying my bottle. I gave it to you."

Margaret accepted the New York cup. "That doesn't belong to me. It's a part of all our pasts. No one owns history."

"Good, because I don't need the responsibility of any more history." I sipped my coffee and sat at the table, realizing this was the first time in almost a week I felt moderately relaxed. "So, tell me what you found."

She plucked a sugar cookie from the box and took a large bite. Her eyes closed and for a moment her softened expression telegraphed her pleasure. "I've been on a low-carb diet for six days. But when I woke this morning I headed straight to the bakery. I know where my sister Rachel stashes the day-old stuff."

I reached for a chocolate chip and studied its perfectly round shape. "How many carbs in this?"

"A million and six, I think. But I don't care. It's Saturday and everyone deserves a day off."

I couldn't remember the last Saturday I took off. There was always work to be done in the vineyard. If my office work was done, then I headed into the fields to help Scott. We both loved the vineyard, so the work never really felt like work. Feeling a little guilty that I wasn't there to enjoy last night's success with him, I bit into the cookie. "Amazing."

"Rachel can cook anything. Anything."

"I believe it. Her cookies would have been a hit at the party."

"They do some catering. Mostly mail-order stuff now. They're only open to the public on Thursdays and Fridays."

"Small retail shops are struggling these days. How are they doing?"

"Storefront does okay," Margaret said. "We have devoted customers. The mail-order business is booming."

"Good for them. Scott and I hope to set up mail order for the vineyard, but that's at least a season or two away." I sipped my coffee. "Did you bring the bottle?"

"I did." She gobbled the last of her cookie, wiped her fingertips on her jeans, and dug an object wrapped in a thick blue-and-yellow-checked towel from her bag. Carefully, she unwrapped the folds until she reached the bottle. She set it on the table.

Without the distraction of the stone removal and the baby, I could see that the bottle was indeed interesting. The wavy surface suggested a handblown glass that was several hundred years old. The bottle's corked neck was three inches tall and the base of the bottle wide and sturdy. "It's kind of amazing that the glass isn't broken."

"Beyond amazing. I can think of only two like this that aren't broken."

"How old?"

"I'd say 1750."

"That's fairly precise."

"I can make several assumptions on the bottle's age based on the glass, shape, and cork, but what zeroed in the time for me was the hearth that belonged to the house on the property."

"According to Dr. McDonald, the land has been in her family for hundreds of years."

"Try 1748," Margaret said.

"That's exact."

"Her family owned a small tobacco plantation along the Potomac. According to a few house accounts of Patience and Michael McDonald we have on record, it did well enough. They didn't get rich but they weren't dirt farmers either."

"They lived in the house with the stone hearth?"

"Yes." Margaret settled back in her chair, her hand resting on her coffee cup. She reminded me of a professor addressing her class.

"Was there mention of Faith in any of your research?"

"Like I said before, the McDonalds bought Faith's servant contract from a ship's captain but some time around 1749 they sold it. Still searching for the buyer."

"Why would they sell her contract?"

Margaret arched a brow. "Maybe they figured out they lived with a real witch under their roof."

Remembering Grace's bottle, I set down my coffee. I hurried into the living room and carefully removed the old green bottle from the mantel. I set it next to the other. They could have been twins. "Remember I said Grace owns a witch bottle, too."

Margaret's brow knotted as she inspected the bottle. "Wow."

"Grace said her mother found it years ago. My Grandmother Shire had an obsession with collecting."

"Did she remember where the bottle was found?"

"No."

Margaret held the bottle to the sun. Light caught the glass and shone into the interior, revealing what looked like metal pins. "Two nearly identical witch bottles."

"Kinda odd."

Margaret shook her head studying the two bottles. "Kinda super, super rare."

After this long week the last thing I ever imagined discussing today would have been a witch bottle. Laughter born of fatigue and frustration more than humor bubbled inside me. "Just what I need in my life, a little black magic."

"To be clear," Margaret said. "The witch bottles are white magic. Not the scary kind."

Amused, I leaned back in my chair. "Right. I forgot. I don't need any more bad luck in my life."

Margaret stilled, her brow arched. "Am I losing my audience?"

"Not at all." I bit my lower lip. "I'm a little tired."

"In the 1750s, any woman found doing magic could be sent to prison. Even protection spells were a no-no. If claims of witchcraft followed Faith to America she could have been in serious danger."

"So why would these two ladies make the bottles if they feared imprisonment?"

"Maybe they feared this woman Faith or some other witch more than the authorities."

I stifled a yawn, wishing I weren't so tired. "So you think the gals who made these bottles feared the same person?"

"I would say these gals knew a woman in their community that aroused suspicion. These witch bottles cast a protection spell. They keep evil away. And my money is on this woman Faith."

"Do you know anything about Faith?"

"Her contract said she hailed from Aberdeen. I contacted a friend of mine at the university there and he's doing a little digging. We might know more in a day or two."

"So they feared for their lives?"

"Most likely."

I glanced in the jars, feeling a sudden affinity for the women who might have been alone and overwhelmed. Darkness, death, solitude . . . they could all stir up a little madness. "What's inside?"

"The one from the McDonald house has four nails, hair, a couple of buttons, and what looks like a scroll."

"How do you know there are four nails?"

"A friend x-rayed it."

"Where?"

"Friend at an orthopedic practice. She slipped it under the machine for me in trade for one of Rachel's pies."

I traced the seated neck of Grace's bottle. "Grace said there could be blood inside."

"Or urine."

"Gross."

"Hey, I don't write the spells." Margaret reached for another cookie and took a bite. "Is Grace around?"

"Let me check her room." I knocked gently on her open door. When I didn't get an answer, I glanced inside and found only her neatly made bed. "She's gone. I thought she was sleeping after last night but I guess she's off enjoying some downtime."

"She'll turn up."

As I passed my room I spotted the portrait of Sarah Goodwin. "Have a look at this picture."

Margaret rose and looked in my room. "Who is this?"

"Sarah Goodwin. One of the first in our clan to arrive on these shores."

Margaret crossed to the picture, studied it closely. "I don't know much about her but I could find out."

"I've got to admit I am interested."

She reached for her cell and snapped a picture of the portrait. "Do you know where she came from originally?"

"Grace said Scotland."

"This gets more interesting by the minute."

I made a couple more cups of coffee and set both on the table. "So what else do you know about all this magic stuff?"

"Around 1750ish, the area was in flux. Tobacco was booming and the lands were being worked by African slaves as well as indentured servants. The land in the area was subdivided into lots and new land-owners were feverishly building their homes."

"Didn't the indentured servants get their freedom after seven years?"

"If they survived. Most didn't live through the indenture. In fact, only about ten percent got out of bondage with freedom and land."

"They came from England?"

"Scotland, a few from Ireland. You know, Faith was lucky in some respects to be transported. The Scots and Brits burned their share of witches back in the day."

"So she's sent here, but how could trouble follow?"

"Someone from the old country might have recognized her or she kept doing what got her into trouble in Scotland."

"Such as?"

"Remember the witch in Chesapeake. She got into trouble for growing medicinal herbs and refusing marriage offers."

"So how do we find out more about Faith?"

"I think the answer to our mystery might lie with the McDonald family. I was thinking I'd ask Dr. McDonald about those family papers she mentioned before."

"Dr. McDonald didn't seem thrilled with us."

Margaret grinned. "I can be persistent."

"No offense, but you rubbed her the wrong way."

"More the reason for her to give me my answers—so I'll leave her alone."

I laughed. "Or you could make her so mad that she calls the cops."

"She wouldn't do that."

"Don't be so sure."

"Would you come with me?"

"Me?"

Her eyes brightened. "You can bring the kid along. Might do you some good to get out of here."

"I've got work."

"What kind?"

"Vineyard. Followup calls."

"It's Saturday afternoon, Addie. No one wants to talk to you about buying wine. Believe me, if it was a success, they're tired and hungover. And tomorrow's Sunday."

"I have those stones to unload and sell."

"Really, you'd rather unload stones than talk history?"

Temptation stirred. *Go. Take the day.* "They've got to be sold."

"Is all your life to-do lists?"

"No." I pushed aside the mental list that ran like ticker tape. "I have fun."

"Like when?" She folded her arms and her eyes narrowed. "When was the last time you did something fun?"

"You sound like a cop doing an interrogation."

"Don't evade."

"I don't know the date."

"I can tell you the date I last had fun. I was at O'Malley's tavern last week having a beer with friends and we laughed until my sides hurt."

Envy jerked at my shirtsleeve. When was the last time I really laughed? Surely I shared the moment with Scott. We laughed a lot. Didn't we?

"You can't remember?"

"It's not that. I've been busy lately."

"Like for the past decade or two."

A sigh shuddered through my teeth. I grew up knowing if I didn't work, the family would sink. Work was safe. Work kept me alive. But for now, I didn't want to work. I wanted to play. "I'm in."

Two hours later Margaret and I were in the front seat of the Shire Architectural Salvage truck and Carrie was settled in the backseat. She wasn't sleeping but seemed content to stare out the window. The kid loved going places.

"Let me do the talking," I said.

"What did she say on the phone?"

"Like I said, she's not open to sharing family papers, but she did say we could see the family Bible. It dates back to sixteen hundredish."

Margaret groaned. "Dates. I need specific dates!"

Grinning, I settled into the seat as the truck rattled toward the McDonald's home. When I pulled into the driveway, Margaret was ready to jump out of the truck and run up to the doorbell . Carrie was sleeping.

I got out, pulled on the baby sling, and carefully slid Carrie into the pouch. She yawned and relaxed back into a deep sleep. "Must be nice to sleep," I said. "I think I have forgotten what it feels like."

Margaret waved her hand. "Sleep is overrated."

"Unless you're not getting it."

We walked up the path and I rang the doorbell. "Remain calm."

Margaret folded her arms and then quickly undid them and slid her hands into her pockets. "Right."

The clip-clop of heels reverberated in the house. "Heels on a Saturday," I said. "Oh, my."

"I'd have worn heels, if I knew it was a party."

I laughed. "You own heels?"

"No."

When the door snapped open to the very crisply dressed Dr. McDonald, we stood smiling like schoolgirls. She wore creased khakis, a white button-down shirt, and, of course, tan pumps. Her hair was pulled back into a neat bun and her glasses reflected her green eyes. "Ms. Morgan and Ms. McCrae. I was surprised by your call."

"The bottle we found on your property is turning out to be very interesting," I said. "I discovered that my family owns a similar one and we're trying to find a connection."

She nodded. "Come in, please. I've a little information for you."

"Great."

Margaret smiled. "Thank you for having us."

The very proper response belied everything about Margaret, but to her credit, she sounded very genuine.

Dr. McDonald escorted us into a parlor, which was as tastefully decorated as you'd expect. A handmade Oriental rug warmed the floor, oil landscapes hung on the walls, and the fabric covering the Chippendale sofa cost hundreds of dollars per yard. "I pulled up images of the family Bible on my computer. It's two hundred and seventy years old and getting more and more fragile. I thought it best to save what I could."

"Very wise," Margaret said.

Dr. McDonald went to her desk and retrieved two pages stapled together. "These are the first few pages of the Bible. It was given as a wedding present to my ancestors, Dr. Michael McDonald and his bride, Patience. They were married in 1745 and sailed to this country a year later. He owned one hundred acres right in this area, and I believe the stone hearth you removed must have been theirs."

She handed me the paper, which I accepted and gave to Margaret. She scanned the page. "Mrs. McDonald gave birth to eight children, but only two survived past the age of ten."

Without really thinking, I patted Carrie on the bottom. "How sad."

"And all too common," Margaret said.

Dr. McDonald nodded as she turned back toward her desk. "And sensing you'd be curious, I also printed a letter that Mrs. McDonald wrote to her mother, but for whatever reason, she didn't send it. It's dated January 1750."

Margaret's eyes danced and I, too, was a little drawn into the mystery of the family. She dropped her gaze to the paper, transfixed by the scripted words.

"'Dearest Mother,'" Margaret read, glancing up. "Regular stuff about farm and family and then, 'I fear our former servant Faith cast a spell on me when I bade Dr. McDonald to sell her. Since she left, our luck has turned sour. I've lost two more children and miscarried another. My hope is to make my witch bottle, as you showed me when I was a child, and chase away her evil and the pain that consumes me daily. May God have mercy on my soul.'"

So Faith lived in the house with the stone hearth. Interesting.

Dr. McDonald fingered the pearls around her neck. "I was a bit curious about the reference to Faith. I didn't realize witches lived here in Alexandria."

Margaret's eyes danced with interest. "Neither did I. Do you have any record to whom Michael McDonald sold Faith's contract?"

"No. But I will have a look. I shall keep you posted."

April 2, 1751

Captain Smyth sets sail today for England. He has taken the profits from his last voyage and plans to invest in a second ship. Dr. Goodwin also invested heavily in the next voyage. The captain will return to England to oversee the construction and then return to the West Indies for more cargo. He has promised to pick up our new furniture and by late summer deliver it to our brick home.

Chapter Fifteen

After I dropped Margaret off at her apartment, Carrie and I headed back to the warehouse. She woke as soon as I climbed the stairs, and we fell into our now-familiar routine. Clean diaper, bottle, burp. Rinse. Repeat.

By the time I settled her back into her cradle, it was close to six and the door downstairs opened. Heavy footsteps sounded on the stairs and Grace appeared. She wore a long gray skirt, loose-fitting blouse, and her dark, silver-streaked hair up in a bun. She carried two sacks of groceries.

"You were gone awhile," I said. "Have a nice break?"

A brow arched. "I'm bone-tired and every muscle in my body aches."

Color rose in my cheeks. "Join the club!"

"Why can't you take the baby to the country? What's the big secret anyway?" She moved into the kitchen and began to unpack her purchases. "Why's this Scott fellow got to be kept in the dark? His wine launched just fine, otherwise you'd have really been dragging in here this morning."

Patting Carrie gently on the back, I followed. "I still haven't told him much about my family."

Grace grunted. "Much or anything?"

"Anything."

She set the groceries on the counter and began to unpack them. "So he doesn't know about your mother or Janet?"

"No."

She paused, a can of formula in her hand. "Why not?"

"You know how it is when you're related to a crazy person. Everyone thinks you might be a little crazy, or if you're not insane, they wonder when it's gonna happen."

She set the can down slowly and, for a moment, didn't speak. "A man who loves you would take the good with the bad." She set the oven to 425 degrees and pulled a frozen pizza from one of the grocery bags.

"Scott loves me. The silence is my fault, not his. I don't want all that madness in our lives."

"In case you haven't noticed, the madness is in your life and mine, girl. No getting around it. Don't you think the universe is forcing your hand?"

"Not yet. I have a little more time to work this out and get my life back."

She tore the pizza box open. "And Scott will never be the wiser."

"That would be nice."

"Would it ruin you two if he found out?"

"No. No. He would love me no matter what." The words held conviction, but whispers of doubt puffed around me like an evil spell. I thought about the witch bottle and wondered if I should make one for myself.

Grace turned and settled her frozen pizza on a round pan. "I got a call for another job today."

Practicality brushed the witch bottle to the sidelines. "Another job?"

"An old house on Prince Street in Alexandria, as a matter of fact. The new owners want to do a gut job of the basement. They want us to clear out the basement and sell what's there."

"Since when did we become pickers? I thought we salvaged architecture."

"Job sounds easy, and I hate to refuse money."

"I'm not crazy about dragging Carrie to another jobsite. It's not safe or efficient."

"I could watch the baby."

"Again? Twice in one week?"

A lift of the shoulder was Grace's only concession to Addie's teasing. "We can use the money. If I were here alone, I'd say no to the job. Fact, I think the only reason we got the job was because you took the last."

"I could call Margaret. She might be willing to work on commission like with the last job."

"She knows the city better than anyone."

Another inch toward this life. It didn't seem like much, but I feared one day I might look back and realize my old life was so far off in the distance that I couldn't find my way back. "Call them and tell them we'll take the job."

"You're sure?"

"Yeah, let's do it. I'll call Margaret."

I dialed Margaret and got her voice mail. "Margaret, it's Addie Morgan. I have another salvage job. A house on Prince Street. More like picking than dismantling. Interested? It's commission-based. In fact, I'll be on the phone today trying to sell the stones. Let me know. Thanks."

I told myself that Janet and I both needed time. She needed to heal physically and mentally, and I needed to find my footing on ground that still remained as slippery as ever. But what I wanted didn't factor into the equation. I needed to see her and assess her status. When we were kids, I could always tell when Mom was on the mend or falling into a spiral. I suppose my method was never scientific, but there was always something about the way she spoke and held my gaze that told me more than any doctor.

I called her doctor and left him a voice mail message. When he called me back an hour later, his voice sounded upbeat. "Your sister wants to see you," he said in his soft accent.

"Great. I can bring the baby."

"She doesn't want to see the baby. Only you."

"Why doesn't she want to see the baby?"

"She's fragile. It's a good sign she wants to see you."

She didn't want to see Eric and now Carrie. Maybe the new combinations of medicines would help balance her thinking and she'd change her mind.

I fed the baby, settled her in her bed for a nap, and with Grace babysitting, I headed to the mental health facility. I arrived at the hospital just after seven. The lost sleep was catching up to me, and my legs and arms weighed heavy with fatigue. At the registration desk I was redirected to the second floor, where I checked in with another nurse. She escorted me to Janet's room.

My sister lay in bed, her eyes closed and her hands resting in an almost angelic fold across her chest. Easy to look at her now and think she was on the mend, but like the eye of a hurricane, the calmness she enjoyed was simply a break between storms.

At the side of her bed, I let my purse drop to the floor as I sat. Memories of visiting Mom in the hospital tugged at me, and before I could stop the clock from ticking back it was twenty years ago.

Mom shared a room with two other women. One of the women lay in her bed, rocking her head from side to side, moaning softly. Another chatted wildly to a son who looked lost and scared.

Mom sat in her bed, her hands neatly folded in her lap. Her brown hair was brushed straight and flowed around her shoulders. She wasn't wearing makeup but, like Janet, was a natural beauty.

I was fourteen and Janet seventeen but I entered the room first. I always took the lead when Mom was sick because her illness shook Janet to the core.

Mom smiled when we entered. "My girls have come to see me. I love my girls."

Janet rushed to the bed and hugged Mom, desperate for any bit of normalcy. "Mom, you look so good."

Mom gently stroked Janet's long blond hair. Her smile was tentative, as if she understood this moment, which was as close to normal as she could now manage, wouldn't last forever. "Are you getting along okay at the apartment?"

"It's all good," I said.

Janet nodded her agreement. "All good, Mommy."

Mom started to jabber about how much better she felt. She said she'd return soon to our apartment and we would be a family again. She'd talked on and on about her grand plans, but as much as I wanted to believe it would be fine, this time I didn't.

Now, as I stood in Janet's room, I couldn't conjure up the rest of that day.

As I sat, Janet's eyelids fluttered open. Crystal blue eyes remained vacant as she looked at me, searching for the identity attached to my face.

"Janet," I said gently. "It's Addie. Your sister. Addie Morgan."

A cock of her head signaled some recognition, and then a long blink as her brain adjusted. "Addie."

Not a question but a statement. Progress. "Addie. Your sister. You called me the other day, remember?"

A slow, slow nodding. "You didn't call me back."

"No."

"You never call me back."

"No." I shifted in my chair. Her thinking might be fuzzy but she clearly remembered I stopped taking her calls a long time ago.

"Why?"

"Because I got tired of dealing with your problems, Janet."

"I have a lot of problems." Her voice sounded far-off and lost. "But I never asked for them."

Mental illness was not her fault. She was cursed, like our mother, grandmother, and great-grandmother. But it was easy to forget her illness when she lobbed a grenade in my life, shattering what I built.

"How are they treating you here?"

"Good, I guess. I've been sleeping a lot." Her fingers unfurled and her hands went absently to her belly. A heartbeat or two passed. "I had a baby."

"You did."

"Boy or girl?"

"A girl, remember? I'm calling her Carrie, but if you don't like the name you can change it."

"A girl." The word carried with it painful undercurrents. "How is she?"

"Physically she's fine."

Janet shook her head. "Is she like me?"

"She looks like you."

"That's not what I mean." Fingers gripped the blanket until her knuckles whitened.

"It's too early to tell about that. She cries unless I hold her."

"She cries?"

"Yes. But when I pick her up she stops."

Janet smiled, nodding. "She knows."

"Knows what?"

"That only you can save her."

I leaned forward, gripping my purse. "That's not true, Janet. You can save her. You are her mother."

"I can't." Eyes drifted shut as she tried to collect and organize her thoughts. "Mom couldn't save us."

Lies could sound sweet and soothe tension, but the relief was temporary and we needed more than my stand-in-mother kind of temporary fix. "No. Mom couldn't save us. But you are different than Mom. The meds today are different than what she took."

"I am Mom," she whispered. "I have it, the curse, just like she did."

"Curses aren't real, Janet."

"Mom said the witch cursed our family over two hundred years ago. She said the curse would always be with us."

"Mom was just making that up," I said.

"She wasn't. Her mother told her about the curse. And the witch."

"What witch?"

She raised trembling fingers to her brow. "I don't remember. But she's real. Sometimes I hear her."

"She's one of the voices."

Her eyes widened. "She's not like the other voices. I always hear her clearly."

"How do the other voices sound?"

"Like they come out of an old radio. But not her. She's clear."

Arguing over what was real or not real wasn't important. What was important was that Janet believed the voices were real. "What did the witch say?"

"She won't break the curse. Only we can break it."

"How?" I thought about Faith, accused of witchcraft so long ago.

Her head turned toward me and she looked at me for long tense seconds. "I don't know how to break it. I don't know how." Tears welled in her gaze and a tear trickled down her cheek. "Do you know how?"

"No, I don't." And for the first time in a long time I wished Janet's talk about witches and curses was real. Without the curse, we all might have a shot at normal.

But witches and curses weren't real. And like it or not, neither of us was destined for normal.

Fresh tension banded my shoulders. "You should rest, Janet. Sleep."

A slow nod. "I'm tired. So tired."

"I saw Eric."

"Eric?"

"Your son."

Her eyes drifted closed. "Son. A boy. No curse."

"He seems to be fine. He's strong and healthy like his father."

"Good."

"Janet, who's Carrie's father?"

"Carrie?"

"Your daughter. The baby you just gave birth to. Who is her father, Janet?"

She shook her head. "A knight in shining armor."

"Janet." My tone sharpened the edges of her name. "Who is the father? I need a real name. He needs to be contacted."

"I don't know his name. He was a charming prince."

"Janet, do you know his real name?"

"No." Her voice drifted. "I never ask for names."

As if she slipped under the surface of the water, she was gone, sleeping. Her face lost the stress and was now beautifully relaxed.

Leaning back in my chair, I rolled my head from side to side. "You cannot do this to me, Janet. You cannot dump your life on me. I have a life."

My words were lost, gobbled up by the empty space between us.

Rising, I reached for my purse and slung it over my shoulder. "We're going to fix this."

Out in the hallway, I leaned against the wall, fearful that the weight of Janet and Carrie and this life would bring me to my knees.

"Are you all right?"

At the sound of Zeb's familiar masculine voice I stood straighter and turned. He wore jeans, construction boots, and a clean gray T-shirt. His dark hair was brushed off his face, accentuating deep lines around his mouth and eyes. Too much frowning, I wanted to say. Janet made you frown too much. I knew, because I saw the same lines forming in my face.

"Yeah, I'm fine."

"Have you seen her?"

"She's sleeping."

Relief flickered across his face. "Eric was asking. I promised to check on her."

"She won't be able to talk to you now. Tell Eric I saw her, and she's better, but she's very tired. She'll be this way for a week or two."

"Okay. Thanks." He studied my face. "You look like you could use some sleep."

"Been a long week."

"Tell me about it."

Images of the cradle came to mind. "Thank you for the cradle."

"It was Eric's and it was just sitting in my attic. Shame to waste it."

"It's really beautiful. You made it?"

"Yes."

"Amazing. Carrie likes it."

A brow arched. "She's slept in it?"

"Right now as we speak—at least I hope she's sleeping. I'll have to get back soon to feed her."

"She's doing better?"

"Better?" I walked toward the exit and he followed. "We're getting used to each other. Basically, she's teaching me that if she wants something, I must stop everything I'm doing and take care of her."

He opened the door with one hand and waited for me to pass. "Eric was a good baby, but lots of work."

"Did he cry a lot then?"

"Not much. I mean, when he was hungry or tired, but he didn't just cry."

"A boy. That makes sense."

"You don't really believe in the curse, do you?"

"In curses, no. In strong genetics, yes, I do believe." We reached the lobby and crossed it. Again, he opened the door. Passing him, I caught the faintest scent of soap and sunshine. It reminded me of Scott. Clean, simple, and very masculine.

We should've been together today. We should have been sitting on the porch, enjoying a cool glass of wine and musing over last night's successes. We should have made love and lingered in each other's arms. I wasn't supposed to be here. Mental hospitals and babies weren't a part of my plan. And yet, here I was.

"Do you really think the baby could be sick?" Zeb asked.

"There's no way of knowing."

"You're not sick."

That startled a chuckle. "Maybe the jury is still out on me."

"No. You're fine. You've always been steady."

"That's me. Steady as a rock. The dependable one."

He stopped on the sidewalk in a sunny spot. I dug my sunglasses out of my purse, and he pulled Ray-Bans from his pocket and slid them on over his eyes. He was an attractive man, but a little judgmental and hard when we first met a decade ago. Black and white. Right and wrong. Zeb knew the answers. He was the steady guidepost in the storm that Janet always stirred. I think at first he liked her mad sense of adventure. She brought a spark of excitement to his very, very steady life. He never said it to me, but he thought I was boring and plain. He found my steadiness unappealing, whereas Scott loved and embraced it.

"You make that sound like that's bad."

"I'm not exciting. Never have been and never will be. But I thought maybe, just maybe, my life turned on a better path."

I couldn't see his eyes but suspected in this moment they held the dissolution I felt. "And then Janet came back."

"And then Janet came back."

A heavy silence settled between us. "Hey, thanks again for the crib. We'll take good care of it. If I don't get back soon, Carrie will be driving Grace into fits, and I don't want either one of us to wear out our welcome."

His brow furrowed. "Grace doesn't want you there?"

"Let's say she wants this to be a temporary situation like all of us." I fished keys from my purse. "If Eric wants to come by and see the baby, he's welcome. Though I'd avoid the five-to-six time slot in the evenings. That seems to be turning into the witching hour."

"Too tired to eat or sleep."

"That's about it."

"Would lunchtime tomorrow work?"

"That would be great."

"Thanks, Addie."

"For what?"

"For allowing Eric to connect. He misses not connecting with his mother."

"Here's hoping Janet gets better, and she can be in his life," I said.

His jaw shifted to a grim line. "Right."

* * *

The drive back to the warehouse was easy enough and by the time I pulled into the parking lot, my phone was ringing. It was Margaret.

"So you've got another job?"

"It seems so. Want in?"

"Sure. I'm open Monday and Tuesday next week. Either would work."

"Great. I'll confirm the details with Grace and get back to you."

"What's the address?"

"Not sure exactly, but it's Prince Street. Captain's Row."

"Captain's Row?" No missing the excitement in her voice. "God I love that street! I wonder who's tossing out stuff?"

"I'll text details as soon as I have them."

"It's a deal."

"Oh, I have more information about your witch bottle."

"That so?" The day warmed and I watched from my parking spot as the midsummer traffic of tourists and commuters moved slowly by. The Old Town district was popular with tourists all year round but midsummer was the busiest. I remember the warehouse saw more traffic during the summer with visitors buying bits and pieces of history to take home with them.

"I'll save the discussion for when I see you. My lectures can put the best people to sleep, and I can hear the sleep in your voice."

I yawned. "Just a little."

"Call me with a time."

"Will do."

I arrived home to a crying baby.

April 30, 1751

I dreamed that Faith crossed the Atlantic on a ship made of eggshells and sought out the *Constance*. She cried out as she peered into the ship's cargo hold and saw people crying and begging for release. She pointed at Captain Smyth and called him "peddler of flesh," telling him that God would make him atone for his sins in hell. With her outstretched white finger, she whipped up the seas and sunk his vessel, which carried with it our future.

I awoke crying.

Chapter Sixteen

The next day, Carrie and I were walking the first floor of the warehouse when Zeb and Eric arrived with a golden retriever in tow. We were strolling for an hour, the baby in the front pouch, me swaying from side to side, patting her bottom and asking her in a very gentle voice why sleep was so terrible.

"Addie!"

I turned to see the two Talbot men striding toward me. Eric, without trying, was a mini-version of his father. They both shared the same stride, the same square jaw, and the same thick dark hair. Eric was smiling, but Zeb, holding the dog's leash, was not. His expression transmitted tension and annoyance.

Yeah, pal, I bet you can come up with at least ten different things you'd rather be doing as well. Tough. Suck it up.

"Eric," I said. "Who's your furry friend?"

"That's Shep," he said, patting the dog on the head. "He's two and he's in trouble with Dad."

"Uh-oh. What did he do?"

"He was barking at a squirrel and he nearly got loose."

"That's bad."

The boy made a face as he looked at the dog. "Dad said the dog was dancing on his last nerve."

Zeb cleared his throat.

I grinned, grateful I wasn't the only one in the down-to-my-last-nerve club. "How'd you like to hold your sister?"

"Sure!" Eric rushed up to me and I leaned over so he could get a look at her red, angry face. "Why's she crying?"

"That seems to be her job. Cry, eat, and poop."

Eric laughed. "You said 'poop.'"

"A week ago I wouldn't have, but there you go, I did say it."

Zeb's shadow cast a long, deep swath over us. "She sleep much last night?"

Shep sniffed my leg and then sniffed the baby's foot. He wagged his tail.

Scratching the dog between the ears, I shrugged. "A few hours."

"And you?"

"A little less."

"You look exhausted."

I pushed back a lock of hair, aware that I wore yesterday's shirt and I needed a shower. "Feeling it. Why don't you come upstairs? I'll make coffee."

"You or Grace mind if I bring Shep?"

"As long as he doesn't pee."

Eric giggled.

"I'll keep him close," Zeb said. "Where's Grace?"

"Vanished once again. She leaves for long stretches and takes walks, I think. Woman must be desperate for quiet. And I can't blame her."

Eric took the lead, clamoring up the stairs, and I followed. My feet felt weighted with lead and I wanted to sit so badly I thought I might cry. Zeb took up the rear, his slow and steady sure steps mingled with Shep's clip-clop.

In the kitchen, I moved toward the coffeemaker when Zeb said, "Have a seat. I'll make the coffee. Maybe Eric can hold the baby. Shep, sit."

Shep plopped on the kitchen floor, but his gaze remained bright and expectant. "I won't drop her," Eric said. "I'm good at carrying things."

"Then let's have a seat on the sofa, and I'll load her in your arms."

"Are you hungry?" Zeb asked.

"Starving."

"Good, I've already ordered a couple of pizzas."

"Thanks. You didn't have to do that."

His back to me as he filled the coffeemaker, he simply said, "We all have to eat."

I settled on the sofa in the living room and Eric nestled next to me. I thought of him as small when we first met, but I could see he was sturdy for a seven-year-old.

Carefully, I hooked my hands under Carrie's armpits and head, supporting the back of her head with my extended index fingers, and raised her out of the pack. A touch of her diaper told me it was empty and dry. "Sit back on the couch, Eric. I'll lay her in your arms."

He scooted back and clapped his hands as if he was ready for me to toss him a football. "I got this."

Laying Carrie in his arms, I cupped my hand under her head. "You've got to support her head. She's not strong enough to hold it on her own."

He studied her face, his nose inches from her nose. "When will she start to walk?"

"I'm not sure. A year maybe? She's got to learn to hold her head up and then sit up before she can start crawling."

His face inches from hers, he studied her closely. "Why does it take so long?"

"She's got a lot of important growing to do. It takes time. When your dad builds a house, does he build the roof first?"

Eric looked up at me as if I were crazy. "No. That's stupid."

I shrugged. "Babies are like houses. They grow from the ground floor up."

He touched his nose to Carrie's. "Carrie, why are you always crying?"

The sound of his voice caught the baby's attention and she stopped fussing. She opened her eyes and searched.

"I think she likes you, Eric," I said.

He grinned and nuzzled his nose against hers. "I like her."

The front bell buzzed, and Shep barked as Zeb moved down the stairs. He returned with a couple of pizzas, which he set out on the kitchen table. "Soup's on," he said.

Eric rolled his eyes. "He always says that, but we never have soup."

"Pizza is a staple in the Talbot house," Zeb said. "We'd starve without it."

The scents of cheese and pepperoni made my stomach grumble. "Smells pretty good. Eric, want me to hold the baby while we eat?"

"Yeah."

Carrie back in my arms, we headed into the kitchen. I settled in a chair and Zeb set a plate in front of me. "Cheese or pepperoni?"

"Cheese."

He pulled out a slice and set it on a plate for me. "I lived on this stuff when Eric was a baby. Hold baby with one hand and eat with the other."

I folded the pizza in half and bit the tip. "I don't think I've tasted food this good in a hundred years."

Eric laughed. "You're not a hundred years old."

"I sure do feel like it these days."

"Why?"

"Baby Carrie," Zeb said. "Babies are a lot of work."

Eric frowned. "Is that why Mom can't take care of Carrie and me? Are we too much work?"

I glanced over at Zeb. His jaw worked, chewing on words better not spoken. "She's sick, Eric. I told you that."

"How long has she been sick?" He lowered his head and his shoulders slumped.

"She's been sick as long as I can remember," I said. "She doesn't like being sick, and she can't really help it. Our mom, your grandmother, was sick, too. She couldn't really take care of your mom or me."

"Is her stomach upset or does her head hurt?" the boy asked.

"No. It's more like sick in the head. Her brain doesn't work right. She gets confused. It's not that she doesn't love you, it's her brain doesn't work the way she wants it to."

Zeb's gaze locked on mine. Gratitude softened the lines feathering round his eyes. "I told you, pal, Mom is sick."

"I want to see her," Eric said.

Zeb set his pizza slice down and moved to the kitchen counter for a roll of paper towels. He tore off three sections and sat back down. "Maybe soon, pal."

"Have you seen Mom?"

I accepted a napkin from Zeb. "I saw her yesterday. She's very tired. And she's sleeping a lot."

"Because she's sick?"

"Sleeping sometimes is the best way to get well. I did tell her you were asking about her."

His gaze grew hopeful. "What did she say?"

"She smiled."

Eric nodded before he reached for his pizza and took a bite. "Okay. Good."

The three of us sat in silence, eating our pizza. Eric tossed Shep pieces of crust, which the dog gobbled up. Carrie settled and fell asleep in my arms. On the surface, the moment was oddly . . . normal.

My phone buzzed and I glanced at the display. Scott calling. I stared at the image of his smiling face, the vineyard, and the setting sun behind him. A glance at the sleeping baby tempted me to answer, but at this point I couldn't risk her waking. There was so much I needed to say to Scott. I let the phone ring until voice mail took over.

Zeb raised a brow, taking in the scene, and clearly coming to a swift conclusion that didn't favor me. "You haven't told him about us."

"No. Not yet. But I will soon."

"Why the secret?"

"It's not a quick conversation. As you well know, the Morgans are complicated."

"Yes."

When Janet first got ill I tried to be honest and open, tackled the problems head on. But open and honest didn't work, and in the end it had all fallen apart, and I was left drained and angry. As much as I didn't want the storm to touch Scott, the hurricane swirled around us, and soon, no matter how hard I shored up our life, the winds were coming.

Carrie squirmed in my arms and I rose, moving to the refrigerator, where I stowed several pre-made bottles. With the baby cradled in one hand, I screwed the top off the bottle and placed it in the microwave. I punched in seventeen seconds and hit Start.

"Can I feed the baby?" Eric asked.

"Sure," I said. "We can sit on the couch."

Eric looked at his dad. "I'm going to feed the baby."

Zeb smiled. "I know, pal. Pretty good."

The microwave dinged and I screwed the top back on. A quick shake and I grabbed a burp towel. "Want to finish your pizza first?"

"No. I want to feed the baby!"

Zeb rose. "Let's wash your hands, pal. And then we can sit on the couch." The two moved to the kitchen sink and Zeb turned on the water. When Eric's hands had been cleaned and dried, he joined me in the living room.

I settled on the couch and Eric moved next to me as before. This time I draped the cloth over his shoulder.

"What's that for?"

"In case she spits up."

His face wrinkled. "That's nasty."

I sat next to him and scooted close. "Tell me about it. I'm still getting used to that."

I nestled the baby in his arms and quickly dribbled a couple of drops of milk on the underside of my wrist to test the milk. Declaring it just right, I nuzzled the bottle into the baby's lips and waited as Eric reached to take hold of it.

Carrie suckled, smacking her lips.

He looked up at me, his face full of wonder and astonishment. "She's eating, Addie."

"I know. She's pretty good at eating. Maybe if you're real good I'll show you how to change a dirty diaper."

He wrinkled his nose. "Yuck. No way."

Shrugging, I held up my hands. "That's part of it. What goes in must come out."

He shook his head, but his gaze remained on the baby. "I'm not changing any diapers."

Zeb and Shep came into the room. As the dog took a seat at my feet,

Zeb reached for his cell and pointed it at us. My insides clenched with tension. A picture would be tangible evidence of my time in Alexandria.

But Eric glanced up at his dad and grinned so broadly I couldn't make a fuss.

"Smile, Addie," Zeb said.

Drawing in a breath, I leaned into Eric and smiled. Shep rose up and put his head on my knee. Zeb snapped the picture. He glanced at the image and grinned, turning it around so we both could see it. Eric's smile was electric as he cuddled his sister close. My smile was decent enough, but it did little to soften the fatigue around my eyes or brighten my pasty complexion. "What do you think?"

"Awesome," Eric said.

"Very nice."

"We should take a picture with Grace," Eric said. "But we're going to have to tell her a funny joke before we take the picture so that she's smiling. She doesn't smile much."

Grace never smiled when I was a kid. Always stern and solemn, she focused on work and chores. And I couldn't remember a time when she enjoyed herself.

I tipped the edge of the bottle up a fraction to keep Carrie from sucking in too much air. Eric talked to his sister in a sweet, soft voice, asking her all kinds of questions. *Do you like trucks? When you're big enough to climb a tree you can come in my tree house. Do you have dreams?*

The chatter went on and on but neither Zeb nor I wanted to rush this moment. Eric was enjoying his sister, and several times she opened her eyes and stared at him with keen interest.

Zeb leaned against the fireplace, content to enjoy the moment. All the antiques and clutter would have made Scott uneasy, but Zeb didn't seem to notice any of it. His gaze was squarely on his son.

When the milk was gone, Carrie drifted back to sleep. I gently nudged the bottle free of Eric's grasp and Carrie's lips. Very carefully, I covered my shoulder with a towel and then lifted Carrie free of Eric's arms. Draping her on my shoulder, I patted her back softly until she burped.

Eric giggled. "What was that?"

"You've never burped?" I asked.

He blinked. "Yeah, but I'm a guy. I've never seen a girl burp."

"Not ever?" I teased. "I bet some girl in your class has burped."

He rolled his eyes. "Marcia does, but I don't like her. She always wants to play kickball with the boys and she pushes and shoves."

"Cut her some slack, Eric," I said. "She wants people to like her."

"Yeah, I guess." He glanced toward the mantel to the picture of Janet and me. "Did you and Mom ever live with Grace?"

"We lived here one summer when I was about twelve."

He furrowed his brow. "Where did your mom go?"

"Work." That's what she had told Janet and me, but I knew she was in the hospital.

He frowned. "Did she like being a mom?"

"I think she did. It was just very hard for her."

He nodded. "It's hard for my mom, too."

"Remember, Eric. Your mom and grandma have the same sickness. Doesn't mean they can't love." The words rang hollow. I was a few years older than Eric when I asked the same questions, and none of the answers Grace offered were enough. It totally sucked when your mother couldn't be a mother.

Zeb cleared his throat. "Pal, we need to let Carrie sleep and give Addie a rest."

"Addie's too big for a nap," Eric said.

"I might have agreed with you last week," I said, laughing. "But a nap sounds really good now."

Eric grimaced. "I hate naps."

Rubbing my eyes, I yawned. "One day you might like them."

"Nope."

Smiling, I rose, my legs heavy and achy with fatigue. "Want to see your baby crib?"

His eyes brightened. "Dad and I brought that over Saturday morning. It's really heavy."

"It's very beautiful." My gaze rose and met Zeb's. "Absolutely beautiful."

The simple nod he offered didn't match the complicated emotions darkening his gaze.

A heat rose, warming my face.

Eric's voice kicked up a notch, not wanting to be forgotten. "I slept in it when I was a baby."

Zeb's eyes closed for an instant before he looked at his son. "Lower your voice, pal. We don't want to wake the baby."

"She's cranky when she's awake," I whispered.

He held his fingers over his lips. "I know."

With Eric leading the way, we moved to my bedroom. I positioned the baby in the cradle and settled her on her back in the center. I tucked a small blanket over her and gently tipped the edge so that the cradle rocked ever so smoothly.

Eric kissed his fingertips and pressed them on the baby before he and I backed out of the room.

Zeb gathered our plates, dumped the excess crust and crumbs in the trash, and stacked the dishes in the sink.

I slid my hands into my pockets. "Thanks again for the pizza. It really hit the spot."

"Thank you." Zeb squeezed Eric's shoulder.

"Sure. As long as I'm here, you're welcome to come visit the baby anytime, Eric."

Eric frowned and when it looked like he'd ask another question, Zeb gently squeezed his shoulder. "Thanks again," he said. "Get some sleep."

"No worries there."

When the two left, I glanced at the dirty dishes, and as tempted as I was to leave them in the sink, I quickly washed them and stacked them in the drier. By the time I sat on my bed, my lower back hurt and my eyes itched with fatigue. Just ten minutes of sleep. Ten minutes. My phone buzzed and I glanced at the display. Again, I considered letting it go to voice mail. As soon as the thought crossed my mind, guilt took hold, squeezing my heart and twisting my stomach until I hit Answer on the screen.

"Scott." I moved into the kitchen, fearful Carrie would wake.

"Addie. Where the heck are you?"

At the sink, I stared out the window at the meandering waters of the Potomac. "I'm back in Alexandria at my aunt's house."

"I've been thinking about this all morning and I know something must be very wrong. You've got to tell me what's going on. This is so not like you."

"My sister is sick, Scott."

"You only mentioned her once. I thought she lived in California."

"She did. But now she's here."

"Is it cancer?"

"It's more complicated than I can really explain. I did see her this morning, and she's improving a little." Guilt clenched by heart a little tighter.

"You said yesterday that it would be a few weeks."

"That's not changed."

A door squeaked in the background as if he stepped outside his office onto the porch that overlooked the mountains. "Babe, what am I going to do without you?"

Hearing his voice coaxed a small smile. "You'll be fine, Scott. If ever there was a time for me to take a break it's now. You'll be fine."

"I'm already swamped with e-mails from the event."

I rubbed my eyes knowing I needed to check my computer. "What are people saying about it?"

"They loved it." A smile buzzed under the words. "Knocked it out of the park."

I stifled a yawn. "That's great."

"The Chardonnay got the best reviews and a few folks suggested we start entering competitions. Time to really step off the front porch and run with the big dogs."

My eyes drifted shut. "This is your dream, isn't it?"

"It's our dream. You and me. I couldn't have done this without you."

My head snapped up, sending a surge of energy up my spine. "This is all wonderful. Hon, how about I call you tomorrow? I'm still dead tired from Friday, and I've things to do for my sister."

"Sure thing. But remember they can't have you forever. You're my treasure."

"Will do."

"Love you, babe."

"Love you, too."

"I'm not hearing much emotion," he said.

I made myself smile. "Sorry, just tired."

"I'll give you a pass this time," he teased.

"Thanks."

I hung up and moved to my bed, lowering slowly, expecting Carrie to wake. Carefully, I eased back and swung my feet up onto the bed.

* * *

As the sun dipped lower on the horizon, closer to the banks of the steady waters of the Potomac, Grace sat staring at the basket nestled in her lap. Inside the basket rested a bottle, several needles, and a small set of scissors. Scents of the river mingled with the freshly cut grass along the path of the Washington & Old Dominion Trail, a forty-five-mile bike and walking trail that connected the Potomac River with the Shenandoah River Valley. She'd walked that trail every year for years, considering it more like a spiritual journey than a hike. She'd once read about the Camino, a long trail that snaked through France and northern Spain. Travelers from all around the world walked the rocky pathway, but she'd never make it to southern France and walked the five-hundred-mile trek into Spain. However she could imagine what it was like as she moved along this trail that snaked from riverbanks to the mountains.

It had been years since she walked the trail. There'd been reasons of course. Work. Bad knees. Poor eyesight. But all those were excuses. The reality was that she could handle the walk, which wasn't all that spectacular in the big picture. It didn't require courage. Or faith. It didn't require real courage or real faith. It required putting one foot in front of the other.

Real courage, real faith, well, that she did not have. Once she was tested and once she failed badly, and for two decades the weight of that failure hung on her shoulders.

Carefully, she unpacked her basket. First the bottle, then the scissors, and then the needles. The Universe had offered her another chance for redemption. It had sent her Addie, Janet, and Carrie.

She lifted the scissors to her hair and clipped several long strands. She tucked those strands with the locks of hair she'd clipped from

Addie's head while she slept. She dropped them into the bottle. Next came the needles. Four. She never understood why each bottle required four needles, but according to her grandmother, the magic number was four. One. Two. Three. Four. Each clinked into the bottle and nestled on top of the hair.

From her pocket, she pulled a small knife and pricked the edge of her finger with it. Blood oozed out in a bright circle, rising higher and higher until it threatened to spill. Before it slid over the edge of her skin, she pressed it to the bottle's mouth and allowed four drops of blood to drip over the glass and into the bottle. Again, always four drops, all of which she was careful to count.

Next came the scroll, which really was a small piece of paper inscribed with her single-word wish. Clutching her fingers around the paper, she repeated the word four times. Redemption. Redemption. Redemption. Redemption.

Finally, she dropped a small picture featuring her, twelve-year-old Addie, and fifteen-year-old Janet taken at the warehouse when the Universe had offered her a chance to break the curse.

Carefully, she wiped her finger on her jeans and reached for the bottle cork in her basket. She wedged the cork into the top of the bottle and worked it into place until it was so secure it would have to be dug out with a knife.

She closed her eyes and drew in a deep breath. The bottle would weave its spell for her and for Addie, Janet, and Carrie.

May 1, 1751

Dr. Goodwin and I strolled along the bluffs today toward the ware-house. I saw Faith outside the tavern. She was threading freshly stripped green saplings into the wattle fence guarding her budding rows of herbs. She is heavy with child. Dr. Goodwin tells me she is a foolish woman. Her indenture will be extended two years as a penalty for her folly. A cold wind blew off the river as Faith turned to look at me. Her blue eyes were heavy with scorn. The seas grew unsettled and cold winds heralded a terrible storm.

Chapter Seventeen

Margaret arrived the next morning minutes before seven, carrying a box of papers tucked under her arm. She wore faded jeans shorts that cut off an inch above her knee, a loose blue peasant top, and very worn, sensible sandals. Her hair remained in the topknot as always and a collection of silver bracelets rattled around her left wrist.

I handed her a cup of coffee. "Good morning. Isn't our job scheduled for tomorrow?"

"I couldn't wait that long. Did you know the house on Prince Street belonged to a ship's captain?" She sipped the coffee and closed her eyes, experiencing a pure moment of joy. "You do make the best coffee."

"I've been making it since I was four. My mom loved it."

"Four is kinda young to be making coffee."

A shrug and a sip. "I knew Mom was happier with coffee, so I learned to make coffee."

"She showed you?"

"I watched her do it. Mom said as I made it, I would swear. She didn't understand why until one day she caught herself swearing as she made coffee. She figured I learned that swearing went hand in hand with brewing."

"I could laugh at that story, Addie. Or I just might cry."

Odd to talk so freely about a secret hidden away for so long. "Mom was sick. She had the same mental illness that Janet has."

"Bipolar?"

"Yes with psychotic features. They can't seem to stick to the medication schedule. Mom was never really regulated and Janet's good periods never last more than a week or two. Nothing long-term."

Margaret sipped her coffee. "So what does that mean for the baby?"

I splashed milk in my coffee and swirled it, watching the color change. "I don't know."

"If Janet can't take care of herself, how can she take care of a baby?"

I smiled but felt no humor. "I'm still working on that."

"Baby's father?"

"So far, Janet doesn't remember who he is."

She tapped a ringed finger against her cup. "Adoption? My folks adopted Daisy."

"I've thought about that. I'm just worried the baby might have inherited three generations of illness."

"She could be like you."

"If I had to place a bet, I'd say she's going to have issues." Emotions welled in my chest when I thought about the road ahead for Carrie. I was Addie Fixer of All Things, and I didn't know how to fix this. I sipped my coffee, needing a moment to steady my voice. "Only time will tell."

"Damn."

"I know. Not a great way to start life."

"Speaking of the kid. She's quiet. Where is she?"

"Sleeping. She's up all night. Sleeps all day."

Margaret shook her head. "My sisters went through that with their babies. Daisy looked like the walking dead for months after her son was born."

"Sounds like she came out on the other end."

"She's crazy about the kid. Stupid crazy, if you ask me. I often ask her where the hard-driving corporate executive went, and she just laughs."

Daisy found happiness in motherhood and that made me a little jealous, because it was a joy I'd never know. Of course, this was not a new realization to me. There'd be no biological children for me. I made that choice ten years ago. But lately, in the quietest part of the night, nestled close to Scott, it bothered me that I also unwittingly made a decision for him. I swore over and over that I could love him enough to make up for what we would never have, but now wondered if that was even possible.

"So tell me about the house," I said. The distraction of work always saved me. "We'll be cleaning out the basement tomorrow. Owner says we can keep it all. You said the house was built by a ship's captain."

"Yes. Ship's captain." She moved past me into the living room and set her box of papers and large satchel purse on the couch. "In fact, the house, or at least parts of it, dates back to the 1750s when building lots were first drawn and sold in Alexandria."

"Do tell."

"Our first owner, Cyrus Smyth, was a Scottish ship's captain who, like his father before him, specialized in human cargo."

"Like slaves."

"Initially, not African slaves, but indentured servants from England and Scotland."

"And you said life for the indentured servant was rough?"

"Very rough. They arrived in debt to the ship's captain or the person who sponsored their passage, so they were forced to work off the debt. The reality was that many of these men and women died before they were ever freed."

"What killed them?"

"Disease, exhaustion, or in some cases beatings. An indentured servant's contract owner wielded about as much power as the slave owners did over their slaves." Bracelets rattled as she brushed bangs from her eyes. "A woman's service could be extended because she got pregnant while in service. Though I might add that the fathers were often the men who owned the women."

"Why did they extend the service?"

"Compensation for the working time lost during the pregnancy and after child birth."

"So why would anyone sign up for a gig like that?"

Margaret arched a brow. "Initially, it was seen as a great opportunity. The promise of land was huge. But by the 1730s, word reached England and Scotland that being an indentured servant was close to a death sentence. But Virginia needed men and women to work the land. So men like Smyth got clever. They lured street children, or any children for that matter, in Scotland, Ireland, and England onto the ships with pennies or promises of a hot meal. They went after men and women who were drunk or in trouble with the law. They paid off the local magistrates to sentence the accused to transportation to America. One way or another, men like Smyth filled their cargo holds with laborers. And once the ship arrived in America, the servants were charged for their passage. Of course, they had no money so they had to be sold to pay off the debt."

"That's some business."

"It was very profitable. Smyth would arrive with people, sell them, fill up his cargo holds with tobacco, and then return to England, where he'd sell the crop for profit."

"Credit for being a good businessman, but no points for humanity."

"Cyrus and his father made a lot of money transporting people."

"How do you know all this?"

"I've been researching the houses in Alexandria." She waved her hand over the pile of papers. "Kind of a hobby, or an obsession according to Daisy. Who knows, maybe one day I'll write a book."

"So what else do you know about Cyrus Smyth?"

"He built the house for his wife, Imogen. She was much younger than he when they married and a deeply religious woman." She sipped her coffee as she rummaged through her papers. "But that's not the best part."

I settled into the couch, enjoying her excitement. The stories were what made this business so fascinating. If not for Janet and her illness, I could very well have stayed. "Tell me the best part."

"Seems Imogen feared witchcraft."

No one usually got rich in the salvage business, but most days were never dull. "Think we'll find a witch bottle at her house?"

Her eyes brightened with a passion I truly envied. "That would be amazing."

My excitement for the job grew. "How do you know she feared witches?"

She thumbed through papers covered with scribbled handwriting and coffee stains. "According to court papers of the time, 'Imogen Smyth, widow of Cyrus, accused one woman by the name of Faith of witchcraft, and under a court mandate, Imogen with two other goodwives in attendance, searched Faith for the signs borne by a witch.'"

"Faith again?"

"She keeps popping up. Funny, but I never really gave her much thought before, and now I'm finding her name everywhere."

"What designates a witch?"

"The usual. Mark of the devil. Hair where it shouldn't be. Birth-marks. An extra nipple."

I laughed. "Really? An extra nipple. Who comes up with this stuff?"

"I didn't say it was logical. I'm only a teller of history. But we know that Imogen did go after Faith and accuse her of witchcraft. And you might laugh or think this sounds insane, but it would have been a very real problem for Faith."

I savored the warmth of my coffee cup. "Why go after Faith?"

"Like I said, evidence suggests she was a midwife and healer, for one. Midwives often fell under suspicion of the church or physicians. If she were good at what she did, she could relieve the suffering of a laboring woman."

"What's wrong with that?"

"God gave women pain in childbirth as punishment for the whole Garden of Eden disaster."

"She was punished for helping."

"Not saying it's right, but life was hard and tenuous back in the day and people were frightened."

"Aren't witch bottles protection spells?"

"Yes. If these women were afraid of Faith, they would have made their bottles and buried them under their hearths, or maybe just inside the front door."

"What else do you know about Faith?"

I waited, watching as Margaret scrambled through more papers. Though the pile looked to be a complete disorganized mess I could see that there was some type of organization, at least in Margaret's mind. She produced yellowed sheets of legal-sized writing paper clipped together with a purple clip. "We know Faith died in 1793 at the age of seventy-four."

"Wow. That's an impressive age."

"It's saying a lot. Most women didn't make it past forty. Childbirth was the big killer. There were a million other easy ways to die then, but that was the big one."

"So born 1719 and died 1793. She would have been about thirty when Cyrus Smyth built his house on Prince Street."

"According to her headstone and a records search at Christ Church, she left behind one son who she raised almost on her own. The boys' father was listed as Ben Talbot, tavern owner."

"Talbot. Like Zeb?"

"I don't know."

I drummed my fingers on the side of the mug. "A connection would be fascinating."

"This kind of stuff is what I live for. I could barely sleep last night when the pieces came together. I almost called you."

"Oh, I would have been awake."

"Go, Carrie."

Yawning, I raised my hand to my mouth. "This is sleep deprivation, not boredom. I know you have more."

Margaret nodded. "There was a suit filed against Ben Talbot in 1750. A farmer accused his indentured servant of bewitching his tobacco crops and making them fail. Ben fought the charges in court and the suit was dismissed. He later released Faith from her contract and they married." She drummed her hands on her knees to build suspense. "I also have a last name for Faith. Care to guess?"

When I shook my head, she said, "Shire."

"Shire. Damn. She's my clan?"

"Wouldn't be surprised."

"The Talbots and the Shires have a long history."

"Maybe." She shuffled through notes. "Imogen's husband, Cyrus, was killed when his ship was overtaken by a storm in 1751. When word reached Alexandria, Imogen was devastated, as were others who invested heavily in Smyth's cargo. Very soon after, the goodwives of Alexandria accused Faith of conjuring the storm. Imogen believed Faith killed her husband with a spell."

"Damn." For a moment I listened, reaching through the silence until I heard Carrie's soft, steady breathing. I counted five breaths before my thoughts refocused. "You think grief drove her?"

"Maybe. Maybe it was fear or a delusion that Faith could somehow stand on the bluffs overlooking the harbor and conjure the seas."

"We have no bluffs in Alexandria."

"We did then. Most of Union Street and a couple blocks north didn't exist at this time. The bay was crescent shaped. Eventually, the bluffs were leveled and portions of the bay filled in so that it's a gentle slope like it is today. We're standing on fill."

"I didn't know that."

Margaret waggled her brows. "I'm a wealth of information."

"What happened to Faith? You said she lived until 1793."

"She vanished from the records until her death notice in 1793."

"How did a woman accused of witchcraft end up buried in the church cemetery?"

"Her son, Marcus Talbot, became quite a successful tavern owner. Word is he was the kind of guy who knew where all the bodies were buried, and I bet he twisted arms when his mother passed."

"If Marcus owned a tavern, that might mean he inherited land from his father."

"That could very well be possible."

"Wow. And here I thought this was just a picking job."

Margaret's gaze gleamed as she sipped coffee. "What are we picking?"

"The basement. The new owner, a woman from New York, is renovating the basement, and she wants the space cleared."

"Enter us," Margaret said. "Aren't you going to ask me who were the other two goodwives who examined Faith?"

"Who?"

"Patience McDonald and Sarah Goodwin."

"My Sarah? I'm connected to two women in this sordid tale."

"I'm still digging into Sarah's life, but I do know she and her husband came from Scotland."

"History has a way of repeating itself. We've met Rae McDonald and today will meet Lisa Smyth, the woman who lives in the Prince Street property."

Margaret rubbed her palms together, her rings clinking against each other as they moved back and forth. "I love this stuff. Love it!"

"So tomorrow works for you?"

"Yes. I have to work at the center today and the bakery tonight. We have a big mail-order shipment going out, and they need all hands on deck. You should come by and bring the kid. I know Rachel and Daisy are crazy for babies, and they'd love to see her."

"Won't you be busy with packaging?"

"Yeah, but we can spare a moment. Hey, you can park the kid in the front pack and lend a hand. Lots of labeling from what I hear."

"What're you shipping?"

"Pies. Thousands and thousands of pies."

"Sure, why not. It's been a while since I saw your sisters. And I owe Daisy a big thank-you for helping with Carrie."

"You'll have a blast. Well, in a working kind of way."

With Carrie tucked in the front pack, freshly fed and diapered, she and I strolled down Union Street toward the bakery. The day cooled from the high temperature, which hit ninety, to a respectable eighty.

Weather was forecasting a cold front, which would keep temps lower for a few days. That suited me just fine. Packing and moving boxes from a basement was hot, sweaty work and weather that cooperated made everything easier.

Midsummer was the height of the tourist season and the streets were filled with folks dressed in shorts and T-shirts and sporting rosy tans that hedged toward sunburns. There was a lot to do here and if you loved the trails, the water, or history, you could get lost in Old Town Alexandria.

When I lived here as a kid history held little of my interest. I didn't take one tour or read a book about the town when Grace offered me the job and I accepted what I thought was a temporary situation. Surely, I'd have a real job by the fall. But real jobs weren't as easy to come by, so summer turned to fall, and then spring.

We took a lot of demo jobs in those days. As I remembered, we went from one site to the next collecting old architectural treasures that we resold for a nice profit. I rented a small room north of Washington Street on King. I wasn't fancy, but it was my place. For the first time in my life, I controlled the space where I lived. With no crazy mom or sister who discarded clothes and trash on a whim, I kept the place so neat and clean that Grace accused me of being OCD. But it was important to me after a lifetime of chaos to come home each night to neatness and order.

I might have stayed in Alexandria longer, even figured ways to grow the salvage business, but then Janet stormed into town, a whirlwind of fun and adventure. Janet's smile and bright laugh promised a life filled with endless highs.

Now I was back here, at the warehouse, without my little sanctuary apartment. I was in the heart of the storm, once again trying to shore up a leaking dam ready to release a wall of water that would flatten all of us.

I should have been pissed. Terrified. Resentful. I sure was when I arrived in town last week.

However, as much as I hated the chaos, there was a rightness to being back on King Street. No made-up pasts here. No made-up family. No thinking twice before I answered a simple question about myself. Just the truth.

Tragedy, trouble, and drama remained, but here, I had no secrets. Everyone knew where all the skeletons were buried, and it felt good to shed secrets that I wore like a too-tight skin.

When I reached the bakery that night, there was a handwritten sign on the front door. *Addie, come on in. Everyone else, we are closed. Margaret, The Management.* I pushed through the door and bells jingled overhead. The front of the shop was painted a pale yellow and the walls decorated with old pictures of the bakery taken through the years. They were enlarged to eleven by fourteen and mounted. Orderly. That was Daisy's doing. The front display cases were empty, but the glass and shelves glistened.

"Addie, is that you?" Margaret's voice boomed from the back.

"Yes!"

"Through the swinging doors."

Carrie and I moved around the display case and pushed through the swinging doors to find Margaret standing at the head of a long stainless steel table. On one side were trays of shrink-wrapped pies and at the other end were pink boxes that read *Union Street Bakery*. Stickers and yellow twine were heaped in the middle.

"Looks like an assembly line," I said.

"As of this moment, I am the line. We have one hundred pies to box and ship." Margaret stood in front of one boxed pie labeled with a crooked sticker. The twine wrapped around the box should have been a bow but looked more like a knotted mess. She rubbed her forehead with the back of her hand. "I'm in hell."

"Where are Rachel and Daisy?"

"Rachel is MIA. Sick kid. Daisy is on her way. Feeding baby. I'm to start this show, but I can't get the damn stickers to go on straight and the twine knots up. It is possessed. Help me."

Laughing, I moved behind the table. "If you don't mind Carrie hanging around."

She blew a lock of hair out of her eyes. "Can she stick labels?"

"Sorry, no."

"Will she sleep?"

I patted Carrie on the bottom. "As long as I'm standing and moving, then she'll be fine."

Margaret reached for an open beer a table behind and took a deep drink. "I can guarantee you'll be standing and moving."

I studied the layout of the table. "Pies in boxes. Boxes sealed with a sticker and then boxes tied with twine."

"That's the plan."

"Right." I moved the boxes to the center of the table, and put the stickers and twine on the far right. "How about you put the pies in the boxes, and I'll seal them and tie bows."

Margaret put her palms together in a silent prayer of thanks. "I can put a pie in the box."

Laughing, I picked up a strand of twine and ran my finger over the rough surface. "I'll do the rest."

"You are a goddess." Margaret pulled the first pie from the tray, put it in a box, and pushed it toward me. The sticker went on easy enough, but it took me a couple of tries before I secured the twine right. Margaret kept filling boxes with pies and shoving them my way, and there was a moment or two that I fell behind and felt a little like Lucille Ball in the chocolate factory. Finally, I found my rhythm and within minutes I was caught up to her. We worked quickly and easily, and by the time the front bells on the shop jingled forty-five minutes later, we were nearly finished.

Daisy pushed through the saloon-style doors, her gaze harried, and her dark ponytail tangled and askew. "I'm sorry it took me so long. The baby would not settle calm. Gordon tried to walk him, but the kid only wanted me." She was reaching for an apron when she realized the job was nearly done. "Holy crap. Have I stepped into an alternate universe?"

Margaret beamed as she plopped a pie in a box and pushed it toward me. "Told you I could handle this. You worry too much."

Daisy's gaze shifted to me. "Addie Morgan."

I tied off the bow and looked up. "The one and only. Good to see you in the flesh, Daisy."

"You're the genius behind this." Her voice still carried the rusty quality I remembered from that long-ago summer.

"Hey!" Margaret said.

I carefully labeled the next box and reached for a string to tie around it. "Margaret was a huge help. She got the party started."

Daisy moved toward the pile of finished boxes. "I just might weep."

"Least I could do. Thanks for helping with the baby the other night."

"No worries." She moved to the standing trays filled with boxed pies and studied one. "This is great. I don't think any McCrae has done a better job."

"I've labeled a few bottles of wine in my time."

She picked up a box and studied the packaging. "You put the label on differently. Off to the side instead of center. I like it."

Margaret pushed a boxed pie toward me. "I'm a helper, too."

Daisy shook her head. "Thank you, Margaret. And thank you, Addie."

Carrie fussed, forcing me to sway back and forth as I reached for the pie box and carefully closed it. I peeled off a label from the roll. "I thought it was easier to read the label with it tucked in the bottom corner instead of centered."

"It works. It really works."

I stopped my swaying and positioned the label on the bottom right corner. Carrie began to fuss again. Label fixed, I swayed.

Daisy smiled. "She's a strong-willed little girl. Gets that from her aunt."

"We Morgan women are stubborn."

"Stubborn is good." Daisy heaved out a breath, releasing an invisible weight from her shoulders. "I have the shipping boxes already assembled. If we can keep this up for another half hour we'll get out of here at a decent time."

"I don't have to feed the kid for another forty-five minutes," I said. "As long as I can sway, she'll let me work. You have me until then."

Daisy's eyes glistened as if she'd cry with joy. "Thank you."

Thirty minutes later, the pies were housed in shipping boxes and labeled. Daisy loaded the boxes onto her stainless steel cart and pushed the entire order into a large refrigerator. "They get shipped in the morning."

Carrie fussed and I knew my time here was fading quickly. Cinderella's party ended at the stroke of midnight. Mine ended when the baby began to fuss. "Great. I have to get the kid home sooner rather than later."

Margaret shook her head. "Kid blows a gasket when she's hungry."

"I get it," Daisy said. "Thanks, again."

"Sure."

As Daisy undid her apron and stretched her back, she rolled her head from side to side. "I hear you two have a salvage job tomorrow."

"We do," I said.

"Cleaning out an old basement," Margaret added.

Daisy laughed. "A dream come true?"

Margaret pulled off her apron. "I can't wait. I'd rather watch paint dry than work in the bakery. No offense, Daisy."

She smiled. "None taken."

Margaret held up her hands. "But give me a dirty basement or attic . . . I'm in heaven."

Over the years, I forgot the pure excitement I felt when Grace and I readied for a salvage job. Always felt a little like a treasure hunt. "Who knows, maybe we'll go three for three and find another witch bottle."

"What's that?" Daisy asked.

"Kind of like a protection spell," I said. "Margaret tells me women made them to ward off evil back in the colonial times."

"I like the sound of that," Daisy said. "I'll take good luck any day."

"We've found two in the last week," Margaret said. "So, so, rare."

Daisy pressed her hand into her lower back. "Can they bring luck?"

"The newer versions do," Margaret said. "I've also heard them called Wish Bottles."

"We should make bottles for ourselves," Daisy said. "Kind of a girls night out. Wine and witch bottles."

"I've been reading up on them," Margaret said. "People still make them."

Daisy laughed. "Gordon's gone with a bike tour Friday night. Want to do it then?"

"I'm game," Margaret said.

Chase away evil. Evil did include curses, right? Even if it didn't, I liked the idea of wine. "I've got Carrie."

"And I've Walker, and Rachel has the girls," Daisy said. "The more the merrier."

"Sure, I'm in."

June 15, 1751

I met Mistress Smyth at the market today. Mistress Smyth looks well and we spoke of my child and the babe in her belly. We blessed God for our good health.

When Faith passed us by, I whispered that Dr. Goodwin believes it's a sin to relieve labor pains given to virtuous women for the sins of Eve. He suspects she practices magic. Mistress Smyth attached great interest to my words and asked me to explain. I mentioned Faith uses herbs but I didn't dare mention that Faith did the same for me, or that my connection to Faith extends as deep as blood.

Chapter Eighteen

Up early the next morning, I made a half dozen bottles for Carrie and left a stack of diapers and clean clothes by the crib. By the time Grace rose, the baby was also fed, changed, and sleeping in her crib, and I was excited and grateful for a hard day of labor away from this place.

"If you need me, Grace, I'm only blocks away and will have my cell phone."

She cradled a cup close to her chest, drawing comfort from the warmth. "We survived when you went to that vineyard place. We can survive a day here."

"She should sleep for a couple of hours."

"You told me."

"Plenty—"

Grace held up a hand. "I know. Diapers. Bottles. Clothes. Got it. Go. I'm curious to hear what you find in the house on Prince Street. I suspect it will be good. The back of my head is itching."

A half smile tipped the edge of my lips. "I forgot that. How your head itches before a demo."

"Not any demo. Just the really good ones. Now you better get going. That Margaret will be champing at the bit. Girl's got a thing for all this."

"She does. She knows it better than I could ever hope to."

Grace sipped her coffee. "You're better at this than you're willing to admit."

"I noticed the stones are gone from the truck. Where are they?"

"Zeb found a buyer," she said. "They came by last night while you were at the bakery."

"That's awesome. Who?"

"Couple in Loudoun County wants to build an outdoor grill. They loved the idea of history."

"Well, it's kind of being repurposed for a use that's historical. The stones held plenty of fires and cooked lots of meals."

"They've promised to send pictures when the project is done."

"I want to see them."

"Why?" Grace fished in her pocket and pulled out a wad of bills.

"I like it when an old item gets a new life."

Grace grunted. "This is the money from the sale. You can pay Margaret and her helpers."

The roll of bills felt dense. "How much did the stones earn?"

"Enough to pay off Margaret, the guys, and a little extra for formula."

"Formula." Laughter rumbled in my chest. "Good-bye, disposable income."

Grace grunted. "Better get going."

"Right." I shoved the money in my pocket and hurried to find Margaret leaning against the truck, arms crossed over her chest, eyes closed, and her face tipped toward the sun.

"Sorry, I'm late." I jerked open the driver's side door.

"I'm trying to look calm. Not scream, 'Hurry up!'"

I slid behind the wheel and shoved my keys in the ignition. "You're doing a good job."

"It's hard. Believe me." Bracelets rattled as she opened the door and hopped into the front seat. "Hey, what's that hanging from your key ring?"

I glanced at the ring and noticed the key hanging on the chain. "I found it here at the yard. I tucked it in my pocket thinking I'd ask Grace about it but I forgot. When I realized I took it, I just kept it."

She leaned over and fingered the key. "Very old. I'd say eighteenth century."

"I never really thought about the age." I studied the irregular heart shape at the end of the key. "I was just drawn to it."

"Totally cool." She settled back in her seat. "I wonder what it opens."

"I have no idea."

I fired up the engine and backed the large truck out of the space. As the crow flies, the trip to the jobsite was less than a half mile, but it took a few passes around the block before parking opened up on the street, and I was able to edge the truck into two spots fifteen paces from the house.

"My guys should be meeting us here," Margaret said as she typed on her phone's keypad. "Parking."

"Great." I reached for my go-bag, filled with essentials including a camera, measuring tape, duct tape, hammer, screwdrivers, and trash bags. A little careful prechecking meant less damage to the items during removal. Nothing sadder than seeing a hand-carved piece of trim splinter when ripped from the ceiling.

We made our way down the cobblestone street to number seven. It was a three-story brick town house with a black wrought-iron hand railing. The front door was solid mahogany with inlaid handblown windows at the top. A large door handle was set below waist level.

"I'm a geek," I said.

Margaret rested her hands on her hips. "How so?"

"Because I noticed that that doorknob is brass, handmade, and period eighteen hundred," I said. "And it's also much lower than the modern-day doorknobs because people were shorter then."

"I'm grooving on the handblown glass windows and this front door. It's stunning," Margaret said.

"Think it's original?"

"If it's not, it was made very close to the time."

I ran my hand over the railing. "How much would this house cost today?"

"Million and a half. More." She touched the lacquered front door. "I can only dream about living in a place like this."

I watched as her gaze swept over the house, much like a woman in love looked at a lover. "Do you need a moment alone?"

Her gaze danced with laughter. "Just a few."

A retort formed on my lips when we heard footsteps in the main hallway and the door snapped open. Standing before us was a young woman with white-blond hair, pale skin, and a petite frame. She was dressed in a black cotton sleeveless top, dark pants made of a light fabric, and red flats. Her clothes were simple but she possessed an elegance that, honestly, made me feel a tad clunky.

"Hi, I'm Addie Morgan with Shire Salvage. And this is Margaret McCrae. We're here to look at the items you have in your basement."

The woman's gaze skittered between the two of us and then settled on me. "Yes. Right. I'm Lisa Smyth."

Lisa couldn't have been more than thirty-five, which led me to wonder how she came to own such an old and expensive home.

Family money? Internet sensation? Inventor of one of those gadgets you see on late-night television? Sold soul?

"I understand you're renovating the basement," I said.

"I'm house-sitting for my aunt," Ms. Smyth said. "She is going to be putting her house on the market soon and I'm here to take care of the details."

Her smooth, angled face suggested a family with money, but a glance at her shorn nails and slightly discolored fingertips suggested a different twist to her story.

"If you'll show us the way we can have a look," I said. "A couple of our guys are right behind us."

"Wonderful. If you'll follow me."

Wiping the bottom of my tennis shoes on the mat, I entered the foyer. The front hallway was long and carpeted with a handmade Oriental runner that extended from the front door toward a kitchen gleaming with stainless steel and white marble in the back of the house. Directly in front of us was a staircase with a bullnose banister that swirled around like whipped cream. To our left stood a set of open pocket doors that looked onto a front parlor. As much as I wanted to gawk in the room, I could only glimpse the marble fireplace, lush leather furniture, and another handmade Oriental.

We passed a collection of black-and-white images framed in white mats and ebony frames leaning against the wall. I wanted to linger and study each print, which captured everyday faces in exotic ways. I could see that the images were shot with a bellows camera and developed with a wet-plate process. I didn't quite understand the entire technique, but knew it dated back to the Civil War. Photographers in those days needed strong muscles to carry the large camera around. They also needed a delicate touch when handling the large glass negatives and chemicals.

"Love the pictures," I said.

"Thanks. I took them."

"Wow," Margaret said, inspecting them closer. "Wet-plate photography?"

"Yes."

"Very nice," Margaret said.

With no more explanation, Lisa clicked on a light and we moved down an old staircase that looked more period than any other part of the house. The stairs were rickety and the railing was coming loose from the wall. Suddenly, one of those horror movies flashed in my mind. People did know where we were, and Grace would sound the alarm if I didn't return, right?

A flick of another switch and a brighter light popped on, illuminating a long, narrow room that stretched the length of the house. The basement room was filled with all kinds of boxes, old doors, furniture, and who knew what else.

"So what exactly would you like us to haul away?"

"My aunt's attorney wants the room completely cleared out."

Ah, the luxury of having someone else oversee the cleanup job. Scott left oversight of everything to me, and by the time the last contractor left the property, just the thought of paint chips, wood samples, and excuses over delays made me cringe. "Do you want us to save anything?"

"No. Your company hauls away junk and that's what all this is to the owner."

Hauls. Away. Junk. I raised a finger to explain that, no, we were a salvage company and that we saved history, but Margaret poked me in the ribs with her elbow.

A glance at Margaret's you-shut-up expression told me to hold my comments. She saw an item that piqued her attention, and I trusted her eye for history. "We can haul it all away. What plans do you have for the space?"

"It's going to be a media room. Wide-screen television, surround sound, and theatre chairs," Lisa said. "Plans look pretty amazing." She hugged her arms around her chest, warding off a cold shiver. "Do you need me? This room has always given me the creeps."

"Nope. We'll clear out the space."

Margaret's phone pinged. "Our guys are at the front door."

"Great." Lisa glanced toward the top of the stairs toward the light. She didn't like this space, whereas I felt an attraction.

"If you'll just let the boys in," I said. "We'll get to work."

Lisa smiled, her relief visible. "Be glad to. Call if you need me."

As her steady steps echoed up the stairs, I glanced at Margaret, who wandered over to a set of three doors stacked against each other by the west wall. Dust and particles rose up and danced in a beam of sunlight shining in from the street-level windows.

"So, what do you think?" I asked.

"I think these doors will make the entire trip worthwhile. I can't believe someone would just store them in a basement."

Resting hands on hips, I surveyed the room. "So, we just take it all and sort it at the warehouse."

"Exactly. I'm sensing lots of buried treasure here." She clasped her hands together. "This is paradise to me. I could rumble around dark scary places all day long."

"Well, we've got about eight hours, so let's get to work," I said. "And to ensure we get out of here on time, no looking or inspecting. We're hauling and moving. We can dig through all the treasures at the warehouse."

Margaret traced her finger along an old dusty chest with a brass lock. "No peeking?"

"None. Search and rescue. Study later."

Her gaze skittered over the stacked boxes, old picture frames, lamps, and doors. "Fine. But when we're back at the warehouse—"

"You can dig and catalogue to your heart's content."

Lovingly, she touched a dusty trunk. "This is the best part-time job, Addie. The best."

And so it went. We spent the next eight hours, along with our two male helpers, Alex and Joey, hauling items from the basement and loading them on the salvage yard truck. By four o'clock in the afternoon, the basement was empty and the truck full. I paid Margaret and the guys with the cash from Grace. Margaret offered to treat us all to a beer and, though the guys readily accepted, I declined. Carrie and Grace were waiting.

As the truck rumbled over the cobblestones toward Union Street, I realized I no longer craved sunsets and cool wine, but long naps. That day was only weeks behind me, but it might as well have been a thousand years. I pulled onto King and into the side alley behind Shire Salvage, where I parked.

Up the front stairs, I found Grace sitting in the living room, rocking in the old chair. Its wooden bones creaked and groaned as the runners moved back and forth. Her eyes were closed and she hummed a tune I vaguely remembered from my summer here as a child. Without opening her eyes, she asked, "How did the job go?"

"We cleaned out the basement. All the goods are loaded in the truck, and I'll unload and sort tomorrow."

"Margaret a big help?"

"She was. I like her."

"Hmmm. Nice family. They've been on this street for generations."

"Where's Carrie?"

"Sleeping. There's cold beer in the fridge."

"Bless you." Quietly, I moved to the fridge, grabbed a beer, and, popping the top, sat on the hearth across from Grace. I needed a shower and was too dirty to sit on the furniture, but I was too tired to move. The beer washed away the dryness and cooled my throat. "How did it go today?"

"Not bad. She cried, ate, and pooped. She seemed easier today. Like she's settled in a routine she's been craving since she was in the womb."

"I haven't stopped to think about Janet's pregnancy or ask where Janet has been the last few years. I have no idea what her life was like."

"I got postcards from her from time to time. Chicago, New York, even Orlando. She waited tables in bars mostly. She's pretty and I know she could charm big tips out of the customers."

"Do you have any idea who Carrie's father is?"

"No." Grace picked up a roughly shuffled collection of postcards tucked at her side. "Here are the postcards. You might be able to find information in them that I couldn't."

I set the beer on the hearth and took the cards. Carefully, I thumbed through them, searching specifically for November and December of last year. Carrie was a term baby so she'd have been conceived around Thanksgiving. A shuffle through the cards and I discovered she was in Orlando for the winter. That postcard featured an alligator with sunglasses. Blue skies were so Janet. She loved warm weather. But by spring the postcards featured Times Square with the bright lights and buzz of people. She'd have been pregnant by then, but I wasn't sure if she'd realized it. Her handwriting wasn't as crisp on this card, suggesting her mental health was likely failing. If that were the case, she could have missed pregnancy signs altogether. "She never contacted me once during this time."

"When she did call last week, why didn't you call her back?"

"Because I can't fix her, Grace. She'll listen to me for a while, maybe a few months, but by winter, she'll be getting restless and day-to-day rules will feel like a straitjacket."

"You don't think this time is different? She just gave birth to her second baby."

"Her son and husband weren't enough. Why would Carrie be enough?"

The rocker creaked back and forth. "Then you adopt the baby. Raise her with that man on the vineyard. Fresh air is good for babies."

Oddly, the idea really appealed for a split second. I tried to imagine Carrie at the vineyard with Scott. No longer did I believe I could take care of all this and never tell Scott. At some point an invisible point of no return came and went. This life was growing around me like thorny vines and getting free wasn't really possible anymore. I was going to have to tell Scott.

"You're thinking you're going to have to make a choice," she said.

"I didn't say that."

"You think Carrie won't fit on the vineyard and Scott won't fit here."

"I don't know." I sipped the beer, hoping it would ease the banding tightness. "I don't know."

"You know. You know."

I brushed away buzzing doubts. "He's not just a guy, Grace. I love him. I've imagined us being married."

A gray brow arched, disapproving. "Has he talked about marriage?"

"We've talked about a future together, but we've been too busy to discuss marriage."

Grace shook her head. "Okay."

"Okay?" My defenses rose. "What does that mean?"

"It means okay." Fatigue rushed behind the words. "This is for you to sort out."

"You aren't a bystander, Grace." She pulled me into all this. "Carrie is yours as well."

"No, she's yours."

I gulped more beer. "She's Janet's."

"No, Addie. She is not Janet's. You've said it yourself. She won't be able to take care of the baby in the long run. Winter will come, and she'll get restless. I saw it so many times with my sister. They're unwilling to take medication. You know. We both can see it coming."

"I survived." A tightness knotted my chest as I thought about all the forgotten birthdays, missed appointments, hungry nights, and Mom's ranting speeches.

She nodded her head. "Yeah, you survived. If that's what you want to call it."

Hands on my hips, I drew in a breath, struggling to steady a heart that beat too fast. "I'm doing pretty damn well."

"You could do better. And honestly, would you have wished your childhood on any child?"

No. Anger churned, scraped at my insides. "Why didn't you step in when I was twelve and keep me? I begged you to let me stay, but when Mom showed up you just let us go."

Grace nodded, accepting the anger like a fist to her chin. "Your mother said you and Janet could stay if she could stay."

"You didn't want Mom."

"I refused to have that insanity in my life. I could see you were gonna be fine, but Janet was showing signs of the curse. I knew you could get by without me. But your mom needed you. You were her lifeboat."

"You could have been her lifeboat."

Grace tapped a swollen, bent finger on the arm of the chair. "No. She and I never mixed well."

"You could have found a way for *me*."

The rocker creaked back and forth but Grace said nothing.

My shoulders slumped with a biting weariness that went beyond the day's physical labor. For as long as I could remember, I ran to keep up with my mother, Janet, Scott, and now Carrie. "Thanks for the beer."

As I rose, her gaze followed me. "Would you take Janet on, if given the choice?"

The answer came quickly. "No. No, I would not."

She leaned forward in her rocker, the frame creaking like old bones. "I might not be perfect. I sure made mistakes, and I've lived with them all. They haunt me. But I'm not much different than you."

The words stung, but as much as I wanted to argue, I couldn't.

Silent, I moved out of the room and into the bathroom. I stripped off the dirty clothes of the day and turned on the shower's hot spray. I moved into the water, hoping it would not only wash away the dirt and grime of the day, but decades of sadness.

Tears filled my eyes and streamed down my cheeks, melting into the spray. What did I do to deserve all this? What did Grace do? We both wanted our freedom from the curse, but the Universe—the curse—didn't care.

July 2, 1751

The days are long, tedious, and the summer heat hot and humid. The baby suffers with the heat. He cries often. I long for Scotland. I miss my sisters.

Dr. Goodwin worries over the loss of the *Constance*. He does not say, but I know he worries over his finances. He travels to Berkeley Plantation today to discuss a loan.

Penny fell ill with a fever. I tended to Penny myself, but no amount of care eased her fever. Desperate and with my babe in arms, I went to Faith at the tavern. She was so heavy with child she could barely stand. Releasing my pride, I asked if she would help Penny. Her sharp blue eyes stared at me a long moment and then she gave me dried herbs and bade me to put them in hot water to make a tea. Once the tea cooled, I was to give as much to Penny as she could stomach. I gave her a silver coin and hurried home. I brewed the tea for Penny and forced her to drink. Her fever broke at midnight.

What would God think of me? The witch had now helped me twice.

Chapter Nineteen

By seven A.M. the baby was fed and settled in a makeshift crib in the warehouse so I could sort the items from the Prince Street property. To keep her entertained, I strung old keys, scrounged from a box, on a wire to make a mobile of sorts. As I hung it above her, a breeze from an open window moved the keys gently back and forth. The *clink, clink, clink* sounds caught Carrie's attention and she stared at them, wide-eyed and amazed. Though I wasn't sure how much she saw, I was grateful for the quiet and the time to unload the truck.

We'd intentionally loaded the big stuff in first. The doors, two stained glass windows, an old farmhouse sink, and a trunk. But the smaller items were boxed into manageable crates so I could unload them. I set up a couple of sawhorses and suspended planks between them, which created a sorting table.

Grace rounded the corner as I pushed up the truck's tailgate. Since our conversation we'd kept our distance, and neither one of us mentioned last night. The very old and painful wound we shared opened easily. Whatever scar tissue we imagined formed was really paper-thin. Band-Aids were applied, but we were both tender and fearful the wounds would reopen.

"All that from a basement?" She brushed her fingers over the mobile keys.

Her tone was lighter, less gruff. Her idea of an olive branch. It would have been easy to keep silent or swat away her effort.

But I was willing to tread lightly. I was tired of anger, which weighed heavily on me for too long. "Hard to believe people shoved this kind of stuff away out of sight."

"When decisions can't be made, items get stowed. Everyone thinks they'll deal with it, but sooner always becomes a lot later."

I grabbed a cardboard box filled with yellowed envelopes, scraps of paper, and a leather journal. We would never hug or say sorry but we could find a peaceful middle ground. "I'll set what I can on the worktable in the front of the warehouse. We can sort, figure out what to sell and what to toss."

Grace glanced in a box and retrieved a crystal doorknob. "Sounds like a plan."

We had doorknobs, windows, and boxes to unload and discuss. All safe. Work would be our way to survive and go through the motions without being too engaged.

Grace tried to carry a few boxes from the truck, but she moved carefully and slowly, considering each step. I offered to unload the rest of the boxes from the truck if she would unpack the boxes in the warehouse. With a nod, she moved to the sorting table, taking her time emptying each box. I moved faster, half expecting Carrie to squawk, and within a half hour the table was full of boxes.

As I set the last box on the long sawhorse table, Grace was unpacking her second box. Books. Glasses. Jars. Old windup toys. There was no rhyme or reason to what the family tossed in the basement.

I plucked a piggy bank made of brass from one of my boxes. A shake rattled coins. The bank would have value and hopefully the coins did as well. "If this business ever taught me any lesson, it was to travel light. Like packing for a trip. Whatever you put in the suitcase, chances are you'll never use half of it. Same with life."

"Hard to get rid of memories," Grace said as she handled an old rag doll covered in mold. "It's not clothes for a trip. It's a lifetime."

"I've made it a policy not to collect more than I can fit in my car." How many times had Scott teased me about my Spartan life?

"Suppose that's natural. You didn't have many roots as a kid."

I picked up an old shoe, and not seeing the mate tossed it in a pile that was officially now trash. "When I look back now, I don't see our moving around as totally bad. It kept me flexible. I can roll with the punches." Not exactly true. I didn't own much, but I wasn't really flexible. I controlled almost every second of my day. Up at the same time. Laundry done on the same day. Pencils to the right on my desk. Phone charged on my bedside table every night. The list went on and on.

Grace picked up an old clock. She frowned at its dusty, dirty face and I sensed she wasn't thinking about the clock. "You're the strongest of us all. Always have been."

"I don't feel strong. I'm treading water, barely keeping up. If I were strong, I'd have told Scott about my family a long time ago. I'd have told him about the decade-old decision that now affected our relationship. I feared our life together would be swept away by the past."

"If it's on solid ground, it won't go anywhere."

Maybe.

As I dug through a box, my fingers skimmed an old, plain, roughly hewn box. Carefully, I flipped the rusted latch and opened the lid. Inside was a bottle. Lifting it toward the beam of sunlight cutting through the front window, I tried to peer through the dark green, dirt-smudged glass. I shook it and heard the clink of metal. The cork top was sealed with wax. As I held the bottle's neck, a wave of energy tingled up my arm, filling me with a sharp sense of sadness. Longing. *Fear.* I put the bottle in front of Grace, anxious to set it down. "Grace, look at this."

She glanced over with disbelief and stammered, "It's a bottle."

"It's just like the bottle we found at the hearth. Like the one you have. Is this a witch bottle?"

Her voice was barely audible. "Yep."

Unsettling energy washed over me. "What are the chances of finding something like this?"

"Rare, I suppose." She held the bottle up to the light. Dust, grime, and the dark hue of the glass repelled any light or attempts to glimpse the interior.

"Rare doesn't come close. What's going on here?"

"I don't know what you mean."

"Grace. Three witch bottles. Three very old witch bottles that have remained unbroken for hundreds of years. Is there a coven of witches in town that I need to be aware of? Have we stumbled into the supernatural?"

Her eyes warmed. "No. The old bottles weren't so uncommon hundreds of years ago. Folks believed all kinds of crazy things. Witches, spells, and curses."

"You know Margaret is checking into Sarah Goodwin's origins. She has a friend in Aberdeen, Scotland, who might be able to find something out about her."

"I'd be curious to know more about her. I only know she came here as a young bride with her husband."

"A doctor."

"Yes." She smoothed her hand over an empty old frame.

"The house from yesterday was built by a sea captain. His name was Cyrus Smyth." I studied the witch bottle. "I wonder where your mother found the bottle?"

"That, I'm not so sure of. The time between has gotten lost."

"The families must be connected."

"Small town. Paths cross."

I rubbed the bottle with the hem of my T-shirt, trying to clear away the smudge. But the dirt and grime were too thick. No amount of staring would wrestle any secrets free.

Margaret leaned back in her chair; her mouth hung open as she stared at the third bottle. "That was in the basement!"

"Yeah. Tucked away in an old box."

The chair hinges squeaked as she leaned forward and stood. We were in the warehouse, surrounded by the contents of the basement. "This is beyond awesome. Do you realize how important a find this is?"

"I know one was odd. Two puzzling. Three is a pattern."

"A pattern of white witch protection." She reached for the reading glasses perched on the top of her head.

"Remember, the woman who first lived in that house was one of the goodwives who went after Faith," I said.

"If she believed that Faith was a witch and accused of the crime, she might be fearful of reprisal. I mean, a witch doesn't need to come after you head-on. She can cast her evil spell and then suddenly you're sick or your crops fail."

"Any more information on Faith?"

"Nothing more than what I found."

"Grace said her ancestor was a doctor who invested in the ship captain's cargo."

"Our Smyth cargo?" Margaret asked.

"She supposes but she's not sure."

She held up the bottle, tracing her fingers along the slim neck. "Okay, I'll see what I can find."

"Great."

"By the way, you still on for Friday? Rachel is excited about making a witch bottle."

Girls night out. Where did the week go? "Yeah. Still sounds fun."

"By then, I may have more info on the Smyths."

"Maybe you can figure out when our family curse started."

"Family curse?"

"The insanity. The madness. Many generations of Shires believed we're cursed."

Margaret smudged a swath of dirt from the bottle. "Have you always called it a curse?"

"Yes. Every Shire has."

"So when did this curse happen?"

"I don't know. It always has been. Madness and curses go hand in hand with the Shire name."

Margaret waggled her eyebrows. "We have a curse. A witch. And three witch bottles. The plot thickens."

I took Carrie for an evening stroll so that we could both get some fresh air. The walk along the crowded streets of Alexandria earned us glances from folks who smiled lovingly at Carrie while also tossing me curious gazes. One lady asked if I was sleeping through the night. Another commented that my figure looked great, considering.

Considering. I smiled, took it as a compliment, and didn't bother to explain our real situation.

When I climbed the warehouse stairs with Carrie, she was growing restless, and I didn't need to look at the clock to know she was hungry. "I have bottles made, kid. Let's eat."

As I moved up the stairs to the second floor, I heard Grace's voice. It was polite but sounded stiff and annoyed. And then came the sound of a man's voice, soft and so low I couldn't make it out. Bracing, I came through the door, running through the list of people who might have paid us a visit.

It was Scott.

He looked great, as always. Crisp blue button-down shirt that set off his deep, rich tan; khakis that skimmed his narrow waist; and polished loafers. A gold watch, which he never wore in the field, hugged his wrist, and his Ray-Ban sunglasses dangled from his fingers.

When he raised his gaze and got a good look at me, his mouth dropped open and he stood, stunned at my appearance. When I was around Scott, I always kept my ponytail brushed smooth and makeup on my face. He liked the fact I looked pulled together. Neat.

Now my ponytail was slightly askew and curling tendrils encircled my head, suggesting I stuck my finger in an electrical socket. I wore no makeup and my clothes were sweat-stained and covered in dirt from an afternoon of sorting in the warehouse. Not to mention I had a baby strapped to my chest.

"Addie?"

"Scott." The air whooshed out of me. All the rushing, hoping, and praying that I could still keep my two worlds apart collapsed. "I wasn't expecting you."

"I can see that." His gaze dropped to the baby. His thumb tapped against the edge of his glasses, as it did when he surveyed the vineyard after a bad storm. "I think we need to talk."

On cue, Carrie squirmed and fussed. She couldn't care less about Scott, me, or anything other than her bottle.

"Let me get her a bottle," I said. "It won't take but a second."

"Sure."

He followed me into the kitchen and watched me pull a bottle from the fridge and heat it quickly in the microwave. The baby cried and fussed louder, unmindful or uncaring that she had less than thirty seconds to wait. Now was all she cared about. My life was collapsing, but that was minor compared to her grumbling stomach.

The microwave dinged, and I quickly shook the bottle and tested it on my wrist before settling in a chair at the kitchen table. I pulled Carrie easily from the sling—this time not catching her legs in the straps—and settled her in the crook of my arm. As she kicked and balled her fingers into tight fists, I popped the bottle in her mouth like an old pro. She settled.

Scott didn't speak, but paced back and forth, glancing at me as if he did not know me. "I think you need to start this conversation, Addie."

A sigh leaked from between my teeth, and I settled back in the chair, the weight of life finally hitting me hard. "I have an older sister, Janet. She called me last week in a panic. Long story short, she was in labor and gave birth to my niece, Carrie."

His pacing stopped, and he stared at me. No missing the surprise and hurt in his blue gaze. "You told me your sister lived in California."

Carrie's eyes closed and her little body tensed at the sound of my voice. "I know."

"Where is she now?"

"In the hospital." I hesitated and then basically ripped the proverbial Band-Aid off the past. "She's in a mental hospital. She's very sick and unable to take care of the baby. She's bipolar." I repeated the speech practiced so many times over and over the last few days. "She has good doctors, and they're trying their best. They tell me she should be stabilized in the next few weeks."

Scott's jaw ticked slightly. "The next few weeks."

He made it sound like forever, and I almost laughed. Weeks were manageable, and I wasn't worried about losing the next few weeks. I was fighting for the rest of my life. "Yes."

His jaw tensed, released. He was annoyed and perplexed and I couldn't blame him. A lie by omission was still a lie. "Were you going to keep putting me off until then?"

"I honestly didn't have much of a plan. I came to Alexandria thinking I could take care of this in a day or two, but the problem was too big. I've been winging this."

"What about Social Services? Can't they help the baby and your sister? Aren't they set up to take care of problems like this?"

"I've met with them. They looked for a family for Carrie, didn't find a suitable one, so I stepped in until Janet was well."

"Carrie is the baby?" he asked.

Indifference humming under his tone clipped the edges of the words. I had no right to be annoyed with him. I hid the truth. Lied. But something inside me still clenched with outrage. "Yes."

"When was she born?" Most people looked at a baby, especially one this small, with interest, but Scott barely glanced at the child. He wasn't a fan of babies, and I clung to that nugget of information, hoping my past choices really wouldn't matter.

"Last Monday."

"That's why you took off?"

"I didn't know what else to do, Scott. My family has a lot of issues, but they're my family."

His brow furrowed. "What about the baby's father?"

"I don't know who he is, and, so far, my sister has been too out of it to give me a name."

He ran tense fingers through his hair, as he did when the weatherman predicted a hard frost. "Why didn't you tell me any of this?"

"I thought I could handle it. And the launch was so important, and I didn't want to upset you."

"You handled it by ditching me."

"I haven't ditched you, Scott." Fatigue warmed to slightly annoyed and then anger. "I'm trying to fix this, so I can return to the vineyard and you. If anything, I was trying to protect you from this."

"I thought there was more between us." His voice rose and the baby's eyes startled open. She looked around and her bottom lip quivered. She was ready to cry.

"Lower your voice. I need this kid to eat so she can sleep and I can have a few hours of peace."

He drew in a breath and released it slowly. "I thought we shared everything. God knows, I've told you all about my past."

"Did you really want to know before the wine launch? Really?" I shook my head as his lips parted to respond. "I don't think you wanted a family drama dropped in your lap last week. You were distracted and worried. I was trying to basically take one for the team."

"I'm the one that pulled her away," Grace said. We both looked at her, having forgotten she was there.

"Who are you? We didn't get the chance to introduce ourselves," Scott asked.

"I'm Grace Shire. The aunt." She folded her arms over her chest.

"She's my mother's sister. I worked for Grace when I got out of college."

"I remember something about you working in a salvage yard. I thought you said she was sick."

The trouble with lies was remembering them. "She's not sick. It's always been my sister, Janet."

"I suffered a stroke last winter," Grace offered. "I needed her."

Some of the fire melted in his gaze. "It's been four days since the launch party."

"I thought I'd have it all fixed before the launch. I really did. But it's going to take a few more weeks." The last of the words came out as a hiss through clenched teeth.

Taken aback by my annoyance, something he'd never seen directed toward him, he held up his hands. "Addie, I didn't come here to fight. I came here to find out what was wrong. I was worried and needed to know why the most dependable person in my life vanished."

"Well, now you know." Carrie coughed, and I pulled the bottle from her lips and rested her on my shoulder. I patted until she burped. Tired and in no mood, I settled Carrie back in my arms and nudged the bottle back in her mouth.

When I looked up at him again, he stared at me for a long moment. "Do I even know you?"

"You know me. But you don't know my family. And that is my fault. When I moved away from Alexandria, I stopped talking about my family because they are chaos. Getting close to them invites mayhem. A few phone calls from my sister, and see how our lives have turned around in the last seven days? I saved you a lot of unnecessary drama by keeping them in the past."

He shook his head, much like a teacher would when dealing with a dull student. "We're a team. Why didn't you tell me?"

Aware that Grace wasn't missing a word, I tried to soften my tone. "Because I wanted—no, I needed to keep a wall between us and the past. I needed to break with the past to survive."

The door downstairs opened with a bang and small steps thundered up the stairs, seconds before, "Aunt Addie!"

Steadier, slower footfalls followed. Eric and Zeb.

Timing is everything, and I couldn't have timed this day better if I tried. I considered asking Zeb to leave but caught myself. Why? Bring it on. Let's air it all out now and let Scott meet the entire clan.

Scott stiffened as Eric came around the corner, a mash of wild daisies clutched in his hand. "Addie, I picked these for Carrie."

The boy glanced at Scott and stopped. The brilliant smile dimmed, and he took a step back into his father, who stood guard over him. Zeb eyed Scott, his stance growing more rigid and his jaw tensing as a swift glance sized up this stranger. "Addie, did we interrupt?"

With Carrie cradled in my arms, I rose. "Zeb, I'd like you to meet Scott. He owns the Willow Hills Vineyard, where I work. Scott, this is Zeb and Eric Talbot. Eric is Carrie's half-brother."

"Half?" Eric said. "What half?"

Any other time, I'd have smiled. "The half that comes from your mother's and my side."

Scott extended a hand and Zeb accepted it. The shake was firm, testing. "I'm afraid Addie's kept me a little in the dark about her family."

Zeb released Scott's hand. "We haven't seen each other in a long time. Makes sense she didn't mention us."

"I'm not very good about sharing stories about my family," I said.

Scott stepped back, rested hands on his hips. "How are you related to Addie?"

"I used to be her brother-in-law. I was married to her sister, Eric's mom."

"But she's still my aunt," Eric said. "That didn't change. And Carrie will always be my sister."

I smiled at Eric. It was hard not to love the kid. "I just fed the baby, but you can hold her if you like."

He grinned and the two of us moved to the couch. He sat, scooted all the way to the back of the cushions, and I laid the now-sleeping baby in his arms. He held her close, lowering his face and whispering, "Good afternoon, Baby Carrie."

Scott, Zeb, and Grace stood in awkward silence for a beat before Grace cleared her throat. "Would anybody like iced tea? I'm sure I could make some up."

"If you don't mind, Grace, I'd like to take a walk with Scott," I said. "We need to talk."

Zeb nodded. "Eric and I will stay with the baby."

"Thanks. It won't be long."

A somber Scott and I walked down the stairs. Neither of us said much as we walked along the brick sidewalk of King Street and then turned south on Union.

Scott ran fingers through his thick blond hair, destroying the neat, slick look. I always considered him rugged and handsome. I appreciated that he always looked so pulled together. In a matter of minutes though, his look turned a bit crazed. I was responsible for that look.

"I should start at the beginning," I said.

"Thank you."

"My sister is Janet and our mother was Elizabeth. Without boring you with a blow by blow, Janet inherited mental illness from Mom. Mom committed suicide. Soon after that, Janet's quirky behavior grew a lot quirkier. Fast forward a couple of years and she met Zeb, fell in love, and was expecting Eric. I hoped she'd found her happily-ever-after life, but Janet is more like Mom than I ever realized. Soon after Eric was born, it was clear she couldn't handle the responsibilities. She took off when he was a baby."

Uncorking the words bottled up for seven years and shaking them loose was as hard as I'd imagined. Some words describing unspoken dark details clung to the bottle, refusing to be freed. "She showed up a week ago, very pregnant, and in active labor. By the time I arrived in Alexandria, the baby was born."

His arm brushed close as we walked, but he didn't touch me, sensing I craved skin-to-skin touch and reassurance.

"I felt like a fool standing up there with your aunt. She must have thought me some kind of damn fool."

My gaze wandered ahead to the river, which meandered past. A gentle breeze touched my face. "That was my fault."

He stopped, those hands curling in frustration. "They know everything about you, and I know nothing."

"That's not true. They know the person I was, and you know the person I am. They may have my past, but you've got the future . . . if you still want it."

Tense seconds, stretched as tight as a bowstring, clicked between us as he stood still and silent, his jaw tense. Tired and too worn to defend myself anymore, I stared off at the river, watching the heavy current meander past. I imagined myself on the water, allowing it to flow and carry me out to the Chesapeake Bay and then to the ocean.

Scott very carefully took my hand in his. Rough calluses brushed each other. My heart beat faster, and the tears, so carefully locked away, escaped. They burned my throat.

"Addie, I love you. It hurts me that you cut me out."

"I didn't plan to keep it all a secret. At first, I was running from a difficult family thing. I just wanted away. And then I started to fall in love with the vineyard and you, and all this would taint what we were building."

"I've told you everything about my life."

I swiped away a tear. "Your glittering, perfect life. That was all the more reason not to talk about mine."

"Don't lay this on me."

"I'm not. It's just that the more you talked, the more lacking I felt."

He traced a calloused thumb on my palm, sending jolts of electricity racing toward my heart. I should have trusted him. I should have been able to share. Why hadn't I? What was wrong with me?

"Are you coming back to the vineyard?"

"Yes. Yes, of course."

"I love you." Blue eyes searched mine. "I do love you. But I'm not ready for a baby in my life."

"Right. Of course. I know that." Ten days ago, I would have been comfortable with all this, but now I was irritated. "I'm trying to fix this."

He pulled me into his arms and relaxed into me. "I want you home soon."

I pressed my hands to his chest, felt the beat of his heart under my fingertips, and savored the warmth of his body. "I'll take care of it all."

"Can I help you? I know attorneys in the area."

"No. That's not necessary. I'm working with a social worker."

"Yes, yes, of course." He smiled and cupped my face. "The child deserves a good home."

"Yes, she does."

"But not with us."

I stiffened. "I know."

His lips grazed mine. "I miss you so much."

"Me, too." Most of the demons had escaped Pandora's Box, and somehow we would survive. I hoped we would be stronger for it, and that one day I'd share the last secret. But to allow the last demon free, well, that terrified me. One thing to hide a past, quite another to alter another's future. "Would you like to stay for dinner?"

"I can't. I have to get back. It was a stretch to get away for the day. Three more weeks and you will be home, right?"

Home. "Not much longer."

He cupped my face and kissed me gently on the lips. "Good. You belong in the country with me."

We walked hand in hand to his car. He kissed me again and then slid behind the wheel of the gray Audi and lowered the window. "I'll see you soon."

"Yes."

"Addie, if you need me, call. I'm here for you."

"Yes. I know. I know."

He backed out of the drive and drove down King to Union Street. I stood watching his car until it turned at the corner and vanished.

He'd smiled, held me close, and told me everything was going to be fine, but he gave me a tenderly delivered ultimatum. Him or the baby.

Closing my eyes, an uneasiness gripped me as I glanced at the warehouse. The choice was clear. And it should've been easy. Scott or the baby. A week ago, it would have been Scott. But somewhere along the line, black and white blurred to a watery gray, erasing the perfect choice. Left or right, up or down, either way I went I was going to lose.

"Addie?" Zeb's deep voice vibrated with curiosity and annoyance.

"Yes?"

He looked around, holding back words, in case we weren't alone.

"He's gone," I said.

That square jaw moved, grinding. "He'll be back."

"You think so?"

"Yes."

I stabbed trembling fingers through my hair, dirty and greasy from sweat and fatigue. "I dumped a truckload of info on him. Stuff I've never told him before. He said it was going to be okay, but a two-hour car ride gives him plenty of time to think."

"Why didn't you tell him about all this before?"

"Do you go around telling the gals you date about the crazy family you married into?"

"It's never gotten to that point with me. But you and Scott have been together a few years."

"I thought time would make a difference. I thought distance would make it all easier to talk about, but the greater the distance, the less I wanted to talk about it. The more time that passed, the easier it was to pretend the past never mattered."

"It always matters."

"Tell me about it."

He arched a humorless brow. "So what are you going to do?"

"I've no idea."

"Like it or not, Janet is not going to be able to take care of the baby. Not now, the near future, maybe ever. Social Services might be able to place her for adoption."

The knot in my gut returned. "I haven't been thrilled with the choices so far."

His expression softened. "There are lots of families waiting for adoption."

"How many do you think know about handling a mentally ill teenager?"

A dark brow arched. "You don't know if she's sick."

"I'm a worst-case-scenario girl."

"Have you considered taking the baby to the vineyard? You and Scott could raise her."

I picked at a loose thread on the waistband of my jeans. "He doesn't want a child now."

"He said that?" His terse tone sharpened each word.

I could feel Zeb's anger. Pulsing. Not a minor storm, but a hurricane that, if unleashed, could destroy everything around it. "Yes. He was very clear about that."

The anger swirled. "You don't want to give her up and you can't raise her with Scott. And we're in agreement that Janet can't do this alone."

"I've got some thinking to do. Choices to make." I smiled, hoping it would make me feel better, but instead my mood soured. One problem with no good solution. Turning from him, I headed inside.

I moved toward the table of trinkets and skimmed my fingers over the top of a collection of china cups covered with roses that we'd removed from the basement.

"The baby is sleeping," he said.

"Great. That means I might be able to get an hour or two of cataloguing done. Be nice if I could sort what we have and get it posted online. Money will come in handy for Janet when she gets back on her feet."

"You can't give her money, Addie. She'll spend it all on junk."

I picked up a bone china teacup covered in roses. How had something so fragile remained intact in the face of so much neglect and abuse? How had it survived when the others in the set didn't? "I know. But I can dream."

He moved behind me, not touching me, but so close his heat warmed my back. "Addie."

My name sounded rough, as if saying it scraped against his throat. "Yes?"

"You're doing a good thing."

Stinging tears clogged my throat, and I knew if I faced him and met his gaze, I'd cry. I had been in Alexandria less than two weeks, but fatigue battered my defenses. Today's encounter with Scott fed the fear, making it grow like a weed on fertile ground.

Zeb's breaths were slow and steady and I counted each. One. Two. Three. He wanted me to turn around and face him. This I could feel. *Look at me. Me.* And God help me, I wanted to face him. Look him in the eye with a defiance that told the world I had this all under control. But Scott's sweet, soft words of rejection stripped my emotions raw.

I didn't turn around. Didn't dare. Because in this moment of isolation and fear, I felt an uncommon pull to Zeb. I sensed or maybe imagined a desire bubbling under the surface for what felt like centuries. To my great shame, I wanted him to hold me, even as logic warned that I couldn't bear the weight of more secrets and lies.

And so I stood stock straight, barely breathing until I heard him release a breath, turn on his heels, and call for Eric. The boy bounded down the stairs, and I wondered when I ever felt that light or free. When had I been a kid? When had I last laughed?

"See you later, Aunt Addie!" Eric shouted.

I cleared my throat, pressed cool fingertips to flushed cheeks, and smiled before I turned. "Later, Eric."

Zeb's head was partly turned toward the door and partly toward me. But if he was tempted to look back at me, he didn't. Instead, he squeezed his son's shoulder and the two left.

Steady, even footsteps mingled with steps full of energy and light.

July 5, 1751

Penny is up and about, feeling more herself today. She has lost weight but she will survive. I didn't dare tell her about my visit to Faith for magic herbs. Mistress Smyth visited today. She came bearing scones and gossip. Faith, she said, delivered twin boys. Mistress Smyth heard the woman barely labored more than an hour before she delivered the lusty, plump children.

Chapter Twenty

I wandered back into the first floor of the warehouse and instead of going upstairs, I moved toward the table of newly sorted items. I walked along the table, touching each item, summoning the energy that some items released. My fingertips grazed over doorknobs, the old clock, toys, shoes, and a mirror, but all the items were stubbornly silent. Served me right. The past wanted nothing to do with me.

The front door opened with a burst of energy and I turned to see Margaret. "Addie. What's happening? I just saw Zeb, and he looks pissed."

"My boyfriend just found out about my family, and then he nicely told me he doesn't want to raise a baby, and left."

Margaret's bright blue eyes narrowed. "Ouch."

"You're telling me."

Bracelets rattled as she rested a fist on her hip. "Boyfriend was mad?"

"Yes, but he handled it well." That was Scott. Cool and controlled. "He's coming back, right?"

"I suppose. I hope. But he has lots of time to think between now and tomorrow."

Margaret snorted. "If he doesn't come back he's an ass."

I couldn't summon a bit of outrage for Scott. "I blindsided the guy. I've never told him about my family. He really is a good guy. It was wrong of me to drop all this on him."

Margaret waved away my defense. "My guess is that Wonder Boy has secrets up his sleeve."

"Scott is an open book."

"No one is a total open book. He's not told you everything."

"I'm guessing he doesn't have crazy sisters or secret babies."

She waved her hand, batting away an imaginary fly. "It'll blow over."

"That experience talking?"

"Not exactly. I can't make relationships or jobs last. I'm your consummate temp."

Her honesty disarmed some of the knives jabbing at my gut. "Why's that?"

"Hell, if I know. Maybe I'm ADD or something. Maybe I just haven't found the right thing. But love me while you can, baby, because I'm a tumbleweed. I'll blow on to the next job or adventure soon."

I smiled. "Fair warning. What's in the file?"

"Found something interesting about Faith."

"Really?"

"Her husband, Ben Talbot, married her two weeks after she delivered twin sons."

"Twins? You only mentioned one son. What happened to the other one?"

"He might not have survived."

"Ah." The birth of twins was not always welcome hundreds of years ago. Twins were an oddity and oddities fostered distrust. "Did birthing twins add fuel to the speculation that she was a witch?"

"Thinking like the good ladies of Alexandria, circa 1751," Margaret noted.

I slid my hands in my pockets. "People don't always add two and two and get four."

"Not only did Ben Talbot marry his indentured servant but he also released her from her contract."

"More magic?"

"It was very unusual and no one likes out of the ordinary." A hitch in her tone suggested she spoke about herself.

"True." Most of my life I hid my past so no one looked upon me with suspicion or worry. But on some level I needed Scott to accept me for it all and today he had not. My anger at Scott rose up unexpected, quick and sharp, and I immediately felt shame. I had no right to be angry with him. No right. I was nobody's rose.

Margaret twisted her bracelets on her wrist. "I'd like to x-ray the other two bottles."

"Why?"

"To see what's inside. Maybe they have similar contents to the first one we found at the McDonalds'. Maybe they can tell us more about the ladies that made them."

"Sure. Feel free to x-ray."

"Think I could get Grace's bottle?"

"That's up to her. But I don't see why not."

"Friend at the hospital is going to do the X-rays. I will be careful."

"I know you'll treat them better than gold. I've seen the love in your eyes when you look at them."

"Oh my God. I think I would die for them," she said with a dramatic flair.

"Don't get carried away."

We headed up the stairs and found Grace sitting in her rocking chair, moving back and forth slowly, eyes closed. "That summer you two were always running around getting into trouble."

I glanced at Margaret, who shrugged. "You talking to us?"

Her eyes fluttered open and for a moment she didn't recognize either of us. "Sorry. I must have been recalling something my mother said to Elizabeth and me when we were young. But you two do look like trouble waiting to happen."

"Grace, can Margaret borrow your witch bottle? She'd like to x-ray it."

Grace pushed forward and stood with a groan. "Why would you want to do that?"

"To compare it to the other two."

"Why?"

"Finding three intact bottles within miles of each other and within a couple of weeks is kinda really super rare, Ms. S.," Margaret said. "I'd love to document it all."

Grace's gaze moved to the bottle, which remained on her mantel. "Sure. But don't open it. That's bad luck."

Margaret pressed her hand to her heart. "I wouldn't dream of it. I promise the X-ray will not damage it."

Grace shrugged. "It's all yours."

The baby fussed, and Margaret glanced toward the sound and then the nearest exit. "I promise to be very careful."

Grace shook her head. "I'm not worried. Take it."

As the baby's cries grew louder, Margaret took the bottle and carefully stuffed it in her bag. "I'll report back."

"Thanks." I turned without thinking and walked into my room. Carrie lay on her back, kicking and flailing her fisted hands.

As I picked her up, I couldn't help but smile. "What are you fussing about, Miss Carrie?"

The baby squawked louder, but I calmly moved to the changing station now set up on the dresser and quickly cleaned her up. Two weeks ago, this had all been awkward and scary and now it felt . . . normal. I lifted her up on my shoulder, and we moved into the kitchen. She nestled her face close to my neck and rooted around as I moved to the fridge and pulled out a bottle. With the baby balanced on my arm, I unscrewed the bottle top, put it in the microwave, and hit seventeen seconds.

"You look like a pro," Grace said.

"You sound surprised."

"I am."

I glanced at Carrie and watched as she suckled the bottle. "Makes two of us. How the hell did we get here, Grace?"

"The curse."

"You don't believe that, do you? Really? Many mental illnesses are genetic."

"I've been thinking long and hard about this. I don't know much about medicine, but I understand curses. I've lived with them all my life. And it's not just Janet and your mother. You and I are trapped by the curse as well."

I could have argued, but I didn't. "Why are we cursed? Is that why we have the witch bottle?"

"It's supposed to ward off evil. But it's not done such a good job. Bottles don't break curses, just hold them at bay. Takes a force more powerful than a bottle to break a curse."

"What kind of power?"

"I wish I knew. I spent a lifetime wondering and thinking about what it would take to break a curse. What it would mean to be free."

Logic aside, Grace believed the Shires were cursed, and looking back over our history, I couldn't argue. We suffered under a bad run of luck for as long as I could remember.

I stared at Carrie's face, and my heart twisted. Didn't matter if I carried the trait for madness or not. A baby would never fill my womb, and I'd never know the elation of bringing a child into the world.

But, of course, Grace was once young and full of dreams. "What held you here?"

For a long moment she didn't speak and then finally she whispered, "Fear."

August 10, 1751

Mistresses Smyth and McDonald joined me for tea today at our newly finished home. There is not a stick of furniture but I made do with the hand-hewn table from the cottage and the rough chairs. It did my heart good to speak to other women like me. We talked first of the tobacco crop and the servants. However, soon our conversation turned to gossip of Faith. Her boys thrive, Mistress Smyth said, and Ben Talbot is pleased with the bastard children he readily claims. Mistress Smyth is appalled a man would claim bastard sons when he should make legitimate heirs with a wife sanctioned by God. Mistress Smyth has promised to speak to the magistrate about Faith. She is certain she has bewitched Mr. Talbot and will trick him into marriage.

Chapter Twenty-one

Playdates. Of course, I knew about them. I might even have looked down on the moms who thought they were fun. But after four days of working on the vineyard and warehouse business and, in my spare moments, feeding and diapering Carrie, I was hungry for conversation.

Scott called me each night and though the conversations were polite, they skimmed the surface. We were gliding across a sheet of ice, too afraid to make a fast move for fear we would tumble.

"I hear you called into the office today and sorted out the orders for the wine labels," Scott said.

I cradled the phone close, standing near the window overlooking the Potomac River. "I did. We should have the labels in two weeks. Plenty of time for the next bottling."

"We begin the first harvest in two weeks. And then the pressing. It's going to be even better than last year's."

His confidence was always intoxicating. No matter how bleak the day, he found a way to be hopeful. I needed that confidence now. I needed to hear that we were going to be fine. "I think so, too."

We talked work for a few more minutes before he said, "I've got to go. Got to get ready for tomorrow."

"Sure." He never asked about Carrie or Janet and, as much as I wanted to discuss this with him, I sensed he considered *this* to be *my* issue.

"Are you doing okay?"

"Hanging tough." Pressing my fingertips to my temple, I turned from the river's view.

"Sometimes that's all you can do. You know, I'll wait for you as long as it takes."

A smile played on the edges of my lips, and the knot in my chest eased a little. Scott was at heart a grower of grapes, and despite his nature, he understood that seeds needed time to grow. Patience was required. It took years for the vines to mature and produce the best grapes. To a man who waited years for grapevines to develop, a few weeks was manageable.

He believed the solution to our problem was simple. Just get Janet on the right meds and she'd be fine. I knew he oversimplified the problem. Even with medications, Janet couldn't sustain a healthy life alone. He also mentioned putting Carrie up for adoption. Another simple solution that really didn't solve the problem.

"I love you."

"Me, too."

I ended the call and stared at the screen shot of Scott and me at the vineyard for a long time. In the picture, I held on to him so tight, fearing the day would come when I would lose him

My phone buzzed with a new call and Margaret's name appeared on the display. "Hey."

"Friday night. Playdate." She stretched out the last word as if singing a song.

The heaviness in my chest eased. "How can you have a playdate? You don't have children."

"But my sisters do, and they share."

"I'm picturing sippy cups with wine."

"Not a bad idea. Still game for making a witch bottle?"

"Yes." Wine, or better, a beer. "When?"

"A half hour."

I glanced at the stack of papers and the baby. She was sleeping but would soon wake. We visited the pediatrician today, and the doctor gave Carrie a clean bill of health and a couple of shots. She was not happy about the shots then or most of the day, but she finally fell asleep. "I'm in. What do I bring?"

"Anything small you want to put in your bottle."

"Have you x-rayed the bottles?"

"I have. I have some tidbits to share."

"This will be fun. See you soon."

I hung up and spent the next half hour searching for jars. Spices in the cabinet smelled stale—at least a decade old—so I dumped out most and rinsed out the jars. I couldn't find nails or pins. One random safety pin. Paper clips and a thumbtack.

I loaded Carrie in the front pack, grabbed a six-pack of beer from the refrigerator, and we headed downstairs. I moved along the long table of goods we collected from the Prince Street house and found a box full of old buttons that ranged from green plastic to tarnished brass. I grabbed a handful of buttons and loaded them in my pocket. A few feet farther on, I discovered a tin filled with keys. I grabbed a handful and we headed out, down King Street and around the corner to Union.

The evening air was warm and filled with humidity that promised rain later tonight. Would the rain clouds reach the vineyard? Funny, working with salvage crews, rain was our enemy. It added risk and delays to often complicated jobs.

The sign on the Union Street Bakery's front door said Closed. I knocked as I swayed back and forth, my hand cupped under the baby's bottom. Margaret pushed through a set of swinging doors and waved as she moved toward the door and unlocked it. "Hey, you made it."

"Witches night out."

She laughed. "Both my sisters are thrilled. They're in the kitchen arranging all the stuff."

Margaret took the beers from me, and I followed her across the lemon yellow lobby and past the empty display case. We pushed through the swinging doors and found Daisy and Rachel sitting at a long folding table. At one end sat two little girls who were about seven. Next to them, in a high chair, was a baby boy with jet-black hair. The boy wasn't more than seven or eight months, and at this moment was more interested in the Cheerios on his tray than anyone else. The girls clearly belonged to Rachel and the boy to Daisy.

Rachel was much as I remembered—short and perky with peaches-and-cream complexion. She was always pretty. A delicate version of Margaret.

Daisy tickled the baby boy under his chin as he laughed. Rising, her gaze swept over the baby sling as she crossed to me, her long legs eating up the distance. A smile warmed her face. "How has the week been going? You look a little rough."

"It's been long. I didn't think time could stop so completely or that I could be so tired. I've fallen asleep at the computer a couple of times."

Daisy laughed. "The first weeks with a baby are rough. It'll get better."

The first weeks. I likely wouldn't have more than the first few weeks with Carrie. She wasn't mine, and it was only a matter of time before Janet got out of the hospital. Like it or not, she called the shots, not me.

Daisy must have read the worries in my expression because her smile faded a fraction, remembering that Carrie would soon leave. I wasn't pretending that Janet would get her act together, but she had legal rights.

Rachel stood, her smile bright and natural. She never faked happiness or forced her good nature. She was happy. Sunshine. "Addie. Don't listen to Daisy. You look amazing!"

I smoothed a hand over my unwashed hair, pulled in a tight ponytail. "Thanks. I feel like a train wreck."

Rachel laughed. "Daisy is right, it'll pass."

I dropped my gaze to the baby, suddenly not wanting our time to pass. "Good to know."

"Can I hold the baby?" Rachel asked, unmindful of the swirl of dark emotions. "I'm a sucker for a newborn."

I found myself hesitating for a split second. Was I actually worried about giving her up? Nonsense. But, of course, I gave her to Rachel. She was a good woman. A good mother who offered a much-needed break. And better to get used to the idea of giving Carrie away, because that was what I wanted, right? "Sure."

As I pulled Carrie out of the sling, she grunted and opened her eyes. Awake and alert, her little eyes widened as she stared at me.

Is this the moment you really give me away?

No, baby. Not today.

I put her carefully in Rachel's arms. She settled, knowing she was born to lie in the arms of a woman like Rachel, a woman who welcomed motherhood.

Rachel cooed as she carried the baby toward the table and her little girls. "Carrie, these are my girls, Anna and Ellie. Seven years old and heading to the second grade in a matter of months." She glanced at the baby, nuzzling her nose close to Carrie's soft, milky skin. "Seems like yesterday that my girls were this tiny."

"Walker was never that small," Daisy said. "Birthing that boy was like passing a watermelon."

I laughed, feeling a little awkward because I didn't have a pregnancy or birth story. I hadn't carried Carrie in my belly nor given her life.

As if sensing this, Margaret rested her hand on my shoulder. "So let's open a couple of beers and start making magic."

Daisy laughed. "Thank God my husband is on a bike trip. Gordon would laugh if he saw me dancing under the full moon reciting spells and making . . . a what? What are we making, Margaret?"

"A witch bottle. Ours is a white magic spell. We're not warding off evil spirits as our ancestors might have done. We're calling on good wishes."

Daisy picked up a handful of dried rose petals on the table and let them fall from her fingers back into the bowl. The table was full of small bowls filled with spices, flower petals, shiny rocks, crystals, and things I didn't recognize.

"Boy, Margaret, you really went to town on the ingredients."

"I've been watching YouTube for days, trying to see what the modern witch bottle is all about. In the old days, and even today, all kinds of personal items fill the small bottle. Next, the larger bottle is filled with liquid and then the little bottle is dropped inside before it's all sealed."

"What kind of liquid?" I asked.

"Water, wine, sometimes blood or urine."

The twins giggled. "That is nasty," they said together.

"I'm with the little people. I'm not peeing in a bottle," Daisy said as she handed her son a cracker.

"We don't have to use urine," Margaret said. She opened a beer and took a long sip. "Like I said, we can use water or wine. Or we can forgo the second bottle altogether and just use one. Totally up to the maker. "

Daisy shook her head. "Why are we doing this?"

"To create good intentions," Margaret said. "Can't have enough of them."

Rachel swayed gently as she held Carrie. "I could use good intentions."

I set my bag of empty bottles on the table, as well as my odd collection of tidbits. "I'm game."

"Good. It's settled."

We each ended up with two bottles: one large and one small. The small bottle was to be filled with the items we chose from the table, sealed, and then dropped into the larger. I sat, grateful to be free of the baby's weight while also missing it a little. I opened a beer and took a long sip.

"You work on a vineyard, I hear," Rachel said.

"I do. For the last seven years."

"So, what do you do?" Daisy asked.

"I started in the fields. That lasted a week and then I offered up my skills as bookkeeper." The story was an old one, and told so many times it sounded a little distant and foreign, as if it belonged to someone else. "I'm doing most of the marketing now. We just launched a new wine."

"Last week's party?" Daisy asked.

"Yes. And thank you again for helping Grace."

Daisy smiled. "That kid has got some lungs."

I glanced at Carrie, content in Rachel's arms. "She does that."

"The vineyard work sounds kinda cool," Rachel said.

I glanced around the bakery kitchen. "My guess is it's just as much hard work as running a bakery."

"She's a master at packaging," Daisy said. "She and Margaret got that delivery out."

Rachel smiled. "I can't believe I forgot to thank you. It was a miracle when Daisy called and said the packages were ready to go."

"Glad to help. It was a nice break."

"So have you heard any more from Janet?" Daisy asked.

"Still in the hospital. I talk to her doctors every couple of days. They say she's doing better."

"I was sorry to hear she was sick," Rachel said.

"Yeah." I really did not want to open up this line of discussion. "It's nothing new."

Daisy fiddled with a mound of dried rose petals. "So what's the deal with the baby?"

"I'm taking care of her until Janet is well enough to make a decision."

"Why don't you take the baby?" Daisy challenged. "You seem good with her."

I watched as Carrie stared up at Rachel's smiling face with wide eyes. "It's complicated."

Daisy frowned, wrestling with thoughts that begged to be voiced. "You're her family."

Margaret clapped her hands. "No serious talk tonight. We should have a little fun. Maybe we all need good intentions."

And so we began to fill our small bottles. I didn't pay much attention to the other women and what they chose to include in their spell. My gaze, my focus, was on choosing the items that would bring me a good future. I chose an old metal button engraved with a rose from the pile. Next I chose a pink crystal, lavender leaves, and then one of the small keys I found at the warehouse. As I held the key, my fingers warmed and the smooth tarnished brass burrowed close to my skin. I thought about Janet and me both as outsiders, locked in by the curse. For the first time in a long time, my heart ached not just for me, but also for her. If I thought my burden was heavy, surely hers was more.

I dropped the key in the small bottle and sprinkled more rose petals on top of it. When the bottle was filled, I sealed it and lowered it into the larger jar.

"What do you wish for, Daisy?" Margaret asked as she sealed her small bottle.

"I wish to hold on to what I have." She circled the top of the unsealed bottle, summoning her wish. "And I would like to be friends with my birth mother."

"That's important to you?" I asked. "I kinda remember Mrs. Mc-Crae as being really great."

"She's a great mom. She *is* Mom. But Terry is a part of me, and I feel . . . I don't know . . . whole, when we talk or communicate."

Whatever happened with Carrie, I knew that I'd somehow be in her life. She needed a solid connection to the Morgans and Shires. We would communicate, so if the time came when she needed my help, I could give it. "Does she want to be close to you?"

"Sort of. She answers my questions without me pestering her. But we aren't really close." She shuddered out a breath. "Someone else answer the question before I get emotional."

Rachel glanced into her bottle filled with rose petals, a ring, herbs, and pieces of paper filled with rolled-up wishes. "I want a life filled with love."

"I love you, Mommy," Anna said.

Rachel smiled. "And I love you, too, baby. I'm talking about a grown-up kind of love."

Ellie grimaced. "Like kissing boys."

She laughed. "Yes."

"I want to be tall," Anna said. Her voice carried a weight and power that belied her petite frame. Judging by her mother's size, she'd be lucky to top five foot one.

Ellie sprinkled glitter in her jar. "I want to fly like a butterfly."

Margaret sipped her beer. "I want a really fast metabolism and to have long legs."

We all laughed as I stared into my bottle.

"Addie, spill. What do you want?" Margaret asked.

As much as I hated Mom's and Janet's mood swings and their disease, they shared a connection. But I was the odd man out. The one who ruined the party. Even with Scott, there were brief moments when I sensed we were running alongside each other. Very, very close, to be sure, but not quite touching. Not quite connected enough for me to tell the whole truth.

I held up my bottle. "I want a normal life."

"Is that it?" Margaret asked.

A smile tweaked the edges of my lips. "That's a lot for me."

Margaret looked ready to argue but instead held up a bottle of wine. "You can also fill your bottle with wine. You being on a vineyard and all that kinda makes sense. However, I'm refilling my glass with wine."

I glanced toward the bottle, half full with wine. Margaret and Rachel filled their larger bottles with water and though it made sense for me to use the wine, I realized I was making this bottle not just for me, but also for Carrie. I wanted to feel connected. And I wanted her to feel a connection as well.

She would never be a part of the vineyard. This, I knew. And so I reached for the water that reminded me of the Potomac River. The Chesapeake Bay. The ocean. All would carry her to a great future. To happiness. To a life far and free of the curse.

The waters crested the top of the second bottle. I sprinkled in glitter and sealed the top. I would bury this at the warehouse, Carrie's first home.

By the time we cleaned up the table and readied to say our good nights, it was after nine. The girls were tired and fussing that they didn't need to go to sleep as Rachel led them up the back staircase to their second-floor apartment. Walker had fallen asleep on Daisy's shoulder and Carrie was again in the front pack, cradled close to my body and sleeping.

"Thanks again," I said to Margaret and Daisy. "It was fun."

"We'll do it again," Daisy said. "Don't be a stranger."

"Sounds like a plan," I said. Who knew if we would keep to our promises, but it made sense in the moment to pretend.

As I walked the street with Carrie, I held the witch bottle in my hand. In the moonlight, I walked to the alley behind the warehouse and found a patch of dirt not covered with asphalt. The day's heat cooled and the evening breeze smelled of sweet grass promises. Carefully, I squatted, and keeping a supporting hand on Carrie's bottom, I found a stick and dug a small hole next to the warehouse foundation. The ground was hard, brittle, and resistant to my digging. But I was suddenly determined to see this through and kept chipping away at the soil. Finally, when the hole was deep enough, I set the bottle into it.

"To be normal," I whispered.

Carefully, I covered the bottle with the cracked, dried dirt and then patted the earth with my hand. "To feel connected."

Rising, I tamped the dirt mound with my foot and then moved out of the alley and around the corner to the front door.

A dog's loud, deep bark cut through the darkness and I turned to see Zeb step from the shadows, holding a leash and restraining Shep, the golden retriever. "Addie?"

His face cast in shadows, he looked different. Darker. More intense. "What are you doing?"

The beer had left me a bit light-headed, enough to explain the witch bottle, but somehow I couldn't bring myself to share something so silly. "Carrie and I were up at the Union Street Bakery. Kinda a girls night out. Now we're just enjoying the evening breeze. I forgot how pretty it is here at night."

"It's beautiful." His voice sounded rough as his gaze held mine. "The baby's all right?"

I rubbed the top of Carrie's head. "Yes. She's fine. Sleeping. Where's Eric?"

"At my mom's. Sleepover."

The dog barked and tugged on the leash.

"I'm glad to see Shep again. Why did you get a dog?"

Zeb gently tugged on the dog's collar until he heeled. "Eric wanted a dog. In a moment of weakness, I said yes."

Shep glanced up at Zeb, sensing he was the topic of conversation. He barked and wagged his tail.

"He's cute," I said.

"He's a good dog." No missing the affection in Zeb's voice.

Relaxed and oddly at peace, I enjoyed the play of moonlight adding depth to the creases and edges of Zeb's face. "That must be nice for Eric to spend time with his grandmother."

"She's been great. A rock."

"I remember your mom from the wedding." The woman Addie remembered was tall with thick gray hair she wore in soft curls around her face. Mrs. Talbot's expression was one of worry at the wedding, clearly sensing the trouble looming around the corner. Days after Eric was born, Zeb argued with his mother about Janet. Janet always found a way to toss a grenade into the middle of everyone's lives. "What brings you here?"

"I found a stroller in the attic that was Eric's. Thought you might be able to use it. Grace let me inside, and I left the stroller in the warehouse."

"My shoulders and my back thank you." Fiddling with my keys, I opened the front door to the warehouse. As I held the keys in hand, the old key found years ago warmed with energy in my hand. Smiling, I tucked the key in my pocket. We walked over to the stroller.

"It's not fancy, and it's older, but it will help."

I touched the well-worn handle and imagined Zeb pushing it alone. "How did you do it? How did you manage your business and take care of Eric?"

A faint smile twitched the edges of his lips. "There are days that I wonder that myself. I don't know how I did it. I'm sure I made lots of mistakes."

"Eric seems to be doing really well."

"Thanks."

Absently, I patted Carrie's backside, which was sagging into the folds of the front pack. "You never heard from Janet again after she left you two, did you?"

"A few postcards but never a phone number or a permanent address. It took three years for me to track her down so that she could sign the divorce papers. I hate to think of the money that private detective cost me."

"Where did you find her?"

"Portland." He glanced at his palm and traced a callous at the base of his index finger. "I flew out there and found her at a diner where she was waitressing."

"I never realized she lived in Portland."

"She wasn't there for long. She looked thin and drawn, and I could see she wasn't taking good care of herself."

"Never has."

I thought about adoption papers and custody agreements. "Did she give you any trouble signing the papers?"

"No. She signed the divorce papers easy enough. It was the custody agreement that made her hesitate."

"She had not seen Eric for three years at that point."

"I know. I know. And it took all that I had not to explode. She kept asking what kind of woman walks away from her kid."

"Do you think she'd sign adoption papers and release Carrie?"

He frowned. "I don't know."

Adoption still made perfect sense. It did. But I no longer imagined a loving couple taking Carrie. I imagined me holding her in my arms and calling her daughter. "What did you say when she made that comment?"

"I invited her to move back to Alexandria and be a mother, if that's what she wanted. Eric was already asking questions at that point. His friends talked about their mothers, but there wasn't much for him to tell."

"But she said no."

"She didn't articulate the words, but she signed the papers. When she did that, my remaining hopes for us died." He shook his head. "I actually went to Portland thinking I could still save us."

"She isn't a bad person, Zeb. She's very sick. She's always been sick."

Absently, he rubbed the top of Shep's head. "In the clear light of day I get that, but when push comes to shove, it doesn't matter why she can't function. It only matters to Eric and Carrie that she can't."

The baby yawned, sensing we were talking about her. I rubbed her backside until she settled back. "Do you think it'll be different with Carrie? Do you think now that she has two children, she'll try?"

"She might try, Addie."

But would she succeed, and for how long? Would she try only to be able to give the baby the life we had with our mother? I survived. Janet survived. But it didn't take a shrink to know neither of us thrived. We both found ways to run away from home.

"What are you going to do about the baby, Addie?"

"Janet's in no shape now to make a decision, but I still believe the baby needs real parents."

"She'll listen to you."

"She never has before."

Absently, he rolled the stroller back and forth. "Kids have a way of getting under the skin. They have a way of taking over."

Sadness curled around my heart and squeezed.

"You're good with her. And she's quiet when you're around."

"Quiet." That startled a laugh. "That's debatable."

"Wait until she starts laughing and crawling and making talking sounds. It's hard to resist."

I watched as she pursed her little lips and then relaxed them. Was she dreaming? "I can't keep both Carrie and Scott. He doesn't want a baby now."

Zeb tensed his jaw, grinding words he wasn't sure should be spoken. "Is there anyone else that would be better suited for her than you?"

"I can handle the illness better than most. I spent my childhood taking care of Mom and Janet. But adopting her means losing any chance I have of a real life with Scott."

He shoved his hands into his pocket, rattled bits of loose change. "All I know is that, sometimes, good luck comes disguised as disaster."

A humorless laugh lurched free. "There must be one hell of a pot of good luck waiting around here somewhere."

He laughed, his white teeth catching in the moonlight. "I've faith you'll find it. Good night, Addie." With a tug of the leash, he and Shep vanished out the front door of the warehouse into the night.

September 24, 1751

Dr. Goodwin, under the advisement of Mistress Smyth, brought a complaint against Faith in court. He suggested she must have used sorcery when delivering a babe of a tavern maid and when she broke the fever of an ailing farmer. No doctor can or should relieve women of labor pains or squash a fever as she does. Ben Talbot spoke on behalf of his wife, Faith. The charges were put aside.

Chapter Twenty-two

The witch bottle forgotten, I'm not sure how the next few weeks vanished into thin air. Zeb and Eric stopped by several times a week. Grace kept doing her disappearing act and Carrie and I fell into an odd routine that felt natural. I wasn't willing to risk bringing a baby into the world, but I was making a point to be there for Carrie, one way or another.

Scott and I spoke daily, though our conversations grew more and more businesslike. It was easy for him to focus on the vineyard. With the harvest just days away, his mind was filled with a million details that, if ignored, would come back to bite.

Several times I brought up the baby, but he found a way to change the subject in a few sentences, sensing what I wanted to say. *Let's raise her together.* I would listen to him run away from the conversation, unable to justify my right to give chase. As we danced around hard truths, I knew the time to decide loomed like a summer storm darkening the horizon.

Margaret and I took on a couple more salvage jobs. They were small. An old schoolhouse needed desks and chalkboards hauled away. A diner getting renovated sold us a neon sign, barstools, and booths.

All the items, when cleaned up, could be turned over for a nice profit. With the warehouse space filling, I was soon searching upcoming flea markets to showcase some of our items. Some walk-in traffic found us, but the big designers and builders didn't have us on their radar yet. We would have to attend more flea market events to spread the word that we were, once again, acquiring.

Alexandria's grip was tighter than ever, and I really didn't mind.

I was cleaning baby bottles at the sink when I heard the faint closing of a car door. The sound barely registered as I glanced toward the baby seat where Carrie lay. Daisy had dug through her storage room and brought over the baby seat, as well as a bassinet, and more clothes than the baby could ever wear. I could admit, the extra equipment made this temporary motherhood job a lot easier, and I was grateful.

The front doorbell buzzed, and I shut off the tap and dried my hands. I picked Carrie up and moved her to the bassinet before heading down the stairs.

I stopped midstep, one hand on the railing. My grip tightened. Janet stared up at me.

"Addie." She looked pale and drawn, but her hands were steady and her gaze clear.

"Janet."

"Blindsided" could easily have described the moment. "I didn't know you were being released."

She twisted the hem of her shirt around her index finger. "I found out this morning."

"Why didn't you call?"

Would I have taken the call? I certainly didn't have a good track record for that kind of thing. A faint smile touched her gaze. "Where's the fun in that?"

Scrambling for words and anything that made sense of this moment, I blurted, "I'm sorry I haven't been back to see you. I don't know where the time has gone."

"It's fine. I don't like those places either."

My gaze skimmed her skinny jeans and fresh white blouse. She'd washed her hair and wore a little mascara and rouge. "You look good."

"Grace brought me the clothes."

"Grace?"

"She came by almost daily."

And so that explained the missing hours. Why hadn't she told me? "The doctors cleared you?"

She pulled a crumpled paper bag from her purse. "He gave me my medicines."

I resisted the urge to inventory the pills and ask her for a detailed description of her med schedule. If I pushed too hard, she'd balk. "Good. You have to take them."

She lifted her chin. "I will. I will this time." She glanced past me. "Can I come in?"

"Sure. Yes. I'm sorry."

She glanced around the warehouse that was quickly refilling with items Margaret and I had collected. "Where's the baby?"

"Carrie's upstairs sleeping."

"Carrie. I remember you said you'd given her a name."

I felt as if I danced on eggshells. "Eric named her. I'm sure if you want to change it, you can."

"No. No. I like the name. It's pretty."

As I moved up the stairs, her footsteps followed steadily behind me. We moved into the living room toward the bassinet trimmed in white lace. I glanced in to make sure Carrie was still asleep. Janet held back.

"This place hasn't changed since we were kids. Even still has the same musty smell."

"Grace didn't change a thing." Janet was hesitant, afraid, and waiting for me to take the lead. I could feel her need to see the baby. Her need to hold the baby. Her need for my approval. As her needs rolled over me, my grip on Alexandria tightened as if I was suddenly on the verge of losing everything.

"Come look at her. She's pretty."

Janet moved across the room, her purse clutched in her hands. She peeked into the crib and, for a long moment, stared. "She's pretty. Real pretty."

"She looks like you," I said. "Your coloring. Your long, lean body."

She shook her head. "I was hoping she'd be more like you."

"Me?"

"Strong. Stable. That's what I want for her."

"I don't know how strong I am, Janet. I've been muddling through the last few weeks. It's not been a pretty picture."

She traced her fingertips along the cradle's smooth wood, as if remembering it belonged to Eric. "When Eric was born, I remember how hard those first few weeks were. If not for Zeb . . ."

"You'd have run away sooner." Bitterness shadowed the words.

"Yeah. And even with Zeb I couldn't cut it." A faint smile returned. "The doctors at the hospital said that we needed to be honest. To face our mistakes. I'm trying to do that."

Janet had been running from her disasters for so long I couldn't imagine her standing still. And the simple fact that she could admit there was a problem gave me a little hope.

"Do you want to hold her?" I asked.

She flexed her fingers before curling them into fists. "She's sleeping right now. I really don't want to wake her."

"She might fuss, but that won't be the end of the world." Pull out a recorder so that I could play my own words over and over again when Carrie woke up tonight at two A.M.

Janet pulled away from the cradle. "I don't want to hear the crying. Not now."

"Okay."

"Can I get you coffee?"

She turned from the baby, her expression relaxing. "That would be great."

"Are you hungry?"

"Yeah."

I set up a cup of coffee to brew before digging a loaf of bread from the red breadbox and pulling peanut butter and jelly from the cabinet.

Janet sat at the kitchen table, smoothing her hand over the surface. "I remember feeling really happy at this table when I was a kid. Grace can't cook worth a damn, but it was nice sitting here. She was steady. Calm. I liked that."

I held up the jar of peanut butter. "As you can see, I'm making the house specialty."

Janet's eyes glistened and for a moment a distant memory connected us. "She liked grape jelly, but I always wanted strawberry."

I pointed to the opened strawberry jam jar. "That was my first act of defiance when I moved in weeks ago. And I bought good coffee. She doesn't drink good coffee."

Janet shook her head. "How does she live?"

"I don't know." The coffeemaker gurgled and spit out the last drops into the mug. "Still take it black?"

"Yes. Thanks."

I set the mug in front of her and just like that we fell into old roles: her being vulnerable and me taking care of her. We were re-creating a scenario that had played over and over a thousand times before.

She cupped her long hands around the warm mug, absorbing the heat before she raised it to her lips and sipped. "You still make great coffee."

"My peanut butter and jelly sandwiches are pretty good, too." I set one in front of her.

She stared at the sandwich and tore off the crust. She lifted the crust to her lips and then hesitated. "It's all backward. I should have been taking care of you. When Mom was sick, I should have been the one to run the house."

"Neither one of us should have been the one to run the house. We were just kids."

She nibbled the crust first, just as she did as a child. I asked her once why she did that. Saving the best for last. An odd comment from someone who always rushed toward the fun as fast as she could. "She hated being sick. She hated not being able to be a mom."

"I know." As an adult I should have understood this and found a way to forgive all the past mistakes. But the child in me still huddled in the shadows and clung to anger and a deep sense of betrayal.

"You're still mad at her."

"Yes."

"I used to be. Not anymore." Her hands trembled as she set the crust aside and chose a piece that was oozing peanut butter and jelly. She ate in silence as I filled a mug full of coffee for myself and sipped, content to let her eat. When only crumbs remained, she sipped more coffee. "You're mad at me, too."

A sigh shuddered through me. "I'm trying not to be angry, Janet. I am trying."

"But you are. You might keep it all together for me and the baby, but you're angry, and have every right to be."

"Janet, you've made some very serious mistakes. You've walked away from one son, nearly killed me in a car accident, and now you left your daughter with me."

"I'm sick."

"I understand that. And as long as you take your medicines and try, I can roll with the punches. But when you toss away the meds and pick up a bottle of vodka, I get angry."

She met my gaze and held it. "I didn't drink at all while I was pregnant with Carrie."

"What about pot?"

Her brow wrinkled. "Some, but none of the hard drugs."

"You didn't take your meds either, did you?"

"No. I stopped about a year ago. I felt so good. And I thought I finally tackled it."

I pinched the bridge of my nose, struggling to hold on to patience. "You can't *tackle* this. You can't will yourself out of this. It's forever."

Her blue gaze cooled to ice. "I didn't ask for this, Addie."

"No one asked for it, Janet. I sure didn't ask for it. And yet here we are." Carrie began to fuss and automatically I pushed away from the counter and went to her. She called. I went. That was our pattern.

I lifted her up, unable to hide a smile as she opened her eyes and looked at me. A sloppy grin curled the edges of her round, full mouth. Might be just a reflex and not a real smile but to me it said she knew she was safe. Knew a bottle was coming soon. Knew Addie would fix it all. I glanced into the kitchen. Janet stared at her mug, tracing the rim with a finger.

I moved into the kitchen. "Do you want to hold her while I make a bottle?"

She flexed long fingers. "It's been so long since I held a baby."

"It's not hard. I got the hang of it pretty quickly."

She rubbed her hands on her jeans. "I should wash my hands. The cab."

"Sure. Wash your hands in the sink. That's a good idea."

With Carrie on my shoulder, I moved to the fridge and pulled out a bottle. With one hand I unscrewed the top and put the bottle in the microwave. I pressed twenty-three seconds to accommodate the extra milk a growing Carrie now required. The doctor said no baby food until she was about three months. Three months. I thought Carrie and I would have parted ways by then, but seeing Janet now, and faced with the thought of giving Carrie away, I knew, *knew*, giving her up would be the hardest thing I'd ever do in my life.

Janet dried her hands with a paper towel and moved to the chair and sat, just as Eric did when he held the baby. I cradled Carrie in Janet's arms. "She likes it when you hold her head up a little. She likes to be able to see what's going on."

Janet's posture was as stiff and rigid as mine was the first time I held the baby. "Eric was a bigger baby."

I fought the urge to nudge the crook of Janet's arm up a few inches. "She was six pounds six ounces when she was born. How much did Eric weigh when he was born?"

She tugged the edge of Carrie's onesie so it rested flat on her chest. "I don't remember the numbers. I should remember the numbers."

"It's okay. I kinda remember he was close to nine pounds. Zeb will know."

Her gaze rose. "How is Zeb?"

"He seems to be doing real well. He lent me Eric's crib and a stroller. And he's done well for himself in his business. Eric is doing great. Zeb's done a good job with him."

"Zeb is as steady as a rock." Faint hints of resentment hummed under the words. "He really tried to keep us together."

I went to the microwave and removed the bottle. The top screwed back on, I shook it and did a quick test on my wrist. "Would you like to feed her?"

"I would."

I draped a towel over Janet's shoulder and handed her the bottle. A part of me hoped she'd struggle and Carrie would squawk at the unfamiliar arms. But the baby stared up at Janet as she gently coaxed the nipple against her lips, and Carrie easily latched, as if this were the thousandth feeding, not the first.

Invisible fingers squeezed my heart, and I imagined myself standing outside in the cold, looking through a large picture window at a party. I was the uninvited guest, longing to be inside where it was warm, laughter bubbled, and glasses clinked.

On the outside. Unconnected.

I ducked my head and turned toward the counter, where I reached for the peanut butter and dolloped out a large spoonful onto the bread. My appetite was gone, but I needed something to keep my hands busy. For a long time, I smoothed peanut butter onto the bread before I dug out jelly and layered it thickly on top. I smashed the top piece of bread into the bottom and cut the sandwich as Carrie's soft, suckling noises swirled around me.

She cried so miserably the first time I held her. Balled her fists, declaring that she knew she was in the wrong arms.

"She feels right in my arms," Janet said.

Sadness squeezed the remaining air from my lungs. Carrie didn't feel natural in my arms the first or second day. It took us time to settle into a routine. But we found our groove, and now, to just surrender her clogged my throat with unshed tears. "She's a lot of work, Janet. I keep her on a regular schedule. That's important for babies."

"I know." Janet's raised gaze held hints of fire. "She's not my first."

"No." It would be easy to remind her of her failures with Eric. The lost days and the lost years. But I treaded on thin ice. With no legal claim to Carrie, I knew if Janet wanted to take her, there'd be little I could do to stop her. "Have you seen Eric? He's been asking about you."

A frown wrinkled her brow as she lowered her gaze back to Carrie. "I haven't seen him yet. I'm not sure who to call."

"I have Zeb's number."

"Zeb. It didn't end well with us. He was so angry."

"He's mellowed, and he's been a help with Carrie."

"His ex-wife shows up and she's knocked up by another man. The old Zeb would have been furious." Resentment simmered under the words.

"I'm sure he's frustrated, angry, and hurt. We all are."

She leaned forward and kissed the baby's head, closing her eyes, savoring the smell. "Zeb built that crib. It took him weeks."

"It's stunning."

She opened her eyes, but her gaze remained on Carrie. "I remember the day he unveiled it for me. I cried."

"He's a good father."

"Yes. He has always been a good father." She let the words trail, hinting there was more to the Zeb story. Janet was fairly steady now, but I hadn't forgotten her talent for manipulating and driving wedges between people.

"Do you want me to call him?"

She rolled her head from side to side. "I don't think I can deal with him right now. I always see my failures reflected in his eyes."

"He wants what's best for you."

"He wants what's best for Eric. Not me. Not Carrie." She smoothed her hand over the baby's forehead, touching her like she were a fragile egg. And she was fragile. Just a few weeks old.

My throat tightened with emotion, forcing me to clear it before I spoke again. "Where are you staying?"

"I have a friend in town."

"You can stay here." I wasn't sure if I wanted her to accept or not. "There's a spare bed."

"No. I don't want to stay here." She glanced around the room, her gaze drifting over the eclectic collection. Like everything else in the room, this place was her second chance. "It makes me uncomfortable."

"All Carrie's baby things are here."

"I'm not ready to take her. I have to figure a few things out."

Relief washed over me. "That's sensible. You need to think about yourself, Janet. Get healthy."

Again the anger flickered. "She's my child, Addie. Not yours."

For a heartbeat, I couldn't speak. "I know."

"Once I get my act together, I want to be her mother."

Words clanged in my head and begged to be shouted. *I've done all the work! I love her! I want her!* But I corralled them all.

Janet shook her head. "You've got that look."

I blinked. "What look?"

"Injured. Pure. The martyr. Addie the Saint."

That's what Scott had called me whenever we disagreed. My Little Martyr.

I tiptoed over more eggshells. "I love Carrie, Janet. I want what's best for her. For you. None of us has to make a decision tonight."

"No. No decisions tonight." But there was a resoluteness that suggested she would do whatever she wanted to do.

Carrie sucked the last drops of milk and instead of nodding off to sleep, fussed and squirmed. Janet set the bottle down and began to jostle the baby. "It's okay, Mama's here."

"She doesn't like to be jostled," I said without thinking. "Do you want me to take her?"

"No." Janet stopped jostling Carrie, but the baby kept crying. "I know how to hold a baby."

"Put her on your shoulder and pat her on her back."

Janet shifted the baby awkwardly up to her shoulder, her ringed fingers snagging the soft cotton of the baby's onesie. Carrie's head flopped, and it took all my restraint not to take the baby. My sister righted her quickly, patted her daughter on the back, and a part of me hoped the baby would hate her touch. This wasn't the way we did it. Carrie liked a softer, gentler pat. But Carrie adapted quickly and released a healthy burp.

Janet laughed. "That's what was upsetting her."

Feeling a little betrayed and lost, I saw connections unravel I had begrudgingly, and then lovingly, woven.

The baby tried to raise her head, and it flopped again before Janet caught it with a ringed finger. "She's active."

"Yes."

"I wonder if I was like this as a baby?"

"I've wondered that myself."

She held the baby back from her body and studied her pink, round face. "She looks like me."

"Yes." Minutes ago she wished the child were more like me, now she took pride in the sameness she shared with her daughter.

A heavy silence settled around Janet. "Do you think she's *like* me?"

Cursed, you mean? "I don't know. I asked the doctor at her checkup but he didn't know. He said it will be a long time before we know."

"How old was I when I started showing signs?"

"When you were little you cried a lot. You were afraid of shadows. Afraid of the dark. But Mom thought it was kid stuff. Quirks."

She brushed a strand of hair from her eyes. "When did you *know*?"

"When you were eleven. Remember when you took your shoes off in the winter and ran around the snowman I built? Your feet were blue by the time I convinced you to go into the house. You kept laughing. Calling me silly. An old woman." Even our mother worried over her daughter's blue toes.

Janet tipped her head back, coaxing the memory from the shadows. "I thought it was so much fun. I thought I was the snow maiden."

"Yeah, I remember. It got worse in high school. The boys. The parties. You never ran out of energy. And then one day when you were in the eleventh grade you didn't get up in the morning. You stayed in your room for two weeks."

"The first crash into depression."

"Yeah."

She cradled Carrie in the crook of her arm. "I don't want her to run circles around snowmen."

"Neither do I. But she might."

Janet stared at the baby, carefully placing her palm under the baby's hand. "Such a tiny little hand. So vulnerable."

A knock on the downstairs door made Janet wince. She couldn't bear any more stimuli and I didn't want to leave her alone with the baby, but I rose and walked to the threshold. A glance down the stairs, and I spotted Zeb and Eric.

Eric was grinning, holding a colorful red box. As always, Zeb's expression remained guarded against the unexpected. Smart man.

"Zeb." My tone added sharp edges to his name.

His hand went to Eric's shoulder, stopping the boy's advance up the stairs. "What is it?"

"I have a visitor."

Darkness hardened the line of his jaw. "Scott."

"No." The baby began to cry. I didn't know how to say this without Eric hearing. There was no softening the blow. "My sister."

The words didn't quite connect with Eric immediately, but they slammed hard into Zeb. His fingers tightened on Eric's shoulders, and he slowly knelt in front of the boy. "Did you hear that Eric? Addie's sister is here. Your mom is here."

The boy's eyes widened, and he jumped up and down. "Mom is here?"

"Yes."

"How's she doing?" the boy asked. "Can I see her?"

Zeb looked up to me, his expression asking: *What kind of disaster are we walking into?*

Carrie's deep-throated cry wafted into the rafters. "The baby is fussy, Eric."

He rolled his eyes. "She's always fussy. Can I see Mom?"

"Sure. But you need to come up the stairs slow and soft."

"Not like a herd of elephants? That's what Dad says when I run up the stairs. Elephants have big feet."

"I know. But your feet aren't that big."

"That's what I said."

"Come up quietly, and you can see Carrie and your mom." I glanced over his head to Zeb. "Give me a second or two head start?"

"Understood."

I hurried back to the room where Janet was jostling Carrie, who grew increasingly fussy. "Janet. We have visitors."

She looked up at me, the flicker of panic clear and sharp. The baby's cries were unraveling her loosely woven composure. "Who?"

"Eric. And Zeb."

Her eyes closed and for a moment she shook her head, hinting this was too much. "That's great."

I moved forward, my hands outstretched. "Let me take the baby." Janet's grip tightened.

"Eric is going to require all your attention." I moved closer. "He's a spitfire."

Just as I spoke, little elephant feet clamored up the stairs, and Janet allowed me to take the baby into my arms. I held her close, so grateful to have her back in my arms that tears burned my throat. She wasn't my child. I had no legal rights, but I couldn't give her to Janet and simply hope that my sister kept her life together.

I rocked Carrie slowly from side to side, and her cries softened as Eric ran into the room. "Mom!"

The baby startled and turned toward the sound of her older brother's voice, accepting loud yells as part of her odd little family.

Janet rose and turned to face her son. Weeks after giving birth, her frame was thin and her blond hair full and bright. Just like all the pictures Zeb saved for Eric.

Janet extended her hands, and he ran toward her and burrowed his face into her belly, hugging her so tight his little fingers whitened. She raised her arms and very slowly tightened her grip. For a long time Eric stood there, holding her, trying to make up for years of no hugs or kisses.

Both Janet's children forgave her. Eric and Carrie didn't care about curses, long absences, highs and lows, or bad choices. They loved Janet. Her spirit or aura ensured that no matter how much trouble she made, she'd always win them back.

I wanted Eric to be happy. I wanted him to love his mother, but it hurt a little to see him so enamored with Janet. When my sister arrived, I became invisible to Carrie and Eric and everyone else. More threads of connection thinned.

Drawing in a breath, I held Carrie a little closer. When I looked up, I found Zeb staring at me. His features hardened, reflecting a brittleness akin to ice. Eric and Carrie may have forgiven their mother, but Zeb had not.

A smile fluttered at the edges of my lips. It was a pitiful attempt to say, *I know. I know.* She's lobbed another grenade into our lives.

He looked away, unwilling to accept an alliance, any connection or kinship with a Shire. His son was all he needed.

Eric kissed his mother. "Mom, I missed you so much! I got all the birthday cards you sent me! I keep them in my room."

Janet looked at him, her fingers smoothing his short-cropped hair. "Cards?"

"The birthday cards!" he said laughing. "The last one had a race car on it."

Confusion darkened her gaze. "Baby, you said a race car?"

"A red one. You sent him a card with a red race car on it. Don't you remember?" Zeb asked, as he shifted his stance. "Hello, Janet."

She didn't quite raise her eyes to meet her ex-husband's. "Zeb. You look good. Eric looks great."

Zeb nodded, but said nothing.

"I've grown a lot since you last saw me." Eric stood a little straighter to exaggerate his height.

"But you still have the same nose and the same eyes," she said.

Eric touched his nose. "How do you know I have the same nose?"

"Because it's like mine. When you were a baby, I could look at you and know you were mine because of your nose."

"People say I look like Dad."

"You do. Every other part of you is him." She touched his nose with the tip of her finger. "But not your nose. That is me."

He giggled and touched his nose again with chubby fingers. "I like my nose."

"Good."

Eric looked toward me. "Addie, you don't have our nose."

"No, honey, I don't. Mine is shorter."

The boy inspected his sister's face. "What kind of nose does Carrie have?"

I glanced at the baby, whose eyes were wide, alert, absorbing it all. "I don't know. It's all hers. Very pretty."

"But not Mom's nose. Not mine."

"No."

He grinned, clearly glad he shared something special with his mother. "That's okay. She looks like Mom more than me."

Zeb cleared his throat. "Janet, where're you staying?"

"With a friend." She brushed her fingers against Eric's cheek.

"Are you staying in town?" The question was soft, conversational, with no hints of the fear and worry I knew raced through his mind. Janet had turned his life upside down once before, and he weathered the storm. But he and I knew we all swirled gently in the eye of the hurricane and it was only a matter of time before the winds picked up and blew faster and faster until they reached a crushing strength. Zeb and I could ride out her next storm, but Eric and Carrie would be swept away by it.

"I don't know." She smiled at Eric. "I've missed my boy."

Zeb's jaw tightened as he slid his hands into his pockets. "How did you get here?"

"I took a cab."

"Eric and I can give you a ride. No sense you spending your money." Her fingers stilled as she brushed Eric's bangs back. She didn't like being told what to do. We all knew that. But her pale, gaunt features and the tremor in her hands told us both she was tired. Rest was critical for her now. Sleep allowed her brain and body to heal. We'd avoided the problem of Janet for the last couple of weeks, but she was here now and wasn't going away anytime soon.

I smoothed my hand over the top of Carrie's head. "Go get some sleep, Janet," I said. "No one is going anywhere, and you do need to sleep."

She turned toward me. The apology that lingered behind her eyes when she arrived had vanished. "Sure, but I'm coming back."

"I know."

She hugged Eric close. "I love my kids."

"No one doubts that," I said. What we doubted was her ability to care for the children.

Zeb rattled the keys in his pocket. "I'm parked out front."

"Always so organized," Janet said. "Always."

She walked toward me and leaned down and kissed the baby. I didn't tense, reach out, and touch Janet or offer her a hug. I was too scared. Too worried that she'd take my baby away.

Eric took Janet by the hand. "Come on, Mom. You can see our car."

She kept smiling. "I can't wait, baby."

"I'm not a baby, Mom."

She rustled the top of his hair with her delicate fingers. "You'll always be my baby."

Eric giggled.

Zeb looked at me. "You have everything you need?"

"I'm fine."

Janet shook her head. "She's like you, Zeb. She's always had her act together. I'm the one that's broken."

Eric squeezed her hand tighter. "You're not broken, Mom. "You're perfect."

"Thanks, baby."

I followed the sound of their footsteps down the stairs and listened as Zeb closed the main door and locked it behind him.

Just Carrie and me. Alone. The tears caught in my throat loosened and within seconds fell down my cheeks.

When Scott called an hour later, I was sitting in the living room with a glass of wine in my hands. Carrie had fallen into a heavy sleep, but my nerves were wired so tightly I wasn't sure if I would ever sleep again.

"Scott." I nestled close to the phone, needing him. *Tell me it's going to be all right. Tell me we are fine.*

"You sound tired."

"It's been a long day. Crazy."

"I saw the e-mails you copied me on. You're staying on top of the business. I don't know how you do it."

That rattled an unsteady laugh. "Neither do I."

"I don't know what I'd do without you." He lowered his voice and hesitated, knowing he entered dangerous territory. "How's the baby?"

"She's fine." I held the wineglass up to the light, turning it and watching the wine slide down the inside of the glass. When the wine dripped like this, experts called this tears. "Janet is out of the hospital. She came by today."

"That's a good thing, right?"

When she was in the hospital, we were all assured a little normalcy. Now, it was anybody's guess. "It should be."

"What's that mean?"

He didn't understand the disease or the curse. Both never fully relinquished control of our lives. "Time will tell. I'm hoping she can hold on to this."

"She saw the baby?"

"Yes." I pictured Janet holding Carrie. Fear circled but I chased it away.

"You don't sound happy," he said.

"I want the best for the baby."

"Isn't being with her mother the best thing for her?"

Carrie had settled easily into Janet's arms. She hadn't cried. She cooed. "If Janet is healthy."

"You just said she was doing well."

"For now."

"You sound like you don't want to give the baby back to Janet," he said.

"Honestly, I don't." The words rushed out before I could wrestle them back.

"Addie, we've talked about this."

"Have we, Scott? You said you didn't want a baby now. I, like always, agreed."

"Like always? What does that mean?"

Frustration scraped and scratched under my skin. I went along, very willingly, with everything Scott wanted up until this moment. He knew what he wanted, and it was easy, exciting even, to follow a dreamer with a plan. I rose and walked into the kitchen and stared out the window toward the busy street below. "I'm not blaming you."

"You're still not explaining yourself." His tone turned crisp, sharp, as it did in the wake of a hailstorm at the vineyard.

I traced my fingers in circles on the counter. Round and round and yet going nowhere. "Janet may think she can care for Carrie alone, but she can't. She's going to need help."

"That's what Social Services is for, Addie."

"No, Scott, it's my job to keep the Shire family on track. I've done it since I could barely walk."

"Then why did you move down here? You haven't seen your family in seven years."

"Time doesn't seem to matter. I'm here, and I'm needed."

"What if Janet doesn't want your help? You're making a big assumption."

My voice sharpened to a knife's edge, freshly honed on a whetstone. "I know. But I will be there for the baby's sake."

A frustrated sigh leaked through what I imagined were clenched teeth. "So you're just not coming back."

And there it was—the choice—stripped bare for us both to see. Scott or the baby. "I was hoping we could figure this out together. I thought we were a team."

"We're a team. But getting between a mother and child is huge. It's also not smart or very legal."

"She's sick." Janet's time in the hospital did not mean she was fixed. She'd never really be fixed.

"Did she act sick when you saw her?"

Frustration rose up within me. "She seemed fragile."

"Was she acting crazy?"

"No." Not yet. Not now.

"Give her a chance."

His arguments all made good sense, and any smart lawyer could conceivably convince a judge that I was overstepping. But I knew it would end badly. "I can't trust that Janet and the baby will be fine. I can't watch her drive out of Alexandria with my fingers crossed and hope."

"You've been the caregiver in that family for all your life. You just admitted that. Maybe you don't know how to be around the family unless you're running the show."

"Do you think this is something I wanted? I thought we had a pretty good thing."

"I thought we did, too. I also thought we were on the no-kid plan. We've always said kids were a very, very distant idea."

My grip on the phone tightened. "I didn't create this problem."

"And you don't have to solve it either. Carrie is Janet's child."

"Janet is sick."

"You haven't given her a chance." After a long pause, he said more softly, "Addie, I love you. I love the life we have. The life we had."

I closed my eyes, wishing for a clear solution. But left or right, up or down, in or out, someone was going to lose this battle. The baby's fussing would grow louder and louder until she got her bottle. "I love you, too, Scott. But I have to go."

"This is not over. We have to talk this through."

"Sure." Talking wouldn't change the choice. "We need to talk again."

"I love you."

I hung up the phone and leaned against the counter as the baby's cries magnified. Scott and I could talk all we wanted. We could examine the pros and cons. And, in the end, a choice would have to be made.

And someone would lose.

October 5, 1751

There was an accident at the tobacco warehouse today. A stack of hogsheads toppled on Ben Talbot. Dr. Goodwin was summoned but he pronounced the man dead. Faith came running to the warehouse screaming when she heard the news about her husband.

Chapter Twenty-three

When the front bell rang the next morning, my first reaction was annoyance. The baby was taking her morning nap, which meant ninety minutes of silence to upload the pictures I took of the salvaged items from the Prince Street basement and get them listed in our new online eBay store.

When the bell buzzed a second time, my thoughts skittered to Janet. She had great timing. When I needed something, so did she. Time, Carrie, none of it mattered. Janet simply took.

Rising, I moved quietly down the stairs, summoning more reasons why the baby needed to stay with me.

Standing on the stoop was a tall, lean man dressed in a charcoal gray suit. His hair was cut neat and crisp around his angled face. He wore dark sunglasses and carried a slim briefcase.

"Can I help you?"

He studied me closely. "I'm looking for Addie Morgan."

"I'm Addie Morgan."

He reached in a coat pocket, pulled out a business card, and handed it to me. Raised letters and a linen stock told me he cost big money. Harold S. Gray, Attorney-at-Law.

"Mr. Gray." I hesitated, doing my best to sound calm. "What can I do for you?"

"I'm representing your sister."

I flicked the edge of the card with my index finger. "In what matter?"

"Is there a more private place we can talk?"

I lifted my chin. I was tired of secrets. Of hiding. "Here is fine. Why are you here?"

He drew in a breath. "Janet Morgan is concerned that you may contest her custody of her infant daughter."

Anger stabbed and prodded, but I kept my tone even. "She told you that?"

"Yes."

I held his card so tightly the fine white linen paper creased. "She certainly works fast."

"She wants you to understand that once she has a place to stay, she'll be taking the baby."

"Really?" The baby/job juggling act was driving me insane. What was Janet going to do when she picked up a waitress job?

"There's a meeting scheduled tomorrow with Social Services at nine o'clock in the morning. The department will be ruling on the child's custody."

My fingers crushed the attorney's card. "Doesn't sound like I have a choice."

"No."

He turned and left, leaving me to stand at the shop entrance, my head a little dizzy with anger. "So I'm supposed to turn the baby over to her?"

He stopped and faced me. "You will be required to follow the ruling of the department."

"And what if I don't like the ruling?"

He pulled Ray-Bans from his breast pocket. "I suggest you get an attorney."

"How the hell am I supposed to afford a guy like you?" My voice rose high and sharp. "And how the hell is Janet affording you?"

He slid on the glasses. "That is not your concern."

"Are you going to be around in five months when Janet can't hack it anymore, and she and the baby are in crisis? Are you going to drive across the country when she calls to bail her out of more trouble?"

"I can't predict the future, Ms. Morgan. I can only deal with the issue at hand."

"Meaning you don't give a shit what happens to the baby! Or Janet for that matter. She can't handle the stress right now." Years of pent-up anger rolled free now.

"Have you ever considered that maybe you underestimate your sister."

Disgust rose up in my throat. "Spoken like a man who's never traveled this path before." I slammed the door, the bang of wood against wood echoing in the warehouse.

Calling Zeb for help was not easy for me. We'd forged a tentative alliance. I understood he was simply looking out for Eric and the boy's relationship with his mother's family, but I needed an ally. Though I considered calling Scott, in the end, I didn't bother. He was always so very clear about what he wanted. He never wavered. Never changed course. How could I blame him? It was me who'd changed course.

I dialed Zeb's number. As my stomach knotted, my finger hovered over the Send button, and I paced the floor. Drawing in a breath, I pressed the button. The phone rang once and then twice before he picked it up.

"Addie. Is everything all right?"

"Not really. Janet wants Carrie."

A long heavy silence cut across the airways. "She said that?"

"She not only said that, but she's hired an attorney to represent her. There's going to be a hearing in the morning at Social Services."

He sighed. "How can she afford a lawyer?"

"She can't. But she knows so many people, and she can be so damn charming. She's convinced this guy to help her, and I bet he doesn't get paid a dime."

"Their arrangement isn't really the problem. He's on her side and helping her. Look, if you need to hire an attorney, I know they're expensive, but I've some money."

Sudden hot tears stung my eyes. "No. I don't want your money, but if you could show up at Social Services tomorrow at nine A.M. and talk to the social worker, maybe you could convince her to give this situation more time."

"How much more time, Addie? Are you willing to raise the baby?"

The question had buzzed in my head for days, but when Janet showed up yesterday, the buzzing grew so loud it blocked out almost all other thought. Breathe deep. Let it go. "Yes."

Silence snapped. "What about Scott?"

"He doesn't want to be a part of Carrie's life."

"So he's not going to man up and help?"

"It's not his fault. I changed the rules. And now I have to figure out what's next. But I can't worry about next if the social worker gives the baby to Janet."

"Okay, I'll be at the hearing."

"I don't want to cut Janet out of Carrie's life, but I see a train wreck coming if she rushes into mothering and working."

"I know."

"Thanks, Zeb."

"Sure."

I hung up and the hot tears burning the back of my eyes spilled down my cheeks. A couple of weeks ago when I buried the witch bottle, I asked to feel normal, but my life was so far from normal now.

The next morning I dressed Carrie in a light blue onesie that belonged to Daisy's son and was one of the nicest garments in the bag of clothes. Light blue, I reasoned, was also suited for a girl as well as a boy.

I rummaged through my clothes, but found only jeans, which would not have worked for this hearing. With no time to shop, I called Margaret and asked if she owned a skirt. A half hour later, she arrived with a pink paisley A-line skirt and a white blouse. Both had a peasant feel to them, and I debated if they looked more "motherly" than a clean pair of jeans and a button-down shirt. In the end, I chose the skirt, top, and a pair of tan sandals.

Grace came out of her room dressed in a simple pair of cotton pants and a white top. She brushed back her gray hair and tied it back into a ponytail at the base of her head. She looked as pulled together as I could remember.

I loaded Carrie into her car seat and slung the baby bag on my shoulder. I was hoping the social worker would see my side, but I knew life never went as planned, so I packed extra clothes and diapers in the bag in case the baby left the building with Janet.

Grace followed Carrie and me outside and as Grace settled in the front seat, I hooked Carrie's seat into the backseat. We made the trip in silence and because the morning commuter traffic had cleared, the journey took less than ten minutes. I parked the car in front, fed the meter, and pulled the baby and bag out of the backseat as Grace closed her front door.

The receptionist was expecting us, and even mentioned that Ms. Morgan had arrived. That prompted a raised brow from Grace. "First time she's ever been on time."

We rode the elevator to the second floor and were directed to a conference room. When I knocked, the door edged open, and I saw Janet and her attorney sitting across the table. Janet looked lovely. Her hair freshly washed, she wore a navy blue pullover dress that hugged slim curves. Bracelets rattled from her wrists and her eyes sparked with a nervous excitement that would be hard to resist.

She looked up at Grace and me, and oddly, the smile did not dim. She rose and came around the table and hugged me. "Addie, I want to thank you for everything you've done for Carrie and me. I don't know where we would be without you."

"You're making a mistake," I whispered in her ear. "Don't do this."

She smiled at the baby. "Why don't you have any confidence in me? Why do you think I'm always going to screw up? This time is going to be different."

"I wish that were true."

Ms. Willis entered the room, along with another woman who was tall and full figured. She wore a blue suit and white blouse with blond hair around her shoulders. "Ladies, if you will sit we can begin."

I glanced over my shoulder, hoping to see Zeb, and when I didn't, my heart dropped..

"Shall we?"

I sat and set the car seat on the table. Janet sat next to me and turned the seat so she could see Carrie. She jostled the baby's socked feet and tickled her under the chin. Carrie grinned and kicked.

I sat and tried to calm racing thoughts. I needed to sound clear and thoughtful. "Yes."

"I am Mrs. Hudson," said the other woman as she opened her file and reviewed the case. "As I understand it, Ms. Janet Morgan, after having spent the last thirty days in a mental hospital, is now stable and would like to take custody of the minor child, Carrie Morgan."

Janet smiled, but it was her attorney who spoke.

He leaned forward in his chair, his gold cufflinks winking in the light. "That is correct."

"Who are you?"

"I'm Harold S. Gray, attorney-at-law. I'm here on Ms. Janet Morgan's behalf."

Mrs. Hudson studied the lawyer and Janet before her gaze shifted to me. "You must be Ms. Addie Morgan?"

I straightened my shoulders. "That is correct. I'm Janet's sister and Carrie's aunt."

"It's my understanding that you did not want the child at first. According to Ms. Willis, you asked her to find a foster home."

"That is correct." I shifted forward in my seat. "News of the baby's birth was a big surprise to me. It took some adjusting."

"And now you want to keep the child?"

"Janet needs time to get on her own two feet. I have no doubt that she loves the baby, but raising a baby, I've discovered, is very stressful. It has always been my experience that Janet doesn't handle stress well."

"I don't think it's fair to talk about the past," her attorney said. "This is about now. My client has already gotten a room in a friend's house and she's looking for a job."

"Who's going to take care of the baby while you work, Ms. Morgan?"

"My friends have offered to help."

The door behind me opened and closed, and I turned to see Zeb. He wore a crisp white shirt, a red tie, and khaki pants.

Janet shifted in her seat. "What's he doing here?"

Mrs. Hudson looked at Zeb. "And who are you?"

"I'm Zeb Talbot." His voice was clear and sharp. The cavalry had arrived. "I was married to Janet Morgan for three years, and we have a seven-year-old son together. I have custody of the boy."

Janet shook her head. "This is not fair. I'm different than I was then."

Mrs. Hudson held up her hand. "Mr. Talbot, how is it you came to have sole custody?"

His expression was stoic, his voice even as if he were giving a report to a superior. "Janet left when our boy was four months old. The stress of mothering was too much."

"That is a biased opinion," the attorney said, rising. "That was seven years ago and does not take into consideration the stresses and strains of their marriage. This matter is completely separate."

Mrs. Hudson wrote several notes in her file. "Ms. Willis, what is your opinion?"

"I've met with Janet Morgan several times in the last month, and I've seen tremendous improvement. She is willing and anxious to take custody of her baby. I've seen where she's living, and it's suitable, as are her roommates. I think Addie Morgan has done a tremendous job with the baby, but Janet Morgan should be given the opportunity to parent."

"If I may speak," I said.

Mrs. Hudson nodded and I continued. "I believe Janet is sincere. I know she loves the baby, but she has the same illness that our mother had, and even Janet will admit, we did not have a stable upbringing."

The attorney shook his head. "Medications and treatment options have advanced radically in the last twenty years. That is not a fair comparison. The past is not a predictor of the future."

Zeb shifted his stance, the tension rolling off of him. "I disagree. I have been down this road with Janet. She is not ready."

Janet glared at Zeb.

Sadness and loss washed over me. The voices around me swirled and grew distant and far off. I knew before Mrs. Hudson spoke I'd lose. When she finally ruled, she ordered that Janet be given custody of the baby with supervised visits from Ms. Willis.

Loss enveloped me like a thick wool blanket, weighing down my body. It took tremendous effort to lean forward and kiss the baby on the cheek, push the diaper bag toward Janet, and leave the room. Conversations buzzed in the background but I refused to make sense of it.

Zeb caught up to me at the elevator. "Addie, we can fight this. This does not have to be the end of it."

"I will always remain close so that if Carrie needs me I will be there." I pushed the Down button.

"So you're going to walk way?"

I faced him. "What do you want me to do? A fight is not going to change anything. It's only going to add more stress into Janet's life and Carrie needs her healthy."

"She can't do this," Zeb said. "She can't."

"Maybe she can." I tried to inject hope into my tone but I missed the mark. "Maybe I haven't been fair to Janet."

The doors opened and I walked inside. "Thanks for coming, Zeb. I really appreciate you trying."

I barely remembered the drive back to the vineyard. The landscape blurred past me as I drove the country roads I knew so well. The first time I drove these roads, I felt broken and lost and now here I was again. Broken and lost and searching.

I pulled up to the vineyard sign and drove up the dirt road. Dust kicked up around my car.

When I parked in front of the tasting room, I got out of the car and stood for a moment. The place was so quiet. No cars. No honking horns. No baby crying. Too quiet. The noise of the city once was maddening, but now the silence was worse.

"Addie."

Scott's voice sounded warm and welcoming and when I turned he was hurrying toward me. He wore a large grin on his face, and he easily wrapped me in his arms. I burrowed my face into the rough shirt that smelled of Scott and sunshine. I loved his smell. Loved his touch. Tears burned and fell. When I sobbed, he wrapped his arms tighter around me.

"It's going to be okay, baby." His warm breath brushed the top of my head. "We'll be fine. I love you."

I clung to his shirt, needing his strength. "I love you."

He pressed his hands on my shoulders and leaned me back so that he could see my face. Carefully, he brushed away a tear trailing down my cheek. "Will you marry me?"

I blinked, struggled to shift my thoughts. "What?"

Grinning, he dug a small box from his pack pocket and held it in front of me. "Marry me."

Hands trembling, I took the small box. Hinges creaked softly as I opened it. Inside was a single solitaire diamond that looked to be at least a carat, or maybe more. It caught the midday light and twinkled. "Scott."

"I've been meaning to give that to you for weeks. I didn't realize how much I love and need you until you were gone."

I stared at the ring. It sparkled in the light. So beautiful. A month ago it was my heart's desire. "It's beautiful."

He took the box and removed the ring. Carefully, he slid it on the ring finger of my left hand. "I love you."

I kissed him, wishing this moment was perfect and enough to wash away the loss that lingered like a specter. "I love you."

He hugged me tight. "We're going to be happy."

A hole gaped, open and raw, in my heart, but I believed it would heal. It had to. "I know."

"And Janet and Carrie are going to be fine." He smoothed his hand over my hair, tucking a loose strand behind my ear.

"You called Grace." My words sounded distant, far off.

"I spoke to her about an hour ago. She told me what happened." He smoothed his hands over my hair. "You're exhausted. You need sleep, and then in a few days you'll be back in your old routine. You'll be fine."

"Right. I know. I need time." The words echoed, hollow.

"I know you think you're the best choice for Carrie, but Janet is her mother. She'll be better off."

"Better off?" The words tumbled out rough and jagged.

"A child belongs with her mother." He spoke as if he were stating a fact I should know. "We both know that. That's why I hired the attorney for Janet."

"What?" Replay. Rewind. "Say that again."

"I hired the attorney. Honey, you're so loyal. You'd have ridden that situation to the end. It would have drained the hell out of you. I knew the best thing to do was end it quickly. You need to get back to your life. *Our* life."

For a moment I wasn't sure what to say. "You decided."

"I did. I did it because I knew you wouldn't."

I glanced at the ring, winking bright in the sunlight. My dreams glittered back up at me. Had this been what the witch bottle always wanted for me? Had it known I belonged here and not Alexandria? Maybe it did know what was best for me.

Maybe.

Very slowly, I pulled the ring off. I placed it in the center of Scott's calloused palm and slowly closed his fingers over the diamond. "Thanks, but no thanks."

His smile didn't dim. He was still so proud of his good deed. "Baby, what are you talking about?"

I cleared the emotion tightening my throat. "You shouldn't have interfered."

The smile dimmed only a little. "Your sister interfered in our lives. She was tearing us apart."

"No, we were doing that. We reached a fork in the road and realized how different we are."

He spoke to me like he were breaking down a complex problem for a small child. "I love you. You love me."

"I sure thought I loved you." Where was the old certainty?

"Thought?" he said, offended. "What does that mean?"

I squirmed free of his touch, annoyed by the weight of his hands on my shoulders. "I've got to go."

"Where?" he challenged. "You can't leave like this, Addie."

The place suddenly felt too small, the air too stale. "I can't stay here right now. I can't talk to you about this."

"Look, you're tired." His was the tone someone used with a child. "Your emotions are all out of whack. When's the last time you slept a solid eight hours?"

"It's been a really long time. In fact, I can't remember. And maybe sleep will do it for me. Maybe I'll lay my head down and wake up and realize that your helping Janet take the baby from me was a good thing."

His eyes darkened with a knowing that was absolute to him. "You're going to thank me."

November 1, 1751

Dr. Goodwin petitioned the courts to have Faith examined for signs of witchcraft. Mistress Smyth asked me to join her in this arduous task. I hesitated, but Mistress Smyth told me this was my duty. Mistress Smyth said Faith's evil magic killed Talbot and likely her husband, the captain. Two good men destroyed by black magic.

When I arrived at the Smyths house for the examination, Faith was there, wide-eyed and pale. Her hair framed her face in a wild, fiery halo. It took two men to restrain Faith so that we could examine her.

When she was told her children would be taken if she didn't comply, she ceased fighting and agreed to inspection. We found no signs of a witch. When Faith dressed, her face was hard and angry and my fears of her were renewed.

Without a word, I knew she levied a terrible curse on all of us.

Chapter Twenty-four

When I drove away from the vineyard, I realized I didn't have any place to go. I had no real friends outside of the vineyard or the salvage yard, and since I knew I'd not return to the vineyard, I followed the pull of Old Town and wound along the country roads, highways, and finally the interstate. By the time I parked in the warehouse alley, it was seven in the evening. The day's temperatures rose above ninety and still, even with the sun dipping lower, the air was thick with heat. A warm breeze from the river brushed my skin in welcome.

Keys in hand, I grabbed my bag and climbed the steps to the apartment. Grace sat in her rocker by the fireplace, staring out the window through the trees toward the river.

"I didn't think you'd come back," she said without turning.

"I went to the vineyard." I set my bag down. "It didn't feel right anymore."

"Why not?"

"Too quiet."

"It's too quiet here. I keep thinking I have to look in on the baby but the cradle is empty. Feels wrong."

I sat on the couch, absently fingering my keys and the fob, now warm with energy. "Have you heard from Janet?"

Grace faced me. "It's only been a half day."

"I thought she might have questions."

When she shrugged her shoulders looked thinner, more fragile. "She should know how to care for a baby. She took care of Eric."

"Yes." After a lifetime resenting being needed, I now missed it. "Never thought about it, but she does have more experience."

Restless, I rose and moved toward the mantel and looked at the collection of papers. My gaze settled on the old witch bottle. "Margaret returned it."

"Yes. About lunchtime. She x-rayed it. Was excited to tell you about something, but I told her you were gone."

"Did she say what it was?"

"That fellow she knew in Scotland found records of our ancestor, Sarah Goodwin. Turns out she was born a Shire."

"A Shire. Like Faith."

"This guy found an old church Bible. Listed Sarah and several other siblings born to an Owen Shire. Also listed a bastard child, Faith. And in the court records there was a Faith Shire condemned of witchcraft and sent to the Americas."

I traced the outline of the bottle with my finger. "Faith and Sarah were sisters?"

"Looks like it."

"One sister came in bondage and the other as a bride. It makes sense that Sarah would fear Faith. Sarah marries a doctor who is trying to make his mark in the world and she discovers her sister the witch is at her doorstep."

"Seems you or I don't have a lock on sisterly relationships."

I tried to peer through the bottle's dark glass so I could glimpse the contents. "She didn't tell you about the bottle?"

"I didn't ask, and she didn't offer. What's in the bottle really doesn't matter."

I picked up the bottle and held it up to the evening light streaming through the front window. It remained stubbornly dark, refusing to let me peek inside. Figures. Shut out again. I set it back on the mantel but for whatever reason did not settle it squarely on the wooden surface. As I released the neck, the bottle quickly tipped and plunged forward. I lunged to catch it, but it hit the brick hearth and in a blink shattered in a dozen pieces.

I knelt down, my hands hovering over the shards. "Shit! I'm so sorry, Grace."

Grace looked up. "It's okay, honey. It's an old bottle."

"It's an antique." I plucked at the broken pieces, the four nails, a coin, a lock of hair tied in a faded red ribbon, and a rolled up piece of paper. "Shit." My hands hovered over the glass. "I'm sorry."

Grace pushed out of her chair. "Stop saying you're sorry. Let me get a bag, and we can bundle it up. Margaret will be excited to see the contents."

I sat back on my haunches wondering if I could do anything right. "Margaret will be upset it's broken. Its value lies in the fact that it was unbroken."

"It's a bottle, Addie." She handed me a grocery store plastic bag. "It's a bottle."

Carefully, I loaded all the glass pieces into the bag. I reached for the scroll, fingering the delicate paper.

Grace handed me a wad of paper towels and I wiped up the liquid on the floor. "Stop fretting."

Tears choked in my throat and I thought at that moment I'd break. "Grace, I'd like to stay here for a while."

"Really?" No missing the hope.

"Yeah." I spoke with more authority. "Think I can make something out of this business again."

She rested a fist on her bony hip. "What about Scotty-boy? Sounds to me like he enjoyed having you run his vineyard."

Scotty-boy. If it weren't all so sad, I'd have laughed. "We're on a very, very long break."

"Why?" She sounded almost happy.

"He hired Janet's attorney."

Grace grunted. "Ass."

I fingered the edges of the scroll's brittle paper. "I'd like to think he thought he was doing me a favor."

She muttered an oath. "I'd like to think dogs can fly, but that don't make it true. What's the note say?"

Frowning, I unfurled the scroll. Delicate script writing covered the page. I read the note out loud. *"Protect me from Faith—my sister is my curse."*

"Faith," Grace said. "The witch?"

"If Sarah Goodwin and Faith were sisters, it makes sense this would be her bottle."

Grace shook her head. "Seems amazing that my mother found that bottle and it has just been sitting here for decades."

"Protect me from Faith—my sister is my curse," I repeated.

Grace shook her head. "No truer words have been written."

As I picked up the remains of the bottle's contents and lowered them in the bag, steady footsteps sounded on the staircase and I turned to see Zeb standing in the doorway. Grace took the bag and made an excuse about checking inventory. She was gone before either of us could comment.

"I thought you left," he said.

"I did for a while. Thanks, again," I said to Zeb.

"I wish it were enough." He crossed the room, stopping feet short from me. "Where did you go?"

"The vineyard." I tried to smile and not look as lost as I felt. "Scott proposed."

A frown furrowed his brow. "He did?"

"I said yes." I held up my naked left hand. "And then I said no."

"Why?"

"He paid for Janet's attorney. He was proud of himself."

"Dumbass."

"You sound like Grace."

He grunted approval. "She's a smart woman."

I wanted to think Scott wasn't evil. "I really think he wanted to do what he thought was best."

Zeb shook his head. "He had no right."

"I've no right to throw stones." I dropped the walls I'd built so carefully around me. "I've made choices that didn't include him."

"You were taking care of your sister's child."

I shook my head. "It's more complicated. See, I had my tubes tied ten years ago. It was right after Mom killed herself. I swore I'd never risk passing the curse on to a child. Scott said over and over he wasn't ready for children. I should have told him about the surgery but I thought I'd be enough."

"Why are you telling me?"

"I've no idea. I've spent a life running from this place, my past, and that secret. I figured going forward, I'm putting it all out on the table."

His frown didn't soften. "That's a hell of a choice to make."

"It is. And maybe one day I'll regret it, but not now and likely not tomorrow. It was the right thing to do for me."

A heavy silence hovered between us. "What are you going to do now?"

"I'm going to stay for a while. Help Grace. This place is perfect for a cast-off. And that about describes me right now."

He hovered close enough that I could feel the energy radiating from his body, but he made no move to touch me. "You're not a cast-off, Addie."

I looked up at him. "Okay, maybe not a cast-off, but I'm in need of rescuing. A second chance."

He shook his head. "You are the rescuer. You don't need anyone's help. You've proved that thousands of times."

We stood close, barely inches apart, and the energy hummed between us. It pulled. Beckoned us to touch. But neither of us moved.

He shoved out a ragged breath and jabbed his thumb toward the door. "I've got to go pick up Eric. He's at my mom's. I just wanted to check in with you."

Sliding my hands into my pockets so that I wouldn't be tempted to touch him, I nodded. "I'm fine. Thanks for checking."

He lingered an extra beat. "I'm glad you're staying."

With so much lost, it didn't make sense that I felt okay with being back. "Me, too."

He turned and walked from the house. I stood listening to the steady thud of his feet on the hardwood and the creak of the door hinges as it closed.

I swore I'd never return to the salvage yard or embrace family. And I did. And now I was alone.

That should have been reason enough to drink or at least cry. And maybe I would soon. But I needed sleep. I needed to wake up clear-eyed and rested.

Maybe I would be glad Scott intervened, but not likely. I thought

I loved him and he loved me, but neither of us trusted that love with the truth.

In my room, I kicked off my shoes and stared at the portrait of the stern woman. As always, she glared as I sat on my bed. "Save it, old lady. I'm not in the mood."

My muscles ached and my head throbbed as I slowly lowered myself to the pillow. I kicked off my shoes and raised my feet onto the bed. Years of overplanning, and now I had no idea what was next.

November 5, 1751

Mistress Smyth, Mistress McDonald, and I gathered in secret. Each of us brought a bottle, nails, and scrolls of paper, but the purpose for these items must remain a secret. Faith left town with her sons. Her whereabouts are unknown but we all still fear her dark magic.

Chapter Twenty-five

When Grace jostled me awake in the morning, the sun was bright and glaring. I sat up quickly, half expecting to hear Carrie's cries and ready to make a bottle. I was on my feet when I realized Carrie wasn't here. She was with Janet. Loss swept over me, hot and searing, and I wondered if it would cool in time.

Blinking, I pushed the hair from my eyes and looked at Grace. "What? Is something wrong?"

She was dressed and looked as if she rose hours ago. "No. Figured you'd better wake up. Janet is outside."

"What?" I rubbed my eyes, struggling to gain my bearings.

"She's sitting in a car, and the baby is in the backseat."

I reached for my shorts and pulled them on. "Why is she outside?"

Grace rolled her eyes. "I don't know. Figured you better go find out."

I tugged on a T-shirt and, rubbing the sleep from my eyes, I glanced at the clock on the wall. I'd slept for thirteen hours.

Slipping on my shoes, I made my way to the parking lot. Janet sat in the driver's seat, both her hands gripping the wheel. Carrie was in her car seat, crying.

I knocked on the window and Janet started. She opened the car door. The baby's cries rushed out with her. Her hair had lost its gloss and her skin looked pale. "Have you taken your medicine?" I asked.

"Yes."

Automatically, I opened the back door and pulled the baby free of the car seat. Resting Carrie on my shoulder, I patted her on the back. Slowly, she quieted. "Rough night?"

With a trembling hand, Janet reached for a cigarette and a lighter. She lit the tip and inhaled deeply. "She's not an easy baby. Eric was easy."

Carrie's cries softened to intermittent moans. "She's a handful."

She jabbed shaking fingers through her hair as she stared at the tip of the glowing cigarette. "She acts like she's crazy, like me."

"That's what I thought at first. But I think she knows what she wants and won't compromise." Her diaper felt heavy. "She hates a wet diaper."

Janet cursed. "I just changed her."

"I know. She's a pee machine."

That jostled a smile that faded quickly. "I want to raise her more than anything, Addie. She's my child. I want to stick around and get to know Eric. But I don't think I can cut it."

The baby rooted her lips against my neck, a sure sign she was hungry. There'd be no peace until Carrie ate. "Why don't you come upstairs? Grace will make coffee. And I can feed the baby. We can talk."

She shook her head and looked up at me with bloodshot eyes. "You'd do that after yesterday?"

My sister is my curse. The words on the scroll didn't ring as true. "Yes."

"Why?"

I tipped back my head, sensing I'd so regret all this one day. Janet would always be a roller coaster. "I couldn't give you a logical reason if you paid me."

A smile flickered and faded. "I can't do this alone, Addie. I love Carrie and Eric, but I can't do it alone. I need your help."

And here I stood at the crossroads. If I agreed, I'd be taking care of the baby and Janet for a very long time. I would be embracing the curse, wrapping my arms around it, and daring it to take its best shot. Experience taught me that the curse would make my life tough in the coming years. I'd question my own sanity. Feel exhausted. So frustrated. That was the nature of the curse, the disease. It affected everyone in the family.

But I was willing to do it. "We'll figure this out together, Janet."

"How?"

I opened her car door and reached my hand out to her. "I don't have a clue. But we'll figure it out."

December 1, 1751

I dreamed of Faith last night. "You denied me," she said. "You denied me in Scotland and here in Alexandria." I watched as she raised her hand and pointed to me. "I curse you, dear sister. Until you claim me as your flesh and blood, your fears will shackle you and yours." I awoke, tears streaming. Dr. Goodwin asked about the dream, but I told him nothing.

Epilogue

Two weeks passed before I heard Zeb's heavy footsteps crossing the warehouse. Carrie was in the baby seat, fussing and grabbing her toes. Janet still lived with her friends, but she came by every day or two to see the baby. Carrie enjoyed the visits and so did Janet, but in the end, each seemed to be relieved to take a break from the other.

"I hear you have a big job coming up," Zeb said.

"We do. An old church in Leesburg. Should be quite interesting."

He grabbed Carrie's foot and jostled it. His touch was rougher than mine, and it caught the baby's attention. She looked at him, wide-eyed. "Janet's been by to see Eric a couple of times. He likes seeing her."

"That's good. She does the same with Carrie."

"And you're okay with that?"

"We're working out a legal agreement. I love them both, but I won't let this disease run the show. The agreement says I have primary custody, and she'll have visitation."

Creased feathering around the corners of his eyes deepened. "You think it'll work?"

"It has to."

"You heard from Scott?"

"No." I grinned. "He's waiting for me to see the light."

"And?"

"I saw it. And that's why I'm here."

A slow grin warmed his face, softening it in a new way. "Good. I'm glad you're here. Real glad."

Making Your Own Witch or Wish Bottle

1 large bottle with lid
1 smaller bottle with lid that fits in larger bottle

ITEMS YOU COULD INCLUDE IN YOUR WISH BOTTLE
Crystals, shiny buttons, or pieces of mirror (to hold the light and
   good energy)
Safety pins or nails (to repel bad energy)
Flower petals
Heart-shaped buttons
Locks of hair
Herbs
Sea salt
Spices such as cinnamon, allspice, and cayenne
Honey
Stones
Essential oils such as peppermint, lemon, or lavender
Paper with your good intentions written down in pencil
Anything you feel symbolizes your wish

Witch bottles are some of the oldest forms of magic that reached a heyday in the sixteenth and seventeenth centuries. They were used to protect the home against troublesome spirits by warding off evil. Most witch bottles were buried near the hearth or the front door of the home because it was believed evil swept down the chimney or through the front door. Once the bottles were buried, they protected the property from the dark forces that seemed constant hundreds of years ago. Today, the witch bottle has morphed into a wish bottle and is used to create good luck or reaffirm positive intentions.

A witch or wish bottle is a jar or some kind of breakable container used to contain bits and baubles assembled to create good intentions or protect against negative energy. If you can, make your bottle at the full moon when energy is considered most potent. Fill the smaller bottle with all the ingredients you think are perfect for your bottle. Seal the bottle and place it in the larger bottle. Fill this bottle with water or wine and then seal. Also feel free to decorate the outside of your bottle with paints, mirrors, or anything that appeals to you. Remember these are very personal, and no two should be alike.

Once your bottle is sealed, hold it in your hands and say, "Healings, blessings, and good fortune." Feel free to bury your bottle near the front door or hearth or simply leave it on display in a special part of your house. Be sure to put it in a safe place because if the bottle is broken so is the spell.

AT THE CORNER OF KING STREET

DISCUSSION QUESTIONS

1. The novel alternates between the eighteenth century and the present time. Does this enhance the storytelling? How do the historical passages shed new light on the contemporary story?

2. Toward the beginning of the novel, Addie says of Shire Architectural Salvage, "For every item, we were a second chance for some kind of life." How does the salvage shop represent the Shire Family, past and present? Why do Grace and Addie gravitate toward this business?

3. Why didn't Addie tell Scott about her past? Was she right to keep it from him? How might their relationship have changed if she'd been open about her family early on?

4. Grace tells Addie, "I'll smash this life to bits. No Shire woman gets a free ride." Do you think she's justified in demanding that Addie step in? Are we bonded to our family even if they've caused us pain?

5. How is Grace different from Addie? Why does she believe she failed her family—and why does she think Addie can prevail?

6. The characters create their own modern-day witch bottles, filling them with their hopes and dreams. What would you put in your witch bottle?

7. Was Scott's interfering in Carrie's custody warranted? What would you have done in his situation? What about in Addie's or Janet's case?

8. Do you think the curse was real? And has it been broken now that Addie and Janet have mended their relationship?

9. Do you think one's centuries-old family history can affect future generations? How so?

10. What do you make of the ending? How do you see the story continuing?